TESTAMENT

BOOK 2

GLYPH SERIES

RONIN ROMERO

1

LADY INIS MERCELLE VII

It kept returning. Without permission it inserted itself into the moments during which her mind was the weakest. Whether in the form of a vision, dream or a flash, the occurrences and images therein remained the same.

Uneven rubble layered the ground for miles around them. A city that once stood proud and strong lay flat and broken, devoured by the cold fangs of Chaos. Its people were chewed up and spat out, left to die in pools of dried blood which dotted the fractured concrete landscape with smears of brown and red. Glass crunched beneath the soles of their boots; the signature sound of a devastated population.

Signs that once labeled the extravagant buildings and streets did nothing but jut corners out of the dirt, reminding them of what the city once was. The city had been a beacon of prosperity, of strength and faith in humanity. Now, it was little more than a massive grave marker for those who gave their lives to try and save their loved ones. It was clear that no one was spared, as the only sound to be heard was the trio's own footsteps.

Behind the mind's blur, the dream wouldn't allow her to read the signs or decipher the faces of the other two people walking along with her. Yet, they shared the sensations and emotions of the moment together, as one.

They walked in the cool night breeze beneath the stars, waiting for a message that would tell them they stood a chance against this enemy. At the center of the city, they stopped to take in the carnage and violence which they could only picture from the remnants of war that surrounded them. Happy to still be alive, but grief stricken over their fallen comrades, they spared no silent prayer.

Thousands of shimmering dots in the sky told them nothing, leaving the three of them in their silence to fend for themselves on a dying planet. All they needed was proof that their struggles had purpose – something that said the sacrifices they had made weren't in vain. It felt as if the hand they'd extended for help was cut off at the wrist, and the bloody stump was slowly draining their lives away.

In their last moment before hope fled and the despair of yet another loss crept in, a collection of blue sparks came together in the sky, shining down on them from above with a warm embrace. Its light rivaled that of the moon, illuminating the jagged pieces of scattered concrete all around them. One at a time, the sparks broke away from the cluster, fell to the ground, and disappeared into the craggy rubble.

The sparks rained down around them, falling faster and faster until the cluster was a cascade of the wondrous lights. A torrent of blue flooded the flattened city, bright at first, but once all of the lights had found their ways beneath debris and into the dirt, the shining pillar's brightness faded, and darkness once again shrouded the ruins.

They waited, once more putting their hearts and souls forth in exchange for that last bit of hope. A small tremor tickled the ground as the sparks settled into their graves and found slumber in their abandonment.

There was nothing left to grasp, nothing to pull back into existence, and no way of going back. They had lost their light.

What had they done? Who were these two figures who felt like strangers at her side? Why was this series of images repeating on a loop in her head? She had become delirious.

These images couldn't be avoided, no matter how hard she tried to pull her mind away. Someone was trying to tell the three of them something, to show them a future without guidance, without light. The message was muddled, confusing, and lacked congruence with the future she had fought and planned for.

Someone or something wanted Mercelle to give up, but her past had been forged on never doing so, even in the face of certain failure. An overwhelming weight of powerlessness always followed the dream, always came after the vision, and never failed to trail behind the flash of the hollow images.

No matter how hard she tried, she couldn't look away, nor could she change what she saw...

HER SKIN THROBBED. Barely able to keep her heavy eyelids open, she winced behind the pain of her sunburn. Blisters were starting to well up in some spots, and she needed to find shade.

A shadow was cast next to a tall sand dune as the sun began its evening descent. She plugged her tablet into the small, handheld solar charger to catch the sun's last bits of energy, then she flattened out in the shaded sand. Her legs cooled in the loose granules, and she buried them until the coolness soothed her skin and nestled around her sore knees.

Over the last four days she'd been getting messages from Feres on the tablet about Chaos squadrons in the area of Sandra. They could have been regiments of replica soldiers or transportation caravans. Either way, it wasn't worth the risk to send anyone out after her until the threat and area were cleared of enemy signals. The Demigods may have been trying to keep an eye on Sandra after their tower was taken down. In a couple more days, Mercelle hoped, she would be back in Sandra, bragging about how she had walked all the way back from the South Pole after taking down a giant tower with Lito.

"Who needs transportation when you have brute strength and endless determination?" she'd ask the soldiers at the gates if she made it back before shriveling into a dehydrated stump.

The longer she lay there, the more she thought she wouldn't make it much longer. Travelling mostly at night and resting periodically throughout the day got her farther than she expected, but it wouldn't get her the remaining eight hundred miles her map showed between her location and Sandra's closest gates.

The wounds she sustained from taking down the massive tower with Lito were mostly healed. The scabs on her legs and arms had fallen off a couple of days ago, and her chin was closed and scabbing over quite well. Bruises ranging from green to brown and purple ran up and down her ride side, making it hotter than her left. She wiggled onto her bruised half to work it into the comfy sand.

None of that helped to give her energy.

She'd run out of vitamin packs two days ago, and

had her last electrolytes yesterday. Dry skin was starting to flake from her parched lips. Smacking her stale tongue against the roof of her mouth procured a bit of saliva which rested on her gums as long as she could keep herself from swallowing. Then the thirst returned.

Air bubbles rumbled around in her stomach. She lifted up granules of sand, letting them cascade from her palm and onto her hip. The sensation was a decent distraction from the holler of her aching side. She thought about taking out the photo of her and her parents, but lethargy convinced her not to dig into her pocket, and that picturing it in her mind's eye was good enough for now.

She shouldn't have felt this terribly after a mere two days without vitamins. Was it the harshness of the desert? It could be drastically cruel to the human body. The idea that Earth's landscape was once dominated by water and vegetation was beyond her comprehension, yet she found herself imagining a clean, fresh spring rolling off the top of the dune and filling her mouth with cold, satisfying wetness.

Memories returned to her of being taught in school about the vast species of flora, and the endless cities that spanned across continents before Chaos arrived. She also remembered learning of the decimation squads which Valk and the others dispatched to dismantle any remnants of humankind while giant machines pumped the deep, salted oceans of Earth away. That the planet had turned almost entirely to desert over the past millennium showed just how much of an impact Chaos had made on Earth, and indicated the obvious future the Demigods had planned for the arid planet. Something she hadn't quite grasped before spending four days alone in the desert.

There was something else she was struggling to grasp.

Each time she allowed her eyes to close, the same dream took over. She was walking through stone and steel vestiges of a destroyed rebel city, feeling as if all hope had been lost. At first she believed it to be another nightmare pulling her back to the loss of Lanna, but this was a different city which the foggy details of the dream refused to divulge. The sense of someone – perhaps two people – close by her sides layered the dream in further mystery. There were lights falling from the sky, blue in color, and as they burrowed themselves into the dirt around her, the physical sensation of hopelessness grew into a dark pit in her stomach.

She wanted terribly to explore the feeling further, but continued convincing herself that dreams were only interpretations of how one perceived their surroundings. At the moment, with starvation and heat ruling her body, hopelessness was something she kept deep inside herself. In her weakened state, Mercelle assumed her dreams were trying to show her how she felt subconsciously, to hold her fears up in her face without allowing her to look away from them.

The only control she had over it was not letting it weigh her down while she was awake and on the move toward Sandra.

It was relaxing to lie there, peeling the dead skin from her arms and neck, waiting for the sun to go down. She exhaled, and let her tired muscles sink into the sand. A gust blew a few strands of hair into her face, tickling her forehead and nose. To avoid irritating her skin further, she pushed the strands back over her head. Only, when she brought her hand back to her face, the strands had pulled loose from their roots and tangled around her fingers.

A sharp thud stung her heart. It couldn't have just been a sunburned scalp. Lito had told her something was wrong, and to get checked out as soon as she arrived back at Sandra. But, Chaos convoys near the city had stalled her time table, and each time fatigue clung to her like a weighted blanket she struggled to decide whether or not to wait for help, or keep trudging along.

Part of her was glad for the delay because it filled her mind with things other than Lito's last haunting words to her or her potential health issues. She'd had the sealed silgen suit on when she was near the tower at the South Pole. Could radiation have leaked through somehow? Were the waves strong enough to penetrate the protective silgen linings?

There wasn't anything she could do about it at this point in time, all she could do was toss the strands into the breeze and concentrate on not breathing hard enough to make the aching bruises and stinging skin worse. With half of her body beneath the sand, Mercelle could feel a miniscule quake rising, falling and rolling through the region, and she wondered if she would have even felt it while walking or standing. She became one with the pulse of Earth, giving all of her mental energy to try and pull her away from repeating Lito's words in her head again.

One final, dreadful thought about a future stuck in a hospital bed, and she was asleep, watching the blue stars twinkle down from the heavens once more.

THE SHADOWS HADN'T MOVED at all when her tablet beeped beside her. She rolled out of the sand and onto her back, tilting the screen toward her face to read Feres's message.

Areas around you and Sandra have been secured. No enemy signals remaining. Retrieval has you locked on and will disembark shortly.

Zooming out on the map, two pink dots began flashing inside Sandra's location, indicating retrieval buggies. A smile lifted her cheeks, and she held back tears of joy to make sure no further moisture left her body. Only one more night and she would be on her way to the closest thing she had left to a home.

Fairly close to her own dot, she spied the area where Chaos had held the hostages and a massive monster inside trailers. The trailers were most likely still there, some on their sides and others corroding away. It was just beyond the next crevasse, the one Lito had baited the monster into. Waving lines on the map showed movement within the chasm.

Mercelle's stomach growled, and she got herself an idea.

THE SUN FINALLY WENT DOWN, and the moon was full in an empty sky. Walking was a slow go, but the crevasse was closer than she thought. Either that or she'd fallen asleep while walking, she couldn't tell.

A faint echo of a screech grew louder as she approached the edge, and went down onto her knees to look over. The drop off of shear stone disoriented her as she looked over the precipice and down into the small chasm. About a hundred feet below was the monster, emaciated to a thin facade of the monstrosity it had been when she last saw it, and blistered worse than her.

It had done quite the job digging at the opposite side of the crevasse, which was comprised mostly of loose gravel. But, it must have run out of stamina before piling enough dirt at the bottom to climb out. Still trying pitifully to pull more sand down, it slid into the lowest part of the pit, screeching with frustration, wanting only to end its suffering.

Mercelle was happy to oblige, licking her teeth with a hungry grin.

Another rumble in her stomach, and a twisting of her vision, told her that her vitals weren't where they were supposed to be. Weakness shivered throughout her legs as she stood, staring down at the creature and thinking about how much meat was left on its bones. The back legs were short and thick. They were the best bet, and they looked delicious.

She had never eaten real meat before, only soy and protein replacements. The former High Cleric, and her late, close friend, Agnitius, had taught her about how the ancient people used to cook meat over a heat source, the same way they cooked their substitutes now. The thought used to make her queasy, but she was far from that feeling as she pictured the monster's flesh turning from pink to...whatever color it was that actual meat turned when it was cooked and safe to eat. She hoped to learn really soon.

Before abandoning the transport, she had given it a final onceover to make sure she hadn't missed any spare vitamin or electrolyte packets. She was out of luck along that avenue, but she had found another small plasma charge in the hold.

She could make fire; all she needed was meat.

The only way down without cordage was the opposite side of the chasm, which was made of the loose dirt the monster had attempted to move down. She walked around to the other side, all the while listening to the cries coming from below. They echoed off of the crevasse walls, bounced off of distant ridges and returned to her ears.

Screeching vibrated inside of her head, and deliriousness stumbled her heavily to one side. She had to question whether this was the right thing to do. It felt like being back in that first tower with Lito, figuring out if she wanted to go one way to revenge, or another to safety. Waiting for retrieval in the safety of a toppled trailer was one option. But hunger was a powerful force behind her decision to sit at the edge of the sandy slope, and slide down into the monster's domain.

It was a long slide downward. Her boots kicked sand up into her face, pulling her from her delirium and waking her up with a rush of energy. The path ahead of her ended near the monster, but once she got close to the bottom it lunged at her.

A claw swiped toward her, but she went flat and avoided it, then tucked and rolled to put some distance between them with her remaining momentum. The monster screeched, then stumbled and fell. It was weak.

Two weak warriors met in a desert crevasse. Who would eat whom?

She unsheathed her knife, gripping it in one hand while clenching the other into a fist. The monster was digging at the sand around it to catch its balance. Mercelle could see its eyes attempting to shut, and she understood the feeling all too well. As long as she did a better job of resisting the urge than the beast, she would have a chance at dinner tonight.

"Come on," she whispered to herself. "Stay awake." A quick, hard smack to her cheek and she was alert, regretting it immediately as her pink skin burned and tingled.

Her heavy soles sunk into the loose sand with each step, and by the time she reached the monster it was still on its side, blinking in long, slow waves. It looked at her with mourning eyes, almost like it knew the end was here.

Mercelle flattened a hand on the side of its scaled head, trying to feel any semblance of recognizable life. There was no pulse, no breathing pattern. If the creature's eyes weren't still attempting to function she would think it was dead already.

Not to be fooled, she pulled the knife back, preparing to stab it into the throat. Suddenly, she became curious as to why the throat would be the most vulnerable flesh in the monster if it had no need to pump blood or breathe air. That's when the lean monster took the opportunity to twist its body around, swiping its tail into her chest and sending her onto her back.

"Emmett's asshole!" she hollered. Operating purely off of adrenaline, she rolled onto her front and pulled herself upward just in time to leap over a second swipe. She somersaulted back into the sand, taking a scoop of it up in her free hand.

The monster rushed at her, and she stood her ground. The crevasse echoed its footsteps as it pounded the ground with heavy talons.

Just before it lunged, she tossed the sand into the creature's broad eyes. It lunged anyway, but screeched and leaned to one side. Instead of going over, this time she slid beneath it, kicking away one of its claws and slicing down its midsection before coming up on the squealing beast's rear.

It was easy to cut open, especially since it was still wounded from the fight for the hostages. The flesh on the underside was tender. She licked her lips. Dark, heavy liquid dripped onto the ground. She couldn't see what color it was in the shadow of dusk.

Jumping into the air while the monster flung its head from side to side, she came down on its back, sticking the blade into something that felt like a spine. She twisted the knife, pulling left and right, up and down, until the back legs went limp and the monster flattened onto the sand.

The eyes blinked in random intervals up at her. The

monster's top half was still alive, and there was no way she was going near that mouth or those front claws to finish the job. Both back legs were immobile, and as she sat atop the dying Chaos creation she realized that she couldn't hack this thing up with a simple knife. That would take all night.

She unclipped the small plasma charge from her belt, armed it and shoved it into the fresh wound she'd just made. Then she rolled off the side of the monster and crawled away until the boom shot sand and flesh into the air behind her.

As fate would have it, a smoking hind leg landed just beyond her head. She grabbed it by the ankle and cooked it over the burning front half of the monster.

She opened her mouth as wide as she could to take ravenous chunks out of the leg meat. The first bite was savored. It tasted like slimy, hard tofu meat, with a little bit of char. Salt would have helped with the taste, but it was bliss. She chewed that first bite into mush before swallowing it and waiting to feel it hit her stomach in a sweet pang of victory.

The second, third and fourth bites went down in gulps, barely hitting her tongue. By the fifth bite she could feel her body absorbing the nutrients into her blood and digestive tracts. Already, her limbs felt lighter, as if gravity was going back to normal after a brief shift.

That was all good and well, but her head was still

fuzzy. With a stomach full of dense monster meat, she let out a belch that rivaled the monster's former screeches, and she lay back down in the cool sand. The flat, rocky wall that was her way out of the crevasse looked more and more tedious the longer she stared up at it.

At the very bottom, something reflected moonlight at her. She moved her head about to try and get another angle on the reflection, but ended up crawling over to it. A piece of glass was buried in the sand, the reflective kind, like a mirror. Only, this one was curved and shaped. She had seen it before.

She reached into the sand and pulled it out. Granules drained out of the inside of the glass and she shook it clean. Lito's armor was as fresh and flawless as the day she'd found it in the temple.

It fit her very loosely, like wearing a wide waste canister around her torso. But she wore it anyway, lying back down and thinking of where Lito might have ended up.

2

ZAKOPAT KRAJ II

White, clean light gleamed from the glossy walls of the small room. The glare only made the stains in his assigned uniform more distinct. Dressed from neck to elbow to ankle with a loose fabric meant to imitate the shape of a human form, Kraj picked at the neck lining of the greying garment.

As usual, only two chairs and a table – made of solid glass – occupied the nearly blinding interrogation room. He hadn't been made to wait this long before. It still beat analyzing human intelligence signals around the clock.

There was no color in the room. The closest was Kraj's brown irises. Even his skin was becoming lighter each day without the sun, and the uniform specially designed to dehumanize the humans was without color

~~also~~. Did the Chaos intentionally make the uniforms that way, or was it just in their nature to misunderstand the humans and their need to be comfortable?

Kraj didn't care about the clothes, although his mind was racing from the heightened level of oxygen. He started to breathe deep, slowly, and relax his lungs for a few seconds at a time. This wasn't the first time he had gone undercover, but this was definitely the most in-depth assignment he had ever accepted.

The rest of Glaven Grad tower wasn't as rich in oxygen as the interrogation rooms. Probably so that the interrogated can be clear headed, or perhaps the opposite, as he did end up getting more of a dizzying effect from it at times. Replicas didn't tend to accommodate for human needs in the general areas of the tower, especially on the work floors.

He missed his woman, Cekanja, and her children who called him father. There was no doubt in his mind that they were wondering where he was, as he was rarely gone this long from his Oasian family and tribe. It was all to help the rebellion, and to create a safer world for them. The only difficult parts were keeping his accent in check and remembering that his name was no longer Zakopat Kraj, at least not until he finished up in Glaven Grad and made his way back home.

Even with a woozy feeling rising and falling within him, he still didn't feel the kind of fear any normal human would feel when about to be questioned by a

Chaos replica. He had done a few of these "evaluations" since arriving in Glaven Grad about a week ago, and as long as he stuck to his cover story he was untouchable. There was nothing they could get out of him.

But, they gave him so much information.

A standing, rectangular piece of the wall slid into the floor, and a Mora stepped through from the corridor. Its long legs bent beneath the table and it sat across from him with a stiff posture accentuated by pointed, bony shoulders.

The replica's garments were more tailored to its body, but still had some lightness to them, and the dark blue skin on the midsection was exposed. Not as elegant as the Demigod Mora herself, the copy was a more tamed version. He had to look up at its black eyes across the table.

It placed something circular and solid between them on the tabletop, about the size of Kraj's palm, and then it flicked a long finger above the device and activated a holographic projection of some sort of file in the Chaos language which he couldn't read.

"Crassa," it called him without looking down, while dancing a finger through the file to make notes in the hologram. All humans within Glaven Grad were referred to as "Crassa", it helped to let them know they weren't equal. "Tell me why you have come to Glaven Grad."

“We’ve gone over this every day for almost an entire week now,” he said.

“You must be getting back your ability to retain new memories.” The Mora stopped to peer at him for a second, suspicion always in its eyes.

These creatures were stupid when on their own – easier to manipulate than a human would have been. But, with the systems and departments Chaos had in place, they had strength in numbers, and could catch on to any suspicious inconsistencies with time.

Kraj made a point not to shift around in his seat. Stillness was an indication of confidence. He did bob his head ever so slightly, just to make sure the replica picked up on his annoyance. “The issues with my memory only pertain to my time before coming here. After I woke up in Sandramedius I escaped. Everything after that I can retain perfectly fine.”

“If you could elaborate on that it would save us both some time.”

It wasn’t a surprise that the replicas failed to comprehend human biology. Try as they did to experiment on the Earth dwellers, their only progress came from trial and error. Slowly, they unmasked bits and pieces of human anatomy, but the brain would continue to elude them. Hence his concise cover story.

“I’m still getting bits and fragments back piecemeal,” Kraj lied. “I’ll have a dream that triggers a memory here and there. So far, what’s come back to me indicates that I was accused of something I didn't do – something bad – and I was serving in the Sandran infantry when they deemed me mentally incapacitated."

"Why?" It kept its eyes locked on the notes it was taking in the hologram.

"Why what?" He liked to ask questions when he wasn't supposed to. It gave him an edge in the conversation. After all, he was here to gather information, not beat his cover story to death. "Why did they blame an accident on me, or why did they deem me as mentally incapacitated?"

The Mora glared at him with vast blackness showing through its eyes. It wasn't going to answer him.

"It was all just an excuse for them to study the brain of a soldier to see if it could be genetically modified for improvement," he replied.

"What kind of actions were taken to obtain data from you?"

"I'm not sure if what has come back to me is entirely the truth. Like I said, anything before my time in Glaven Grad returns in flashes and waves. I believe they tracked certain alpha patterns within the bloodstreams of my brain while subjecting me to blasts of electricity and charged particles of some kind. A few dreams I had showed me being tortured and starved in order to create certain chemicals in my cortex muscles to be harvested. I can only assume that what they took out of me was used to create tonics to test on others.

"I remember escaping from Sandra, and coming here to make sure I was fighting for the right side."

"You no longer have alliances with the humans?"

"They betrayed me. I feel I did them a service and they used that to their advantage and tried to kill me for their own benefit. They're terrible, selfish creatures. I would never go back to them. I couldn't, even if I wanted to."

"Do you remember your human name?" it asked.

"I do. My name was Olim Jasusa," answered Kraj. "But I don't use that name anymore."

\The replica took a moment to document his words into the hologram floating above the table. He almost went on to give more details of his supposed origin, but knew that giving unprompted information only helped them in ways he didn't intend. The Moras were trying to find a flaw in his background. That's why they made him repeat it every day during every interrogation. He was at the point where he couldn't even tell if he was being interrogated by the same Mora as the day before. Good thing he knew his cover story inside and out.

"What isn't making sense, Crassa, is why you would remember these details and nothing else. You can recall everything from our previous interrogations, but nothing specific before your imprisonment in Sandramedius?"

"Again," Kraj repeated. "What they did to me impacted my ability to recall memories prior to the traumas they induced. Anything that happened after that has no problem sticking. I can create and remember new memories. The old ones are just more difficult to access. They come with time."

"I am starting to understand why you were kept alive," it said. "Especially since most other defectors run through their usefulness quite quickly."

All of his loose ends had been covered. He could answer any question they threw at him. "Anything that comes back to me I have reported directly to you. I'll continue to provide you with any and all memories that resurface. As an officer in the infantry I must have had access to some weapons and special initiatives that you will need to know about."

Anything to show discontent toward his fellow humans would help him secure his life, and his position within Glaven Grad.

"So far," the replica began to scroll to another page. "You've given us specifications on battle formations and resource allocation, but nothing more. If you are unable to give us something more than that you will no longer be allowed to live in Glaven Grad, or anywhere else for that matter. Is that understood?" It didn't wait for him to answer. "Have you remembered anything new from your past since your last debriefing?"

This was where his job became difficult. Creating

new details to add into his rock solid cover was something that had to be examined from many angles before he spoke.

"I had a dream last night about transporting some kind of weapon from Lanna to Sandra," he fabricated. "Canisters, I think. I remember knowing that what they had inside was a gaseous substance, a new element they had created. If it was the gas I think it was, then it's a compound designed specifically to disrupt seismic energy when released into the atmosphere. It can cause isolated ground quakes large enough to shake any structure loose from its foundation, or collapse mines."

"Can you tell me when the memory took place? How long ago that might have been?" It scribbled details into its notes.

"I couldn't say." Leaving open ends like this made the Chaos chase after details that may or may not emerge. "If it was long ago enough, the weapon may already be operational."

The Mora stopped notating and stared deeply into his face, trying to find any kind of facial twitch that would give away his dishonesty. Every muscle in his face and body did exactly as he wanted it to, and he was in complete control of even his most subconscious tells.

He gave the Mora a confused look back, as if he didn't understand what she was doing. Someone not versed in the psychology of their enemy wouldn't be aware of their own actions, and would find them strange. Therefore, this Crassa reacted accordingly.

"This information will be escalated to the Demigods for consideration," it said, going back to the hologram and flicking its finger around on it to create shapes and glyphs he wasn't familiar with. "If they believe this to be of any importance, you will be allowed to stay another day until our next debriefing, at which point you will be required to provide more specific details via your memories. Failure to do so will result in your position within Glaven Grad being re-evaluated."

"As always," he responded, nodding his understanding.

It shut down the hologram and picked up the round device from the tabletop, standing from its seat. He knew he wasn't to move until a Valk came in to escort him back to his working station, so he stayed put, and was a little taken aback when the Mora stopped at the doorway and turned to ask him another question.

"As a member of their species, do you believe that what was done to you was wrong?"

Kraj let out a single, scoffing chuckle through his intentionally derisive smirk. "War causes people to do things they wouldn't normally do in order to survive. Entire societies will forego their values and beliefs if they think it will lead to them beating their enemies. I can't blame them for wanting to procure an advantage by any means necessary. Strength lies in loyalty and numbers. If one has to be sacrificed to make a hundred stronger, then that is what must happen. I only hope to someday make them regret allowing me to escape. They made me what I am, and I intend to pay that back." He gave the Mora a hexing glare, tilting his head forward at it as he did. "Do you believe it's wrong for your Chaos to torture and experiment on their own kind for the sake of advancements?"

"That's the difference between our species, Crassa. It doesn't matter what I think. The Demigods were trusted to oversee this takeover of Earth, and that's what will happen. A species grows weak when power is spread too thin. You humans will never understand the importance of obedience." It waved a hand and the door slid back into the floor. A second later the Mora was gone, and the door slid up again.

It answered his question. That was the first time he had gotten a Mora to answer something he had asked. The Mora wanted to see if his frame of mind had switched from the human to the Chaos. He failed the test on purpose by showing that he was operating off of emotion and vengeance as opposed to blind devotion to the Demigods. Anything else would have been too obvious, and would have given him away.

Humans, Kraj believed, got their strength from struggling against those who ruled over them, which was why he was one of the few Oasians who believed in contributing to the war. Usually, peace and neutrality were the ways of the Oasian tribes. When he'd heard about the peaceful uprising against Lord Cakram, he decided that peace and victory could both be had, but that it had to be fought for. That was when he began trafficking information between the superpowers of the human rebellion. Humans were smart, and full of a flaming passion for what they believed in, and they believed in ridding the planet of Chaos.

With the replicas under such tight control, they were loyal, and they robotically did what they were assigned to do. This made Kraj wonder why they called themselves Chaos when they were more organized than any human government.

He couldn't wait to get out of this highly oxygenated room and clear his head.

The door slid back down. A Valk stepped in to escort him away.

KRAJ STEADIED his breathing to get accustomed to the thin air in the corridor. It was back to moving slowly, conserving energy and meditating when possible. The rest of the Glaven Grad tower was not a healthy environment for humans, but Kraj distracted his conscious mind by reminding himself of the additions made to his cover story. Everything needed to stay synced. They were always looking for a contradiction or flaw.

The story he'd fed the Mora about the ground quake compound was brilliant. That would lead to the Demigods ordering replicas to reinforce any subterranean structures of all towers around the world, as well as strengthen foundation supports. It was a wonderful waste of time and resources. This brilliant little liar knew that the rebellion would only attack a tower from above ground. Only Dredger could penetrate a subfloor, but Kraj suspected that he wasn't going to start taking down towers any time soon.

Lito and Lady Mercelle had already taken down two towers on their own. The towers' true weaknesses lay within. As the Mora had indirectly reminded him: humans are smarter than the replicas, maybe even the Demigods. All it took was two crafty individuals – one who may or may not be a God – to infiltrate the towers and tear them down from within. Chaos could spend as much time and resources as they wanted reinforcing their structures, but the humans would still tear them down. He was more sure of that than whether or not he would be making it to his workstation alive.

The Valk jerked Kraj's arm around a corner, and led him down a long hallway with tall windows along the left side. Kraj and the Valk were very high up, and he could see the surrounding city amongst the ground below, enveloping the base of the tower.

Giant engines with what looked like thruster attachments on them were being mounted to the outside of the tower – silver funnel shaped units jutted out of the bases. There was no telling what the replicas were up to; they could fashion random components into almost anything. Wheels and tires melted down into flooring. Electrical devices changed around in order to route power to certain lights and terminals based on the locations of the Chaos population within the tower. Even parts of human transports had been seen mashed together with unfamiliar stones and metals to create workable apparatuses.

But, what were these new couplers going onto the building's exterior? Surely the Moras couldn't have constructed them to help with structural support so quickly after hearing about his fake dream. He had just left the debriefing. And there was no possible way they could have heard about the fake ground quake gas prior to him making it up. He would have to snoop around and see what he could find out about those shiny, silver attachments. Luckily, he was good at sneaking around the tower at night.

He had been assigned to Workfloor 86. Numbers were the only things in human language, and they only existed so the humans in Glaven Grad could know where to go for their assigned jobs. Workfloor 86 was where he poured over human communications ad nauseam and edited them into transcripts that would then get passed through a translation program to put the information into something the replicas could read.

It was easy to alter the information how he saw fit before passing it along to the program. He took mental notes about what intelligence he saw coming through to Glaven Grad, and managed to keep his video transmitter hidden while capturing the documents on his screen, reporting it all back to his superior. The tough part was: when he transmitted his data out, he knew he would never hear back about it, not even as much as a confirmation of transmission.

Communication between Kraj and his handler was a one-way street, one that would give until it wouldn't anymore. His life was a means to an end, and although he was invaluable, he was also expendable. Faith in his powers of observation and reconciliatory skills had convinced him that when the time came, he could make his escape and return to Cekanja before bartering for his next assignment.

The Valk grunted as he shoved Kraj through the door to Workfloor 86.

Rows of terminal screens with low benches in front of them lined the floor from front to back. With a perimeter that would take Kraj at least a few minutes to walk around, the massive space held hundreds of workers. Only a handful of those workers were human.

The vast ceiling was a single screen that reached to the corner of each wall. Besides the humans, all of the other seats were occupied by Newlyns mindlessly tapping and scrolling through unreadable documents.

Kraj always wanted to try and learn Chaos, but the language was so strange and distant to his understanding that he thought he would just stick to what he knew.

He made his way into the center of the floor where his assigned seat was waiting for him. His terminal was one of two connected to a frame that was bolted to the floor. The other terminal was being used by a Newlyn that looked exactly like all the others. But, Kraj had become familiar with the replica's eye movements and tapping rhythms, which were the only things that set it apart and revealed each day that he was sitting next to the same replica.

All of the other humans looked like they were on the edge of death. They didn't fare well in this harsh, oxygen sparse environment.

"Good afternoon," he said as he took his seat and logged in to his terminal with the alpha pad.

The Newlyn grunted at him without taking its eyes off the screen in front of it. Below the Newlyn was steel grating which drained away any dripping goo that came off of the replica. The draining system was throughout the entire floor, and the Newlyns here didn't leave their stations much.

"Cheery as always, I see," he replied to the creature's silence. The intake file was full, and more reports were coming in. He tapped on one and brought it up. It was a wind pattern report from Naselba.

He changed the figures to make it look as if the city had been experiencing extremely harsh winds during the past few weeks. To make sure the report would likely indicate a false stressor, he also added unusually high seismic activity to the record. Chaos would see this as proof that the planet was reaching the end of its habitable status.

There was no harm in giving the Demigods a big head, as it would ultimately help the humans.

The new information went into his final report forms, which were then sent to the translator program to be made into Chaos glyphs for the replicas to process. All in all the fudging took less than a few minutes, and he went on and on throughout the day, making his changes and sending the reports up.

When he looked over at the screen next to his, the Newlyn was working on something he couldn't read, blocks of text surrounding the inner cross section of either a mechanical engine or an organ of some sort. The screen was scrolled away before he could make out the picture.

"Working on something important?" he asked the Newlyn. It was never a bad time to try and pry intelligence from unlikely sources.

"I wouldn't know," it finally replied. "I just do my job to make sure the right files get to the right replicas for processing. What happens after that is anyone's guess, and truly not my business." As it spoke, bits of goo slid down its neck, rolled over its rotund body and dripped down through the grating.

"Surely you're smart enough to know what's important and what's not?"

"That's not my job. They'll execute me if I try to work outside of my parameters."

"As long as we make our quotas we should be fine," Kraj said nicely. The Newlyn was hard pressed to speak to him most days, and was quite good at dodging baited questions.

The next report he pulled up shocked him. It was a transmission from Sandra to Kerk outlining the take-down of the southern tower by Lito and Lady Mercelle. He was already aware of that, but what surprised him was that Lady Feres had spoken to the pair, and was cross-referencing data with Dredger indicating they were in the desert, separated, and travelling to different locations. Mercelle's location was listed in the intelligence briefing, but it was also stating that Lito had not been heard from since reporting the tower's destruction.

This was a great opportunity to filter what went up the chain.

He changed the timestamp of Feres's last communication with Mercelle and Lito to just before the tower came down, and removed the content. The rest of the report was altered to state that neither of the two had been spoken to since approaching the tower, leaving the replicas to surmise that they died in the collapse.

He wiped sweat from his cheeks, and stopped to take a few deep breaths of stale air. Sometimes, when he was in the depths of altering a report, he would forget to steady his heart rate to counteract the lack of oxygen. Short bouts of meditation here and there also helped. After a quick review of his work, he sent it through to the program.

Kraj leaned back in his seat, stretching his arms above his head. "Only a few more left before I'm all caught up. What about you?" He didn't care about the Newlyn's workload, only that eventually small talk would turn into something useful for him to get back to his handler.

"Fine," the Newlyn grunted.

He looked around the room, trying to find something to point out so that the Newlyn would have a reason to look up from its screen. Nothing caught his eye. "I sure wouldn't mind a change of scenery. You know? Maybe an outside job or something."

"They want you inside, Crassa, so they can keep you contained," it said.

"That makes sense, I guess. How long have you been at this?" He motioned a hand toward the Newlyn's terminal.

"I haven't been away from my terminal for more

than a minute at a time since they assigned me here many years ago."

A sudden daydream – more like a nightmare – sped through Kraj's head. He pictured himself as an old man with a white beard down to his knees, sitting at the same terminal, coming up with cleverly faked memories each day in order to keep himself alive. So close to feeling pity for the replica, he thought about what kind of person he was to lack empathy for such tribulations. The creature had never experienced freedom, but Kraj didn't really care about anything that didn't have the potential to preserve his position or provide him intelligence.

"If I keep up with my quota I'll be moved to a factory floor. That will allow me to move around more," it sadly stated.

He had decided not to feel sorry for it. Besides, he wasn't here to feel bad for the enemy. His only important friend was the one receiving the information he sent out.

"I'm happy for you," he said. "That'll be better for you, I think."

The Newlyn didn't reply, it just went on working, and he did the same. It was only a few hours until the screen on the ceiling flashed a distinct orange color, and a Mora's face came into frame announcing that it was "Crassa out time".

All of the Newlyns on the work floor took a moment

to let their heads go back. When they relaxed, their necks sucked into their bodies and their faces pointed up at the ceiling. It was a gross, unsettling sight to see, but every one of them was hoping to get called away for something. Maybe even reassigned to another occupation. Instead, they had to endure the daily call for "Crassa out time".

All of the humans stood and began filing out of the room for their eight hour block of rest time. This was the only time allotted for humans to eat and sleep, to rest and refuel. The slop given to the Crassas was nothing more than a thick protein-based substance that was definitely missing some key vitamins.

As he said goodbye to the Newlyn next to him and stood to file out with the rest of his kind, Kraj stopped short of walking into another man who was shuffling his way to the door. The man's face was blank, staring ahead and paying no attention to Kraj. The skin on his face was beginning to sag and turn a greenish pale color. The man would die soon.

No humans lasted long in Glaven Grad. Slowly slipping into anemia and fatigue, they would give up, one by one, and fail to show up to their jobs. That's when they were removed to either be executed or experimented upon. He wasn't sure what any of the others were there for. Focusing on his own tasks kept him mostly under the radar and out of trouble.

He was glad to be getting away from his terminal.

Even when he did sleep, all he saw were reports and descriptions of intercepted communications repeating themselves as projections on the insides of his eyelids.

The Crassa quarters were nothing more than cordoned off sections of corridors with thin pads on the floors and basins of water every twenty feet or so which smelled like feces and chemicals. He did his best to survive off of the cleanest smelling basins, and they were lucky enough to have them cleaned out every few days and refilled with a clear liquid smelling more of chemicals than human excrement.

He tried to spend the least amount of time in the human quarters as possible.

Walking brusquely, he realized that he was exerting too much energy and slowed himself. His chest felt heavy, tight. So he closed his eyes for a second and let his mind slip into a place where his pain and discomfort didn't exist. Then he continued on toward the exit of Workfloor 86.

When the small crowd of humans emerged from Workfloor 86 and into the corridor, Kraj clung to the wall and let them pass by. Everyone went toward the human quarters, but he broke from the pack and snuck in the opposite direction.

Having memorized the routes and times of the Valks patrolling the halls, he avoided discovery. Within minutes he had found the utility closet he needed in order to access the electrical ducts.

The ducts were wide and round enough to fit more than just himself. Made of a black glass that could almost be seen through at certain angles, they held jumbles and tangles of thick cords. He placed himself at the center of the jumble, and moved slowly through the maze of ducts to make his way upward.

All of the more secretive goings-on happened toward the top of the tower.

Being surrounded by the heavy cords and enveloped in the lilac light shining through the glass, he almost felt as if he were underwater. His motions to push himself along were very much like swimming, and it made him thirsty.

Sweat beaded off of him, and trailed inside the ducts. Perhaps he was more like the Newlyns than he thought, just with sweat instead of slime. It was nearly hot enough inside the ducts to give any sensible human being a heat stroke, but he maintained, making his way through a dozen floors. It may have been more, but he meditated as he inched along, causing him to lose count as he instead focused on steadying his vitals.

Most of the rooms were dark, and either empty or used to house random machines and parts. He navigated up to the next floor, and the duct cut through a room full of Moras that were sitting around a circular table, each with their projector screens on and notating into their respective holograms. It looked like a think tank. Probably brainstorming ways to use the fake information he gave to them earlier that day, Kraj thought.

Curling into a ball in the corner of the glass tube, he reached down and pulled off his shoe. From inside it fell a flat transmitter that was flexible enough to take on the shape of the sole of his foot and hold his weight as he walked on it throughout the day. He bent it flat, and held it up. The screen facing him showed what the lens on the opposite side was picking up.

Chaos glyphs and texts glowed on the Mora's holograms as they spoke and discussed something he couldn't make out. Tapping the button on the side of the transmitter took images of the replicas and their notes. Even if he couldn't read what they said, the images automatically went back to his handler, who had likely developed a program to read Chaos writing.

He held the transmitter tight as the shoe went back on, then he made his way along to what resembled a hospital room with steel tables along one wall. All fours kinds of replicas, along with one human, were lying on the tables, hooked to lines and machines, seemingly unconscious.

Moras were wearing face coverings and going down the line injecting the subjects with different substances. More images were taken and sent off before he advanced through the ducts and into a laboratory.

That's when Kraj found a hatch, and climbed down into the vacant room.

The door was open, and the next room over was a chamber used for mass experiments, surrounded by an observation deck separated by a large pane of glass. He crouched behind a metal shelf full of beakers and canisters with unreadable labels, and steadied his lens between two containers. From there he could see through the double doorway and down into the experimental chamber.

He had dreaded being taken to one of these horrible chambers ever since he found one during his first snoop a few days ago. This was the only time he had actually seen one about to be used. He began recording the scene playing out before him.

The glass chamber inside the observation walkway had another line of replicas and humans. He counted five humans, and nine replicas of all four varieties. They stood facing the entrance as another human led a cart of different colored beakers in. She handed a purple vial to a Valk in the line. The replica took it and drank it without instruction. The next Valk got a green liquid, and when she came to the first human he got a sickened face and the man pulled away from the vial.

The woman looked back through the entrance, and two more Valks entered, grabbing the man by each arm and forcing his mouth open. The traitor clenched the man's throat and shoved the vial into the opening.

The man gagged, and almost managed to spit some liquid out, but the Valks shoved his jaw upward, shattering the end of the vial. With a closed jaw, the man could only swallow as blood dripped down his front side.

The next human was more cooperative. She took the vial and sipped it down, cringing at the taste of the brown fluid before handing the empty vessel back. If she looked sickly prior to taking in the mystery liquid, she certainly started to approach death afterward. Her eyes darkened, and she barely held herself upright with a hand on the wall.

Once they were done poisoning the rest of the line of humans and replicas, the woman giving out vials stood in front of them with her hands held behind her back, eyeing each of them. Some of them swayed in their stances, others fell to their knees. A few were showing no symptoms at all.

The traitor eyeballed each individual, observing what was happening to their bodies. A human voided their insides onto the floor, and then collapsed forward into it. That's when the woman stepped out of the chamber and sealed it shut. By the time she made her way up to the observation walkway, a reddish water had started to pump up through the floor of the chamber.

All of the replicas relinquished themselves to the flood, going limp and allowing themselves to float in it once it got high enough. The humans, however, panicked and flailed about, trying to keep their weak muscles going and their heads above the surface.

Kraj had no way of identifying the liquids being used, and neither would the recipient of the feed. He moved the lens to capture the labels on the sides of the canisters and beakers that filled the shelf. By the time he had panned back to the filling chamber, there was no air left at the top, and all thirteen bodies were floating along the ceiling.

Replicas didn't need to breathe, so he didn't understand exactly how they were meant to take in the liquid. The submerged humans convulsed, reaching the end of their lung capacities.

One at a time, air bubbles spewed from the humans' lungs until none were left to writhe beneath the fluid's death clench.

He felt nothing for the lost beings. They were defectors. Prisoners were experimented on right away, not kept until they were weak and frail like these individuals. These people must have given up some type of information to secure their lives long enough to get sick and useless. Bad part being that their information was likely true, and had the potential to provide an actual advantage to the Chaos.

He wondered what the woman administering the doses had done to secure her spot in Glaven Grad. There had been rumors floating around the desert and Oasian tribes about the Demigods kidnapping pregnant women and keeping their babies, raising them in Glaven Grad in the ways of Chaos. Perhaps she had been born and raised here, and was accepted as another replica.

A gurgling sound arose from beneath the floor, and bubbles shot up from drains as the reddish water began to lower. All of the bodies lowered with it until they were lying on the floor, unresponsive. The replica test subjects must have been given poison as well, he thought, since they couldn't die by drowning.

The traitor stood, observing from above. Next to her was a Mora that she was conversing with, likely about the poor results of whatever it was they were trying to accomplish. No, it wasn't *a* Mora. This one was taller, had longer hair, and wore the Chaos glyph on her garments. It was *the* Mora, the Demigod.

Kraj focused the transmitter's lens on them for a moment, but a disturbance within the chamber brought his attention back to it. The doors were opening again, and Moras were entering to examine the corpses. But, one of the corpses started to move.

One of the dead Newlyns, blubbery and fat, trembled and shook. A Mora rolled it onto its back, and the Newlyn's body rippled and spat about, slime slinging all over. The other Moras got closer, trying to see what would happen, like a pack of curious children waiting to see if their makeshift bomb would go off when triggered.

This bomb went off.

The front of the Newlyn expanded, puffed out. Its wet skin stretched farther than Kraj thought it could, and became taut as goo slicked down onto the floor.

From neck to crotch, flesh tore in a vertical split that sprayed darkening slime into the Moras' faces. Dripping deep purple, and resembling tendons and bones, a turning mass protruded out of the Newlyn. The replica's skin deflated and the new creature emerged into the chamber.

The sound of bones clicking together as the bulging mass reached a long claw out, scratching at the floor to pull free from the remnants of the Newlyn's exterior. Oozing strings of thickening flesh wrapped around the bony limb. Growing another extension, the monster slashed the new claw outward, gashing an on-looking Mora's face wide open.

The replica held its wound shut, and turned to leave the chamber, but Mora had already activated the failsafe, and locked it down. It ran straight into the glass door, and clawed at it to open. A second later the rest of the Moras were alongside it, tapping at the keypad and pounding weak fists into the panes, hollering to be released.

While they exercised futility, the monster flipped over on the floor, splitting open yet again on its back. Teeth pointed out from the edges of the newly formed opening. At this point, it was almost entirely round, aside from the two bony extremities that were still getting thicker and growing muscles, with a spewing gash of a mouth on its back.

Kraj couldn't believe what he was witnessing. He wouldn't be the only one to see it since his transmitter was still operating. Perhaps he would need to rewatch the recording later just to make sure he wasn't hallucinating.

Slow, deep breaths through the nose.

It was crawling now, with a third leg starting to take the same shape as the other two. An awful mixture of throat sounds and screeching filled the room as the monster jumped onto the Moras' backs and tore into their flesh.

Limbs, muscles and parts were tossed left and right and some even stuck to the glass walls, sliding down and leaving grey trails of Mora blood.

Up on the observation walkway, the traitor and Mora were smiling at each other. A job well done.

KRAJ THOUGHT about the prospect of sleep as he snuck his way back to the humans' quarters. None of the water basins smelled okay enough to taste, and he figured it would just make him vomit anyway. There was no sense in trying.

Regardless of whether or not he felt he could sleep, he needed to try.

A few hours were managed before the morning sirens went off. It was back to Workfloor 86, and trying as hard as possible to hide his exhaustion.

3

LITO VII

Lito opened His eyes.

Desert sand was all He could see in every direction. The wounds that covered His body four days ago were already healed, including the bullet holes. With the collapsed southern tower days behind Him, He walked in the direction of the Shard's dig site.

Time alone helped Him to steady His thoughts, clearing the dismay from His mind regarding the strange feelings He had for Feres. Tiredness came and went, but the closest Lito felt to sleep were His occasional daydreams. He wasn't sure what they meant, or if they meant anything at all, but they flooded in when He let His mind rest during long bouts of walking.

There wasn't much else to do. The dig site for the Shard was still hundreds of miles away. He could see the map in the memories behind His eyes, and recognized the flat valley He was centered in. Every time Lito closed His eyelids He ran the risk of falling back into another flash of images that came and went with such speed that He wasn't able to fully comprehend them. They were all the same, and they never varied.

Stars fell from the sky, bringing dark voids to replace the hope He and the others had garnered between each other. He couldn't tell who was walking along with Him, nor could He recognize the ruins of the city over which they walked.

The only certain piece of the flash was the turmoil accompanying each star as it fell from the sky. It almost felt like a message, or a warning. But, from whom?

Done with the map He was remembering in His mind's eye, Lito sensed the beginning of another lucid daydream. It started with an airy sensation that cooled Him throughout. That brought on thoughts of victory, and an alacritous zeal for it. He wanted to examine the vision further, and perhaps discover something He had missed before. But, nothing enveloped His arduous psyche this time, and Lito trudged on through the scorching desert, feeling His senses going in another direction as He held His eyes shut.

The daydream had Him walking through ruins with two others. Could they have been Mercelle and Feres? Now, He was sensing a presence, and getting a mental impression of eyes on Him. Was there a fourth person He couldn't see? Were their eyes truly on Him? When He opened His own eyes, the desert greeted Him, empty and arid.

Hearing crunching of granules to the left, He turned and saw something that made Him question whether He was in the throes of another flash of images. A tall shadow stood many feet away, completely blackened even in the daylight. Lito shaded His face to get a better look at it.

It was taller than Him, and held something at its side. The shape was similar to a human's, but He couldn't see clearly enough until the wind died down and the sand settled back into the rolling dunes. Two broad shoulders, thick waist and arms, bulging legs. It was indescribable to Lito's senses, but felt like an aura of ancient, undiscovered energies, which held no candle of logic to His current, exhausted thought processes.

The object in its hand was a steel staff with a dark, round stone fastened to one end. He didn't perceive a threat, but rationality guided Him to wariness when the shadow looked Him up and down, and stepped closer.

"Stop," Lito ordered with a hand out. "Don't come closer than that."

Halting a few paces away, the shadow became clearer, and Lito could make out the details on its skin.

It wasn't a shadow at all, but a man with a complexion darker than a starless night's sky. Pitch black, and a flawless face, but the man's body was full of old scars, like the four jagged claw marks paralleled and grey across his muscular breast. The mark had the pattern of a scar, but it was flushed to the skin, like a birthmark. His eyebrows were the only hair Lito could see, and they were a plain, bright white. The top of his head shined with a clean baldness. All the dark man wore was a single piece of bent steel strapped around his pelvis and genitals. Lito thought that strange for a human in the desert.

"You hooman?" the man asked with a deep, penetrating voice.

He didn't answer, but replied, "You are."

"Yes." the dark man answered. Then he continued in a language that Lito didn't understand. It sounded like a quick series of low, guttural tones that rose and fell in cadence, and his tongue moved in an unfamiliar fashion. His body language indicated he was asking another question. When Lito didn't respond, the man spoke slowly, "Language is primitive. You is speak...?"

"I speak this language, yes," Lito told him. "But that other one is new to me. It'll just take me a little bit of time to learn it."

"I is bilingual, is learn some light skinned language. But, no mistake you is make, I is stronger than others you is know." The mysterious man pointed his staff at Lito. "I is mean no harm. If I is need to, I is fight." He reached behind his back and brought forth a green object that he held out in one hand. The item was bright, a yellowish-emerald color, and looked like the pictures Lito had seen of cacti or mushrooms from the ancient times. "Or I is feed," the bald man finished.

Lito was surprised to see such a diplomatic nomad this far out in the middle of nowhere. How did he survive?

"You are kind," He said. "Thank you, but I don't require sustenance."

The man let the green item drop and dangle at his waist by the string tied around it. Then he bent his knees, lowering his body and aiming the staff at Lito.

"No is eat?!" he shouted. "You is Chaos!"

"I assure you, I'm not." Lito put His hands out and calmly stepped back, but the stone on the end of the man's staff was already coming at Him. He leaned to one side, slapping the heavy pole away and hopping over a leg swipe attempt. "Please. I'm not going to hurt you."

The man wasn't hearing it. He spun the weapon over his head, trying to disorient Lito before striking. A curling of his body, and the man swung low.

Lito simply lifted a knee to block the strike, then caught the other end of the staff when it turned toward His face. "Enough," He said, pulling the rod free from the man's grip and tossing it aside. "Chaos is your enemy? It's mine too."

Astonished, the hard-headed fighter pulled a short blade from the back of his steel loincloth. "I is no believe you!" He came forward, swiping at Lito's midsection at every angle, but He kept rolling and turning to just miss the blade each time. The dark man was quite the warrior: quick, agile, and from the sounds of the blade swiping through the air, Lito could tell he was very strong.

Lito finally found a chance to wrap His hand around the swiping wrist and hold it still. The warrior let go of the knife, dropping it into his other hand and slicing upward. Reaching over His occupied hand to catch the wrist before the blade could make contact, Lito moved to end this futile dance.

With both of the man's wrists in His grip, Lito put one over the other and pulled them in opposite directions, causing the warrior's arms to cross at the biceps, and their faces nearly touched.

"Calm yourself, warrior," Lito told the squabbling man as he tried uselessly to shake from His grip. "I am not Chaos, nor am I human."

"You is liar!" the warrior shouted at Him. The man's face was bent with ferocity. His brow wrinkled as he shouted.

"Listen!" Lito pulled the man as close as he could get. "Look into my eyes! I am Lito, the God of Order!"

"Lies!" The warrior was persistent, and continued to struggle in Lito's grip. He pulled and yanked, shifted and pried, trying to get free, until he finally looked into the glowing cerulean of Lito's irises. A sudden shock froze the man, and he was stupefied.

That was the first time Lito noticed the man's eyes were white around black irises, but the pupils were encircled in thin red lines, allowing their borders to be faintly apparent in the glint of bright sunlight.

"I'm telling you the truth," Lito said. "Even if you don't believe who I am, at least believe that I won't harm you." He raised His eyebrows at the warrior, who was blinking himself out of a stupor. "I'm going to let you go now. Okay?"

The warrior nodded, his bald head bending a reflection of the sun's rays.

Loosening His grip, Lito let the man's arms go, and took a step backward. "We speak a similar language. We understand each other. Yes?" More memories came back, and He thought about the day Mercelle had woken Him in the temple, and taught Him "yes" and "no". It was more instinctual than anything when He had immediately understood the words.

"I is understand," the warrior replied. "You is true? You is Lito? Order God?"

"I am. And you are?"

The man squeezed his eyes shut for a moment,

returning his knife to the back of his metallic waistband. "I is Bewapen. Is warrior."

"You are quite the warrior," Lito praised. "I'm sure your enemies fall by the packs."

Bewapen walked over to his staff and picked it up out of the sand. "I is never kill other man before. Clan is avoid battle for millennia. I is never see other man fight way you do. You is true. Is God."

"That's right. So you're obviously human. Why haven't I seen more people like you?" Lito looked around in case others were sneaking up on Him. No one was there.

"We is stay hide from other hooman. Clan is alone." Bewapen's hand gestured toward the distant horizon.

That would explain the variation in language, thought Lito. Bewapen's dialect had simply evolved in a different direction than the rest of the human population due to their sequestering. "Is your Clan nearby?" Lito asked, curious to see how many others there were like Bewapen.

"I is take. You is travel from afar?" He started walking in the same direction Lito was already headed in.

Lito followed.

Within an hour of walking, Lito was led around the edge of a long ridge, and once His view was clear of the mountain He saw thousands of pitch black men spread about the base of the hidden ridge and the valley further down. Fires were burning and smoking with circles of the dark males standing around them, eating and conversing in small bits of clothing, jewelry and intricate hair designs using beads, colored wires and clasps.

Red and orange flames peeked out from small holes in the ground where men were forging steel objects. Without gloves, the men handled the red hot material like it was tough dough in their hands, shaping with the force of their fists and palms before it got too solid, then they moved on to using hammers and anvils. Lito was shocked to see bare skin against hot metal without it burning or searing off. Even He wasn't capable of withstanding such temperatures.

Each man stopped what they were doing and looked up at the pair as they headed further into the valley. One man had reflective, metal rings clinging tightly to his arms all the way up to his biceps, and white bangs that led back to a thin layer of hair. When he looked at them, Bewapen looked back and said something Lito felt was a greeting, but couldn't be sure. Then he said, "This is Klere. I is say that I is make new friend, Lito. I is take to Kop Stamhoof."

The translation helped Lito to match certain tones and words in both languages.

"Is nice to meet you, Lito," said Klere. "I is never see light skinned before." He glanced suspiciously at Bewapen, muttering something foreign.

"You is no worry," Bewapen advised with a small wave. "Is friend. Is mean no harm. Lito, Klere is royal dressmaker. He is make all clothes for Kop and Queen. Anything you is need, he is make."

"I is see you is no have arm guard." Klere tapped the rings on his own arms. "I is make for you."

"That isn't necessary," declined Lito. "I don't have a good record of keeping track of my armor. Things tend to fall off of me and become lost to the desert."

"You is speak ancient tongue, is old dialect. Is interesting. You is want jewelry? Is small." Klere pulled a small, dark stone the size of Lito's fingertip from a steel bowl next to the working bellows. "Here. Is no gaudy, is easy to make smooth."

Taking the stone into His hand, Lito looked over the shiny surface of the small mass of onyx. Perfectly round, the marble rolled back and forth across His palm until He shoved it into His pocket.

"Thank you. I'll try to keep this safe."

Klere laughed. "Is nothing. Is stone. Is much more within Earth. If you is lose, I is give another."

"That's kind of you." He didn't know what to make of all of this, aside from the fact that kindness wasn't lacking here. "I'm afraid I don't have anything to give you in exchange."

With a smile and a wave, Klere turned away and went back to stoking his flames with the bellows.

"He is flirt with you," Bewapen pointed out. "You is no worry. Is harmless. Come. We is speak to Kop. He is need to know who you is." He exchanged farewells with Klere.

Lito followed him again.

Pairs of warriors were sparring with staffs, clubs and battle hammers as tall as they were. Each Clan member continued to stop and gaze at Lito as they walked by, and He wondered how long it had been since they had seen someone from outside their Clan, if ever. He couldn't help but feel like an outsider. Bewapen bowed his head back at the gawkers, keeping a steady pace as Lito trailed behind him, returning smiles to those watching Him pass and listening in on their dialect.

The human cities He'd seen before were quite different from this one. These men only had their bodies, their steel, their fires and their weapons. Nothing else decorated footpaths or living areas. At the base of the mountain He saw openings, like caves entering the Earth. It was clear to Him that these people lived underground in the safety of the caves. He thought about Dredger in the subterranean city of Kerk, and the similarities between the two peoples. Like Kerk, Lanna and Sandra, everyone seemed to have a purpose or occupation in which they specialized. Something about this society felt much more placid and serene, as if it had been working seamlessly for countless generations, at peace with the planet.

Agnitius had told Him that the Crimson, Grey and Black bloodlines had all died out over the millennia, leaving a mixture of what remained. All the late High Cleric had to go off of was what was included in the Book of Order and what was recorded and salvaged during the reign of man, and nothing else.

Agnitius had it wrong, and Lito was glad for it.

Dark skinned men dotted the landscape, and without guidance Lito would have never suspected a group to be living in this area. The crowd grew more and more abundant with men stopping curiously to silently greet Bewapen. As they passed by, the men started following closely behind, gathering and whispering to each other.

Bewapen stayed quiet, as if he was waiting until they arrived at a specific place before explaining Lito's true identity. A sudden thought occurred to Lito that Bewapen may have been leading Him into a trap. He refused to believe that, and brushed the idea from His thoughts.

Up ahead was a billowing fire, a burning heap of the same object Bewapen had offered to Lito as food. Were they burning their food sources?

Standing in a perimeter about forty feet out from

the fire was a tight circle of straight-backed men, facing inward and holding their weapons at their sides. The weapons of choice seemed to be long handled tools with something heavy on the end.

Bewapen walked Lito right up to the back of one of the men, and tapped him on the shoulder. The guard turned and gave him a confused look, but motioned them both through before closing the gap. All of the men following behind the pair stopped and waited outside of the circle.

Where were all of their women? Lito shuddered to think that the Clan kept their women hidden, or that there weren't any. Women were equals, leaders and warriors in the rebellion. Was it not the same here?

Next to the fire was a fully clothed, older man sitting on a finely crafted chair – like all of their other tools and clothes – made of steel. It looked like the sitting man was wearing a thick trench coat of rusted chain-mail that went down to his ankles. A tall hat made of metal strips sat atop his head with a wide brim all the way around, and lengthy, thick tendrils of bright white hair hung out from under it, reaching his waist. Beneath the long chainmail jacket the man wore nothing but a shiny loincloth and steel strips around his waist, biceps and thighs.

When the man saw Bewapen and Lito approaching, he stood, looking away from the fire with arms open.

He spoke through a smile, it seemed and sounded

like another friendly greeting. Random trinkets that Lito didn't recognize hung from the man's belt. One of them was a round device with numbers ranging from one to twelve around the outside, and two brass bubbles on the top. Another was a plastic looking piece of equipment – with a small screen and buttons inside – that looked like it could fold and unfold at the middle. More numbers were on the buttons.

"Day is good," Bewapen said. The men grabbed each other's forearms in a sort of handshake greeting. "I is bring friend. Friend is Lito, is to meet Kop."

"Lito is welcome." The man held out his arm, and Lito copied Bewapen's greeting. "I is Kop Stamhoof. I is Kop of Clan, is happy to meet you." His speech was exactly the same as Bewapen's in tone and accent. He turned and said something to Bewapen, who replied in the same language.

To Lito it sounded as if the Kop was seeking more information, and He heard His name from Bewapen. "I am happy, also," Lito responded, not wanting to reveal His confusion just yet. Upon closer inspection, He could see metal gears and cogs decorating the Kop's coat, he even had one above the brim of his hat. Some were shiny and reflective while others were corroded and pitted.

Stamhoof motioned to the three other men standing from their seated positions around the fire. The first wore his hair flat and pulled back, while donning copper shorts clinging tightly to his thighs and holding a hammer taller than himself. He bowed his head as the Kop introduced him. "You is meet First Prime Neemoor. He is my advisor, is second in command."

The lean yet muscular Neemoor took Lito's arm in greeting. "I is happy to meet you, light skinned man."

"Please, First Prime Neemoor, just call me Lito," He replied.

Next was a man with long tendrils bunched atop his head, decorated with wide beads and clasps of silver, bronze and gold. All over his body were dangling piercings with small stones and shiny, polished metal. They were on his forearms, biceps, thighs, even his stomach, chest and sides.

"This is Second Prime Virou-Malik," the Kop said. "Is third in command, is in charge of warrior training, is commander of Clan army."

Virou-Malik smiled behind the multi-colored powders accenting his cheeks, lips and eyelids. He wore a skirt made of metal strips bound close together which came a quarter of the way down his massive thighs. With a strong grip, he shook Lito's hand.

"I like your jewelry," Lito complimented. "Did Klere make those?"

"Klere is make all my jewels," Virou-Malik answered with a surprised look. "You is meet him already? Is good friend. He is make my skirt and jewelry for sparring."

"Sparring?" Lito couldn't understand why jewelry would be necessary to spar.

"Yes," said the man. "I is train warriors. When we is spar, we is not stop until trainee is pluck one piece of jewelry from my body."

Lito looked over Virou-Malik's skin. There were many small scars from places where rings had been attached and then ripped out. It seemed like an interesting tactic, but effective, leaving his trainees with a souvenir from besting their trainer.

"And I is Third Prime F'Briek," inserted the other man as he stepped around Virou-Malik and shook Lito's hand. His skin was rough and calloused, especially on his fingers and palm. "I is blacksmith. I is responsible for weapon production and sappidge cultivation."

"Sappidge?" asked Lito. "Is that what you're burning here? A plant of some kind?"

Kop Stamhoof kept smiling, but didn't seem interested in answering Lito's question before asking one of his own. "Why is you visit Clan, light skinned man?" the Kop asked.

Lito looked to Bewapen to answer, since self-proclaiming His God status seemed to be a bit off putting.

"Lito is Order God," Bewapen obliged. "Is original. Is come to visit, search for Shard."

"Is God you is say?" Stamhoof chuckled, hissing air

through his teeth and letting his long, white dreadlocks fall over his face. He spoke to the Primes in their native tongue before returning to their shared language, and Lito picked up a couple of words, but couldn't put together the entire sentence. "Is long time since I is laugh so hard. Hoomans is not God. Hoomans is stupid to claim so."

"It is not a claim," Lito told him flatly.

"Is true," inserted Bewapen. "Lito is best me in battle."

"Best? Pish!" The Kop laughed out loud this time. "Light skins is no best than Clan in battle. You is need more training."

"I beat him in battle because I'm stronger than humans, light skinned or not. I do have to admit that I'm still learning some of my own abilities and limitations. Now, Bewapen told me that he is aware of the legends of Order. That means you must know of the legends." They were a complicated Race, but He was determined to get through to them. He couldn't walk away without them knowing that they had an opportunity to help fix their planet before it was too late.

"I is aware of Order, but you is not Order God. Order God is myth, is lost, is false hope. You is no allow to lie to me or people of Clan. Go away." The Kop sat back on his steel chair, watching the flames char and burn the glowing green flesh at its center.

The three Primes and the Kop conversed, and the

Order God listened. He locked eyes with Bewapen for a split second, and by the look on his face Lito could tell that Bewapen knew He was listening.

Repeated phrases and words began to become familiar. Tones and body language revealed further meanings and intentions, and within a few minutes Lito could tell they were in disagreement. First Prime Neemoor seemed to be calmly opposing Kop Stamhoof's outright dismissal of Lito. They were throwing a certain word around, and once Lito was able to piece it together in a couple of contexts He recognized the word as "proof".

"I can prove it to you," Lito said. "If you would allow me the opportunity to show you something you've never seen before, I think I can change your mind." Something within Him made it a requirement to change their minds. If He could convince them of His true identity, He might be able to reignite their faith and enlist their help unto the rebellion. They had more power to fix their circumstances than they knew about, and He needed them to know about it.

"Hohaha!" Stamhoof taunted. "You is learn Clan language fast." He waved a lazy hand. "Lito is allowed. You is show me Godly powers. I is waiting." He crossed his legs, leaned back in his seat, then folded his arms. It wasn't anticipation, it was sheer, challenging doubt.

"My blood has the ability to speed up healing in open wounds," Lito revealed. He pulled up the bottom of the tight shirt Mercelle had given Him, and took it off. Scars adorned His skin from His chest to His stomach and back. All of them were closed, and almost completely healed. "I received these wounds four days ago when a warrior from Lanna helped me destroy a Chaos tower, far to the south. Have you ever seen deep lacerations heal this quickly before?"

"Pish!" The Kop scoffed, pointing an accusatory finger at Him. "All other hoomans is liars. Light skinned is not trusted. You is show nothing. Young hooman is stupid!"

"I'm not as young as you think I am."

The Kop grinned at Him. "I is one hundred seventy-two years old." That was shocking to hear. The oldest human Lito had met since His awakening was in their eighties, and looked about the same age as the Kop. "Bewapen is ninety years old. You. You is young, light skinned." He waved Lito away.

Bewapen looked almost as young as Mercelle. There was no way Lito could believe what He was hearing, but He didn't need to judge a people of whom He had very little knowledge.

"I'm not exactly sure how old I am – my memories of time before Earth are still on their way back – but I know that I've been on this planet for at least sixty-five million years."

The Kop's head snapped to attention. This seemed to pique his interest. "Lie is very specific. Order is known in light skinned people, is no surprise. Hoomans is masquerade as Gods. Is not true. This is showing nothing of God. How is I think you as God? Not from this."

"With faith," Lito answered. "The people of Lanna found the Book of Order just over two decades ago. Since then the outside world has developed their own faith around it."

But, the Kop was having none of it. "Book of Order?" Stamhoof scrunched up his face. "Thing is no such."

"There is such a thing. The people I created wrote it after they buried me in a temple. Your ancestors provided a page as well."

The Kop stood from his seat, ready to entertain Lito's suggestion. "You, prove," he said, drawing a short blade from his belt. He held it out to Bewapen, who took it from him.

Lito looked around at the surrounding men, making sure they didn't take this as a signal to attack. He didn't feel like proving Himself in battle was the best way to go about this, especially since He had already bested Bewapen earlier. He hoped beyond hope that they weren't going to have Him fight Bewapen to the death just to prove His ability to fight better. He'd refuse.

"Prove," Stamhoof repeated.

Holding the hilt tight in one hand, Bewapen gripped the blade in his other palm and pulled the blade from it, spilling blood into the sand below. Then he handed the knife to Lito.

Lito took the blade and ran it along the inside of His own palm, drawing blood. It was the same crimson color as Bewapen's.

After handing the knife back to Kop Stamhoof, Lito hovered His bloody hand outward. Bewapen took it without hesitating, squeezing and massaging their wounded palms together to get Lito's blood worked around. Stamhoof, Neemoor, Virou-Malik and F'Briek cringed at the sight of it all, and Lito felt the eyes of the entire surrounding circle of guards on Him.

Lito avoided eye contact during the long awkward minute that Bewapen worked their hands together. When Bewapen finally let go, he looked closely at the open cut, crouching down to rub it into the sand. Then Kop Stamhoof grabbed him by the wrist and wiped the whole mess across his chainmail jacket. A very close examination of the palm, and Stamhoof's eyes seemed to have discovered something spectacular.

"You is look!" he excitedly ordered the others as he pulled Bewapen's hand toward their faces. "Is no bleed!"

"Is true then," Bewapen said, showing Lito his healing wound. "Blood is healing! Lito is Order God!"

The slice had gone from the knuckle of the pitch black thumb to the base of the pinky. Flesh that was red and bloody a few seconds ago was now covered in thin, fragile skin, aging the wound by at least a couple of days. His healing abilities must have been progressing – nothing He had healed before went this quickly.

Even His own palm had stopped bleeding.

The Kop shook his hips in a celebratory dance that made the trinkets dangling from his waist jingle. All of the other Clansmen joined in, and Lito was announced to the growing crowd as "the Order God is arrive".

It turned out that a large majority of the Clan was bilingual, and Lito and the Kop spoke about the Book of Order while the others listened on; its pages unique to each other, and individualized by the vastly different glyphs used in their texts. They talked about the Shard, and Lito gave a detailed account of how He and Mercelle had torn down two towers together.

Kop Stamhoof had an endless barrage of questions, and Lito thought it best to get them out of the way before commencing with His own. Everything from His resurrection to meeting Bewapen in the desert was detailed, and most of it repeated when the Kop would ask for clarity on certain things like radios, tablets, frequency weapons and reactor cores.

They talked through the afternoon, and well into dusk. He told them about the fall of Lanna, rescuing hostages and fighting a monster. He also told them about Feres, and the way He was strangely attracted to her like a magnet.

He eventually asked His first question. "I couldn't

help but notice that you have no females here. Is your entire Race only of one gender?"

Stamhoof took a breath, as if to prepare for a long explanation. "*You* is original. You is creator of hoomans, should know."

"What should I know?" There was a lot of hidden history to this Clan. Lito felt He was on the cusp of discovering something that could potentially aid the rebellion.

"When you is create hoomans, all Races is equal male and female. All is same, but not us. When you is create Black Race, you is only create one female." The Kop looked as if he was doubting Lito's ability to understand.

He repeated back His interpretation of what was being said, just to confirm. "Your Race was made with only one female?" How could He have done that? His respect for the Clan grew even more as He considered the obstacles He had likely created for the Race in failing to provide more females.

"Yes. Order Book is tell light skinned about Order, and Seven Races. Clan is know of Order since beginning. Some stories is lost with time, but we is never forget where we is come from. Since thousands of years, Clan is stay underground, away from light skinned hoomans, protect bloodline."

"When you say 'light skinned'," Lito asked him. "Who are you referring to? Everyone else?"

"Yes. Other hoomans not Clan is light skinned. Clan is keep bloodline pure, live longer. Maybe we is made last, you is too weak to finish us."

"That's possible. I may have lost consciousness before creating enough of you. I'm sorry about that." Lito directed His apology at the entire crowd.

"You is not to be sorry," the Kop said. "Clan is create right way, as should be. You is thank."

"I can only take credit for your origin, I can't take credit for how you've protected yourselves. You've grown strong and independent as a people. I couldn't be more proud to call you my creations."

"We is proud to be your creations. You is create us strong, independent."

"You said that your people stayed hidden away from the world to protect your bloodline. Why did your Clan come out of the caves, out of hiding?"

"Planet is change. Sacred plant is living off of light from liquid magma deep underground. Underground magma rivers is dry up. Is no magma. We is come to surface. Only fire is feed plant now."

"Plants that grow by fire light," Lito said with a hint of amazement. "I'm sure the rest of the world would like to hear about that."

"Is sappidge," the Kop pointed out. "Succulent-fungi hybrid, is flammable, is edible, is very nutritious."

"Do you know what happened to the Crimson and

Grey bloodlines?" Lito asked, His curiosity getting ahead of Him.

"Story is long. Black Clan is only pureblood Race still alive. Crimson is die out first. Grey is not dead. Is much more to this story."

What felt like a bolt of electricity rushed through Lito's chest. Could the Grey Race have been living somewhere on Earth? Hidden away from the rest of the world the same as the Black Race?

"So, the Grey bloodline still exists?"

"Long ago, Grey is dying. Infertility. They is come to us, is mix bloodlines into Clan to carry on." He stood up, and pointed to the grey birthmark on Bewapen's chest that looked like claw marks. "Grey is alive still, inside some Clan."

"The gene carried on to some of your people?"

"Yes. Not all. Some have. Clan is careful with procreating. Only is one female for birthing, although, is change in time. You is meet her?"

"I would like that," Lito accepted. He couldn't imagine what lengths the Clan had gone to in order to stay alive with only one female. Even with their technology being centuries behind the rest of the world, they seemed happier and just as smart as the rebels. Perhaps, thought Lito, their separation from the rest of the world allowed them to avoid turmoils like war or politics. Every new piece of information He received about the Clan or their history intrigued Him even more than the last.

"I is take you." Stamhoof stood and walked out of the circle surrounding the fire. The crowd broke apart to let him and Lito through.

As they walked toward the cave entrances, Kop Stamhoof explained how the Clan only birthed one female each generation, and that female gave birth to all of the males. The sole female in the Clan was referred to as the Queen, and late in her life she would birth one female. Whenever the Queen would give birth to a female, she would die, and the Clan would have to wait a few decades until the newborn reached full maturity, and could mate to create more offspring.

And so the cycle had continued for millions of years.

"Your Clan has done a great job of keeping your Queens safe from harm. By the way, other humans reach full biological maturity within thirteen to twenty years. They also have a life expectancy of about eighty years."

"Yes," the Kop entered a carved opening in the side of the mountain. "We is living two centuries, more sometimes. I is think is because we is want to be there to fight Chaos God. We is always know Order God is return. We is know Chaos is here when magma flows is dry up beneath ground."

"You knew? Then why did you say that the Order God was a myth?"

"Is a gambit," Stamhoof smirked. "I is want to challenge your claim, but Clan is always know you is return to us."

Clever and aware, the Kop was humbly leading the perfect hidden society of warriors and blacksmiths. The fact that they had managed to keep true to their beliefs, traditions and bloodline throughout the last sixty-five million years was astounding. He couldn't feel bad for not creating more females when He originally made the Black Race, because it had made them that much stronger and smarter in the end. Perseverance was truly what had cultivated strength in all humans, Lito thought, and the Clan was much better at maintaining their perseverance than any other society He'd seen or learned about outside of their village.

"I'm glad you held out hope," Lito said, smiling back at Stamhoof.

AFTER A SHORT WALK THROUGH A CAVERN, the Kop brought Him to an opening that was capable of housing hundreds of people. The stone was carved out to create a high ceiling, and the space was large enough to fit a field of the glowing sappidge plants. There were groups of sappidge stalks growing around central flames, and when He looked closer He could see that the flame at the center of each group of plants was actually a burning sappidge.

He thought it ingenious that the Clan used the plant to assist in cultivating itself. It kept them warm, and fed them. There was no wonder in His mind as to why they held the plant in such high regard.

"Here is all is left of sappidge fields," Stamhoof said, continuing to walk the dirt path between patches of the plant. "We is have endless fields of sappidge along magma flows, until Chaos is arrive. Then, planet is change, shrink. When magma is dry, we is come to surface for better chance to survive. We is find tower, to north. It is take magma from underground, is take it all away."

"So it's a tower that's harnessing all of the Earth's magma? That explains the shrinking, and the quakes."

The Kop bent down and plucked a sappidge plant from its thick stem. As they walked, he pulled the fist-sized clove into two halves, exposing a moist and meaty inside.

"Liquid is flammable," he explained. "Is hydrating too, full of nutrients."

"It's strange that it will burn, but doesn't cause harm to your insides. I haven't seen anything like it since I woke up. Anything flammable is usually toxic as well."

"Sacred sappidge is secret kept from other hoomans. Clan people is travel to outside world sometimes. Is no often, but sometimes one is want to leave Clan, and to leave is meaning a great sacrifice, and must not tell of sappidge."

"What do you mean it's a sacrifice?"

"One is to leave, must sacrifice member of bloodline first, is symbolize severance from Clan. If I is leave, I is sacrifice child of mine, since no direct ancestor is alive."

"Have you ever thought about changing your laws? Allowing your Clan's people to leave freely?"

"Law is law. No is change. It is keep our people together. No one is want to leave."

Lito surmised that it was a form of control and deterrence to require departing Clan members to kill off a member of their own bloodline. That must have been part of what made their Race resilient. He thought it better not to question their ways any further, as their laws clearly worked to keep them harmoniously alive in the long run.

"Do they ever return?" He asked.

"They is come back, sometimes, with knowledge from light skinned people. Is how we learn language. No one is leave in centuries, since Chaos is arrive."

They reached the opposite end of the cavernous field of sappidge. Just as they were entering another walkway going out of the fields, Lito spotted a black sarcophagus pinned high up on the wall above the burning sappidge, held in place by aged ropes and rusted steel stakes.

"That casket in the cavern back there," Lito said. "What's in there?"

"Is old relic," the Kop answered. "Is weapon. Is not important."

Lito felt Himself lacking belief in the Kop's answer. Perhaps He needed to build more trust with the Clan before intruding further on the matter.

"Is Ridder," said the Kop, pointing to the man standing next to an open door with a large staff in his hand. "Is Queen's bodyguard."

Ridder stayed silent and stared deliberately forward, only relenting a slight nod as the Kop took Lito through the door.

The opening at the end of the small tunnel led to a rocky chamber many feet below ground that was airy and had yet another high ceiling. Blankets spotted the floor in piles, and pots of water boiled underneath open shafts that He assumed led to the surface. Humidity dampened the cave, and smaller chambers leading away were doored off in a few places. In the corner, a stack of books as high as Lito's eyeline leaned against the wall. Pages of actual paper were rustled between the covers.

"This is Queen's chambers," the Kop pointed out. "She is live here, is give birth here."

Lito looked around. Not much was contained in the chamber aside from the water boiling over grates of burning sappidge, and a peculiar smell that made His nose tingle with the scent of new life.

"She's with child?" He asked.

"Is pregnant, always," the Kop answered. "Must be."

A door creaked open on its rusted hinges to His left, and a slow foot emerged, planting itself into the dirt and stepping through. She was bulging at the midsection, and pressing against her back with one hand as she wobbled heavily from side to side. Her long, thin garment did little to hide her features. Ample breasts embraced the beige fabric above her protruding belly.

Lito took in the beauty of the Queen, like nothing He had ever imagined. Flat, ivory hair cascaded over her shoulders, and hung far down to her ankles. A few locks even dragged behind her, mindlessly collecting dirt on their ends. Lashes and brows matched the same white hue. Pitch black skin, moist and refined, and pupils only separated from the irises by a single red circle.

She wiggled her toes into the soggy sand. "Hello," the Queen said with a soft, lovely – motherly – timbre in her voice. "I heard there was a visitor. Why don't we sit?"

The Kop took her hands, and lowered her onto a tuft of blankets. "You is sit," he told Lito. They both chose piles and sat.

"I'm Queen Maagda," she started. "Or the Queen Mother, or Mother Aeterna...or just Maagda."

“Pleased to meet you, I’m Lito. The Kop has told me a little bit about you and your-”

“I was told that you claim to be the God of Order,” Maagda cut in. “Is that true?”

“Yes. I’m on my way to retrieve an artifact that might help the humans destroy the Chaos Demigods. Excuse my asking, but, how is it that you speak differently than the others I’ve met?” The question had piqued His interest since she first spoke.

“I have my own artifacts,” she said, nodding to the stack of timeworn books in the corner. “The ancient people wrote stories, kept records. They called them religious texts. Sometimes it’s hard to tell one from another. I find reading texts in the old tongue to be refreshing, especially poetry. I’m also working to translate our historical records into the old tongue, which is what you and I are speaking now. The men speak a version of the language which has gone through generations of brevity and transformation. They learned it by hearing it, whereas I learned it by reading it.”

“Queen Mother is like reading, is always reading,” the Kop added.

“I spend much of my time in my cave. My books help me travel to other places, other times. The language hasn’t changed since the Demigods arrived so it’s been easy to learn. I’m even trying to teach it to the other females.”

“I thought the Kop said-”

"He must have saved some details for me to explain. First: Girls!" She clapped her hands twice in the air. "Come in here please!"

The same door Queen Maagda came out of opened again, and this time four girls came out. The first one looked to be a young teen carrying an infant in one arm and holding the hand of another little girl. The last female came out behind them, shy and hiding behind luscious white locks.

"There are two more that are too young to come out just yet, but these are the first four girls born to our Clan without killing their mother. Since you created our Race we have only had one living female at a time. Birthing a girl used to be a painful, violent process that always ended in the death of the Queen, but things have changed for the better in the last two decades."

She introduced the girls, and they each smiled coyly at the sound of their name.

The youngest Hidre, she was six years old, but looked much younger. She was being held by the oldest named Klo, who was the first ever female born to the Clan to nurse off of and meet her own mother. The other two were Leidra and Gera.

"You're all very lovely," He complimented. Then He looked back to Maagda. "What do you think caused the change?"

"It was foretold millions of years ago, by the Queen Mother at the time. You see, every time the Queen has given birth, she has entered an ethereal realm that provides her with visions. These visions can include the future, the past or the present. Sometimes they hold precious information, and sometimes they show nothing of importance at all."

Visions? Thought Lito. He was becoming familiar with a vision of His own, but figured that was a question for another day.

"How many children have you birthed?" Lito asked.

"I'm not sure, a few hundred at least. A vision has accompanied every one of them. Everyone in the Clan that's under a hundred and ten years old is mine."

Lito thought of the flashes of lucid daydreams He'd had while in the desert.

She winced, shifted her weight, and rubbed her belly. "Ooh this babe. This one will be ready in a few days if it doesn't come early."

The Kop's expression beamed across his face, and he reached a hand forward to caress her stomach. "Child is mine, is new Kop when older."

Queen Maagda put her hand on his, and beamed back at him. "Once the Kop reaches a certain age he creates an offspring to take over after he dies. He – or she – will be in charge once they reach maturity."

"Hope is female," Stamhoof said, sweetly admiring his unborn child. "First female Kop is what I is want. But, I is love it no matter what."

"As long as it's healthy," she returned. "To clear it all

up: back when the Grey people were living in hiding just like us, they came to us asking for help to preserve their Race. Over the course of centuries the Greys had slowly become infertile, until they eventually started giving birth to asexual beings instead of males or females. Their last fertile male came to our Kop and begged him to allow a mating between him and the Queen in order to produce an offspring and carry on with the Grey gene.

"The Kop allowed it, and after the mating ceremony the remaining Greys left to die alone. Three months later when the Queen at the time gave birth to the Black-Grey hybrid boy, she had a premonition that only came true in recent years."

Klo handed Hidre to Maagda, then ladled some boiling water from the pots, pouring it directly into the mouths of Leidra and Gera. They gulped it down like it was the tastiest thing they'd ever experienced. Even the children had tougher skin than Lito.

"From what I've read, and what we've been told by those who leave the Clan and return again, other humans have a gestational period of nine months. I can give birth up to four times in a single year, as long as the mating rituals are on time."

Lito felt a pang of empathy for the strong woman. "That must take a toll on you, physically, I mean." The adaptability and diligence of the Clan continued to impress Him.

"Not really." She cradled Hidre, lowering the top of her dress and exposing a breast for the babe's mouth. "I get rather depressed between pregnancies. It's an empty, lonely sensation. Anyway, the first Grey-Black hybrid baby born to our Clan gave the Queen a vision that let her see millions of years into the future. When she came out of it, she said that she saw the first ever successful birth of a female without the mother succumbing to instant death. It was something our Clan had never heard of before, but was happy to hear at the time. She told the Kop that the female's birth would signal the coming of the Order God – the return of our creator, the original – and that the Queen Mother who performed the birth would forever be known as Mother Aeterna. But, please, just call me Maagda.

"Over the millennia, the story became nothing more than lore, losing traction and becoming more of a fairy tale as time went on. It stayed that way until Klo was born."

Lito watched as Leidra and Gera splashed each other with steaming hot water, laughing and soaking their dresses. They bantered in their native language.

"When you had your first girl, what vision did you have?" He asked.

"Klo was a difficult birth," Maagda sighed. Hidre began to fuss, so Klo came and took her away. She adjusted her gown to cover her breast. "We knew she was a girl as soon as the contractions started. They are always excruciating, to let the Queen know that her end is near. Birthing boys is easy in comparison. Our only fear at the time was that Klo's father is a hybrid, and isn't a pureblood, which meant the end of our untainted Black bloodline. However, we were elated to find that she didn't kill me during the birth, and that I could continue birthing more purebloods, which the other girls are. You see, girls don't want to emerge from the womb. It's like we think that's where we are supposed to live forever. We are typically cut from the Queen in a bloody mess, but with Klo, something told me to start pushing. I don't remember much after that. I passed out, ready to die and let my life flow into her so she could arrive into the world as our new Queen.

"But, I didn't die. It's as if the Grey blood within her kept her calm, and kept me alive. I had a vision of a fat, bald, light skinned man stepping on a strange book in the desert. It was quick, but I'll never forget it. Then, something else that was new happened. I had a second vision of a light skinned girl being born to what I assumed to be a Lord and Lady. We've tried to figure out what it means, but I suppose only time will tell, if it decides to. Some visions are meaningless and tell us nothing. Others will warn us of coming wars or disasters. There really is no way of knowing for sure, not right away, anyway."

Lito was putting the pieces together. "I don't believe

you were seeing the future, Queen Maagda. I believe you were seeing the present."

"Is that so?" Her face revealed the surprise of this information.

"Very much," Lito replied. "The man you saw in the desert, I believe that to be High Cleric Finlin Agnitius. He discovered the Book of Order on the same day that my friend Lady Inis Mercelle was born."

"So, these people are alive now? That would mean that the old visions were true. The coming of Mother Aeterna – myself – *was* the sign of your return. All at once the Book was found, our first successful female was birthed without incident, and your friend was also born."

"That's right. However, Agnitius died recently when Lanna was attacked and destroyed by Chaos forces. Lanna was where Mercelle was born."

"I'm saddened to hear of Agnitius's passing," she empathized sweetly. "Forgive me for asking, but, why is your friend so important that I should see her birth in my vision?"

"She's the one who found me. She's worked to translate many of the texts in the Book, and through those translations she was able to locate my temple, and wake me up. Without her, I wouldn't be here."

He looked over at Klo, who was pretending not to listen to their conversation while she and Stamhoof tickled Gera. For a small moment, their eyes met, and

He could make out the red rings around her pupils. It wasn't an easy task for His mind to accept the fact that Klo was the same age as Mercelle. Klo looked like she was still maturing, and that told Him that the Clan aged slowly. That would explain the impossibly long life spans.

Now that He was apprised of their history, He wanted to know something about their future. "What will happen to the girls? Will they all become Queens and provide offspring for your Clan?"

Maagda's eyes lit up with enormous heart and love as she watched her daughters and Stamhoof play in a heap of blankets on the floor. "They are all Queens," she said. "And as long as there is more than one birthing Queen, the choice will be up to her once she reaches maturity. If my next child is a girl then she will be the first female Kop and have the option to birth children."

Kop Stamhoof seemed delighted at the thought of the next Kop also bearing children for the Clan, as he stopped playing with the girls and stared up at Maagda for a few seconds.

A moving bulge pushed out from Queen Maagda's stomach, and shifted toward one side. The Mother Aeterna sucked air in through her teeth, and leaned to the right to alleviate the pressure, placing a hand on her back again.

"Having experienced births of both genders," she

said through a wince. "I don't think this one is going to be a girl. The pain is too manageable."

"You're in pain," Lito told her. "I appreciate you talking with me, but I really should leave you to rest." The words felt strange to say, but it was as if His confusing feelings for Feres were expanding to deeper abilities of sympathy for His creations.

"I am happy to talk with you, Lito. Thank you for sitting with me, and thank you for creating our people so strong and determined the way you did. We wouldn't be here if we had turned out any different. After you find your artifact, please come back and visit. I'd really like to meet your friend Inis someday."

"I surely will."

He stood with the Kop, tipped His head to Queen Maagda, and they made their way back out into the evening air.

IN THE MOONLIGHT, the Clan peppered the sandy valley beneath the mountainside, sparring and eating next to pits of burning sappidge. Mercelle would have loved to see such strong warriors, and might have even sparred with one or two of them just for the fun of it.

Lito had a growing respect, and a bit of attachment, building for the Clan the more He learned about them. A formidable force of soldiers living in harmony with the Earth, He knew they could help the rebellion. Though their values and histories were vastly different, their purposes were the same, and if they wanted to survive their goals and efforts would also need to align with the rebellion's.

After the Kop offered Lito a place to rest His head for the night, Lito explained how He hadn't slept since being awakened by Mercelle, and that time was of the utmost importance if He was going to reach the Shard and use it against the Demigods. The Kop led Him to the northern edge of the mountain, ready to send Him off. Lito had to plant the seed of partnership before leaving the Clan behind, always remembering that the decision would not be His.

"The human rebellion is strategizing a way to bring an end to the Demigods," He said as they broke from the crowd. "I believe you and your Clan could be a great help to that cause."

Barely taller than Lito, Stamhoof lifted his hat and pulled his dreadlocks up into it before placing it back down. He figured the Kop was stalling to think about how best to respond. A decent leader always thought before speaking, and especially before acting.

"Clan is one to decide," he answered with confidence. "I is talk, choose with them. Queen is decide also."

"If you told them to join the rebellion's cause, would

they listen?" Lito was pushing a certain button, testing the Kop's actual power over the Clan.

"They is always obey, but I is hate give orders, commands. People is choose to fight, or choose not. Just as people is choose to survive, or choose not. I is not decide life or death for people."

"You don't want to force them to fight."

"You is right. Clan is over five thousand strong. Caves is deep in mountain. People is not want to leave home."

"I understand," Lito said. Could He blame them? "May I tell the others about your Clan? They could learn a lot from you."

Kop Stamhoof stopped, and turned to Lito with optimism in his eyes. "You is tell everyone about us. We is above ground now, is welcome visitors."

"Thank you. I'll let them know. But, what should I call you?"

"We is Clan. Is no name."

"They'll need something to identify you by, something that represents your people."

Stamhoof gazed at the dark, round stone mounted at the top of his staff. "Onyx," said the Kop. "We is Onyx Clan. You is tell other hoomans."

"The Onyx Clan," Lito tested it on His tongue, feeling the marble in His pocket that Klere had gifted Him. "It sounds proud, unyielding."

"Name is perfect."

HEADING NORTH from the mountain ridge, Lito was full of energy and life. Something about finding the Onyx Clan, and making contact with a pure bloodline of His own creation, was empowering. It fed the internal impulses which kept His feet moving ever closer to the Shard, one in front of the other.

4

LADY TI-ERIN FERES III

Much to her relief, the presence of Chaos transports between Sandramedius and Mercelle's location had thinned out and eventually disappeared altogether. She was fleetingly worried that something was being coordinated, but once the area and path were cleared, she was happy to give the order to Mercelle's retrieval caravan to depart. It had left earlier that day, and Feres was still waiting to receive confirmation that Mercelle had been picked up and secured. The last time she checked Mercelle's tracker, she was in a deep crevasse near the Chaos encampment where the hostages had been saved. She could only hope that Mercelle was taking shelter there, and that she hadn't fallen in or injured herself.

The walk from the mechanical buildings to the Library was easy, and she was healing nicely. Even her limp was gone, and she was back to wearing heels that were a couple inches high. Something about those inclined boots making her taller was comforting, and brought on an unexplainable self-confidence she couldn't help but emanate. From time to time she'd close her eyes and picture Lito's blood running through her veins, and it made her want to be near Him even more.

Each time the healing wound itched about her stomach, it would remind her of His face, His smell and of the unfamiliar attraction she had toward Him, which she still refused to talk about. Mercelle had to have some idea, as she knew Feres better than anyone. Lito was somewhere between the South Pole and the location of the Shard's dig site. Without having the slightest idea where He was beyond that, she pushed the yearning from her mind, and tried as best as she could to focus on the task at hand.

The name Olim Jasusa was one Kraj had come up with while they worked to formulate an impenetrable back story. The only indications she had that he was still alive were the transmissions that came here and there. As sporadic as they were, they showed the inside of the Glaven Grad tower in a way that couldn't possibly be seen by any other means. Feres had never heard of a human making it out of Glaven Grad alive.

Sitting alone in the exchange room below the Library, Feres made sure the door was locked before accessing the private channel that only she and one other individual knew about. The transmitted pictures stored on the channel contained clean rooms where Moras were operating on humans and replicas, injecting them with strange tinctures. When she got to the video file, she was shocked to see a live account of the Chaos experiments she'd heard so much about.

It wasn't the treatment of the humans in the glass chamber that pulsed a vengeful anger through her veins. It wasn't even the fact that the experiment successfully yielded a live monster, or that Mora allowed it to tear her own replicas apart. What struck her nerve was the woman standing next to Mora.

How could a human being do something like this to another of their own species? What was in it for them? What could Chaos possibly have to offer someone like that, especially long term? Didn't this woman know that a war was going on? It made Feres wonder if maybe Chaos was raising their own obedient humans, capturing them young and teaching them to hate their own kind.

Kraj was the same man who had provided her with the warning about the tower to the south, which had allowed her to send Lito and Mercelle to scout it out. She hadn't known they were going to tear it down. But, she was glad they had because the communication lines were much clearer. Not to mention the fact that the frequency weapon had been disabled, and the entire human Race spared from a terrible, shared death.

Zakopat Kraj was very good at being stealthy and holding up a ruse. When she'd initially proposed an additional assignment to him, he accepted it without hesitation, even stating that he wished he could do more, and take on more than the simple role of intelligence courier. She immediately knew what to do with him, and after a rock solid back story was created, he became the best placed asset in the rebellion's war against the Demigods.

A decision hadn't been made yet as to whom she would be sharing this information. As far as she knew, she was the only one aware of Kraj's presence in Glaven Grad. Most of what she had received from him substantiated much of what they already assumed to be taking place in Chaos territory. Perhaps she would wait until something a bit more substantial came back before divulging anything to anyone.

She didn't expect to see him alive outside of Glaven Grad ever again – his mission didn't include an exit strategy since he'd seemed confident enough to improvise one when the time came.

"Stars above!" She jumped, reacting to the bell on her terminal and shutting down the video feed in a rush. She ran a finger over the screen on the tablet to open the line. "Lady Ti-Erin Feres here." The face on the screen wasn't who she expected. Instead of Lady

Edeen of Naselba, she was looking into the posh face of an older man with flawless, pale white skin, and a pointed nose she hated looking at as soon as she saw it sticking up at her. "Who am I speaking to?"

"Hello, Lady Feres. My name is Deputy Secretary Sovetnik Vtoro. I'm Empress Edeen's second in command."

"Where is Lady Edeen?" she asked with a disappointed look which conveyed that Edeen's absence was unacceptable. "And when did she start calling herself 'Empress'?"

Vtoro cleared his throat. He was nervous. Good. "The *Empress* felt it necessary to ascend her status when Lanna fell, and Naselba became the largest human city on Earth. The Naselban High Courts believe we need a single authority over the rebellion in order to hasten decisions and expedite the removal of the Demigods."

"Sure." She rolled her eyes, and made sure he could see it. "I think she's just a little too full of herself. We were supposed to have a meeting. Where is she? Counting her concubines?" Lady Nevistini Edeen was known to keep an assortment of sleazy companions at her disposal. Mostly of the female variety, but Feres wasn't brushed up on Edeen's latest proclivities.

"The *Empress* is currently indisposed, and is busy with other matters. She tasked me to sit in her place in order to convey a message."

"A message?" she asked with a hint of aggressive confusion and adding a bit of angling in her eyes.

"More like a request," he replied. She felt his tension, and his struggle to keep a steady voice while throwing around weight that he couldn't carry. His voice trembled when he spoke, and she enjoyed watching him squirm. "But, I'll wait until everyone is present."

Feres leaned back in her seat, putting her arms out to her sides in an enormous shrug. "We're all here. Mercelle and Lito are still on their way back from the tower they destroyed – you're welcome – and I haven't been able to reach Dredger since he found the Shard's location and began excavating."

"The Empress extends her gratitude for clearing up the communication lines," he said through a phony smile.

And saving their lives in the process, she thought.

"Our pleasure," she snarked. "Always happy to do all the work while you Naselbans divide up power between each other and play with your credits. Tell me, Vtoro. Is it easy being rich when *you* decide how much currency circulates?"

"It's easier than following a tall tale about Gods and Races," he snapped back. She was impressed, yet he was still sweating. "The meeting will have to take place with just the two of us. You'll be required to pass along the Empress's message to those you failed to procure."

"Required? Ha! Tell your 'Empress' that I'm not required to do a Kaisering thing unless I deem it necessary. I don't work for her and I'm certainly not going to accept any criticism from a woman who can't even show up to a meeting *she* scheduled, and sends a secretary instead."

"*Deputy* Secretary," he rectified. "I'll relay what I'm here to relay so we can end this conversation. I have better things to do."

"I'm sure your Court is waiting to swoon over you as we speak. I think your feet may need to be cleaned. Maybe their swooning tongues can polish between your toes."

Vtoro clenched his jaw. "The Empress is calling for a summit meeting of the remaining leaders of the human population to establish a proper chain of command within the rebellion, and to potentially decide a course of action in order to overthrow the Demigods. The summit will take place in ten days from now, in Naselba. All Ladies, Lords and supposed Gods are to attend, along with any protection and members of your High Courts you may require."

"I'll have it arranged," she said. "Is that all?"

"That is a-"

She ended the connection. "Power hungry...little ingrates," she grumbled to herself. "Pretentious, Kaisering bastards. 'Empress'? My ass."

It wasn't going to be easy convincing Dredger to

attend a meeting of the rebel minds. Luckily, she had Mercelle for that since her relationship with him was much stronger and older. Part of her wanted to cut Naselba off completely from the remaining rebellion, and coordinate an attack on Glaven Grad without them. But, Vtoro was right: Naselba held the bulk of the remaining human population on Earth. If an attack was to be planned on the Demigods, it would have to include every soul humanity had.

As difficult as it was to admit to herself, they couldn't do it without Naselba.

Lady Edeen wanted to establish herself as "Empress", but Feres had something else in mind for this little summit. She would propose a coordination of efforts in order to plan a final attack on Glaven Grad. If Edeen wasn't going to be willing to contribute, then she would leave Naselba to themselves, and consider them neutral, no longer part of the rebellion. She was only afraid that Dredger would refuse to attend, leaving just her and Mercelle to plead their case.

A message had come through on her tablet while she was speaking to the insufferable Naselban. A quick tap, and the confirmation of Mercelle's retrieval was waiting for her review.

Some of the weight on her shoulders lifted with her knowing that her sister was safe and on her way back. It returned when she remembered what Lito had said about Mercelle needing to be scanned by the medical Scholars.

She lifted her shirt, running a finger around the bumpy scar that had formed after Lito's blood got into her wound. For a moment, she closed her eyes again, and pictured His face. That smooth, deep, peachy complexion around those glowing irises. And those damn muscles that she wanted so terribly to touch and caress.

The Sandramedius Library had records of pictures and videos showing the ancient people harvesting and eating sweet fruits. She swore she could smell Lito's essence, and it reminded her of what she always thought the produce's scent would have been. Sugary, and succulent.

Her mouth salivated, yearning to feel His lips on hers.

5

BLED I

The lights were off throughout the expanse of the room. He sat in the center, boney legs crossed and back straight, focusing on starting the chain reaction in his brain that was the catalyst for his replication process.

Valk had perfected his craft of creating new copies. As the oldest of the Demigods, Valk could replicate regularly, creating dozens of copies of himself every few days or so. Mora, although younger than Valk but still much older than Bled or Newlyn, could replicate a single being two, sometimes three, times a day. Even Newlyn replicated sporadically, but often enough to build up and support a massive workforce. Newlyn's handful of copies emerged about once a week, sometimes more often than that.

Bled was the same age as Newlyn – just over a

millennium old – but still couldn't quite master the spark that began inside, and ended on the outside in the form of new beings. The last time he'd replicated was months ago when he'd built up an army of hundreds of replicas. Now, due to Mora's endless experiments and the attack on Lanna, his copies were dwindling in number, and he knew Valk would have his head if he didn't change that, and soon.

Completely motionless, his cold claws wrapped around his knees, he willed his body to go in and out of the visible realm. Liquid electricity surged through his spinal column and accumulated at the base of the Demigod's skull. A concentrated push of chemicals from his glands flooded the brain, and further oscillated the electrically charged particles.

The only thing he could equate the process to was trying to induce an orgasm via deep meditation. Sexual organs were biological traits that were specific to the Demigods – their genderless replicas weren't so lucky.

Spreading, pulsing, circulating through his limbs, the particles pushed out of his greenish, papery skin. Smoking and blistering, Bled clutched his knees, and with a deathly growl he burst into white flames. The ethereal fire had no visible effects on his skin or flesh, but the tearing sensation ravaged every nerve and cell included in his physical entity, until he was afraid to open his eyes and see himself in countless atoms, floating about the dark room.

An empty void pulled energy from his center, greedily filling itself with life and ripping free from Bled's hold. Another void continued to drain him of his essence, and they kept coming, each ripped void suddenly got replaced by another. Bled tightened his muscles, ligaments, vessels, everything he could to keep the scorching chemical from retreating back into his glands. The white flames swirled higher into a column that flicked at the ceiling.

Soulless, putrid ghosts were stealing his aura. Over and over they pulled from him, and broke away like a limb or memory that could never return. A dozen. Two dozen. Would he have anything left?

He lost count, unable to keep track while pushing a self-induced acid through his arteries. Before the flames died, Bled blacked out.

It couldn't have been for long, because there was still a fine smoke clearing from the room by the time he opened his eyes. There was nothing to see. But, he didn't allow the disappointment to set in just yet.

Bled squinted, concentrating on any slight movement over the floor. New Bleds weren't capable of manifesting an appearance within the visible realm until their physical bodies were strong enough. That only took a minute or two. Any trace of pale body parts would catch his attention straight away.

In the back corner, something stirred, but it was gone by the time his pupils zeroed in on it. Toward the center of the space a leg appeared, vertical and alone. Signs of muscle strain told him that the limb was holding something up. It went in and out of sight, as if a curtain of invisibility was blowing in the wind between them. But after the replica got its bearings, the whole body was clear to see.

Standing there, peering around at the new world, was the first and strongest of the batch. It wasn't alone, and when it locked eyes with another fully formed creation, Bled started counting. They appeared along the walls, crowded in the corners, and sporadically throughout the space – pretty much wherever their fetal voids landed after separating from their creator.

His energy had plummeted, and Bled steadily pulled himself up off of the floor. After a full rotational count of the room, he was up to over a hundred replicas in total. This was a very successful batch, and he was proud of what he'd done as the heat subsided from his skin.

"You." He pointed a claw at the first Bled that had appeared. "Come." It started walking toward him. "The rest of you, report to intake for processing. Bottom floor of the ship."

They all lined up in front of the door, but he had to go engage the opening function for them since they were yet to learn about mechanical and electronic machinery. He was able to instill basic information – like language and obedience – in them during their creation, but the rest would have to come later. Their real births occurred when they stepped out from the ill-lit room and into the brightness of the Mastership's corridors.

Fatherless and alone, his creations were now under the control of Valk, unless they were reassigned back to him or another Demigod to guard towers and shipments around the planet. It was with great joy that he kept one behind for a special task that would help to put him back in Valk's good graces. If such a thing even existed.

"Come, child." He beckoned the Bled to come closer, placing a claw on its head. "You will go straight to sensory testing and attend basic combat training before returning to me for your assignment. I have something very important for you to do that you must keep a secret. It is only to be discussed between the two of us, after you're taught to speak, of course. Is there anything I just told you that you do not fully understand?"

The replica kept its eyes on the floor, and rotated its head from side to side.

"Good," Bled rasped. The next time we meet I'll start teaching you about stealth. You'll learn to move about entire buildings and spaces by keeping completely still for as long as it takes, and only moving about when no one is present to see your physical form. This will teach you to remain undiscovered until your task is completed. Are you prepared to keep the details of your assignment a secret?"

It shook its head again; honesty was an automatic response so early on in its development. The replica would need to learn basic skills before getting the full scope of its assignments.

"Then I'll see you after your training. Come, I'll take you."

MORA WAS ALWAYS easy to find. She was either in the Glaven Grad tower overseeing her experiments, or exaggerating her success in Valk's throne room at the head of the Mastership.

He swung by the upper floors and snuck by Valk's open door. The fact that it was open was enough to tell him that Mora wasn't there. As he passed by, he locked eyes with a Bled that was speaking with Valk, probably something about a compromised shipment overtaken by the desert tribes. His replicas, once fully developed in the maturation bay, were intelligent enough to manage their own departments and shipments – they didn't need him anymore.

This Bled in particular was being scolded, creating a great opportunity for Bled to keep walking, and he made his way all the way down to the shuttlecrafts at the back of the Mastership.

He stood in an empty shuttle, waiting for the door to close and the descent to Glaven Grad to commence. Every time a group of newly developed Valks, Moras or Newlyns tried to enter, he would growl at them, showing teeth and claws until they moved on to the next craft. The doors closed. He felt the air evacuate from the craft's openings and lower to the temperature of space.

The Mastership was pressurized and filled with oxygen to help the new replicas adapt to the Earth's climate, and to support the few Crassas on board. But there was no need for Bled to pressurize the craft since he didn't breathe air.

Gravity shifted a few times, and he stood in the center until he felt the jolt of the interlock between the Glaven Grad tower and his shuttlecraft. He delivered another low growl to the replicas who tried entering the same elevator as him.

Mora was many, many floors down from the top, in the midst of celebrating the creation of a new monster in one of her experimental chambers. Her success was always something to be envied.

He stood across the chamber from her, silently holding his hands behind his back. Replicas avoided eye contact with the greenish-pale Demigod as he glared down at them. Mora spotted him standing there, and powered down her terminal. She crossed the observation walkway, and Bled followed her into an empty lab.

"I take it you were successful?" she asked after sealing the door.

"After days of intense meditation, yes. Over a hundred replicas are reporting to the intake bay as we speak."

"And the one?" Mora's eyebrow twitched with anticipation, that's when he saw dark lines leading to pits under her eyes. Her skin was abnormally dry and she looked tired.

Strange, he thought, because Demigods didn't sleep like humans did. Humans got exhausted. The poor, frail creatures needed rest and sustenance to keep them mobile, alive and useful. Creations of Order were weak and needy because their God didn't provide for them the way Leto had created each of His Demigods with a conduit through which His Chaos energy flowed. Bled didn't know why Mora was showing such peculiar, human-like traits.

"Are you feeling okay?" he asked after she blinked so many times he thought her eyes would simply close altogether. "Are you having problems with your replicating?"

"Just tell me you chose a candidate," she said impatiently.

Bled truly didn't care whether or not she was doing well. He just wanted to try and scope out a hidden weakness, if possible. “It’s completing basic development, and returning to me afterwards to go over the assignment specifications. As long as we have the information we need everything should be on schedule.”

“The Newlyns have compiled a file for you,” she reported, rubbing her puffy eyes. “It’s ready, and it contains all of the layouts for Naselba, as well as their security protocols. Funny thing is: they don’t have any protocols for an assassination, or even an infiltration. It seems all they’ve attempted to prepare for is a small attack.”

“That’s why this is going to work, they won’t be expecting it.” Bled’s scratchy voice was low, and secretive. The thought of Mora beginning to crack made him want to earn her trust even more. “If it does then we can begin training more independent replicas from each batch.”

“Only if you can replicate more batches,” her tone deepened.

“In due time,” he lied.

“You better hope so. I’ll let Valk know about our progress.”

Bled wasn’t about to let Mora take credit for his project. She may have helped him come up with the idea, but the formulation and execution of the assignment was left up to his ability to prepare his replica. “Don’t tell him anything. I’ll talk to him once I know the replica is up to the task. Otherwise there's no reason to say anything at all."

"I'm not trying to manipulate you, Bled. Valk wants more productivity, more results and more replicas. If he doesn't get it he's likely to remove one of us from his ranks. I just want to make sure he removes the right one."

"Newlyn."

"Newlyn's been useless and weak since we arrive on this rock. His replicas do the jobs of the Crassa. We could replace all of his creations with human slaves. Who says we have to kill the entire species?"

"He has been plotting against you relentlessly," replied Bled.

"And you," that eyebrow twitched again. "Don't be fooled by all of that innocent blubber and goo. There's a spiteful little pit of anger deep down under it all, and it's filling up. There's no telling what he will do to try and look more useful."

"That whelp has always fancied himself a genius, trying to outwit us at every turn. I'd be surprised if he wasn't after Valk's spot."

"I suggest you move up your timetable," said Mora. "Once the assassination takes place we'll be able to better convince Valk of Newlyn's uselessness. But, you need to start replicating more, or there won't be anything I can do for you."

"Any luck on the chemical acetylator?" he asked.

"I'm still working on it. I can't seem to balance the acetylation effects with the electrical output."

"I'll just have to meditate whenever I'm not training the new replica on its mission. The humans are growing stronger in Lito's presence. My hope is that Valk won't risk losing the armies of Bleds by executing me." That had always been what provided him with a bit of security under Valk: the fact that without his replicas, Valk's army would comprise of nothing but oafish, reptilian dolts. The tact and stealth of a Bled was unmatched by any other replica.

"Valk will do anything to send the right message, especially if the orders are coming from above his head."

"Do you think Leto knows about His brother's awakening?" he asked.

"I suspect not. We would have heard of His departure for Earth by now." Her voice broke, and became hoarse. She coughed lightly and rubbed her throat, looking at him with a scowl in a way that said 'stop looking at me', and so he did.

Again, her well being was more of a detriment to his overall agenda, and he reminded himself that he didn't need her to complete his plan.

Bled only felt like less of a Demigod when Leto's name was mentioned. It had been a thousand years since he had met the God of Chaos, and it was only briefly before he was assigned to harvest Earth under

Valk's command. He would never forget the overwhelming power that came from such a small being. Leto looked just like the people of Earth, and exactly like the supposed savior, Lito. Yet, He commanded and created masses of Demigod armies, and endowed them with abilities which matched that of His brother. If that didn't seal His superiority as God-King over the universe, Bled didn't know what else could.

"The plan is on course," he told Mora, reaching for the door. "Newlyn won't be allowed to step over us on his way to replace Valk. It's likely that the Demigod who tries to take Valk's power will be the first to go. I'd be more than willing to provide testimony on such an individual."

They shared a visible affirmation through eye contact and smirks. Then he left, and made his way back to the Mastership to meditate in the dark room.

6

ZAKOPAT KRAJ III

A report came through his terminal detailing the functionality of the turbine systems in Kerk. He lowered the energy output levels, and made the system seem much weaker than it actually was, before sending his rendition of the report through to be translated.

It had been a long day of attempting to start conversations with the Newlyn next to him. The replica, as always, was enveloped in its work, responding with short replies and keeping the talk to a minimum. Kraj would have to work harder to get onto its good side. Regular compliments and checking in on its mood helped, but he would have to do more to get through to the Chaos creature.

The Newlyn was proving more difficult to woo than

any woman he'd had success with during his younger years.

Getting friendly with the Newlyn got him closer to potentially accessing its terminal. Kraj didn't know how to read Chaos, but if he could navigate the menus, he could try to send some images back to Feres to be translated. There had to be something on the Newlyn's terminal that could help the rebellion learn about Chaos' overall plans and strategies.

He took deep, steady breaths, constantly reminding himself to allow his body time to absorb what little oxygen he was taking in.

"It's almost over," Kraj tempted the Newlyn. He stretched, reaching into the air and arching his back. "Anything interesting today?"

"Nothing I am allowed to speak about," it said back.

"Would you even know the day was ending if I didn't come or go each time?"

He could tell the question sparked some inner thought because the Newlyn stopped working to answer. "I don't believe I would. The days blend together without a view of the sky. Oh, how I miss the sky." It was like watching a child pout over the snack they'd received.

"I would die if I never saw the sky again," Kraj prodded. "Have you ever thought about dying?"

"Sometimes. But, how would I complete my duties? I couldn't possibly die until I've helped my peers sort and process all data going up to the Demigods."

"I don't think they'll ever run out of data for you."

"Then my work will never be done, and I'll never have to die," it replied without hesitation.

The Demigods truly had created the most obedient and loyal of replicas, even if they weren't the brightest. He thought about asking it straight-up if it would allow him to use its terminal, but the gamble on whether or not the replica was that stupid was too steep. It was a better bet to try and get the Newlyn away from the spot which it had occupied for multiple consecutive years.

"Thinking about death can lead to depression," he told the replica. "I was depressed once. A friend brought me a gift, and I was fixed right away. Never had another sad day in my life."

The Newlyn looked away from its terminal, then turned to face Kraj, finally taking the bait. "What was it?"

"The present? Oh, I don't remember. My memory is so tricky. I can recall some occurrences throughout my life, but not certain details of those occurrences. Why don't I bring you a gift tomorrow? That might bring your spirits up."

"I've never received a *gift* before." It pronounced the word as if it was its first time saying it. "What will it be?"

Having very little room to grow and develop an interior life, the replica had failed to mentally progress past the point of a child. There was a cheerful, hopeful, naive kid somewhere inside the Newlyn, and Kraj just needed to ease it out, little by little.

"A surprise."

The Newlyn turned back to its terminal, being obvious as it hid a smile with a globular hand. Kraj's plan was starting to work.

A blue ping came up in the corner of his screen. This was either an indication that his work was being monitored by a Mora outside the room and he needed to get back to being productive, or it was yet another summons to the interrogation room. It was the former, so he pulled up another report to alter.

A convoy was departing from Kerk to provide supplemental equipment to Dredger at the Shard's dig site. After changing the topographical path of the convoy, and relaying the report to the translator, he noticed that another ping was flashing red, and there was a Valk standing behind him.

Clicking on the new ping, he realized that it was, in fact, a summons.

His heart rolled over in his chest. He hadn't prepared a follow up to the fake memory he had last time. And the Mora who debriefed him said that he would need to procure more information on the seismic weapon he had described, or he would be one dead Crassa.

A plan began formulating in his head as to the

options he had to make an escape. Being so far within the Glaven Grad tower, surrounded by Newlyns with a Valk at his back, his chances were slim. He compartmentalized his urge to run, and instead fixated his focus on coming up with something for the Mora planning to speak with him.

The Valk grasped his forearm from above, and pulled him to his feet.

"Goodbye, Crassa," came the voice of the Newlyn behind him.

"My name is Olim," he told it. "Olim Jasusa. I'll see you tomorrow." This time, the replica didn't hide its smile. All it took was a little connection, and an offering of friendship to convince the Newlyn to open up. Now, he just needed to come up with a gift to bring to it tomorrow.

Kraj threw it a quick wink, and smiled back before the Valk yanked him away with unnecessary force. He hoped it wouldn't be his last friendly interaction before an untimely death in a blinding interrogation room.

"As I've said, your case is new to me. I'm just finding it difficult to understand how you have been processing sixteen hours of human data each day, and nothing has triggered the complete return of your memory." The

Mora was noting unintelligible things onto its holographic notepad.

They had already gone through the usual review of his memory issues and his fake back story.

"I always tell my story to a new Mora every day," Kraj said. "If my case would stay with just one of you I wouldn't have to go over the same details every time. Although, it does make me wonder what happens to the Moras who interview me. Lost to the experiments, perhaps?"

It looked at him with a punishing glare. "Then tell me something new. If you want to continue living, that is."

Oxygen was plentiful, and he could breathe easily. He had to control his rhythm so as to avoid taking in too much and inebriating himself. The dizzier he got, the more likely he was to forget about hiding his true, Oasian accent. "I think something did come back to me. A meeting with the engineers and Corporals overseeing the seismic weapon."

"The one you said can create ground quakes by altering the pressure of the particles in the air?"

"Right." Sleepiness suddenly washed over him, and he almost let his eyes close. His breathing would have to slow way down if he wanted to stay awake. "I remember...where they plan to activate it."

The table dragged across his vision, and he realized he was swaying in the seat.

"Where?" it asked.

"Yushud." He cleared his throat, blinking rapidly, uselessly. "You should...turn down the oxygen. It's too high...I-I can't remember." His spine went limp against the back of his chair.

"If the memory has already come back to you then you don't need to remember it again. The truth doesn't require a good memory." The Mora was playing a trick on him.

He started to sweat, and he knew the stiff replica could see it.

"They uh, they plan to...dig a cavern." The hand in front of his face blurred, and he soon figured out that it was his own. "Deep underground. To maximize the seismic impact...and...and cause more damage."

The room spun around him. The walls rotated, rising and falling in unison. He turned to the side in his seat, putting elbows on knees, and bowing his head in between. Blood needed to saturate his brain to help him balance out his oxygen levels.

"Where?"

"If you don't-" His lungs shuddered, and he hiccupped. "If you don't turn down the oxygen...I'm gonna...gonna pass out."

"It's not just the oxygen that's making you feel off, Crassa."

"What are you do...what're you...what are you dosing me with?"

"You don't ask the questions here. I do. If you tell me where they plan to dig the cavern I can turn down the compound I've put in the air, and perhaps I can help you stay alive for another day."

Kraj rubbed his face with a flat palm, tossing his head back and staring up at the bright ceiling. The light pulsed different colors in rhythm with his strong heartbeat, and when he closed his eyelids he could still see the colors rotating from one to the next and back around again. His memory was the opposite of what he claimed it to be, and he easily recalled the details he thought up while the Valk escorted him here from Workroom 86.

"Tell me where they plan to activate the seismic weapon, and you can go back to work."

He grinned, and let out a tiny, childish laugh. "Here," he said, pointing at the floor. It was all he could think to say as a sudden burst of unfocused energy rose up from a surge of adrenaline. "They're digging beneath Glaven Grad...Ha! Deep underground. They think they can swallow the city..." He hiccupped "...and the tower up in one go! Ha! Haha!"

His finger was pointing at the Mora's unimpressed face. Its expression was blank, unresponsive.

"I regularly review the subterranean scans beneath and around Glaven Grad for miles. There are no signs of approaching cavities or caverns." That made cold flash over his sweat covered skin. This Mora was good.

"I suppose I'll let you return to work. I can't speak on how long you'll be there. Your information will be passed up, but once tomorrow's scans reveal that we are still safe from any underground threats, I'm sure the Demigods will commission your execution."

"Wait," he slurred. "They have the capapa...the capability of drilling...hundreds of miles...in just a few hours." His lies were getting thinner in his stupor. The only option to survive was to keep providing them with false information to keep them occupied while he provided true information to Feres. "And," he hiccupped. "There's only one man on Earth...who can drill that fast."

"Dredger is planning to assist the rebellion in trying to destroy Glaven Grad?" the Mora asked, a bit shocked.

He nodded, slowly, and let his eyes close to keep the throes of the motion from dizzying him. Regret snapped him out of it. As soon as the replica repeated it back to him, he knew he shouldn't have said that. Kerk's entire neutral stance on the war could be put in jeopardy. Kraj could be the catalyst that causes the deaths of hundreds of thousands of innocent people.

"I shouldn't have said that," groaned Kraj, pressing his palms into his eyes.

"I'm glad you did. I may be able to help you after all, Crassa," it said, scribbling more glyphs into the hologram. "'Out time' began some time ago. You may return to the bunks until tomorrow."

He stopped himself from speaking any further as the door slid down behind him, and a Valk helped him limp out.

It wasn't a good feeling to vomit in low oxygen, while coming down from an elusive gas and being dragged by a large reptilian barbarian. Figuring out how many times he'd passed out while being dragging along behind the Valk was impossible. But, he felt much better afterward, physically at least.

HE WAS FINALLY LET GO JUST OUTSIDE of the Crassa corridor. Stepping through the doorless opening for a moment he waited until the Valk walked away, and then he scurried in the opposite direction, toward the access panel to the dark glass ducts.

Despite coming down off of the elusive drug the Mora had put into the air of the interrogation room, Kraj felt the need to do what he could to get what information he could tonight. Tomorrow, he thought, they'll up the dose and get him to say something even more stupid. How could he have implicated Kerk like that? What was he thinking?

Maneuvering between the jumble of cords inside the duct, he pushed himself along by the toes of his boots. Then he climbed up a few floors until he came across a medical procedure being performed on a human. He kicked off his shoe to get to the transmitter, and recorded the operation.

A Mora was wearing a facemask, hovering over a human who had been sliced open from pelvis to sternum. Many of the organs had been removed, as there were empty voids where certain parts should have existed. Somehow, the human was still breathing through tubes, and was still alive.

The human was stripped of so much of its innards that Kraj couldn't determine a gender from inside the dark tube. The duct came out of the ceiling, dipping into the far end of the room. Even with his perfect view, it was impossible to figure out how the human was being kept alive.

A Valk was standing next to another steel table, and the Mora motioned for it to lie down. It followed the instruction, and Kraj spied the other two Valks covering the door.

Without warning, the Mora began cutting into the silent Valk, clipping the ends of its flesh to prongs that pried the replica open at the middle. He watched as organs were taken out of the Valk and sewn into the human.

Vessels were connected, veins were reconstructed, and by the time the shell of the Valk's body was removed from the operating room, the human's midsection was no longer a cavity, but a compartment housing unrecognizable biological organs. Stitches outlined each one as it sat, waiting for life to pump through it.

Did the human know what was happening? Could it feel anything? He wondered all of these things, knowing they were irrelevant to his purpose.

The Mora moved a machine across the ceiling that looked like a scanner of some kind. It placed the glass side of the machine above the human, and stepped to the edge of the room. A light beamed down onto the body, causing small pitters of smoke to rise from certain places where the replicas were attempting to attach Valk organs to the human system. He had little hope that this would yield any success, and none that the human would survive.

He gulped back the urge to vomit again. Doing so would certainly compromise his hiding spot.

Light from the cauterizing beam reflected off of the steel table, glaring through the dark glass that surrounded him. Trying to wriggle into alignment with the horizontal cords, Kraj kicked and pushed, knowing the light shined right onto him. Even if it was for the briefest second, it was enough to catch an eye.

The light went off, and the whirring of the machine died. He held still, breathing at a quick, but rhythmic pace to keep his pulse from spiking.

"I think I saw something," came the Mora's voice from below. "There, in the ducts. I thought I saw a Crassa boot up there."

His pulse spiked, and he would have to focus on getting it down after he got out of there.

Stomping from the Valks got harder and louder until he heard the scraping of their claws on the access panel next to him. He scrambled, using the cords to pull himself away from the panel before it came open. His bare foot was rough and sweaty, and it had good traction on the glass.

The sound of the lever pulling free on the panel warned him that it was about to be too late. He reached toward the corner of the duct, catching a lip with his fingertips and sliding himself over to it. He slid sideways, out from under the cords' jumble, and kicked his legs over his head, rolling back into the wider space of the duct's interchange.

He lay flat, still and silent. Only the noises from the Valks nostrils, snorting and hissing, filled the duct. Slight rustling for a moment, and the panel closed back.

"How did a boot get up there?" the Mora asked. "Gather a team and have them sweep the ducting system. The entire thing. Go!"

The Valks rushed out, and Kraj noticed a copper wire, about a foot long, hanging down above his face. It was thick, and would make for easy bending. He reached up and yanked it free from the ceiling.

The human on the steel table was dead, and the Mora had it disconnected from the machines and dumped into a large bin next to the table.

His other boot had to house the transmitter and the wire as he crawled his way back to the panel on the floor with the Crassa corridor, where he stole a pair of boots from a man who looked like he was dead in his bunk.

A few hours of sleep would help him clear his head, if he could find it after the day he'd had.

THIS WAS THE DAY.

The heat was on, and his position within Glaven Grad was wearing thin. His meeting with the Mora the day before hadn't gone well, and he feared he may have let some of his cards show. If there was a time for him to make a move, it was now.

He breezed past his seat in Workroom 86, stepping to the back of the Newlyn he'd been working on for the past week.

"Good morning," he said gleefully to the working replica.

"Hello," it said back, turning away from its screen. "Is it morning already?"

"Yes. And I have a message from the Moras. They said they want you to report to interrogation. Some kind of debriefing. They wouldn't tell me anything more."

"Strange," it quirked its face into confusion. "They haven't called me away in such a long time."

"I think it has to do with me. They might want to debrief you on what it's like working so closely with a Crassa like me. They think I'm hiding something. Which I'm not, of course."

"You're not a Crassa, you're Olim," it said. The Newlyn stood up from the steel bench, its sticky skin peeling audibly away from the surface of it. Slime oozed down its backside and into the grating below. It stretched, poking its stubby arms back over its fat head. "Oh! It feels good to move," it howled before stepping into the aisle.

"Hold on." Kraj stopped it before it got too far away. "I remembered what was given to me as a gift all those years ago that made me feel happy. It was a round pin that reflected and refracted light. It made me feel lighter, happier. So, I made this for you." Reaching into his waistband, he took out the twisted copper wire that he'd pulled from the ducts the night before. He had twisted it into the shape of a five-pointed star, with a little extra slack going across the back to form a pin. "It's like the stars, so you can take the sky with you wherever you go."

"A gift?!" It snatched the wire from Kraj's hand and pinned the monstrosity onto the brim of its high-waisted pants – just below its bare, wide breasts. "How do I respond? I don't have anything to give you in return."

"You don't have to reciprocate. That's not the point of a gift." No. The point of the gift was to make the Newlyn feel as if it owed Kraj something. Just in case anything came up about possible suspicious behavior in the future. If only the Demigods understood their replicas' capacity for emotion, they could make them far more loyal and productive. All it took was a bit of care and kindness, however forced or faked, to open the replica up emotionally. Even if it was just a little bit, it was all he needed.

"Oh! I hope they aren't reassigning me. If they are, I'll try to decline! Wait, no. They won't allow that; they'd just execute me." Its face drooped to a heavy frown. "If I never see you again, Olim, I'll never forget you." At that, the replica turned and left.

He watched it disappear through the door on the opposite end of the room, then he stood between the seat and the terminal, trying to make sense of the chaotic menu on the screen. Nothing was in human, and the Newlyn seemed to have been looking at a list of some kind. Tapping on the list did nothing, but the options along the right of the screen changed the main image when he pressed on them.

A quick look down both ends of the aisle, and he was clear. The transmitter fit perfectly in his mouth as he slid his fingers over the screen, navigating through as many images, specs, plans and documents as he possibly could. Even if he couldn't read them, Feres had the resources to create a translation program.

Pictures of successfully created monsters from Mora's lab. Unreadable graphs. A video simulation of a human's circulatory system. A glowing, turquoise baton which seemed to be acting as a power source or battery to a larger machine. He even saw what looked like the subterranean scans of Glaven Grad the Mora was telling him about. The images looked clear of caverns, as expected.

The next series of images were all from the same file, stringing along in succession. Each image showed the next stage in some kind of reconstruction of the Glaven Grad tower. Everything was captured by his transmitter, and by the end of the series, the tower had transformed into a craft fitted with thrusters and fuel tanks.

That was what he'd seen being built onto the outside walls a couple days ago. He would have to try and get images of them before his time in Glaven Grad ended. Feres could use them to judge how far along in the process Chaos was. The Demigods planning to leave meant the end of their harvesting agenda, and the end of habitability on Earth.

A blue ping came up on his terminal. He tried to close out the file of the Glaven Grad tower, but only pulled up more detailed prints of the interior. There was no way he could get back to the screen the Newlyn had left it on.

He retreated back to his own seat, and just as his backside hit the cold metal, a voice came from behind him.

"They didn't need me for anything," said the Newlyn, squishing into place. "I guess they were wrong when they told you they needed me."

"Guess so." He wiped slime from his fingers, trying to keep it hidden beneath his leg. The fact that the replica still believed Kraj and blamed the Moras for the mix up was a good indication of the trust he had built. He would have to use that to his advantage at another time. Today's risks had been taken, and he didn't want to push his luck any further.

"Why are the tower's specs pulled up on my terminal?"

"Is that what that is?" Kraj laughed it off. "I couldn't tell. I can't read anything that comes up on your screen." He tapped the blue ping, and cleared out the order to increase his productivity.

The Newlyn shrugged, and continued working.

7

LADY INIS MERCELLE VIII

The electrolyte tablets she had on the way to Sandra were the best she'd ever tasted – synthetic rehydration at the tips of her fingers. She was thankful for the retrieval team, but still looked at them with heat in her eyes when they told her she could only have one vitamin pack. Apparently, she was scheduled for medical testing upon her arrival, and couldn't have too many calories in her system. Luckily she was still kind of full from the monster's leg she'd munched on in the crevasse.

All she looked forward to was a shower, and some sleep in an actual bed. The thought crossed her mind multiple times to ask about Lito, but she figured the retrieval team wouldn't know anything regarding His whereabouts, and she was too tired to muster the words anyhow. He could handle Himself.

They radioed ahead to Sandra to make sure the gates would open right away and let them in. It seemed their precious cargo was on a rush order.

Captain Shou greeted her inside, and escorted her on the walk to her A.L.C.O. so she could get cleaned up before reporting to the medical building.

"Feeling better, Lady?" he asked kindly, probably noticing her favoring one side with a subtle limp.

"I'll be better with some rest, and maybe an amputation or two," she joked. A cringe took over her face, and she held onto the rail of the staircase as they descended. "I'm sure I'll be right back out there in a day or two, cutting down replicas."

"As one does." They shared a modest chuckle. "We received word from Dredger about the Shard's dig site. The Scholars made it there fine, and they've uncovered what they believe to be an entrance of some kind. But they haven't made it inside just yet."

"Why not? Don't they have everything they need to blow a hole in the side of it?"

"Dredger fears they might compromise the contents by using explosives. I guess the structure is small and very old."

"Hector, Calvin *and* Emmett! I wish I was there. Any word from Lito yet?"

"No. He hasn't showed up at the dig site according to our last report. Not yet anyway."

They stopped at the door to her A.L.C.O., and he opened it for her.

"Thank you, Captain. I'll take it from here." She limped through the threshold to see Feres sitting in her room.

Lady Feres came to the door. "Captain. Could you oversee the next scouting rotation please? And make it wider. I want to expand our ground coverage."

"Yes, my Lady." He disappeared around the corner.

Once the door was shut Mercelle got a hug that almost knocked her over. "Whoa! I'm really glad to see you too. But, if you don't mind, I need a shower to wash five days of desert off of me."

"I'm not stopping you." Feres let go, and spread out over Mercelle's bed with a heavy sigh, staring at the ceiling. It clearly took it out of her to work around the clock most days, but she couldn't have been as exhausted and sore as Mercelle. "You have no idea how happy everyone is that you and Lito tore down that tower. The comm lines are clearer than ever."

Mercelle pulled her shirt off over her head. "You should have seen Lito. He saved me again, multiple times, and He was the one who blew up the tower after I had managed to disable the launch site on top of it. But, I'll take some credit. I see you're feeling much better."

Feres's eyes glazed over, most likely picturing the

God in action, and pining for His touch. Mercelle tossed her smelly shirt into her sister's face.

"Lovesick!" Mercelle teased. "What do you think He was trying to say to you over that radio before He stopped Himself?" She unbuckled her belt and straps, setting the cluttered mess of knives, ammunition, guns, a tablet and her parents' picture onto her bedside table. There sat a fresh set of clothes, folded and left for her by Feres. A press on the corner wall panel made it slide to one side, exposing a shower unit with a single button beneath a head.

Feres rolled onto her side, spreading her hair over the sheet. "I don't know if *love* is the right word for it. He's a God. Everyone pines after Him. Right?"

"I don't," she replied without hesitation, sliding her pants down over her blistered heels and kicking them aside. "I feel connected to Him, like a brother I never had. We understand each other in ways I've never understood anyone." She hit the button and stood under cascading water. It smelled like disinfectant at first, but cleared away quickly.

"No one but me?"

"Well, yeah. No one is closer than you and me, but..." Water ran over her head, and she smeared the precious liquid over her body, knowing she'd be out of time soon. "Lito operates on a different level. He knows what I'm going to do before I can even finish planning it out. It's like he can see my thoughts before

I can. Or maybe we're just predictable creatures to a God."

"He's something..." Feres trailed off, obviously avoiding the entire explanation or exploration of her feelings.

The timer ended, and the water shut off. Mercelle lathered up a cleanser over her wet skin and in her hair, reaching around to get every inch of her sandy back. "Shou said you heard from Dredger?"

Feres hopped up from the bed, pacing around the room. "Not Dredger himself. I haven't spoken to him directly in some time. I think he's avoiding me. Ashlan and Seemik have been relaying reports between us. Lito is still out there somewhere. I should have given Him His own tablet so we could track Him."

"He can handle Himself," she replied, hitting the button again to rinse off. "When are we talking to Edeen?"

"I had the meeting this morning, no one else was present so I just spoke to some Deputy Secretary. You know she's calling herself 'Empress' now? She's calling for a summit meeting in Naselba in a week and a half's time with all Ladies, Lords and High Courts requested to attend. Speaking of which, have you thought about joining Sandra's High Court? As the former Lady of Lanna – and my sister and best friend – I'm sure you wouldn't have a problem getting in." Feres continued to pace.

"No thanks," Mercelle said with a small scoff. She slicked clear water down her body and into the drain as the head shut off again. "I really like the freedom to leave when I want, to pursue the missions I choose, and to go and kill some replicas without having to work under orders. Besides, I only came back so I could be in that meeting, otherwise I would have gone to the dig site with Lito. We can't wait over a week to plan our attack on Glaven Grad." Stepping out of the shower unit, she dried herself under the strong blast of warm air under the duct's vent, combing fingers through her wet hair. More strands than usual came off in her hands. Without reacting or alerting Feres, she simply shook her hands off into the drain and closed the shower unit.

"Yeah, I'm sorry we couldn't get to you earlier. But this'll give us some time to try and convince Dredger to come along. It's time he stopped fooling around with his sensitive little stance on the war. He needs to grow a pair, or go into hiding before we begin our attack on Glaven Grad."

"It's no wonder why he's avoiding you," Mercelle pointed out. "I don't think he wants to be convinced. It's not in his nature to go with the group. He's always been independently successful, which is why he does so well keeping Kerk neutral." She picked up her new silgen clothes, black and clean, and shook them loose from their folds.

"Either way, we need to try and convince him to attend."

"And just how do you suppose we do that?"

"Not we," Feres sat back down on the bed. "You. You're the closest person to Dredger within the rebellion. Who else do you know that could talk some sense into him?"

"You want me to get in touch with Dredger *for* you?" Mercelle slipped into a fresh pair of form-fitting tactical pants, and moved all of her items from her last pair over, putting her belt and straps back into place, and making sure to stuff her parents' picture into her pocket without tearing it.

"I want you to go to Kerk and talk to him face to face. After he retrieves the Shard he'll wait for Lito to arrive and return to Kerk. Deliver the request for him to attend the summit, and if he declines, well, you'll have to convince him otherwise. We need all the numbers we can get, and without him it's just going to be you and me trying to overthrow a damned 'Empress'."

"A little self-assured, isn't she?" Mercelle zipped up her shirt, losing her breath for a split second, but catching it back and keeping it hidden from her sister. That was strange, she thought, before shaking it off.

"That's what I told her secretary. She is a descendant of the unholy Kaisers, after all. And it's all the more reason Dredger should help us build a united front against whatever nonsense she has planned for us.

I wouldn't be surprised if her plan was to wait the Demigods out while her servants braid her hair and polish her nails."

"I'll see what I can do," Mercelle told Feres with a sigh. "But, if he decides not to come, don't blame me. You know that man makes up his mind and sticks with it. He's as stubborn as we are."

"I know how hard headed he can be, especially when he believes he's protecting his people. Stubborn is an understatement. He hasn't even been responding to any of my messages. Go figure. You and Lito destroy the tower disrupting our communication signals, and he stops communicating."

"He'll talk to me," Mercelle insisted. "But, you're right, I'll have a better chance of getting through to him in person. I'll take a clipper tomorrow morning, should arrive in a day or two tops at those speeds."

"Afterwards, you'll return here with the Shard, and with Lito and the others. We'll put the Shard in for analysis and regroup before the summit."

"I thought I said I didn't like being ordered around." She smiled and sprawled out on her bed next to Feres. "If you don't mind, I'm just going to pass out until tomorrow," she said with a lengthy yawn, hoping Feres had forgotten about the appointment with the medical Scholars.

"Nice try, Lady." Feres stood up, straightening the wrinkles out of her clothing. "Up."

"Can't we change it to tomorrow morning? We could go before I leave for Kerk. I'm sure they aren't going to find anything anyhow."

"You look Kaisering awful, and you're lucky I let you take a shower before escorting you to the medical bays."

"I just spent the last four nights in the desert. Of course I look terrible. I just need some rest. Look, my eyes are already closed."

"I can't believe you sleep in your tactical gear." Feres shook her head. "If your pistol goes off in your sleep, the medical Scholars won't be able to cure a gunshot wound in the head. Lito said He felt something growing...or dying...inside you, or something. Now, I don't know about you, but that scares me."

Mercelle thought about the sick people who used to live in the eastern blocks of Lanna. Some barely able to walk or speak, they led miserable, pitiful existences, useless to the rest of the world. She would rather die suddenly – preferably in battle – than slowly succumb to a descent into fragility and frailty. Living a life of disability meant becoming a spectator to the war, and she'd sooner choose to end her own life over watching her comrades killed because she couldn't save them.

She just wanted to get the tests over with, and maybe confirm that nothing was wrong. If Lito was right, and something had infected her, then the sooner something was detected, the sooner and more possible a cure or treatment could be delivered. She couldn't deny that fact.

"Uuuuhhhhggg!" she groaned into her bed pad. "Fine."

It was no surprise when Feres got a call as soon as she turned her radio back on. She had to go help solve an issue with the charging stations in one of the parking structures, leaving Mercelle to walk the last street to the medical bays by herself.

Even with the bustling foot traffic that made the reputation of Sandra what it was, she still felt alone again, like she had in the desert. It wasn't clear to her if it was because she was starting to miss all of her old comrades who had fallen in Lanna, dealing with thoughts about her health which she couldn't put into words, anticipatory anxiety about talking to Dredger, not knowing where Lito was or a combination of everything.

The one and only times she'd seen fear in Lito's eyes was when He nearly poured His heart out to Feres over the radio, and when He said He sensed something dangerous inside of Mercelle's body. Since then she had bounced back and forth between justifying denial, and avoidance altogether. What she was really avoiding was the fear of the results.

She was tired, and still felt uneasy in her stomach and brain. Could it have simply been attributed to the days in the desert, and her crass decision to ingest the meat of an experimental monster whose origins didn't even lie on this planet? She highly doubted that the medical Scholar would blame it all on something she ate.

AFTER ARRIVING, and having multiple vials of her blood removed – which only made her want her bed even more – medical Scholar Rakta smiled and asked how she was feeling.

"Dizzy, now that you've drained me dry."

"Here," said the older woman, handing Mercelle a sealed pack of tablets. "Sugar, lipids and a few other compounds to help you get your strength back. Take one every few hours until you run out, and get some sleep."

"I'd love to," Mercelle responded, rubbing her tired eyes. "But these tests are making me feel...agitated."

"A little apprehension is normal under these circumstances."

"Not for me," she half snapped. "I've killed countless replicas, travelled the world, ruled a city, awakened a God, even survived the attack on Lanna. A little blood test should feel like nothing."

Rakta gave Mercelle a motherly look, tilting her head to the side and taking on an overly gentle tone. "You're afraid of having to face an enemy you aren't prepared to defeat. You can't fight illness with combat. If that was possible, I'm sure your abilities would cure almost anyone of anything. I want you to know that you're doing the right thing by coming in as early as possible. The earlier we catch something, the more..."

She zoned out, falling sleepily into delirium while staying upright and holding her eyes open. Weakness this heavy had never overwhelmed her like this before. The medical Scholar had become a faceless, voiceless facade of a person as Mercelle attempted to accept her helplessness in the situation. There was a block in her mind, a monolithic stone – harder than diamond – keeping her from fully seeing her ability to overcome this invisible enemy, if there was one there to overcome. It was impossible for her to deny her symptoms, and all she wanted to do was sleep.

But, things were growing increasingly out of her control.

"What about radiation poisoning?" she interrupted as Rakta continued her required, pre-fabricated speech about doing everything they can.

"I'm sorry?"

"Radiation poisoning," she repeated. "How do we treat that?" She ignored the woeful, pitying look Rakta gave.

"That can be a very evasive sickness. If we find traces of radiation in your blood or muscle tissue we would need to start treating you right away with potassium iodide, radiogardase and DTPA to move the particles out of your body. We would have to replace your blood as often as possible with multiple transfusions depending on how bad it is. That would help to decrease the risks of cancers, bacterial infections or any other terminal ailments, but it wouldn't completely take you out of risk."

Her eyes went to her boots. "Will I still be able to fight for the rebellion?"

"It all depends on the results. We should have a complete test done for everything known to humans within a couple of days at the most. In the meantime, get some rest, try to get your energy back up and keep your stress levels down if you can."

"Yeah, sure," she said with no emotion. How was she supposed to react to something she didn't understand, and couldn't overpower with guns, knives and fists?

"I don't know you personally," the medical Scholar told her. "But I knew your parents, and if you have any part of them in you still then I guarantee you will die in battle, and not from any illness. Whether or not you're healthy enough to fight, I know you'll go through anyone and anything you need to in order to be front and center against Chaos."

Her words helped very little, and not enough to

draw Mercelle's attention away from the racing in her head.

Was Mercelle's thirst for vengeance so obvious that even a complete stranger could smell it on her? It was true that she craved a legacy similar to her parents. But, the idea of perishing from this world while the Demigods still held it hostage from its own people made her gulp down the sensation of oncoming tears.

The medical Scholar was still giving her a motivational speech, and explaining possible treatments, when Mercelle stood up and walked out with a blank look of emptiness.

Her cracking exterior was beginning to reflect her breaking within.

8

DREDGER III

Earth. Dirt. Silt and dust.

The planet was almost nothing but desert sand and rocks. Dredger had seen trees before, in the places they called oases where small amounts of water remained on the surface. He had driven by them a few times and saw the desert tribes' mud huts and clay ovens puffing with smoke.

Everything else was the same procession of granules, sand drifts, mesas and mountains. Dull brown was all he ever saw.

He was thankful, however, for the lightness of the sand. It was easy to remove, especially when it wasn't too inundated with stones. Throughout the millions of years, how was it possible that the Shard's temple was left undiscovered by humans? Lito's temple was buried inside the hard rock of a mountainside, but the temple before him was simply needing to be exposed from the millennia of silt atop it.

Dredger wondered whether or not the Demigods were aware that their stripping away of the planet's resources helped the rebellion to find lost temples like this one by thinning out the ground. Order was the ultimate weapon against Chaos, and Dredger was helping to move Order along. He convinced himself that he only did it to secure food and resources for Kerk, but he truly wanted to aid the rebellion – without risking the lives of his people.

Neutrality was a slippery slope upon which a chilling sleet was beginning to fall.

He hadn't spoken directly to Feres in about a week. Messages were conveniently routed through Seemik and Ashlan in the hopes that he could avoid her altogether. Not knowing exactly how she would react to finding out he'd given up over a hundred and fifty prisoners to Chaos, he thought it best to keep his distance for the time being. He doubted she would judge him for making such a decision, as leaders often require sacrifices for the greater good. But, he feared simply hearing her voice would bring forth a surge of guilt which he had been hoping to dodge.

Ahead of Dredger and Seemik was a miniscule shack made of ancient stone. The door on the front side looked barely big enough for a single person to get through. Problem was: they couldn't get it open.

"The scans are complete," said High Cleric Seemik, tilting the tablet to face him. "Here."

Dredger examined what looked like scans of a vertical shaft going down into the ground from the stone shack, dauntingly narrow. Many feet down, the bottom of the shaft ended at a horizontal tunnel. These openings were much too conveniently placed to be natural occurrences.

"I don't see any support beams holdin' up the walls," Dredger pointed out on the screen. "It's only big enough for one person, and any slight movement could be causin' a cave in."

"Is that why we're not using explosives to blast our way in?" asked Seemik.

"Ashlan and I have already explored that option. Mercelle wouldn't be happy with us collapsin' the tunnel, I'm sayin'. Ya got any ideas? I'm open."

The four-walled temple sat there, taunting them with its strange puzzle. High Scholars Sheller and Maalamon were looking over the small structure to try and find a lever or a handle of some kind. The only thing they were able to find was a pair of handprints on the front of the door that looked like they had been pressed into the stone when it was in a malleable state.

"We can try putting more pressure on the door," Seemik suggested. "But any machine would cause heavy vibrations and risk collapse. Do you think you could dig down to the tunnel?"

"It's too far down. We would have to displace hundreds of tons to get down that far. I'd rather we be smart about it, I'm sayin'."

"Hmm. Time is important though."

"We could drill through the door," Dredger said. "But the drill I have here is too shaky. It sputters a bit too much for this kind of job. My other drill is bein' brought from Kerk, I just don't know when it'll get here. Tomorrow maybe. I don't get it. Why was it so easy to get into Lito's temple, but not this one? Mercelle pushed that other door open usin' just her boot."

"The design and glyph patterns on this temple seem varied slightly from what I've seen before. I'm guessing that this one was built much later than Lito's temple, and even later than the last temple which we thought had the Shard in it. It looks like it may have been constructed by a whole different people entirely."

Dredger paid attention to Sheller and Maalamon as they closely examined the exterior of the stone shack. Sheller was squinting at glyphs, and documenting things into her tablet. Maalamon was running a hand over some symbols that were carved, picking dirt out of them with his fingernail.

"You may want to check on your people," Dredger told the High Cleric, poking his chin at the pair.

"Maalamon!" Seemik shouted as if scolding a child. "Eyes! Not hands! I swear, I'll never work with an insubordinate Naselban like him again. As soon as we get back to Sandra he's on clerical work only."

Sheller came around the shack, smacking the back of Maalamon's hand and sticking a finger in his face. Her grey brows furrowed in pointed impatience.

"He just needs to be kept busy," Dredger said. "If he was doin' somethin' with his hands besides touchin' ancient relics we'd be in good shape, I'm sayin'."

"Poor Sheller has become his mother," Seemik added.

A message popped up on the tablet, blocking the scans. Dredger took the device, and held it closer to his face to read. "It's from the perimeter," he explained. "Someone's here."

THE TRANSPORT KICKED up sand as it approached and stopped at the edge of the dig site. Ashlan hopped down from the driver's seat. "Look who I found wandering around the desert," he said.

From the passenger seat came Lito, unscathed, and certainly not looking like someone who had just spent five days exposed to the elements. Dredger supposed that was the signature of a God: invulnerability.

Lito walked straight up to Dredger, and put a hand out for him to shake.

"Glad to see you're doin' okay," Dredger told him,

taking his hand. It was the most solid shake he'd ever experienced.

"Likewise," Lito replied. "You haven't made it inside yet?" He let go of Dredger's hand to shake Seemik's.

"Hello, Lito. We're still taking notations on the exterior glyphs," explained the High Cleric. "There's a door, but it won't budge. We were hoping you might be able to look at it from another angle, and maybe see something we don't."

Sheller was heading over to greet the God, but Maalamon pushed passed her to get to Lito first.

"I'm happy you're still with us, Litooo," Maalamon spat out through his thick, overplayed Naselban drawl. "I've been waiting for you to arrive so you could help us out with the doooorrr."

Sheller ignored the childish Naselban, and Dredger could see that she was reaching the end of her rope with him. "You look well, Lito. How is Lady Mercelle doing?"

"I haven't seen her since the tower. I hope she's okay."

Ashlan scrolled through messages on his tablet. "The last I heard she arrived in Sandra yesterday."

"Welp, then I expect her to be along any minute," Dredger added. "She never likes to miss a dig."

"Feres's last transmission said she was going to send Mercelle to Kerk to deliver a message," added Ashlan. "If we finish up here fast enough we can beat her there."

He put a hand up to his ear piece for a second, then said, "I'll message you with any updates," and headed back to his rover.

The High Cleric stood beside Lito and stared at the stone shack pensively. "Any thoughts?"

The group walked over to the door, and Lito felt the engraved shapes of human hands on the front. They were positioned in such a way that it looked like one would place their hands in the markings and push.

"We don't have any solid confirmation that the Shard is here," Dredger said. "But we're hopeful, as always."

"It's here," Lito informed him. "I can feel it, an energy similar to mine. It's deep underground, though."

"There's a tunnel below," Seemik responded, showing Lito the scans.

Thankful as he was to have Lito present, and knowing that He was probably the only one who could figure out how to get inside the temple, Dredger kept himself from feeding into Lito's ego by letting Him think He was in charge.

"I have a drill comin'. Should be here tomorrow sometime. That should help ya out."

"Have you surmised what these might be for?" asked Lito, pointing at the handprints pressed into the center of the stone door.

"I saw them firrrssst!" Maalamon chimed. "But we don't quite know what they're foorrr."

Dredger stepped in front of Maalamon. "I tried puttin' pressure on it, but nothin' would budge." He kept quiet while Lito leaned down to get a closer look at the prints, as if He would find a detail they had missed. "You're more than welcome to try it yourself. Maybe you're strong enough to get it open."

The Order God pressed His hands into the prints, leaning into them and applying pressure. It was quite the sight to see a God pushing on an unrelenting wall in an act of total futility. He was shocked to see Lito fail at something so small, and lose a battle against an ancient door after He had just survived a full scale attack on Lanna, and then took down an entire tower.

Grunting, Lito put all of His weight and strength into His arms, digging His boots into the sand as it gave way beneath Him.

"Dredger," He groaned. "Push on my back. We need more pressure."

"Ya want me to..." Dredger was skeptical. "...to push on your back?"

"Yes." Lito replanted His slipping boots.

"Okay? I'll try."

Dredger got behind Lito, placing his palms on the God's upper shoulder blades and giving all of the force he could muster.

The door budged – their first indication that it wasn't a solid piece of the structure, but a standalone portion that could, in fact, move. It was only a slight movement, but it was all they needed to know that progress had been made.

High Cleric Seemik got behind Dredger, extending the line of pushing men and increasing the pressure on the door. The sound of stone grinding on stone could be heard shortly, but no openings had been made yet.

"More pressure!" cried Dredger between Seemik and Lito.

"Go on," Sheller directed Maalamon. "Help them."

The snotty High Scholar folded his arms at the elderly woman. "I'm sorry, but I've been instructed not to touch anythiiing."

"Ingrate," she grumbled with a head shake. Rolling up her sleeves and taking position behind her High Cleric, Sheller gave it all she had, pushing Seemik against Dredger, who was pushing Lito against the door with taut arms.

Dredger's elbows trembled, and he didn't know how long he could hold his spot before they buckled. Arms straight, he closed his eyes and tensed up, keeping his back firm and strong.

In an instant, he was on the ground eating sand and bumping his forehead on Lito's boots. Seemik was on Dredger's back, and Lito was sliding forward.

The door had given out, falling into the shack and wedging itself into the entrance of the shaft that was the floor of the interior. Lito was falling headfirst down the hole beside where the door had gotten stuck.

"I got ya! I got ya!" shouted Dredger as he grabbed at the boots trying to make their way out of his reach. He got a hand around each one, but Lito was heavy, and he was pulled forward until Seemik and Sheller rushed up to assist.

The helpful duo grasped one leg, and Dredger had the other. Together they dragged Lito backwards out of the thin shaft. They all got to their feet, leaning their heads in through the doorway to take in the interior of the shack without falling in. With the corner of the door sticking up out of the shaft, the High Scholars swiftly took out their tablets and began recording the inscriptions on the walls.

Dredger wasn't a Scholar, but he was sharp enough to notice a repeating pattern on the walls that looked more like a decoration than a message. Just inside the threshold, a lever pointed downward out of the wall. Seemik's attention went to it.

"Do ya know what it says?" asked Dredger.

"I'm more interested in what it *does*," answered the High Cleric. "The glyphs around the temple are just a repeating symbol interwoven into itself over and over. It spans each wall and loops around this lever here. There's no way for me to be entirely sure, but the closest I can translate it to is: 'abandon'?"

"Is it in the form of a question or are you just that unsure?" High Scholar Sheller asked in the same tone as a teacher or mentor would, guiding him to an answer.

"It's a question."

"The temple is askin' if we wanna abandon," said Dredger. "That's off-puttin'. Best we leave that lever alone until we're on our way out, I'm sayin'."

Everyone turned to stare Maalamon down.

"Agreed," Seemik replied.

Qabda's face came into Dredger's mind, and he knew what she would be thinking in this situation: if Lito obtained the Shard, it would only further corroborate His power, and the more powerful a God became, the more likely they were to crave more power. Having spoken to Qabda about keeping Lito's control over humanity limited, he started to fear that he may be doing the exact opposite. Lito's ego would need to be kept in check. Dredger needed to make sure He knew His place, and that certain boundaries wouldn't be overstepped. There was no telling how Lito would react or change upon finding the Shard, and he could only hope that he was doing right by his people and by humanity.

Dredger was sure of one thing: he wasn't going to be the one going down that shaft. Lito's Shard: Lito's shaft.

9

LITO VIII

Mechanical pulleys were attached to steel mounts, and Dredger had run a cord through them to hook on the harness around Lito's pelvis. Then he handed Him the button pad.

"You'll dangle from the front," Dredger said, tugging on the cord to make sure it was secure in its fastening. "Green button gives ya slack, red pulls back. Got it?"

"Yes," Lito answered. It was simple enough.

"Good," Dredger replied with a bit of unexpected combativeness. "Should be easy for a *God* to remember. Right?"

Beneath his words existed entire thought processes, which Dredger seemed to be having issues keeping in check. It was a good thing, however, because it revealed to Lito the underlying tension Dredger held toward the

Order God. Lito could only imagine the type of threat He presented to Kerk's anti-war stance, and He thought it a good idea to address it head on.

"It doesn't matter what the Shard does, Dredger. I don't intend on ruling your people."

"I don't intend on allowin' ya to," he said back with a passive aggressive smile as he tightened Lito's straps.

Lito was getting better at picking up traces of sarcasm, especially in facial responses and tones of voice, but still kept Himself from feeling mocked, as it wouldn't serve anyone involved. "A true leader is given power by their people, as opposed to taking it from them. Even a God can only truly thrive off of the faith others have in them. That's what makes me different from my brother."

This man was in a peculiar position. But Lito didn't know if he could ever get past the point of skepticism and push through to faith.

He could feel energetic particles rushing up from the shaft, and He knew the Shard had to be down there somewhere. Once it was found He could finally prove to Dredger, beyond a shadow of any possible doubt, that Lito was the God of Order.

Something told Him that wasn't the problem, that Dredger had belief in Lito as a God, just not as the leader of mankind. Lito could accept being solely their savior, and didn't require power over His creations to do so. Humans were made to be independent, rebellious, and with the strength to stand against Chaos if necessary. To exercise control over them would mean to kill their endowed spirits.

"Listen Lito," Dredger said. "I'm as happy as anyone else to have ya awake, alive and helpin' the rebellion. But, if ya want me to have faith in ya, I need to know that ya don't plan to stick around. Humans need to make their own way, and you owe it to us to keep us alive, I'm sayin'. After that, I don't see a need for ya to stay here. Truth is I obviously won't really know what you'll do until ya do it. I'm a bit peculiar like that."

If telling Dredger His intentions didn't work to alleviate suspicion, Lito would have to show instead of tell. "Then there is still hope that you will have faith in me and my intentions one day."

Dredger didn't say anything back, and Lito was starting to see why some would assume that he hid his lack of commitment behind a facade of neutrality. Lito knew better than to believe that Dredger had an inability to commit, even if he didn't realize it.

The Lord of Kerk pushed the red button on the pad in Lito's hand, pulling the cord into the reel on the back of the transport. "In my experience," he said. "The important artifacts tend to be at the end of the tunnel. Be careful. Believe it or not I prefer to see ya back up here unharmed, and I *don't* wanna have to dig ya out."

"Thank you, Dredger. That means a lot."

"I'm glad," said the stoic man blankly, turning and

heading back to the transport. He had said it as if he didn't mean it, but, again, Lito knew better.

Maalamon must have seen an opportunity to have private words with Lito, because he started speed walking toward the stone shack just as Lito hung free from the pulley system they had set up above the shaft's opening. Lito really didn't want to get caught up in a self-serving conversation wherein He expected Maalamon to ask about putting in a good word to Feres regarding more responsibility. Did the man understand the difference between responsibility and notoriety?

Just before the pesky Naselban approached, Lito hit the green button and lowered Himself down into the darkness of the temple's shaft.

Black surrounded Lito, making Him sense the oncoming of the flash of images with the blue lights, and the rubbled city. He pushed it away, not allowing it to fill in the dark parts of His sight.

The entrance above Him was a distant sparkle of light that faded away while He went lower. Something moved the air in strange ways, getting stronger as He neared the floor of the shaft. A particular energy that felt similar to His was tickling His senses, drawing Him in to a force that was ancient, familiar and comforting.

According to the suspiciously speculative humans,

the Shard could have been anything from the boost of power He needed to overthrow the Demigods, to a booby trap set by Chaos eons ago. The best case scenario would be that the Shard could allow Lito's ability to create replicas again like the Demigods could. Worst case could mean He was walking – or rappelling – into a snare of some kind.

Holding the green button down, Lito finally felt His feet hit the floor. He stood and let out more slack from the pulleys. Above Him was the dot of light from outside. Ahead was the tunnel, holding an object many feet away in the narrow passage that glowed a pale, faint blue. It would light His way.

Indistinguishable voices hollered down at Him, and He shouted back that He had made it to the bottom. After a moment of silence, a tiny item fell past His head and landed by His feet. Bending down to pick it up, He shoved the earpiece into place.

"I made it to the bottom," He reported.

"Everything's calm up here," said Seemik. "Do you need any light down there? We could toss one down."

"I've got all the light I need. I'm entering the tunnel now."

"Okay, Lito. Go slow, and scramble back to the shaft as fast as you can if you feel anything start to move. Confirm."

"Confirmed," He repeated back, lowering Himself onto elbows and knees.

Head first, Lito crawled into the tunnel. It only allowed Him to go a few feet before it narrowed even further, forcing Him to scoot along on His stomach. The bed of the tunnel was made of flat rock, worn over many centuries of running water. It was safe for Lito to assume that the shaft was once an ancient well that tapped into an underground river. That begged the question: was the Shard placed there for safekeeping, or was it dropped into the well? As difficult as it was for Him to imagine, Lito considered that at one point throughout human history the Shard was disposed of.

It must have been important enough to someone, because whoever put it down here had certainly thought ahead enough to carve clues as to where it had been moved into the first Shard temple Seemik and Dredger had found. That was an alarming thought: that the simple failure to document the Shard's new location millions of years ago when it was moved could have prevented Lito from ever finding it. Without knowing what it did, Lito couldn't decide whether or not to be grateful for the clues.

Just beyond the next bump was the dull blue light, moving about slowly as if it was shimmering through moving liquid. He pulled His shoulders, then His hips through a tight squeeze of a passage, and was on the mysterious object.

Half buried in sand that had spent countless years

making its way down to this spot, the Shard twinkled weakly like a fading star. Wondrous and entrancing.

It was glass, with an airy liquid inside, clear and swirling around with hundreds of blue sparks that had managed to stay lit after all this time. The sparks swam through the clear parts, flowing and bouncing off of the inside of the glass. It was the size of His fist, triangular and pointed on the corners. The top point had a stone clasp on it, carved with a precision He was yet to see in that kind of material.

A silvery dust trailed away from the clasp, leading Lito to think that the Shard had been attached to a type of chain or lead that had dissolved throughout time. Dense energy packed the tunnel, and it almost felt like the whole thing would collapse without it.

When He touched the Shard for the first time, His fingertips attracted all of the blue sparks to the glass, like magnets attracting to His skin, fighting to get out through the glass. Electrical sensations surged through His arm, through His chest and dissipated in His nerve endings. Within a second, as if awakening from a slumber, the sparks were glowing bright enough to nearly blind Him.

The tunnel disappeared, and He found Himself standing on uneven ground, staring up at the blue lights as they fell from the sky, bringing an unrelenting gloom unto His heart. Were they the lights from the Shard? They seemed to be. Despair with a hint of regret taunted Him, and when the lights retreated into the dirt and faded to darkness He snapped away from the flash of images, seeing something entirely different.

Mental pictures of the first Races, the temple and the Book of Order sped across His sight. Falling, dropping, flying through the air behind the pull of new gravity, He hit the ground of a once bountiful planet, weak and dying. His nerve endings changed from a comforting vibration to a shock of impact. Everything was coming full circle, and the Shard was but a checkpoint in that journey.

Euphoria, and a perception of completeness overwhelmed Him – a body coming back into contact with its soul – and He turned onto His back to let the feeling wash over His existence.

AT THE TOP of the shaft, Lito handed the Shard off to Seemik. The sparks had faded from their blinding light, but still remained brighter and more lively than they were when He had found them.

"May Humanity and Order reign!" shouted the thrilled High Cleric. "We found it!"

He thrust the Shard into the air multiple times, and then handed it to Sheller.

While Dredger disassembled the pulley rack from within the stone shack, Lito unclipped the harness from around His waist and let it drop to the ground, watching Sheller gaze at the moving sparkles within.

"Magnificent. We'll have to see what it does."

"The energy it puts off is very similar to mine," Lito said, trying to put His thoughts into words. "It feels like a part of me, something I lost long ago that I've waited a long time to return to."

Sheller gave the Shard to Maalamon before he could snatch it out of her hand.

"Can you feel it?" Lito asked. "The energy?"

"I'm sorry, but no," Sheller answered with a head shake and a touch of disappointment. "It is spectacular to look at nonetheless."

"I can feel iiit!" declared Maalamon.

Lito didn't believe him, but felt that all human imagination should be fed and encouraged. It was what made them who they were. "Good for you," Lito told him, realizing after the words left His mouth that He was successfully mastering sarcasm. "I think it might be time to see what the 'abandon' lever does, now that we're done with the temple." He held out a hand for the Shard, and Maalamon reluctantly gave it back. "Would you do the honors?"

"I would love tooo," said the High Scholar, stepping into the doorway of the temple.

Lito picked up the harness, and motioned for Sheller and Seemik to hastily follow Him over to the transport where Dredger was loading the last part of the pulley rack into the back of a rover.

Altogether, they stopped and turned around to watch.

Maalamon poked a curious head into the shack, looking down into the blackness of the shaft. One hand on the lever, he pulled it upward until it shifted into a vertical position against the wall.

Lito felt a rumble far beneath them right away. It extended long arms up toward them until the rest of them could feel it too. At first, His reactionary impulses told Him to get Maalamon away from the stone shack before it was sucked into the ground, but He decided not to say anything at all, and to just enjoy the spectacle instead, knowing Maalamon was just out of the collapsible area.

Dredger cupped his hands around his mouth, about to shout to Maalamon to vacate the area, but Seemik put a hand up to stop him.

"Let him learn," requested the High Cleric.

Lito liked that man. Part of the importance of free will was allowing one to learn from their own mistakes.

As the ground trembled below their feet, sand began to fall into the shaft. The tunnel collapsed and a stream of air rushed up through the shaft and shot out of the entrance, blowing Maalamon many feet into the air. The High Scholar's robes kicked up and he went head over heels, careening and cart wheeling away from the epicenter of the small quake.

He landed at their feet, nearly making it all the way to the transport, but falling just short. Coughing and spitting out sand, Maalamon ran hands over his body parts to make sure everything was still there. Lito was more amused by the reactions of the others than the involuntary flailing performance He had just witnessed.

Sheller promptly bellowed out a hysterical laugh, swaying to one side and bumping into Seemik on accident. "I guess we know what it does?!" she hollered between breaths.

The High Cleric helped to steady the elderly High Scholar in her stance, barely able to contain himself as he asked, "Are we going to be touching anything else?"

Maalamon shook his head, and sand poured out of his ears.

A small distance away, the stone shack toppled inward, and the shaft became a slight dip in the desert landscape. Lito felt ashamed to lose such a relic, and was disappointed that Mercelle would only see the stone shack in pictures and recordings. But it was worth it, because they now had the Shard, and a new hope for victory.

Plus, they all got to see Maalamon flail through the air.

"I'm sayin' we accomplished what we came here to do," declared Dredger, smiling at the High Scholar as he dusted himself off. "And I think we can say we had a little fun doin' it."

Lito was having fun with the harmless shared joy, learning yet another emotion. He was just thankful that this new one was a good and simple feeling. The fact was that this was the most fun He'd had since waking up.

10

MORA II

This experiment had failed hundreds of times. She and her replicas had never successfully implanted a working acetylator within living flesh to full functionality. Although Chaos bodies held up much better than human ones, all were failures.

Decades ago, Mora had tasked an entire team of her replicas to research and develop only the acetylator. They worked to perfect it, but even with the assistance of her best surgeons, she couldn't accomplish a perfect operation. If she could get this right, she could greatly decrease the likelihood of her subjects succumbing to the harsh exposure of various chemicals, radiation and treatments. The acetylator essentially changed the composition of particles being taken into the body, and turned them into something the flesh could use to sustain itself while becoming stronger and more durable. It only had to be tweaked properly for each subject.

This had to be the one, she thought. She could feel it in her bones that this was going to work. She could also feel a great deal of mysterious pains running up and down the sinuous muscles of her elongated abdomen. Rubbing and massaging them did nothing to help. When the pain shot up, it went all the way to her head, ringing in her ears, and she rubbed her eyebrows to try and keep from cringing behind the strange, intense ache.

She was watching the implantation procedure through the round window atop the operation room. From there she could see everything her replicas were doing. One monitored the subject's internal reaction on a screen against the wall, making sure the Valk wasn't starting to reject the implant. Another Mora was inserting the long, needle shaped probe into the freshly sewn incision, while the third assisted with instruments and probe readings by holding a small screen in its hand for the operator to watch.

None of her replicas caught it, but a slight spike in frontal-neuro energy flow came up on the large screen, and the subject's claw tips twitched. This was an indication of an oncoming rejection to high levels of gamma charged tachyons used to lubricate the surge of experimental compounds. She had seen it many times before, and the subject would die soon if she didn't prevent it.

"Decrease tachyon output," she said through the speaker.

"Affirmative," replied the operator before it tapped commands into the small screen.

"As soon as I tell you to, bring the output back up." She needed to keep a constant flow of tachyons through the Valk's flesh while making sure not to overload it.

"Affirmative."

Mora's eyes stung, and her ears vibrated with a strong ring. Sprays of scratching sensations ran along the folds in her brain, making her see light that wasn't there. She closed her eyes to catch her equilibrium.

"How long are we to wait, my Queen? Now? Hello? If we wait any longer the specimen will crash."

She rubbed and rubbed until her scalp no longer felt like it was on fire. The episode was the worst she'd had yet, and she was glad it was over. "Yes," she sputtered out, opening her eyes. "Bring the levels back up."

But it was too late. Rejection reactions alerted in all sensors, and the subject was no longer responsive. All three replicas looked up at Mora with confusion on their faces.

"This specimen is lost," she instructed. "Dispose of it." She shut off the speaker, and let her eyes close again.

Hands of a replica went around her forearm.

"My Queen," said her main hand. The replica must have picked up on her physical ailments and came to her aid. "I believe it's time for you to replicate. Come, I'll bring you."

She allowed the replica to guide the path of her steps out of the observation deck, and into the private room at the end of the corridor. It hit the button to slide the glass door shut so that no one could see in, but Mora could see out through the one-way glass.

She sat down on the lone chair in the small, dark chamber. Shutting her eyes again, she concentrated on pushing out all of the charged energy from her core, catalyzing the replication process. She thought about how the meditation could possibly help her to ease the mobile stinging and scratching moving about her insides and resting in her brain.

Before she could even out her emotions and use the created energy to separate a replica from her body, she felt the flesh of her newest creations pulling away from her own. It was the normal sensation of tearing muscle and cleaving ligaments, but she had given it so little effort it was as if it was going to happen whether or not she willed it to.

She looked back and forth at the two newborns, and they stared back at her, waiting for her guidance. The main hand was still standing outside of the door, and Mora stood to hit the button and open the door. Both replicas stepped through the opening when she waved them away, then she closed the door again and sat back down, reviewing the last conversation she'd had with

Bled as her new replicas walked by her main hand and went down the corridor.

Even though the two were born together, Newlyn and Bled never acted close. They were both on the same level of incompetence, but at least Bled had the good sense to align with Mora before Newlyn did. It didn't matter, because it was only a matter of time until Valk saw Newlyn for the useless blubber and goo he was and destroyed him. Once that was taken care of, she'd only have Bled to deal with. All she had to do was take credit for Bled's little 'assassination' experiment, if it turned out successful. Then, Valk would be even more in her favor, causing him to take his guard down even further.

Her plan perfectly coincided with the eradication of the human Race. It wouldn't be long now before the Glaven Grad tower was outfitted with thrust engines that could lift it away from Earth, and guide it through the cosmos alongside the Mastership. Within a month's time, the planet would be devoid of remaining resources, and its atmosphere on a rapid decline. Even though the renovations were Newlyn's design, they didn't need him to complete the project and make it work. She just wanted Newlyn gone, and Bled at least a distant thought by the time she and Valk floated away from this planet, side by side, each with their own ship.

And if Valk refused to take her as his Queen, then she'd have to figure out how to get rid of him too. It could be easy, or it could involve many arduous steps along the way.

Her thoughts brought about a rushing on of more mystery pain. She concentrated on meditating, trying to quell the sharp stings before they accumulated inside her head again. Instead of the meditation helping, the relentless stinging intensified far past the extent of any episode she'd experienced thus far.

The scratching sensations peaked in her brain, signaling an end to her episode, but it didn't end. It shot back down into her belly, and when she ran her hands over her stomach to find the source of the pain, she felt a small lump next to her silvery-blue belly button.

It moved as her fingers graced the skin covering it, twisting and shifting upward through her organs. Internal tearing racked her senses, and she felt tissue being pulled apart in order to allow a path through her body through which the strange, round abscess travelled. Mora lurched over from the pain, crying out for a quick second and causing the main hand outside the door to reach for the open switch.

"Leave me!" she called out before the main hand could reach the switch. At that, the replica hesitantly turned and walked away.

Without knowing what was happening to her, Mora wanted to keep any possible weaknesses to herself. She couldn't risk word getting out that she was in a vulnerable position. If Newlyn or Bled knew just how weak she was, they would certainly come after her. Even trusting her own replicas was out of the question, as they ultimately answered to Valk over Mora.

The lump reached her chest, pushing bones out of the way, and tossing Mora to the floor. She writhed, wriggled, even convulsed a little bit to try anything that might be able to make it stop. Nothing helped. In fact, every movement she made only increased her level of bodily agony as the mass rolled through her chest and reached the poison gland at the base of her throat.

All around the gland's opening began to swell and roll about, stretching and gaping wider and wider as if something was about to come through it. The hole grew, the skin surrounding it peeling back to expose the surface of the lump.

Mora's head ticked all the way back. Her gland opened wider than it had ever opened before, and what emerged was a small, round and white object that plopped itself onto the floor beside her. It was covered in the noxious acid that usually shot out of her gland when she wanted to immobilize her enemy.

So small, she could have swallowed it in a single gulp. But, as the pain subsided, and the internal pieces of Mora's body went back into place, she gazed at the thing, taking in the wet, smooth texture of its exterior, and the tiny movements coming from within.

She sat up and leaned against the wall, gagging and spitting as she waited for her throat to remold itself back into its normal shape. Within a minute she was checking herself to see where the pain had gone, shuddering to think that it may return again. When it didn't, she relaxed, letting her muscles rest, and enjoyed the freedom from the agony.

Her body felt lighter, like she could float up to the ceiling and look down at herself. Instead, she rose to stand, then bent down to pick up the lump from the floor. Turning it over in her hand, it looked like an egg. She and Valk had decimated many egg-producing species during their shared conquests. But, how did one come out of her?

Chaos didn't procreate, the Demigods replicated instead. It was the power bestowed upon them by the great God-King Leto to help them spread the influence of Chaos across the universe. The beings she had encountered who were capable of making such biological objects were only able to do so because of eons of evolution, and Chaos didn't evolve. Not anymore, at least.

The first Demigods of Chaos had the ability to evolve in order to improve their biological adaptability. But, as time went on, the God-King learned to make beings that no longer required improvement, therefore, removing their abilities to evolve beyond their created states. Now, any creations of Leto's were perfect upon conception, and there was no need or room to improve upon such wonders of advanced existence.

Still, the egg sat in the palm of her hand, tickling her skin with the small protrusions that pressed out against the egg's exterior. Drops of her internal acid sat atop the white external layer. She brought it close to her eyes and watched the egg absorb the acid into itself. Curious, she brought her other hand up to her gland, inserted a sharp fingernail and pulled out a few more drops. Rubbing the acidic substance over the egg, she saw it disappear once again through the thin skin. Then it seemed to wriggle about slightly, rolling this way and that within her wide, flat palm.

It was cute, adorable, and it was a piece of her.

Had she changed her genetic makeup somehow through the centuries spent on Earth, slaving away at trying to use the durable human body to create more efficient, biological killing machines? Had she accidentally done something to herself along the way? The questions didn't seem to matter. Their weight was something she didn't care to carry with her. She had a successful, live being which she had created all on her own. It was perfect, and for the first time in her entire existence, Mora felt love.

She had existed outside of her own physical body countless times via her replicas, but her connection to the easily controlled Moras was nonexistent. They belonged to her; however, once their flesh was separated from hers, they were mere objects, basic beings under her command. Part of her lack of emotional, physical or even existential connections with her creations was the fact that they were under Valk's control also. In fact, Valk's word superseded hers, as did Leto's.

Experiencing the ultimate freedom of having something she created be hers and hers alone – independent from the bridled oversight of Valk and Leto – Mora beamed a wide smile at the tiny, oblong ball she held. She pressed it to her chest, holding it close and trying not to weep at her new secret.

No one was to know about the egg, not even her other creations. It would be her escape, her solace, and her freedom when she felt constrained by the wrenching claws of her superiors.

She would have to hide it. Deep beneath the Glaven Grad tower were endless subfloors left abandoned by the previous centuries of ruined experiments. Valk never saw fit to refurbish them, or even bury them, as they had all expected to make it off of this round rock so much sooner. Her precious egg would have to be kept out of sight, and away from prying eyes. Bled or Newlyn would almost certainly use it as leverage against her, and Valk, she thought, would likely put a hoof on it and crush it into oblivion if he felt something could possibly exist outside of his rule.

Mora wasn't going to let that happen.

Holding the small, squishy egg between two fingers, she lifted her skirt and placed it high between her thighs. Her small muscles were soft, and the egg nestled perfectly between them, and walking wouldn't be a problem because the sway of her legs tended to be smooth, elegant and close together.

Taking a quick lap around the small chamber, she tested the hold of the egg between her thighs. It didn't slip or budge. She would have to keep it there until she was deep under Glaven Grad, and no one was around to witness its existence.

Readying herself, and holding back the glow of her accomplished smile, she hit the door switch and stepped out into the corridor. Right away, the trio that was previously operating on the Valk surrounded her.

"Is there something else we can try, my Queen?"

"Did we miss something?"

"We'll try again, and get it right this time."

The main hand came from down the corridor and asked, "Everything okay, my Queen? You were in there longer than usual."

"I'm fine," she answered. "Just running some scenarios in my head."

"You look much better, my Queen. Should I shoo these three away?"

The operating team stepped back, all three of them staring down at the floor after the main hand's suggestion.

"No," said Mora. "I'd like you three to come up with two hundred scenarios each on how we can increase our odds of success during the next attempt at installing the acetylator." She looked at the main hand. "And I'd like you to supervise. Narrow down the best proposed scenarios and compile them into a single file to be ready by nightfall."

The main hand nodded its obedience, then stepped to the side to let the operating team scurry away and start their work. Then it came closer to Mora.

At first, the Demigod felt the need to step back and away from the highly ranked replica, but stopped herself so as not to arouse suspicion of any kind.

"We won't let you down, my Queen. Our success is yours to have." It looked her up and down, and Mora clenched her thigh muscles nervously, keeping a stern face. "I must say, my Queen, you are simply glowing after this last replication. I fear one of your newest creations may have been making you sick. I'm glad you got it out. Should I have the newest pair of replicas disposed of in case they aren't up to standards?"

"If there's anything substandard about them then the scans in the maturation bay will pick it up and dispose of them. I have a meeting with Bled I have to get to, and you have scenarios to narrow down. I suggest you get to it if you want to make your deadline."

"Yes, my Queen." The main hand dipped her head before turning and following the operating team back into the labs.

Mora waited for the corridor to empty out, then got

to the stairs and went down them, rolling the small egg back and forth between her thighs with each step.

Earth's specimens weren't the most remarkable she'd ever come across. In her opinion, the most interesting species she and Valk had eradicated during their conquests was a planet of seven-legged bugs the size of the Mastership. They called the planet Verservero, and the gigantic creatures communicated with low resonating frequencies which were picked up by very fragile, meaty pendulums they kept stabilized inside their brains.

Having never encountered extraterrestrial threats, the Verserveron bugs lived lives of tranquility and comfort. They travelled their massive planet, feeding off of secretions from a strange, blue weed that had grown miles thick over the entire surface of Verservero, leaving behind trails of excretions that glowed, dried, floated into their thin atmosphere and then rained down to further pollinate the blue weeds.

The Verserveron's communication organs were so sizeable and rich with molecular reproduction that Mora could harvest and use them to replace damaged tissue within her and Valk's replicas, bringing them back to optimal health. Her experiments were easy, and yielded much success in the way of providing Leto with data on their biological makeups. They didn't fight her, and gave very little resistance to Valk's decimation of their planet and species. Mora had simply assumed that they lacked the intelligence to understand what was happening to them, even as she swiftly created Verserveron-Chaos hybrids as hunters to wipe out the planet of bugs and leave the plant life intact for harvesting.

Soon the entire self-sustained environment collapsed on its own. It was a shame that she had to leave behind a smoldering wasteland before fully understanding the symbiotic ecosystem the Verserverons had created and maintained. Their peace was destroyed by Chaos, and the pair of Demigods had done their job well, sending endless loads of the rich weeds back to the Great Wall for Leto to have for Himself.

Evolution was something Leto struggled to understand, or even accept. He saw it as a sign of inherent weakness within flawed a biological design. He chose to pick and choose which parts to keep for Himself, and which pieces to eradicate. It was always Leto's intention to either ransack or raze, and it was always His choice. Valk just followed Him blindly, with no regard to the beauty of symbiosis they seemed to be removing from the universe.

Verservero was a memory she'd hold on to for all eternity, she only wished she could have the same success with figuring out how to mesh the complex structure of human D.N.A. with Chaos.

She recalled her early experiments on the humans as she trekked through the hundreds of deserted floors beneath the Glaven Grad tower. Passing by small stalls lined against a long partition, she looked over the corroded wires that hung down within each one. They used to deliver electrical charges directly into human renal systems so she could track the absorption of the radioactive particles used in those times. Humans had no tolerance for radiation, which was her main tool when trying to manipulate genetic structuring of a being in order to allow it to mesh with foreign bodies.

Creating Chaos hybrids was their way of keeping their numbers of replicas high, and it wasn't until they came to Earth and failed to create such hybrids successfully that they were forced to use their own replicas for battle against the ever resistant human species. It all put more pressure on the Demigods to learn how to replicate faster, and with bigger batches.

A few more floors down, and she found the empty tanks – their glass long shattered – wherein she had barely managed to keep a genetically altered human under water without it drowning. She only kept bits and pieces of the data from this experiment, as it only served to improve human functionality, as opposed to creating a weapon they could use against the human population. Somehow, she had greatly increased the specimen's lung capacity and capillary operation, allowing it to take in water, extract the oxygen, and exhale only hydrogen. When she determined that all had been learned from this experiment, she allowed the hydrogen levels in the closed tank to go unchecked, and the specimen slowly suffocated.

That had to have been over half a millennium ago, and she wondered how long it had taken the tank to break, and how long it had taken the body she'd left behind to break down into dust.

The Kaisers, who ruled Earth following the Great Exodus, used to provide Glaven Grad with countless human subjects. They had considered them rejects because they hadn't inherited the same genes as the three first Kaisers, and were labeled "unclean". Mora couldn't tell the difference, as most of the gifted rejects were perfectly healthy until she got her hands on them. Now, centuries after the decline of the Kaiser's empire, her only means of acquiring new subjects was by incarceration, or defectors who came to Glaven Grad out of desperation.

Another few floors down, and she came to a wide experimental chamber. It was circular, layered with dust, and the center of the floor had collapsed many centuries ago. She couldn't descend any further, as the remaining floors beneath her were likely filled with debris. This would have to do.

Along the outside of the round chamber were small

operating rooms. She chose one and stepped over the toppled tables and shelving units. Back during the days when these rooms were functional, the walls were used to store and transport many unstable compounds. Glass and polymer tubing was used to pump sensitive chemicals from vats into the labs for careful use. The lines were long dead and empty, and she imagined this would be the safest place for her egg to be kept.

Popping open one of the wall panels, she took one last look around her to make sure she wasn't being followed, and listened for the slightest of stirring noises. The air was clean, and there was no scent of sentient life around her, aside from the egg which she carefully pulled from the warmth between her thighs.

The soft, small ball moved, and dark parts of whatever it was that lived inside kept pressing against the opaque exterior. It was trying to speak to her, or, at least, that's what she chose to believe. She wanted to speak back, but couldn't understand how to speak a language driven by love or attachment. Her own Chaos energy resonated within the egg; she could feel it responding to her pulse of ethereal flows. It was as if she held a piece of her own existence in her hand, and she didn't want to leave it alone, but she had no choice. Parting with the small, defenseless newborn was its only hope of surviving.

An uncomfortable, unfamiliar yearning to care for the object boiled over inside of her. There was no fighting it, and she felt that the nurturing impulse she was feeling was the result of the subsiding pain from the last few days. Instead of hurting physically, her energy was fighting her, and unwillingly focusing her attention on ensuring the health and safety of the egg. For such a small thing, Mora could feel an overwhelming tug of gravity luring her in, and she didn't care whether or not it was a trap, because it fulfilled her.

She tensed the muscles in her neck, pressing them against the gland in her throat and excreting acid from the opening. Holding the egg close, she rolled it around on her neck's opening, soaking it in the excretion until it was dripping in the provided sustenance.

Holding back a tear, she placed the egg within the wall. "I'll come back for you," she told it. "I promise you."

Then, Mora closed the panel and ascended the hundreds of flights of stairs to get back to her operational laboratories. Without the egg in her possession, she returned to the emptiness which had become her darkened reality.

11

HIGH CLERIC ASTOR SEEMIK II

After the small tidbit of fun they'd had watching Maalamon learn a lesson about touching things he shouldn't, Seemik noticed that Dredger had retreated into himself. While packing up the caravan and gathering up the security perimeter, he hadn't said a word to anyone. He rode with Seemik, scowling out the window in deep reflection the entire time. Seemik thought – more than a few times – to ask him what he was thinking about.

Assuming it had something to do with the Shard proving to actually exist, and Lito becoming more powerful the more Order was fed to the masses, the High Cleric decided to wait until Kerk to bring anything up regarding the political change the Shard had the potential to make. He would rather have a conversation with his fellow Sandrans there to back him up, and not while the loud roar of heavy engines surrounded them. If Dredger was feeling as if his power was being threatened by Lito or the Shard, then a discussion was necessary. He needed to know that they were all on the same side, neutral or not.

Seemik spent the night in the large, rumbling trailer-pull thinking of ways to convince Dredger of this. Certain words would have to be avoided, while others would have to be pressed upon. The most important thing the High Cleric wanted to keep in mind was his tone. Dredger wasn't Seemik's mentor or Lord, nor was he Seemik's subordinate or subject. A balance of tone would need to be maintained in order for his ground to be held, as well as to avoid disrespect or condescension. Once inside the tunnels of Kerk, Seemik would be his guest; however, some topics were unavoidable, and would likely require a controlled amount of aggression. For instance: the summit.

If the rebel minds were going to be convening, any human leaders left out would be easy targets for Chaos. That was a point Seemik was willing to hammer home, no matter the cost of tone or offense. Dredger's power existed within the solidarity he held with his loyal followers. Seemik only hoped that he hadn't been blinded by it.

THEY ARRIVED THE NEXT MORNING. Dredger led everyone to a cafeteria many floors down from the entrance, and had some rations brought to feed them.

Seemik had some crispy soy chunks seasoned with salt, and some electrolyte tablets, while Maalamon, Sheller and Ashlan enjoyed their meals of protein patties and cold water. Lito examined the Shard for hidden clues.

The High Cleric put his clean, ceramic plate in a bin that sat in the center of the long table. "Once we get the Shard back to Sandra we can get it into analysis and see what we can find," he said, wiping salt from his lips. "We need to figure out how to use it as soon as possible."

"Good idea, I'm sayin'," Dredger replied. "That thing could be dangerous. It's ancient, and if it's from space then it could be radioactive. I'd like to avoid any of my people gettin' infected or sick."

Seemik doubted it was dangerous. Lito was quite astute at sensing danger, and would have said something straight away.

"I can assure you it is completely harmless to humans." Lito was trying to alleviate Dredger's worries.

Dredger scoffed at Him, and shook his head. He was taking Lito's words as a challenge. "If I don't feel my people are safe around the Shard then I'll remove it from Kerk myself if I need to."

It was atrocious the way Lito was being spoken to,

and Seemik couldn't stand by and allow it to continue. "There's no need to speak to Him like that. Lito's just trying to help us any way He can. Now, He said it wasn't harmful. We can believe Him."

"Ya believe what ya wanna believe. I'll be the cautious one who says 'I told ya so' when it all gets Kaisered up. How do we even know that Lito knows what He's talkin' about?"

"Because He's a God," Seemik answered, trying not to shake his head.

Lito stayed quiet, and Seemik assumed He was simply allowing the mortals the chance to decide for themselves what to do next. The Order God emanated the ideal of free will, even if Dredger couldn't see that.

"This is why I don't like dealin' with fanatics like ya. It's all about piety, blind trust in a hope that seems to be takin' up all your time. Humans are gonna win your war, not some ancient God."

Bolting to her feet, Sheller stepped in front of the angry man, pointing a finger at him the way she had done to Maalamon at the stone shack. "One day you and your city will be called upon to help fight the Demigods. You'll-"

"Legend!" Dredger shouted over her, much to Seemik's surprise. "Will *not* dictate policy! In! My! City!"

Muddled frustration overtook the young High Cleric, and he dropped his guard, asking with a very pointed tone, "How can you call it 'legend'? After all you've seen? You've been at every dig site and expedition with Lady Mercelle ever since the search for proof of Order began. You were there when proof was found – when He was awakened. You are more of a testament to the truth of Lito's power than anyone else in this room! Your life force is linked to Him, same as the rest of us!"

It was painfully baffling to Seemik why Dredger would be so resistant to Lito's words. He asked himself whether or not Dredger knew he was making a fool out of his reputation as a level-headed diplomat and leader. The whole world would soon see him as the man who helped Lito but failed to trust Him. Did he not see that Lito was meant to be the end of the Demigods' hold over Earth?

"I don't believe in destiny," Dredger snapped back. "I won't give the credit of my hard and gruelin' work to someone who's only been a part of our world for a couple of weeks." He stood up, balling a fist at his side and jamming a finger into his own chest as he spoke. "I built this city! I created a place for the rejected humans of the world to live! Nobody did that for me! I helped Mercelle because she's like a daughter to me! That's what her parents wanted! I owe my life, and the lives of my people, to her parents, Feres's parents and everyone else who helped me defend Kerk from Chaos! I owe it to those lost lives to provide for my people! That's all I'm doin' by diggin' up your precious temples! Ya don't get to question me." He made sure they all caught contact with his seething eyes as he looked around the circle.

High Scholar Maalamon was too frightened during real situations to pipe up. First Officer Ashlan wasn't much into politics. Security, combat, following orders and killing replicas were better uses of his abilities. Sheller's eyebrows were arched in a way that said she didn't think her words had the power to correct anything at all.

Lito looked like He was standing by, waiting for them to come to an agreement that Seemik didn't see working out. The High Cleric was still a little shocked by Dredger's reaction to their suggestions. He didn't think anyone had ever seen Dredger this passionate about an objection.

Heavy boots stepped through the door, and they all looked up to see who was interrupting their little debate.

"Oh," said Seemik. "We were just talking about you."

Up until the hostage rescue that Feres, Lito and Mercelle led, Seemik had only known Mercelle by reputation. He didn't think Mercelle would give in to awkward silences, and as she looked around the room at the fuming individuals he could tell she smelled the tension like a methane leak. Something was also a bit off with her. The areas under her eyes were greyish, and she looked like she had lost a few pounds since he last saw her. It hadn't been *that* long ago.

Dredger avoided her eyes, tapping his foot on the floor and adjusting the goggles on his head until he finally took them off and hung them on his belt. It was like a father not wanting his daughter to see him angry.

Sheller took a seat between Ashlan and Lito, across from Maalamon. She may have figured that being between the calmer bodies would slow her frustration. Lito stood and came to greet the Lady.

"I see you're finding your way around," she told Him with a smile. Then she hugged Him around the neck.

"Did you do what I asked?" Lito questioned with a serious, stoned face.

"The results should be waiting for us when we get back to Sandra. Not something I'm looking forward to. But, I do have to say that I'm feeling a little more clear headed than I've been in the last few days. More energy all of a sudden. I feel good."

Was she sick? Was something wrong with the impenetrable warrior Lady Inis Mercelle? As she stood before him, Seemik saw her as flawless. She contained her burdens and exuded a steadfast confidence unlike any other woman he had met who was around his age. It was like she had seen it all and done it all, and would forever be bored with the world if she wasn't constantly pushing the boundaries of humanity.

"Is that it?" she asked, pointing to the Shard on the

table behind Lito. He couldn't even answer before she scooped it up and held it in front of her face. "So the glyphs were right. It was moved." The pale blue sparks flowing in the clear liquid shined onto her dry cheeks, and Seemik noticed that her lips were peeling in one spot.

For a moment, she stared at the Shard, then looked away deep in thought, before looking back at the swirling blue sparks.

Constantly pushing, even under the weight of illness. His admiration for her only grew after seeing the flaws in the details of her skin.

Seemik cleared his throat. "Dredger thinks it might be dangerous," he said. "He wants it removed before someone gets hurt. How are you feeling, by the way? I heard your transport broke down on your way back from the tower."

"Getting better," she replied, handing the Shard back to Lito. "Thanks for asking. How was the dig? Anyone get hurt this time?" Everyone looked at Maalamon. "What did you do?"

Seemik wanted to laugh at the thought of the High Scholar careening through the air, to allow Mercelle to see the subtle curl of his lips, as he saw hers, but Dredger was stirring more and more with each passing, agitating moment.

"Forgive the atmosphere," said the High Cleric. "It's still filled with the steam of our heated discussion."

"What were you talking about?" she asked, looking to Dredger.

"We touched on some important things," Seemik answered when Dredger didn't. "The war. Order. Chaos. Fear. Neutrality. Inevitability."

"You covered a lot of ground," Mercelle said. "I actually have something I need to talk about with Dredger – something everyone should be aware of."

"What is it?" Dredger asked, putting his goggles back on the top of his head.

"*Lady* Edeen is now calling herself the Empress of the rebellion, and thinks she's in charge. She set a date for the summit of all Lords, Ladies and High Courts to meet in Naselba. It's just over a week away. I wouldn't ask you to go, but we need to stand up to her and show that we're united, and that we're willing to work *with* her, not *for* her."

Seemik would have to let the air clear out for a few moments before trying to bring that up. He knew that Feres was going to contact Lady Edeen in order to schedule the summit, but knowing it had a date – and so soon – he was glad to see Mercelle taking control of this argument.

Dredger seemed to make a much better attempt at putting on a polite face when speaking to Mercelle, even as he argued back. "Ya don't need me for that. I'm not a Lord, and my people ain't gettin' tangled up in your rebellion."

Seemik couldn't help but continue where he had left off before Mercelle showed up, and he let it all out at once. "It's only a matter of time before Chaos sends another army to your door. Sandra can't justify defending a city who cannot defend us back. I assume the purpose of the summit is to plan the attack on Glaven Grad. The rebellion is moving to end the war as Earth approaches a drop off point of habitability. It's either us or them. Chaos will come after you if they beat us, but we'll have a better chance at victory with you involved."

"Plan your attack," Dredger retorted sharply. "I can't force my people to fight in a war I promised to avoid. Ya have no idea what I've done to keep away from the violence of Chaos *and* the rebellion. My city would shun me."

Mercelle stepped closer to him, squatting down to level her face with his as he sat on the short stool alongside the long cafeteria table. "They will stand by you as long as they understand how much they're needed. Think about it. Even if we win the war, without your help Kerk will forever be a city of outcasts. This is your chance to change that."

The High Cleric picked up on the scent of a secret, as he was sure all city leaders had plenty. Dredger was being a bit too obvious with his circumvented rationalizations.

"Turnin' on Kerk would be your choice. If ya want

me to have faith in somethin', I'll hold onto the hope that the rebellion will save Earth from destruction and win the war, and that you'll keep your humanity intact afterward."

"Coward," Seemik blurted out. Mercelle gave him an admonishing glare. "I'm sorry, but you can't sit idly by while the rest of the world fights to protect you. Never forget that your people fought before to defend the city in the attack on Kerk – they can fight again. Many people from the rebellion died during that battle, fighting for you!"

"I won't be threatened by a child," Dredger yelled at the High Cleric. "Ya haven't lived long enough to recognize the dark places of the world by sight, and how to sidestep them in order to survive, I'm sayin'."

Seemik shook his head. Dredger just wasn't getting it. "I'm not speaking from experience, I'm speaking with logic. We don't need to compare our pasts; we need to salvage our future. Once a strategy is formulated to attack Glaven Grad, the rebellion will allocate resources from somewhere. You'll soon find yourself without income or work, and Kerk will be left to its own devices while the rebellion cuts you off to funnel efforts into the attack. Lady Mercelle, are you aware of any upcoming plans to commission Dredger for work?"

She didn't look anyone in the eye when she solemnly told Dredger, "Now that we have the Shard, there are no other breadcrumbs to follow in the search for Order artifacts. And with Naselba and Sandra being the last remaining rebel cities, there isn't any construction needed either."

Seemik felt terrible for contributing to what looked like a gang up. They were all letting into Dredger, and in his own city where he had the right to have them all executed if he so chose. But it had to be done. Keeping the people of Kerk from the war would only bring future strife.

"Kerk's citizens will adapt," Dredger insisted. "Or they'll starve." He peered over at Lito sitting quietly with the Shard. "Would ya allow humans to suffer like that?"

"I don't 'allow' anyone to do anything," Lito answered with a flat tone. "It will be within their abilities to exercise free will and decide for themselves whether or not they want to follow you, as all power is accompanied by adversity."

"Then I'm exercisin' *my* own free will. The rest of ya are just shadows, following Lito's influence however He speaks it."

It caught Seemik off guard to see Maalamon stand up to interject. "You must attend the summit, Dredger-rrr. Otherwise it will look like an act of resistance against the Empresssss."

"Quiet, Naselban! It's ridiculous to accuse me of resistin' a rebellion. Maybe you're the ones takin' over Earth with your tyranny and your *orders*. Kerk will learn to survive on its own. I won't keep repeatin' myself to ya."

Sheller rejoined the conversation. "You know that's impossible. Humans need each other to survive. It's in our nature to make friend or foe of each other. Neutrality was a good plan to protect Kerk, but we're approaching a do-or-die breaking point, and staying neutral was never meant to last."

"I agree," said Seemik. "Come to the summit, figure out a way to contribute to the war effort – I promise you the war will be over soon – and you'll need to bring some Marshals from your board."

Now, Dredger was acting as if they were the ones who weren't getting it, staying silent and fidgeting with his goggles again, pretending they were more important than what was being discussed.

Mercelle reached out, putting a hand on his knee. Dredger held her hand, reluctantly, rubbing it with his thumb.

"I think it's about time ya all headed back to Sandra," he said, eyes still on the floor.

They had berated him enough, for now.

"Sheller, Maalamon," ordered Seemik. "Prepare the convoy for departure."

"Go with them, Ashlan," Mercelle told him. "Wheels up in thirty."

"Got it," replied the First Officer, stuffing his mouth with the last of his protein patty.

Lito stood up with the rest of them. "I'll take the Shard out to the transports. Be well, Dredger," He said, and followed them out.

Seemik and Mercelle stayed behind for one last shot at convincing Dredger to do the right thing.

"You've been like a father to me ever since mine died defending Kerk. Even before that we were like family."

"I know. And ya will always be like my daughter," Dredger responded solemnly. "That will never change."

"Everything changes with time," she told him. "The war is changing. It's coming to a head, and if you don't make the right decision, Kerk won't survive. That isn't a threat. You know it's true."

With a sigh, Dredger put his inner inner unrest on display. To Seemik's surprise all it took was a plea from someone Dredger trusted and believed in. Lito had to of known it wasn't Him, that's why He left.

"By comin' to the summit I won't be able to consider myself neutral any longer. Even if I did come, Edeen would never accept the allegiance of a desert digger."

"We can't plead a case for you unless you're there," responded Seemik. Ignoring the damning look from Dredger, he thought about how the fate of Kerk's people rested on this pivotal moment. How could Dredger not see that this was the best move – the only move – that he could make to secure his peoples' future?

Begrudgingly, Dredger gave a subtle nod to Mercelle. Seemik let out a long sigh of silent relief.

Mercelle jumped up, thanking Dredger and putting her arms out to hug him. Instead of reciprocating, he put a hand up between them, and swiveled on his stool to face the end of the long table.

Her reaction was a swift change from elation to a forced poise and acceptance of the fact that he was making a decision which he wasn't happy about.

"I guess I'll see you there," she said, straightening up and turning to leave, a pinch of regret in her eyes.

"You're doing the right thing," Seemik told him before exiting the cafeteria. There was no response.

It couldn't have been easy for Mercelle to convince Dredger to do something like that. His refusal to hug her afterward must have really hammered the feeling in. Tempted to offer her his own hug, Seemik tried to think of a way to say something comforting to her. He ultimately kept quiet, not knowing how she would react to a consoling friend, and not wanting to look too sensitive in front of the immaculately gorgeous and strong woman.

LITO TOOK a large case of weapons from Ashlan. Seemik followed, talking to Lito as He carried it to the transport to load it up. The handful of Sandran transports were lined up just outside the giant opening that was Kerk's main entrance.

"We'll have to open a line of communication with this new Onyx Clan, somehow. It's funny how the human records have no traces of their existence."

The case went into the rear hold of a four wheeled transport. "They've kept their bloodline pure," Lito explained. "Only mixing with the Grey Race at one point in time, millennia ago, before it died out, but most of their Clan is pureblooded."

"Interesting," he was riveted, having already accepted that any and all information pertaining to Order had been revealed or recorded. "So the Grey lineage lives on within the Onyx Clan? And they live over twice as long as the rest of us?"

The Order God returned to Ashlan for another full weapons case which would be far too much for any normal human to carry alone. "That's correct. They're very formidable warriors and would make for helpful allies. Luckily, their ideals of an Earth free from Chaos match ours."

A whole Race, kept nearly pure through the millennia, and secret too. If he could get the Book of Order and bring it to the Clan, he thought, perhaps they could help in translating the Black text, especially if his theory of purer blood leading to easier translations of the relevant text was true.

"How is it that they've kept hidden all this time?"

"They used to live underground," Lito answered, sliding the case in beside the last one and closing the hold. "There's a plant that they call sappidge, and they use it for food as well as fuel. It thrives off of the light from magma flows, but their Kop – their leader – told me that the magma has dried up over the last few centuries, which is why they've decided to surface. Some crops are kept alive in caverns by fire light."

"Most likely a side-effect of the Demigods' removal of precious resources."

Ashlan shouted back that there were no more cases to load, and bodies started finding seats throughout the caravan of transports prepared to take dozens of soldiers and the High Scholars back to Sandra. Only a few vehicles were still finishing their charging cycles.

"Hey, Lito," Mercelle shouted, coming up on them with something shiny in her hands. "I brought something for you." She handed Him the torso portion of what looked like glass mirror armor, reflecting His face back at Him. Seemik recognized it from the night he and Lito first met during the battle for the hostages.

Lito put it on over His shirt, smiling and thanking her. "How did you come across it?"

"Long story," she replied. "But, I finally killed that monster you left behind."

Seemik was sure there was a joke in there that he wasn't privy to, but Lito didn't get many jokes.

"The High Cleric and I were just discussing the Onyx Clan," He said.

"I heard. I was half listening to be honest."

"After speaking with their Kop – and experiencing their battle techniques first hand – I believe they could make strong allies. But first, there's something we need to do to help them."

"How?"

Seemik remembered Lito speaking about free will earlier. Yet, now He was talking about performing a favor in order to persuade a Clan to help the rebellion. Was He learning the function of politics, or just trying to provide a hand to a group of humans in the midst of hardship?

"I passed a Chaos tower as I was walking north from their village. It's made of a clear material, likely glass, and looks like it's lifting magma from deep underground."

"If we take down the tower they may be willing to forge an alliance with us," said Seemik. It was the obvious next step that Lito didn't seem to want to say, but He led them to it instead. "I'm sure Feres would supply the firepower, if you gave her a few days. Could we do all of that before the summit?"

"We have weapons," Mercelle smirked.

"We could get there today by transport," Lito threw in, as if that was where He planned to take the conversation all along.

Seemik shook his head. It was quite a swift left turn from suggesting a favor. "Not to doubt either of you, but we haven't even figured out what the Shard does. If we regroup at Sandra, you can gather a small force and then hit the tower."

"It can be done," Lito assured. "This tower is much smaller than the last one."

Mercelle perked up. "Good. I'm starting to feel better, so, I think I could use some exercise."

"Take this," said Lito, handing the Shard to Seemik. "Run your tests. See what you can find."

He shook his head again. "What about giving me a day or two to scrounge up some backup? If I call to Lady Feres now-"

"Backup?" Mercelle held back a laugh. "Hey, Ash! You up for some off-mission fun?"

Ashlan, who was waiting for a charging port to complete its cycle, pointed at her slyly to display his excitement. "Always, Lady."

The smile she gave Ashlan was one Seemik wished would have been saved for him. Women liked the tough types, men who were up for sudden danger. That wasn't him. He was the Library mite with his first round of beard stubble still patching his jaws and cheeks. She would never see him the way he wanted her to.

His heart shriveled slightly.

"There's our backup," she replied. "Ashlan, Lito and I will take separate transports to this tower and see what we can do. If we're successful in taking it down we'll speak to the Clan and discuss an alliance before heading back to Sandra. In the meantime, you can run your tests."

"I'll oversee the convoy," said the High Cleric with a sigh. "Please get back to Sandra as soon as you can. We leave for the summit in seven days' time, with or without you."

Mercelle was visibly excited, smiling harder than he'd seen so far. "The less we have with us the better. We're just going to take a couple of clippers to save on time. Ash, this one work okay?" She smacked the side of a clipper that was hooked across the back of the six-wheeler.

"Everything's fully operational as far as I know," he answered. The burly man stood in their circle, and Seemik tried not to be jealous of the muscles and thick layer of stubble on the man's jaw and upper lip.

"I got it," Seemik lied. In a sudden rush of confidence, he unhitched the clipper and lifted it from the rack. As soon as it came free the two-wheeler dropped to the ground, falling onto its side and sending Seemik to his back.

So much for trying to be the tough guy.

Familiar laughs came from the backseat of the six-wheeler. Sheller and Maalamon were enjoying the show. The most embarrassing part was still to come.

Mercelle, biting her lips together to restrain a chuckle, reached down to help him up. Or, at least, he thought she was trying to help him up. When he attempted to take her hand, it instead went to the handlebar of the clipper, and his fingers wrapped around her wrist.

"Uh," she awkwardly grabbed his wrist back. "Oh, sure." She helped him up before lifting the clipper upright with a single hand.

His youth was showing, but he was too nervous to stop himself from acting like a fool. "Sorry about that. It didn't look that heavy. It just caught me off guard was all."

"Of course," she replied, finally letting her chuckle out. He was relieved that she was playing it off. "Thankfully, these things can take quite a beating. I don't see any *serious* damage."

His heart stung for a brief second when she looked at him. Ventilation systems within Kerk filled the city with fresh air, pushing the stale air out through the great entrance. The breeze blew through their parked caravan as they stood in the sun, and it swept her hair over her shoulders.

The only thing he could think to say back was what a beautiful neck she had, and shoulders, and everything down to the rounded ends of her boots. Being the intelligent High Cleric that he needed to be, they stayed as thoughts.

"Feres would kill me if she found out I was going to try and take down another tower. I'm supposed to be resting while I travel. But I gotta do something to take my mind off of things."

Just hearing her talk to him about herself put his anxiety at ease, and he was able to speak again. "What things? Your test results?"

"Yeah. They should be waiting for me once we get back. Not that I'm in a hurry. And not that I think anything will even come of it. I don't know. Lito, do you still feel something...off inside me?"

Lito nodded, offering a feigned smile.

Seemik hoped that Lito would keep her safe until she returned to Sandra. The fact that she could take care of herself turned him on, but fighting Chaos meant always knowing to expect the unexpected, and Lito was the best at handling the unexpected.

"Don't worry," Seemik said. "Sandramedius has the best medical Scholars in the world. Nothing is going to keep you down. Right?"

"I'd rather not think about it," she cringed, turning away from him.

His heart shriveled a bit more.

12

ZAKOPAT KRAJ IV

A star: a symbol of hope represented by a burning ball of flame and plasma in the sky. It could also be used as an expletive alluding to one's inability to understand certain aspects or details of a situation.

"Stars align," grumbled Kraj into his monitor. "I can't make sense of this report."

The end of his sixteen hour shift always brought on double vision and a tendency for Kraj to cross his eyes when staring at an endless influx of reports to process. He considered taking the night off from snooping to catch up on some sleep. Although, he still wanted to get shots of the additions to the outside of the tower.

Still wearing the wire star Kraj had fashioned for it, the Newlyn next to him tapped away on its terminal screen.

"How much longer until you transfer to the factory floor?" he asked the replica.

"Only a few more days they said. It'll be nice to have a change of scenery, and to work on something other than a screen. I don't think I would have been able to keep my sanity if you weren't here to provide small bits of excitement through our little conversations. None of the others talk unless they're ordered to. I've really enjoyed working near you. You should ask about being transferred to the factory with me."

"I don't think the Demigods would allow that."

"You're smarter than the other Crassa," it said. "Maybe they would make an exception."

After a week of nudging his way into the replica's good graces, Kraj had it eating out of the palm of his hand. "I doubt it. But, if you put in a good word for me first, I'd have a better chance."

"I will. On my first day I'll tell them about how efficient you are, and different."

"Do you remember the day I told you my name?"

"You said it was Olim Jasusa," it confirmed.

"That's right. Humans have names to tell each other apart, to make a person different from everyone else. Have you ever thought about a name for yourself?"

"Replicas don't get names. It keeps us from feeling unique. We work better as a whole, and terribly as individuals."

"That's intriguing," Kraj told it. "Humans are similar, just not to the same extent."

A piece of his heart went out to the Newlyn, knowing that his efforts to try and establish an individualized personality within the replica would not only serve to gain Kraj access to new information, but it was also likely to lead to the replica's death if discovered. Part of him felt like he was raising a child, only to use it as a means to an end for purposes of espionage.

Feelings aside, the Newlyn was being properly manipulated, and it was only a matter of time before Kraj found an opportunity to use it to his advantage again. He just hoped he lived long enough to see it.

Deep down, his beating heart wished he could escape with the poor, exhausted, tortured replica. Restless nights kept him busy wondering if the human population would be willing to accept a defector any better than Chaos did. He doubted that would ever work.

It was doomed to sit in its pitiful, tedious existence until it wound up in one of Mora's experimental chambers. The tired smile it wore did nothing to quell the sadness Kraj could see behind its empty eyes. He would just have to keep sneaking snaps of its screen when it wasn't looking. Kraj was getting good at using the transmitter undetected.

He was taken aback when his terminal's screen went dark, as did the Newlyn's next to him. Standing up, he watched as a wave of black screens swept across the room. A power outage?

Suddenly, a large glyph showed spanning the entire length and width of the ceiling.

"What's that mean," he asked the Newlyn.

It was already on its feet. "Stand," it replied.

The wide doors at the entrance of Workroom 86 swung open, and Valks filed in, snatching humans and Newlyns alike, removing them from their posts. This felt precarious, like something bad was unfolding in front of him.

"Some kind of security protocol?"

"I assume so," the Newlyn answered.

The replicas obeyed perfectly, holding out an arm and waiting for the Valks to drag them out by it. The humans seemed to be the problems. One human felt the need to try and explain to a Valk that he hadn't done anything wrong, refusing to offer an arm. He was swiftly lifted from the ground and tossed against the wall, his body creating quite the echo when it hit. The man lay, gasping for air, on the floor.

Poor guy had the wind knocked out of him. The Valk paid no attention as he rubbed his chest and wheezed heavily, it just dragged him out by a leg instead of an arm.

"Something must be up," Kraj insisted, pressing the Newlyn to see if it had surmised anything further since the violent interaction they just witnessed.

"This is normal," it nonchalantly said. "Some humans just don't understand the chain of command, or the consequences for being disobedient."

It was baffling for Kraj to see that from this side of things, humans were the savages, and Chaos were working in order. They were well organized. One thing humans and Chaos had in common: they both attacked when cornered.

Through the open doors, he saw that the humans were getting strip searched before being led away bare skinned with their clothes in their hands. This was it: they had picked up on his transmitter's signal during one of his transmissions to Feres. As soon as they got to his terminal and pulled him away, he'd be done for.

Not just yet.

Shoving the heel of his boot into the other's toe, he pried his foot free, kicking the boot over to let the flat transmitter fall out. It slid onto the metal grates beneath his seat, but was far too wide to fit through. The boot slipped back on, and he lowered the sole onto the device, twisting it back and forth, crushing it into pieces small enough to fall down into the goo trap.

Just as two Valks came around the Newlyn's terminal, he swept as much of the mess away as he could with a single kick, leaving behind a few small bits of black plastic and screen polymer. Pleasantly, the Newlyn offered an arm and was taken away.

The second Valk glared down at him, waiting for

him to act up so he could be thrown against the wall. Kraj thought about how many of them he could possibly take out before either the Bleds were brought in or the floor was sealed and gassed with everyone still inside. It didn't come to very many when he played out the scenario in his head.

If he had been made, then why were the other humans being searched? They must only suspect something. This was more like an investigation than an arrest. There was a chance at him surviving the whole debacle, but no way of sending information out without his transmitter. His only choice was to wait until he was in a more opportune position to either make his escape, or to do some damage before he went out.

Kraj aimed an elbow at the Valk, and was removed from the room with minimal force before receiving his search.

THEY DIDN'T ALLOW him to put his filthy clothes back on until the Valk got him into an interrogation room. It was at least a mile in the cool air of the Glaven Grad tower, walking with all of his sun-starved skin exposed to any Crassa or replica who cared to stare.

This room only had a clear chair standing in the center, and he paced around it for what felt like hours. Thinking, meditating, worrying, suspecting.

Were the replicas questioning everyone on the floor? Could someone have seen him accessing the Newlyn's terminal a couple of days ago? What would happen to the other humans? To him?

If only the interrogation rooms had access panels to the ducts. He would have been half way gone by now. The replicas knew something, and if he was made he would need to try and take out as many of the damned things as he could before being executed. The last thing he wanted to do was become a part of Mora's experiments.

It was back to the same old plan and back story: play dumb, let them continue to think he was still trying to recall his memories, and figure out some bit of information to keep leading them on for more.

"Sit down," came a Mora's voice from an invisible speaker.

Kraj did as ordered, taking the only seat in the center of the room.

A sliver of a door came up in front of him, and in came two Moras who stood on either side of the opening, and two Valks that took stances in front of them. Lastly, a single Bled entered, almost floating as it passed Kraj, and disappeared against the wall at his back.

He kept still, pondering the idea to fake a touch of fear.

One Mora pulled up a projected hologram on which

it was already taking notes on his reactions. The other stepped forward to begin the interrogation.

"What was your rank in the militia at Sandramedius during your time there?" it asked as the door slid shut.

With eight eyes on his front, and a Bled at his back, the room felt smaller. The walls were closing in on him.

"After all these interrogations you still don't have a file on me?" he countered.

The Mora replied with an annoyed squint, and before he could react the Bled sprung from the wall, its curved, shiny talon around his neck. Skin started to peel under the force of the blade. Kraj prepared to die.

Warm liquid dripped down his neck, but only a few drops, and he kept himself alert despite the fact that he wasn't getting fed a more potent oxygen mixture this time around. When he opened his eyes, the Mora's flat nose was inches from his.

"I can assure you that the next question you ask us will be your last." Its cold eyes didn't blink. "We are paying you the courtesy of allowing you to be truthful. Depending on your answers your life may be spared. *Refusing* to answer questions will *not* work in your favor."

"I understand," he rasped out, trying not to move his throat against the edge of the Bled's talon.

The blade moved away, and retracted back into the Bled's arm before it disappeared against the wall again.

"I'll repeat myself this one time only," said the Mora,

standing up straight and pacing slowly between the Valks. "What rank were you in Sandramedius' militia?"

His hand was busy checking the skin on his neck. Blood covered his palm, but he wasn't bleeding much. Only a small slice of skin was peeled back. He steadied his pulse.

Like a looming cloud of poison gas, the Mora glared down at him.

"Sorry, I uh," he blubbered. It was time to show some fear, even though he never understood the function of such a distracting emotion. "Corporal, I believe."

"You believe? Why do you say 'believe'?"

He stopped himself from itching the back of his neck. Fear was his target, not nervousness. Nervousness indicated a secret, whereas fear was what they wanted.

"The only thing I remember for sure is waking up in the asylum in Sandra, and being told that I did something while on duty that injured a lot of people. I...I don't know. I snapped or something. They had performed experiments on me to try and make some kind of...drug, and it erased my memory of everything before that. I escaped and came here."

"Some of those memories come back to you from time to time?" it asked.

"Anything I remember is spotty. I can't tell if they're recreations of former memories, actual recollections or merely dreams. I tell you everything I can because I want you to kill the people responsible for taking my life away."

"We can't say you've told us much, and the Demigods are starting to question whether your life is worth maintaining."

"I-I've told you about the weapons I remember helping them develop. Vehicles they used. Battle formations and plans."

"Have you reported any information to the humans since you've arrived in Glaven Grad?" It stopped pacing, and faced him with its feet spread apart.

The question, though subtly toned, hit him like a ton of bricks. As long as it didn't show, he knew he could keep them dangling.

"What?! There's no possible way for me to communicate with the outside world. The terminals in my workroom are only linked to a closed network, nothing can go out from them. I don't even have any family...that I can remember, anyway."

A real memory came back to him of his woman Cekanja. In the memory she was with the children, back at the Oases, divvying up sweet cane for the children. Kraj had more than anyone, and ate until his stomach hurt and all three young ones passed out from exhaustion. Now, they likely still fed on the rations he'd scored from Dredger before accepting Feres's proposal.

"Have you accessed any unauthorized terminals

during your time assigned to Workroom 86?" questioned the Mora, continuing to pace.

He *was* seen. "No, absolutely not." The Mora waited for something more. "I can't read Chaos glyphs," he said with a shrug.

The Mora turned to pace the other way, keeping its gaze locked on him as it rotated. "You're sweating. Why?"

"I'm afraid."

"Of what?"

"I'm afraid that I'm going to die no matter what I tell you."

"Then you're willing to lie in order to better your chances at survival?" It rotated again, still without blinking, and paced in the other direction.

Allowing perspiration to drip down his face, and pretending to shiver, sold his fear. He feigned a frozen posture as he spoke. "Wh-whether or not I tell y-you the truth w-won't make a difference."

"Fair enough," it said, standing still again. "I don't think you're lying; however, I don't believe you're telling us the whole truth."

He had no choice.

"Th-there is something else I-I need to t-tell you."

Again, he was left in the interrogation room, alone, for hours. Left to ponder what he had told them before they gathered up and left. The lie he had previously fed them about Dredger's potential involvement in the fake tunnels being dug beneath Glaven Grad was a bad example of him selling someone out to save his own skin. That was under duress, and Kraj was heavily intoxicated at the time by some unknown substance. It was hard, but he had to sell out someone else in order to secure his position. Picturing Cekanja's face in his mind helped him come to it.

In his shaking voice, he delivered a made up story about his neighbor – the Newlyn whose terminal was next to his – accessing other humans' terminals after the out time alarm. Even stating that the Newlyn was seen pulling up files on his own terminal as he was arriving one day, and that he would find dried goo on his screen when logging in.

The Mora's reaction was one of doubt, and he couldn't tell if it believed him or not. The replicas left in such a rush afterwards. If his word was taken at face value there was no telling what would be done to the Newlyn, who happened to be completely innocent in the whole situation. Innocent, aside from the fact that it was working against the humans by processing stolen files and transmissions from rebel communications.

But, he thought, the Newlyn was as much of a hostage as he was.

Feeling guilty for his words only made the hours stretch longer, into torturous eons of regret which he talked himself down from, over and over again. When the door finally slid up and open, Kraj was sprawled out on the floor, meditating to keep his breathing steady.

Two Valks entered. They could have been the same ones from earlier, or different ones entirely. He had no way of telling them apart. Both of them stood in the doorway until he came over to them with an elbow out. He was swiftly pulled from the room and walked down the corridor to a different kind of room with a floor made out of metal grating from wall to wall.

A Newlyn was standing in the center of the grating. It was wearing the star pin Kraj had fashioned for it on the brim of its high pants.

"What's going on?" questioned the frightened Newlyn. Kraj felt its fright grow, and resisted as the fear nearly transfer to him. "I've already told you everything. Why is he here?"

One Valk held his arm tight while the other motioned at the wall behind the helpless Newlyn. A Bled emerged from thin air, swiping a taloned blade forward and taking the Newlyn's head clean off with little effort.

Kraj let out a holler of panic, compartmentalizing his guilt to show the Valks that he was afraid and disgusted. The disgust was real, but fear had never served him well, therefore, he kept himself from feeling it. He gagged as slime flowed from the opening where the replica's head used to be. It spilled over the grating, splashing on his legs and draining away as the Newlyn's leftover exterior flattened on the floor.

At his feet, its head drained out, leaving just the deflated skin, and the dark eyeballs rolled about, getting stuck in the grates. The Valk holding his arm let go, and stomped on the eyeballs until they fell through. Horrified, Kraj tried to act confused in case any part of his cover had remained intact.

"Wh-why...?" He remembered what the Mora had said about asking questions. Valks didn't communicate beyond grunts, snarls and growls anyhow, and he wouldn't be getting any information out of them.

A thick hood went over his head. Kraj waited to be decapitated, for the Bled to finish the job that was started earlier and cut all the way through his neck. Breath continued to make its way into his lungs, and instead of meeting his end, he was walked through countless floors, and descended stairs in utter darkness.

By the time the walking finally stopped, his feet were sore, he was starving, and his skin was drenched with sweat. The hood came off of his head, and just before him was an empty cell with walls made of metal stripping. It was heavy material, and resembled the same bars humans used to imprison their captives. Even the same hinged door. The only difference being that the strips were sharpened to dangerous edges.

Inside was nothing but a cold, stone floor. A human definitely had a hand in designing these cells, as they were very much different from the white-lighted interrogation cells he was accustomed to.

"I take it you aren't bringing me back to my station," he quipped. "Human out time must be over by now." It was hard to tell if the sun was up or not. There were no windows or portholes looking out, and he suspected that he was somewhere below the Glaven Grad tower.

A low growl came from one of the Valks as it shoved a claw full of broken plastic and polymer pieces into his chest. He caught them, mindlessly holding them together in his palms as he realized that his position had in fact been compromised.

There was no more Workroom 86 in his future. He'd be damned if they were going to experiment on him instead. The purpose of his infiltration of Glaven Grad was to hinder the Chaos effort, not to provide assistance to it in any way.

The hard shove of a Valk claw against his back pushed him into the threshold of the door, where he tripped on purpose and leaned against the frame. During that split second, he jammed a piece of triangular plastic into the door latch while blocking it with his body. A swift kick from a Valk hoof sent him reeling into the empty cell.

He tucked his head, and rolled on his back until his feet came down onto the ground. Labored breaths hissed in and out of his lungs, and he dreaded that he might have broken a rib.

Clanging sounds came from the door as the pair of Valks attempted to shut it, but the latch wouldn't take with the plastic triangle lodged perfectly into the hole.

Clang!

Embittered snarls came from the Valks, trying to figure out the mechanical malfunction between two small, reptilian brains which were more bent on aggression than problem solving.

Clang!

It was only a matter of time before the piece moved and he was stuck in their custody for good. He held his chest, heaving air in and out and mounting the soles of his boots on the jagged floor.

Clang!

Honing in on his last chance to show Chaos the true extent of the human spirit, he sprinted forward, gaining what little momentum he could before reaching the door and putting his full weight into a timed kick.

Clang!

His boot made contact with the steel door, and it swung open, slamming into the face of one Valk while the other stumbled backward to avoid its fall.

Quick to strike, the unfazed Valk whirled a sword around at him, but he ducked, letting the blade hit the steel strips of the cell. He crushed the replica's wrist with another kick of his heavy boot, and the sword fell free. Before it hit the ground his hand was around the hilt, and he impaled the recoiling Valk straight through the chest as the other one came up behind him.

Another duck avoided another sword swing. Would the Valks ever get smart enough to see that move coming? That left him open for a second kick to the back, which he dodged with a roll to the side, clamoring the blade down on the Valk's extended leg and hacking halfway through it.

The limb dangled from the infuriated replica, and Kraj brought the blade back up in one last slice that sheared off the pointed face of the Valk, leaving it squirming and scratching on the floor.

The weight of the replica's sword would only hinder his ability to run, so he ditched it there, and sprinted from the corridor. Surprisingly, the rest of the cells were empty. They must not have kept many prisoners.

One door led him to a balcony that showed the various floors above and below him. His only options were up or down, and since he could recall descending so many stairs while the hood was over his head, he needed to head back up toward the surface, at least until he found a view to the outside.

Hopping onto the railing, he balanced himself,

stretching upward and reaching for the floor above him. His fingertips went above the edge, and he used their grips to pull himself taller and work more of his fingers up.

The floor shook around his hands, and he looked up to see a Valk staring down at him from above, its hooves on either side of his desperately clawing fingers.

A hoof went up, then came back down at his hand, but he was quicker than the beast.

Kraj let go, falling backward, down into the chasm of the tower's sublevels.

13

LADY INIS MERCELLE IX

Results from her blood work awaited her a thousand miles away in Sandra, and Dredger's misplaced anger festered back in Kerk. It was shaking to watch his solid will bend under the weight of reasoning. She had never seen him so stiff and closed off as when he'd agreed to attend the summit meeting.

Feres would be pleased to know she'd been successful in her mission to persuade him to come. Pulling herself back in to focus on the mission at hand, she peered up at the shimmering tower. From behind the fields of boulders where they hid themselves and their clippers, they could see the whole thing.

It was made of clear, reflective material, with the four corners shrouded in a black, pitted rock that looked like it had been formed by rapidly cooling magma. She imagined the replicas had used some of the harvested lava to build structural supports on the tower's corners, otherwise the entire structure seemed to be made of glass. All the way through to the center of the tower, Mercelle could see a glowing red pillar spanning from the base to the tip, which was high, but not nearly as high as the southern tower that had reached well into the atmosphere.

"Is that...glass?" wondered Ashlan aloud.

"Yes," Lito verified, slipping the reflective body armor over His arms and head. "I assume it's to manipulate the sun's rays and refract the heat back into the middle of the tower in order to keep the magma column in the center from solidifying. Supports on the outside keep everything sturdy."

The sun bled through from the other side of the tower, bending its light into intense beams of white that spotted the ground for miles in every direction. It reminded Mercelle of the crystal antennae at the top of the last tower. Glaring red emanated from the inside of the building, and there were no walls to stop it, just glass floors and beams.

"They must have tapped into a magma vein," she said. "Which means they've drilled deep into the Earth's crust, maybe even down to the core. Now we know what's causing the planet to shrink."

"We have the clippers," Lito suggested.

"We won't need them," she replied. "You see the

dark rock going up along each corner? It's pitted pretty well. We can climb up one of the corners quietly without being noticed."

Ashlan was of the same militarized mind as Mercelle. "How many bombs do we have?" he asked.

"Five," she answered. "And they should have quite an impact since the whole thing is made of glass. I'm just worried we won't be able to damage the internal column enough. As long as the rest of the tower is destroyed around it the column should solidify over the next couple of days. We could always simply disable the pumping system."

Lito came back with "No. The entire tower needs to come down. Most of the structure is below ground. Remember the silver and copper mining tower? It's just like that. To completely destroy it we need to melt it into the substructure. The magma will do most of the work for us, we just need to puncture it high up enough to leak down over the structure, while damaging the floors closer to the ground level to let it flow."

"I love a good collapse," she grinned. "Get the magma to bleed over the floors, it'll melt away the supports on the outside, and harden as it flows until everything falls in on itself – easy. I'm guessing that the pumping mechanisms are subterranean. Damaging the lower floors will help to disable them."

"Sounds like fun," said Ashlan, stretching his meaty arms.

"You know, I enjoy our little talks." Mercelle was glad to have Ashlan there. As long as he could keep up, he'd be a ton of help. She especially liked the fact that he didn't take their intimate encounter to mean that she wanted to spend the rest of her life with him, as men tended to do after experiencing her in that way. She knew his type all too well, and having sampled his skin on her tongue, she found that she wanted someone more unique, more unpredictable. Ashlan was a great lover, but his "plaything" flavor had gotten old quite quickly. Mercelle found herself wondering whether or not she was yearning for a more fulfilling relationship, like the one her mother and father had. Toys like Ashlan simply wouldn't cut it anymore.

"As do I," Lito agreed. "We'd be better off splitting up and dispersing the blasts throughout the tower."

"Who wants top?" she asked, looking into the sky.

"I'll go high," Lito said. "The heat will be more intense the further into the tower you go. If you two focus on spreading bombs over the lower and middle floors, I'll get as close as I can to the column higher up. The farther up the puncture the more likely this is to succeed."

"Then we have our plan," she affirmed, handing a bomb to Lito, and two to Ashlan.

"Not yet," pointed out the First Officer. "What's our exit strategy? I'm not sure jumping from enormous heights suits me."

"Not your style?" she quipped. "Don't worry, you'll take the lower floor. I'd say ten or twenty levels up. I'll go toward the middle, maybe forty high, and Lito will go higher from there. It looks like the tower has around seventy or eighty levels. Breaking the inner cylinder at about sixty levels should drain out the magma from higher up."

Lito nodded.

"Yeah, uh," Ashlan was still toiling on the details. "I'm not going up until you tell me how we're coming back down."

Mercelle kind of enjoyed keeping Ashlan waiting. "Chutes," she told him. "I grabbed a few before we left Kerk. You'll be closer to the ground so you'll have to pull your cord as you jump, otherwise it won't open enough. Got it? Let's strap up."

She opened the side compartment on her clipper, and handed out the parachutes. Ashlan had his sidearms, and so did she, along with a couple of short blades each. Aside from His singular bomb and pair of trench knives, Lito also agreed to take a pistol this time. He must have learned how useful they were when He'd had a couple dozen of them firing at Him all at once.

Just for good measure, Mercelle showed Him how to drop a clip and reload, and how to do it in under two seconds flat. The leftover grappling hook was hers.

"Should we contact Feres and wait for a vesp or two

to arrive?" asked Ashlan. "We could use the extra feed, and maybe a scan of the layout."

Lito replied, "It may be best that we don't tell her about this until afterward."

Mercelle agreed. "Right. This isn't exactly an approved operation. Even if we succeed, there's no telling how she'll react. I know she won't be happy with me either way. Besides, the sooner we can take this down and talk to that Onyx Clan, the sooner we can return to Sandra with allies and prepare for the summit."

"I'm grateful that you chose to help me with this," Lito told them. "I would have done it by myself if you didn't come. How are you feeling?"

She hadn't even thought about how she felt since leaving Kerk. There was no stomach pain, no exhaustion, her head was clear, and she felt an energy which had been absent from her being since the last tower. "I feel great," she said. "I'm ready."

"Well! Hector's hairy twat!" Ashlan hooted, pumping himself up. "Let's do this!"

There was nothing Mercelle liked more than the moments just before destroying some Chaos. Although they couldn't see any from where they stood, she hoped there would be some replicas to tear apart.

Sand shimmered in the beams of light reflecting off of the tower's glass floors. Shadows were cast from the four rocky supports, and the dark trails reached almost all the way over to where the trio crawled across the ground. They agreed that keeping as low as possible in the darkest of the four shadows was their best route to approach, lessening their chances at being spotted before they'd even made it inside.

Coarse granules clung to her sticky forearms. Shimmying along was hard work, and it was just under a quarter mile's distance from the clippers to the base, where they stood and tried to get a good look inside the tower.

"It's the strangest thing I've ever seen," she gawked. Even from the bottom level she could see into much of the tower, through many floors. If there were any replicas in this tower, they were either high up enough to be out of sight, or they were Bleds, lying in invisible wait for unsuspecting victims.

Aside from wide glass pillars, the floors she could see were empty. Hundreds of thousands of square feet each, the levels blended into each other more the higher up she looked, until they blurred to indistinctness.

"There used to be billions of you humans," Lito said, sounding nostalgic. "Now there are only a couple million, left concentrated into cities and tribes. So few that whole towers like this can exist for centuries without the human population even knowing about it."

Ashlan joined the God in His bout of extrospection. "That just makes me feel like a sand flea in a Demigod's world."

"This isn't really our planet anymore," Mercelle put harshly. "It won't be until the Demigods are dead. It's our job to take it back from them. Now, are we done with the little pity party? I don't feel sorry for either of you." She peaked an eyebrow at them.

"Ready, Lady." Ashlan winked back.

Lito nodded.

"I'll go first," she said. "Ashlan, count twenty floors and then go in."

"Got it, Lady."

"The charges are all rigged to my detonator. Here are your earpieces. Keep in contact while we're separated, and let me know once the charges are in place and you're clear of the blasts. I'll trigger them all at once." She put a hand over her mouth, and whispered "Testing, testing."

"Loud and clear," said the First Officer.

"Remember," Lito reminded them. "We're not here for revenge, we're here to offer the Onyx Clan an alliance by providing them a gesture of loyalty."

She knew He was referring to her. "I'll keep myself in check. It doesn't look like there are any replicas guarding this thing anyhow."

"Just because you can't see them doesn't mean they aren't there. Chaos can be clever too. Remember."

Lito was right, Bleds could be placed anywhere, with an eye out for intruders just like the three of them.

They used pits in the black rock of the corner supports to climb, and made their way steadily up the side of the tower.

SOON, Ashlan was off, and Mercelle was nearing her floor. Sunlight assailed the tower, and it shone out around them like its own beacon of celestial force. She felt strong conquering the monstrous building, and didn't let Lito out-climb her. Suspended hundreds of feet in the air with nothing but their grips holding them to the craggy rock, they pumped their muscles, floor by floor. Feres would have been surprised to see her exerting herself like this so soon after looking the way she had in Sandra.

She stretched her foot, pushing her weight up from the toe of her boot. Her fingertips fondled the pit that she was trying for, but her toe came loose, and she fell. Before she could even start scratching at the rock to regain her grip, Lito had her by the wrist and held her to the rock.

"Calvin's corpse, that was close. Thanks, Lito."

"Still feeling okay?"

"You don't need to keep asking me that, you know. Why don't I just let you know if I start to feel particularly terrible? How's that?" This was beginning to feel a bit like having a nagging mother around.

"That will suffice," He replied. "This is the fortieth floor."

"Is it? I lost count." She moved over and put a foot on the floor of the open tower. Her head went through next. "Looks clear. I'll wait for your contact."

Lito nodded, and she went in.

It was like being in another dimension. Stepping over the glass floor, she had to keep reminding herself that she wasn't going to fall through. Wide pillars of the solid, clear material – she counted six – came from the identical floors below, and continued up through the ones above. The air was much hotter inside the tower than outside, despite the lack of walls.

A glint of light told her that something was moving to her left, and when it jumped so did she.

Throwing herself right, she heard the swipe of a curled blade at her ear. Instinctually, she put a hand on her gun, but realized that the noise would draw more attention and went for a knife instead.

The Bled's talon retracted, and she saw the replica's position just before it went out of sight again. She flipped the knife around, holding it by the blade and hurling it at the empty void. Its tip met the target, and the replica choked in pain, coming back into view to show that the wound it had taken on its midsection was leaking profusely.

It grasped the hilt, and slid the blade out of the hole, dropping it to the ground. Then the enraged Bled rushed her with both talons bared. She rushed back at it, sliding onto her back at the last second and kicking its feet out from beneath it.

Her boots stopped her next to the knife, and she took it back up as quickly as the Bled got to its feet. With not a fraction of a second to spare she hopped back up off the floor and began blocking swipe after swipe until one caught her forearm, splitting it open. She put a hand over the wound to keep it from opening further, but that only distracted her while another talon came forth.

The shiny steel of the Bled's blade came to a sheer point that could peel skin off in thin layers, and it was heading for her.

A hand caught the Bled's arm, stopping it in place. Lito bent the arm back, cracking it in multiple places. Then He cut upward with His trench knife, separating the arm from the body at the elbow, and using the extruded talon to decapitate the wounded replica.

"Lito!" she said, shocked. "What are you doing here? I-"

"Wait," He told her. His palm went around the blade and He pulled it out to draw blood. "Move your hand."

Resisting the urge to vomit, she slowly took her

hand away from the wound. In any normal combat situation, this wound would have meant that she was done until medical attention could be administered to stop the bleeding. With Lito, however, all it took was a quick swap of D.N.A. and the bleeding stopped.

"Ashlan," she called through the earpiece. "Keep an eye out for Bleds. We just had a run in with one."

"Confirmed," he replied.

"Thanks, Lito. That's a little gross, but thanks."

"You're welcome. Be careful."

"I will."

She gave Him a couple of minutes to vacate while she scoped out the area. Alongside the giant glass pillars were shafts that connected the floors – straight drops that led through each one, reaching as far down through the tower and as far up as she could see. They would make for hasty escape routes should the occasion call for an evasive retreat. If she had learned anything from taking down towers with Lito, it was that the main supports were also the weak points. This was going to be easier than she thought.

Slower, more cautious steps were taken, closer to the pillars surrounding the glowing red cylinder at the center of the tower, which she didn't dare get near. Heat enveloped her, growing more intense the further in she went. Soon, the sweat started to vaporize off of her skin, and she led with her fingers until the tips of them burned, and she pulled them back.

The closest pillar to her got a plasma charge stuck to it, and she circled around to the other side of the red column to place the next one. Nothing in her peripherals stirred, and she kept her head constantly rotating and bobbing, always ready to duck. As close as she was to the column – though still many yards away – she could see the orange and red liquid swirling within the glass containment, flowing upward to what she was sure to be a launch site of some kind. She was glad not to be at the tip of the tower this time.

Her second bomb went onto a second pillar. This strategy had worked on the first tower they took out, and given the much weaker structure of this one, she was sure it would work just the same if not better.

Heading back out toward the exterior, she whispered through to the others, "Mine are planted. How are you two doing?"

Gunshots snapped off above her, echoing down through the shafts that opened up to each floor. She felt the entire tower shiver with the reverberation of the sound. High overhead, visible flares of gunfire popped, she could barely make them out through the many layers of glass. They were coming from right next to the column of magma.

"I've planted mine!" Lito shouted into the comms. "But I'm under fire!"

It went dead, and she assumed He was putting more

effort into defending Himself than communicating further.

"Charges armed and ready!" called Ashlan. "I'm on my way up!"

"No!" Mercelle dashed in the direction of the nearest vertical shaft. "Plant your bombs and get out! I'll get to Lito and blow the charges!"

"Confirmed!"

There was no railing around the shaft, and no staircases to help navigate the levels, just an opening that went through the ceiling and floor. The grappling hook was heavy in her hand, and she aimed it straight up the middle of the round, hollow shaft.

She pulled the trigger, and the spearhead shot out, zipping cord from the coil within until it stuck into something, and the cord went limp. There must have been a much bigger replica presence higher up, and she hoped Ashlan wasn't running into any trouble beneath them on his way out.

Her fingers tightened around the trigger and the grip, and she reversed the wind of the coil, pulling the cord taut until it lifted her off the ground. Faster and faster, floors flashed by her eyes, and Lito came into view.

Surrounded by Valks and Bleds, Lito was barely visible even from below. Limbs maneuvered at high speeds, and His body twisted and dodged so fast that she couldn't follow the movement. Just like before, the

Valks were outfitted with firearms. In the pandemonium, it was impossible to tell whether or not some of the shots being fired were coming from Him. Bullets ricocheted off of the reinforced glass floors and ceilings, bouncing around until the crushed slugs either found the proper angles at which to lodge themselves into the panes or lost momentum and fell onto the floor.

She questioned what options she would have at assisting Him so close to the column. Her skin would surely melt off of her flesh that close, she thought.

With only two clips, and close quarter weapons beyond that, a better game plan would have to be devised to keep her from helplessly watching Lito get pummeled. Also, she couldn't blow the charges until He was cleared from the blast area.

Lito could defend Himself against attacks sure enough, but the circle surrounding Him was closing in.

There was no telling what would happen once the lava started flowing from the center tube.

She wished she had a suit to help her breathe. The air was growing thinner and thinner as she ascended the floors to get to Lito through the shaft, and she practiced her steady inhales to keep her blood pressure from rising.

Nearing His level, she let go of the grappling pistol and let it continue upward, using her momentum to land both feet on the glass floor. A set of Valks noticed her right away, and ran to attack. Drawing her firearm, she quickly took out their legs, knowing handgun rounds did little to damage thick Valk bodies.

All of them went down, just as her ears picked up the subtle swiping sound of a Bled's talon. Always ready, a dip moved her around the swipe, and when it countered back she turned the barrel of her gun sideways and deflected the blade away. As strong as Bled steel was, it could never cut through Lanna hardware. She forced a boot into the replica's gut with enough force to push it back a few feet, and while it recoiled she brought the gun up and put one in each eye.

Even if the damage wasn't terminal, at least it would be blinded.

Turning to see Lito's status, she saw Him take a claw to the side of His armor, then shove a shoulder into a Valk's side and slice the back of its knees open in the same spin. He went to block the next strike as shuddering stomps got louder.

She whipped around, aimed at the rushing Valks and blasted away at their meaty thighs until they went down. Something hard and heavy hit her ankles, nearly snapping the bones. Had her boot maintained any better of a grip on the floor her feet wouldn't have slid out from under her, and either her calves or ankles would have snapped like overloaded support beams.

Air pressed out of her gut and through her mouth when she hit the floor. A Valk's hoof was circling around, and its blade was coming down at her. She gasped involuntarily, kicking herself out of its path.

Bleds closed in on either side, and her only clear path away was back down the shaft, but she couldn't leave Lito behind. There was no telling how many injuries He was currently fighting through, and even though He would most likely survive, if He was overwhelmed or overpowered, He could end up in Chaos custody.

He was doing another spinning move that allowed Him to make contact with each barrel of the firearms attached to the Valk's hands. Every time one faced Him, it was promptly struck away, and an additional blow was made to the wielder.

The Valks were better off with their swords, she thought.

She ran toward Him, ignoring the rising temperature, until a hoof caught her in the side and sent her reeling and coughing. The force of it kept her rolling until she stopped herself just short of falling down a shaft. As she gasped for breath, a sword narrowly missed her head and she rolled away from it, tumbling into the shaft. Only falling one floor, she caught the edge and dangled. It took a moment of deep panting to calm her lungs, then she realized she had dropped her gun. Hooking her leg over the edge of the floor, Mercelle pulled herself up.

Finally, some room to move. The entire level was

clear, but Valks were already hopping down from floor to floor, descending the other shafts in order to surround her.

Still clearing a space around the glowing red column, Lito stuck a Valk in the gut multiple times, and used the lifeless body as a shield to push the others out of the way. Unfortunately, that gave the replicas the opportunity to fix their barrels on Him. Only, this time, He didn't seem to notice the ones aimed at His back. He'd taken gunshots to the back before, but if His chute got damaged, she thought, He may not be able to make it out safely.

With no way of shooting through the glass to provide suppressive fire, only one option came to mind. She took out the detonator, then she suddenly became aware of how close Lito was to the bomb planted beside the red column and her hasty thumb came off of the button.

As if her thoughts had transmitted to Lito, He tossed the Valk cadaver aside and ran in wide bounds straight toward the shaft she had just come through. Gunfire erupted from behind Him, but He slid across the glass floor on His hip and allowed the bullets to fly over Him. The distance between them and the glowing red column was just enough, and as Lito came over the edge above her and entered the shaft, she discharged the bombs.

Flames, spits of magma and shards of glass sprayed

out over the replicas and blew them out from the center of the tower.

A red geyser flooded the floor, spilling out above her, and as Lito fell past, she threw herself over the edge after Him. As quickly as she'd come up, she was heading right back down again, this time with Lito's boots just ahead of her face.

Mercelle hadn't thought about the fact that their chutes couldn't possibly open in the small shaft. She momentarily realized that wasn't the main issue as the floors far beneath them began to buckle, and the shaft was collapsing around them. Entire floors were shattering, creating oceans of thick shards swirling around in smoking, red liquid.

Cool, rushing air stung her cheeks and nose. It was difficult to get her bearings and figure out exactly where they were in the midst of all the movement. Below them, two red bursts of flames from her charges blasted through walls and supports. Before her mind could begin to calculate their position within the tower, the entire shaft moved, and tilted to the side.

Her shoulder bounced off of the next floor, and she went reeling, unable to tell which way was up. The two of them rolled onto an empty level that was slanted enough for them to slide across once they stopped tumbling. The high end of the level fell, and the floor evened out slightly, bringing them to a halt.

She caught her breath again, trying not to inhale the

fumes or specks of dusted glass in the air by breathing through her silgen shirt. Lito pulled her to her feet, which meant that they needed to run, and now.

They sprinted toward the edge of the building as magma poured out of the cracks throughout the center column and ran over the tempered glass.

The clear material the tower was constructed with was withstanding the heat of the lava, but many of the glass bolts and bindings were starting to shake loose, creating breaks in the ceiling and causing panels to drop and shatter.

A portion of the floor above fell in, blocking their path to the outside. Openings were all around them, they just had to get to one of them before being surrounded by either magma or replicas, and with the integrity of the floor holding up, magma began pooling from the middle outward.

A panel dropped beside them, splashing liquid hot lava over their arms as they blocked it from their faces. The stings were enormously painful, especially the chunk of smoking red magma that clung to her thigh and slid down the side of her leg. She could feel an opening being created in her flesh, but knew it wouldn't bleed due to the cauterizing effect of the lava. The pain – and the heat – made her sweat, but as long as she could overcome the pain she could stay mobile.

Changing course to evade another falling panel, they neared an opening with a clear path. The side of the tower went down, closing the entire edge off in front of them. It was only a matter of time until the whole floor went. They came to a sudden halt to keep from being crushed.

Running along the collapsed edge of the building, they tried to make it to the corner before anything else caved in, and before the flow of lava reached their boots. Lito led the way, slowing down as He always did to make sure He wouldn't lose her.

A greenish-grey blur cut across in front of her, and Lito was gone. Sliding to a stop, she saw Him to her left, against a crooked pillar with a Bled's talon pointed at His neck. Lito's hands were around the Bled's arm, holding the blade back. He rotated around, pushing the Bled's back to the pillar.

"Keep going!" He shouted to her.

It should have only taken Him a quick second to dispatch the replica, but once she turned toward the opening He let out a cry of pain she was yet to hear from Him. Regular humans cried out in pain as an automatic response, and if a God was doing the same, then something terrible had to be going wrong. The sheer fact that Lito hollered was enough to rattle her nerves.

Spinning back around, she saw Lito's hands around the Bled's throat, with a Valk at His back. The Valk's sword was sticking out from the bottom of Lito's armor in the back, somehow managing to make it around the lower edge.

"Lito!"

She tried to get to Him, but a row of panels dropped between them, landing sideways and creating a see-through barrier that she couldn't get over or around. Bright red splashes dotted the floor around Lito and the two replicas.

He twisted the Bled's neck until it separated and pulled apart. Then He reached around, pulled the blade from His back and from the Valk's grip, and threw a high kick into its chest. It went onto its back, and a flow of magma ran over the hole above them, cascading down and bathing the replica in the hot liquid.

It roared, then screeched and writhed for a second, flinging the mess all over the vertical glass panels that surrounded it and Lito. She ran to one side, stopping herself short of falling into a wide crack in the floor. Around the other end she was foiled by a pile of melting rock from the tower's exterior. There was no way to get to Him, and He had no way of getting out.

Another flow of magma ran over the edge above Lito and began filling the space inside the panels. It was like she was watching a tank fill up from the opposite side of an observation barrier.

He looked at her with terrified eyes as the pooling lava reached His boots. Smoke rose from the melting soles. Her only way to go was through the last remaining opening and over the edge of the outside of the tower, which was maybe a dozen paces behind her. Lito was trapped, surrounded by collapsed portions of floor that had piled up and blocked each direction.

"Lito! I can't get to you!"

A panel dropped above her, and she crossed her burned forearms over her head to take the impact. The weight of it brought her down to her knees, and when the corner of the panel struck the floor the whole thing shattered, raining shards over her.

She stood, ignoring the blades of glass falling off of her back, and the small sharp bits sticking out of her skin all over. Her legs were shaking, and her throat tightened as if she were in the throes of some sort of episode.

Lito's boots were completely under the surface of the magma, and the bottoms of His pants were alight with flames. He wasn't moving, just holding still, waiting for it to be over like He had given up. No more pain showed on His face, just a confused countenance that didn't know where to look or what to say.

"Lito..." she said, limping toward Him and flattening a hand on the glass between them as she watched the glowing magma rise above His waist.

Trying to keep His hands above the climbing surface, Lito mouthed the word "go".

"No! I can't!"

His mouth formed the words "I'll be fine" in a calm,

collected manner that didn't stop the tears from dripping off her chin, but did put a chink in her onrush of panic.

"Promise me!" she screamed. Another panel fell behind her, and she stepped onto a pile of shards to keep out of the magma that came with it. "I'm not going until you promise me that you'll be okay!"

"I promise," His calm lips dictated. The lava was up to His chest, and flames from the shirt beneath His armor enveloped His face. The skin licked by the flames didn't melt, and Mercelle recalled Lito's immunities to extreme temperatures.

Everything within her wanted to reach through the glass and pull Him free, but it simply wasn't possible. Her only option was to save herself and come back for Him once the lava solidified. She gave Him the same nod that He had always given her – stern and quick – only this time flames and glass separated them. Then she pushed herself away from the searingly hot panel between them.

Lava coated the floor all around her, and it was impossible to see how thick it was. The pile of shards she was on was shrinking beneath the rising surface. She couldn't breathe behind the bombarding puffs of black smoke filling the air. A nauseous feeling shot up from her stomach, and she forced it back down, closing her eyes for a second to gather her inhibitions back together.

A dozen paces. Less if she took them wide. She would have to be fast, and hope that the lava had started hardening.

She hopped down into the lava, rippling the liquid outward. The half inch of soles on her boots sizzled underneath her feet, and she powered forward, using all of her strength to pull her boots out of the thickening substance. Four steps into the sprint and the bottoms of her feet began to burn as she walked barefoot through liquid fire.

Just as the soles disappeared and her skin started to sear off, the glass wall at her rear broke open from the weight of the built up magma, and it rushed at her back like a torrent of heated death.

Air pushed on her back and singed the ends of her hair. If the chute on her back was melted it would be useless, and she'd hit the ground with full force. Still unsure as to exactly how high up they were, Mercelle knew her only option to survive was to jump, leaving Lito behind.

The rounded corner of a glass pillar stuck out of the floor, and she used it as a stepping stone to kick herself out the side of the building, and ahead of the lava swell, praying to Lito that her chute would open properly, and that He'd be okay.

14

BEWAPEN I

The woman was injured, frazzled and frantic all at the same time. He had never seen one this light skinned before, nor had he ever seen a woman act with such vigorous importance, or jump out of a building.

After he was able to get her away from the crumbling tower, he and the Kop assembled a large force to rummage through the smoking, steaming, solidifying stone for any sign of Lito, or their friend named Ashlan. Lito was found, and only because He'd managed to get a few fingers to stick out of the magma before it began to harden around Him. But, there was no sign of the other man.

The light skinned woman was flecked with burns all over her body, but Bewapen's hands took the heat of the lava without a fuss. Lighter skin was weak and thin,

Bewapen surmised. He and the other members of the now named Onyx Clan hoisted Lito's smoldering mass of stone from the glass pile, and rolled the whole thing a dozen miles back to the village along the side of their mountain.

"You is no touch," he told her, pointing to the sappidge soaked bandages around her feet. "Is heal."

"Thank you," she replied, clearly in less visible pain than she'd been when he'd found her. Their first encounter was a mixture of trying to understand what she was saying through screams of pain, and attempting to calm her down enough to allow sappidge bandages to be applied to her smoking wounds. "No sign of Ashlan?"

"You and Lito is only ones find," he said. "We is still look."

With the tower downed, the Clan was celebratory, especially to know that Lito was there. Lito and His female friend rested for the night, but not for long. They were both up before the sun.

Bewapen held her hand, helping her limp over to Lito's scorched body.

"Clan is happy tower is destroy. Kop is thankful."

"We did what we could," she told Bewapen, cringing in agony and hesitating with each step. "The magma won't be returned to the ground, but we made sure that no more will be taken out. Eventually, the Earth will begin creating more on its own."

She smelled like sweat, burned skin and sappidge juice, which formed a very enjoyable combination that Bewapen didn't mind in the least.

He lowered her onto a metal stool next to Lito, keeping her deeply burned thigh straightened. The Order God had been enveloped in the red hot liquid before the rest of the tower collapsed into the sand. They had to chisel Him out and pry away the malleable stone as it hardened around His muscles and limbs. All of His skin was burned off, leaving exposed flesh, bones and teeth. His eyes were also discolored to the point of being unrecognizable.

The light skinned woman's reaction to seeing a skinless face and body was disgust and concern at first, but once He started to move Bewapen saw relief wash over her.

"As long as He's alive He can heal Himself," she reminded Bewapen, who had already witnessed Lito's ability to heal not only Himself, but Bewapen's wound as well.

Within hours the skin had started to grow back, letting them know that He was strong enough to withstand drowning in liquid hot lava, while further solidifying the Clan's belief in His power and purpose. By mid-evening, He was able to close lids over eyes and lips over teeth, and Bewapen carried Him to a cot to rest for the night.

He was only used to seeing burns on young ones, as

their skin grew thicker with age before thinning out late in life.

With a much happier visage now that she was sitting, the woman scooped cups of warm sappidge juice from a basin next to the cot, and dribbled it over Lito's blisters, just like Bewapen had shown her.

"Is this your home?" she asked.

He looked around at the timid cave. All he had was his cot, and two pots: one for water and one that he usually used for food, but had filled it with the healing liquid for Lito. "Ommteek eesill," he spoke from his diaphragm, forgetting that she didn't speak Clan. "Is home. Is mine."

The last he heard the Kop was helping Mother Aeterna through some labor pains, attempting some tried and true methods of inducing, if she allowed him to. Second Prime Virou-Malik still watched over the search parties as they rummaged through the downed tower to find Ashlan. It was an eventful day for the Clan, and the population of just over five thousand was dividing their attention between the arrival of the guests, the search for Ashlan around the tower's remains, Mother Aeterna's impending delivery, and the celebration of the downed tower.

He shooed the onlookers from his cave, and only the few who could fit their heads through the threshold stayed behind to gawk at the light skinned woman and the Order God. Mercelle was beautiful. It was the way she moved with intention, and spoke like she was in charge, almost like she feared nothing but others being in pain. That was how women were supposed to speak. Tales from ancient times said that women in the light skinned cultures were more demure and submissive to the wills of men, which made little sense to him.

"Eestoo!" shouted the Kop from outside the cave.

The gawkers parted and let him through, the jingle of his trinkets and chainmail trench coat preceded his entrance.

"Aa'ol meen Lito," Kop Stamhoof said. "Is heal?"

"He is," Mercelle answered. "Thank you for your help. I'm not sure what I would have done if Bewapen and his friends hadn't come along."

"You is welcome," Bewapen replied. He pointed to the gawkers and ordered them to fetch more warm sappidge juice. "Tee'al moot sappidge, gee too'al, haast." A couple of them disappeared behind a sea of faces crammed into the cavern outside his home.

Bewapen customarily relinquished his seat, and the Kop sat beside Lito's cot. The two of them were brothers of ultimate power. Order and Onyx. Origin and creation. He couldn't wait to see what the Kop's reaction would be once he learned who was sitting across from him.

"Lito told me about you. Said that you lead a strong Clan of warriors. He's the one who convinced me and Ashlan to help you by taking down the magma tower."

"I is forever grateful" the Kop told her. "Clan is forever grateful. You is strong warrior, is help us very much."

"Yeah, well, your friends helped us too so we're even, personally, at least. I still have something else to ask of you, of your Clan."

Lito stirred, blinking and moving His mysteriously blue eyes around. Bewapen almost rushed over with some water for Him to drink, then remembered that Lito didn't need to eat or drink anything.

"You is okay?" asked the warrior. "You is need something?"

"No, Bewapen." Lito's voice was dry and harsh, like that of a very old, dying man. "You've been kind enough."

The Kop put a hand on Lito's arm and helped Him to scoot back and sit up. "You is kind also, but must rest."

"I don't need to rest. I'll heal just the same whether I move around or not, and I would rather move." He looked over His battle partner. "Your feet."

"Yeah, I know." She looked down at her cane and wrapped feet with a half smirk. "There are little burns over most of my arms and legs, but my feet got the worst of it. My boots are gone – melted. I guess it beats being boiled alive."

Bewapen thought everything about her was perfect, even the way she downplayed her injuries.

Lito looked down at His body. He must have just realized that He was wearing nothing but sappidge soaked bandages over every bit of His skin, aside from His eyes and mouth. Bewapen had tied them around His torso tight to make sure they wouldn't slip off, and continued to wet them with juice from the pots.

"Mercelle," He said. "My armor."

"Relax. It survived and it's safe with the clippers."

"You name is what?" asked the Kop.

"Stamhoof," Lito replied for her. "This is Inis Mercelle, the Lady of Lanna I discussed with you."

"O'uwo gee! Praise you! You is born day Book is found, day Mother Aeterna is give birth to first female. She is see you in vision."

"That's right," she admitted. "He told you about me too? Huh. You two must have become quite friendly during His short time here."

"Lito is good friend," said Bewapen, smiling at her a bit too wide for a reason he didn't quite understand. "You is good friend too?"

"I am now." She waved a hand over Lito's bandages. "We're allies now."

Two men in steel loin cloths carried metal pitchers into the room, pouring the steaming sappidge juice into the pot, then hastily made their way back to the door to observe.

"Lito is tell me about you," said the Kop. "Say you is leader, like me."

"That's right. And there's a meeting of all the human leaders coming up in less than a week. We're going to talk about a strategy to take down the biggest Chaos tower on the planet, and hopefully the Mastership along with it. I would like to extend an invitation to you and your Queen if you would like to come."

The Kop rubbed his chin, and flung his white dreadlocks over a shoulder, as he typically did when thinking hard. "You is want alliance? We is discuss it together, not now. Now is birthing ceremony. You is come. My son is birthing."

Bewapen had been waiting for Kop Stamhoof to mention the ceremony. There was nothing more treasured to the Clan than the birth of a new member, especially their next Kop. Bewapen remembered the day his son, Geboor, was born nearly forty years ago. It was the most important birthing ceremony of his life. It wasn't until recently that Geboor had left to find his own cave, leaving Bewapen alone in this one.

Lito seemed elated. "You want us to witness the birth of your son?"

"We'd love to!" Mercelle tried to stand up in her excitement, but didn't get far into the endeavor before plopping herself back down with a twisted face of discomfort. "We might need a little help moving around is all."

"We is take care of you," said the Kop, rubbing her hand. "Someone is want to meet you."

Although he was tempted to stay and spend time with Mercelle, the warrior Lady of Lanna, Bewapen knew his work would be much more appreciated elsewhere.

"Kop. Friend is still missing, Ashlan. I is go help?"

"That's Lady Feres's First Officer," Mercelle told them. "I didn't see him after I jumped out of the tower. He might not have made it out before the bombs went off."

"We is find," Bewapen assured her. "Kop. I is join search?"

"No. You is stay with us, carry Lito to ceremony."

The Order God, mighty and unyielding, shifted His feet over the edge of the cot and lowered them onto the floor. "I think I can manage on my own."

"I can't," said Mercelle, looking down at her wrapped feet. "Got anything with wheels?"

Without hesitation, Bewapen slipped one arm behind her back, and another behind her knees, picking her up like a light blanket. She smelled salty and sweet, and with their faces so close together he couldn't help but look into her eyes as she gasped and smiled all at once.

THE CELEBRATION WAS in full swing. Under the setting sun performers spun flaming ropes through the air.

Couples held hands, kissed and compared skills in sparring matches. Young boys jumped over the fire pits, laughing whenever one would fall into the flames and come out without hair. Drums were pounded as feet danced through the sand. Talks of possible lava flows bountifully springing back to life abounded all around them.

Mercelle had an arm around Bewapen's shoulder. Lito and Stamhoof led the way, having their own conversation. Each time they got caught in the crowd Mercelle would stop holding on so tightly and rub the muscles on Bewapen's back. He had a few knots, and she was finding them one at a time while running the fingers on her other hand over the Grey claw mark on his chest.

"Your people really know how to have a good time," she said when a group of celebrators bumped into them.

"Light skinned is no have good time? Is no celebrate?"

She squirmed a bit after he asked her that. "You know, where I come from – the rebellion – skin color doesn't really matter. We range anywhere from dark Brown to completely pale, but nobody cares or judges or uses terms like 'light skinned'. We're all equal."

Bewapen struggled with how to reply. "Eepsa'al. I is uh...is sorry. Clan is sequester from rest of world for long time. Is always call others outside of Clan 'light skinned'. Is no intend to discriminate. We is proud of our bloodline, is proud to have purebloods. But I is no pureblood. I is like you, is mix Race. Is no make me different from purebloods or light skinned. You is right, skin color is no matter. We is all hooman, is made by Lito."

"Skin color may not be important." She traced a finger over his chest. "Race is real though. Nobody can argue with that. Some may argue that even though there were Seven Races we are actually one Race, as is Chaos. If we can cross breed Races, learn the same languages, or love each other, then we are definitely more similar than the Book of Order expresses."

"I is believe that. Race is important, is define us. But I is no believe mix Races is bad, or light skinned is bad. We is only need to remember our past. Is never forget history, or tradition. Is only learn from it, together."

She smiled up at him. Her reactions were heartwarming, and he took pleasure in discussing the Clan's heritage and histories with her. She had some gaps in the information Lito had provided, and filling them in was just another excuse to keep talking to her.

After reaching another entrance to the vast cavern system, he showed her the underground sappidge fields, which were being picked more than usual due to the party going on in the valley. Then they passed by Ridder as he stood guard outside the Queen's cave.

"Hwee'o," greeted Bewapen.

"Hwee'o," replied Ridder.

"What's that mean?" Mercelle asked.

"Is greeting. Is hello, or welcome." He wanted to teach her the Clan's entire language.

Inside Mother Aeterna's cave, the youngest female, Hidre, was crawling about the floor while Leidra, Klo and Gera scooped water from a basin and tossed it over Mother Maagda's back. Steam rose from her hot skin and filled the large cave with the scent of struggle and new life, mixing with the grey smoke from the fire in the corner. Two of the three Primes – Neemoor and F'Briek – were already there, sitting in their designated seats with an empty one between them for Virou-Malik.

Along the upper parts of the walls were carved out windows that were full of peering faces. Bewapen brought Mercelle to the back of the large room, and placed her on a pile of blankets beside Lito and Kop Stamhoof.

Pots of sappidge juice lined the walls, waiting to be lit for the end of the ceremony.

"Huuuuhhhhhh!" moaned the Queen, waddling over to Lito as another cup of water was splashed over her. She held one hand on her back, with another on her giant stomach, a wince crinkling up her face. "Lito," she groaned after a contraction. "Good to see you my friend. You seem to be healing nicely, and very fast."

Lito shook her hand, and water slicked from her hair over His blistered arm. "Good to see you also," He said. His voice was slowly returning to normal as His throat began regrowing the singed skin and inner membranes. It was difficult for Bewapen to process the rate at which Lito was recovering from being submerged in lava. Men from the Clan wouldn't have taken on any burns, but would have likely suffocated. Regardless, even the Onyx men didn't heal as quickly as that, not even with the assistance of sappidge juice. "I brought another friend for you to meet. This is Inis Mercelle, Lady of Lanna."

Mother Maagda pursed her lips and blew air out. "Oh. The one I saw in my vision? The one you were telling me about? The warrior?"

"I guess you could call me that," Mercelle said, shaking her hand. "How are you doing?"

"I'm just waiting for the contractions to merge," Mother Maagda replied. "After birthing a few females the males don't seem bad at all anymore. Hmmph!" She tightened her hands into fists, staying on her feet through a seizure of her internal muscles. Bewapen never understood how one person could bear so much constant pain. "There's another one! HooooHHHH!" An easy breath relaxed her. "And it passed. A few more and we'll be able to finish the ceremony."

Kop Stamhoof flattened a hand on her belly, and Bewapen remembered feeling that same belly when Geboor was inside, kicking and twisting to get out. That womb had birthed so many of their Clan, including

Bewapen himself. It was an enchanted portal, bringing new life from somewhere beyond this world. She was his mother, his son's mother, the entire tribe's mother. She was their Mother Aeterna.

"Geboor is at celebration, likely," Bewapen told Mercelle. "Is my son. Is born from same womb. Is warrior, like me."

Bewapen was proud of his son. Nearing his fortieth year, Geboor was about to reach full maturity. He didn't know if his son had taken on a lover yet, or if he was like Bewapen and only had affections for the Queen. It was an individual's choice whether to remain celibate beyond the Queen's mating requirements, or to make a home with another male member of the Clan. There weren't exactly options beyond that – at least not until the other females came of age and made their own choices.

Having experienced the love of other men, Bewapen never felt completely fulfilled by it. The thought of being alone his entire life lacked the fully realized satisfaction he craved. There was a time when he considered waiting until one of the young females came of age to court her, but by that time he figured he would be too old and undesirable.

"That's sweet," Mercelle cooed at him. "If he's anything like his father he must be kind and strong...and handsome."

His cheeks got warm, but he couldn't tell if Mercelle

could see any redness showing through his pitch black skin.

"How old are you, child?" asked the Onyx Queen, putting a hand on Mercelle's knee.

"I'm twenty one."

"Then you were born the same time as Klo here. Her birth was what made me become Mother Aeterna. I saw your mother and father hold you for the first time when you were born. They were so happy to receive you. I understand it was the same day the Book of Order was found?"

"Right," Lito answered. "That's when the human rebellion began searching for me."

"And when the balance of the war finally started to shift in our favor," Mercelle added.

A bald man pushed his way through the dense crowd in the doorway, calling to the Kop, who got up and went over to speak to him.

"You is part of Clan," Bewapen said. "Is for longer than you think. Since Lito is left us last, we is speak of you. We is believe that you is important to salvation of Earth. We is believe that you is born same time as first female, same time as Order Book is found."

"It was all seen in my own vision, as well as a vision from millions of years ago when the Clan first gave birth to a Grey-Black hybrid child." Mother Maagda cringed at the onset of another quick contraction.

"I don't think so," Mercelle told them with a

doubtful shake of her head. "It must just be a coincidence that I was born at the same time. I mean, dozens of people had to have been born on that same day, maybe hundreds."

"We is not believe in coincidence," responded Bewapen. He wasn't about to let her confidence be shadowed by self-doubt. She was holy, ethereal and the center of his attention at the moment. "We is believe in Fee'u. Fate. You is here now. Vision is true."

Maagda blew out another breath, wiping sweat from her neck. "Everything happens for a reason. Sometimes those reasons are very specific, and are made clear to us. But, mostly we are left to see how these 'coincidences' relate to the happenings of the world. So far, we haven't had any motivation to distrust them. OOOOooooouuuuuhhhhaaaa!" This time, Bewapen's mother went to her knees, and chatter arose from the spectators. "It's tiiime! Hwee'o oondeetah!"

The Kop rushed back over. "Search party is report," he said to Mercelle and Lito directly. "Is no sign of friend Ashlan, but is still looking."

"Thank you," Mercelle replied, standing and looking to the pained Mother. "We should go. You're-"

Maagda's hand grasped Mercelle's wrist. "No. UUUhhhhhoohoohoo. Staaay. Hwee'o oondeetah."

Bewapen couldn't read the expression on Mercelle's face as well as he hoped. She was either relieved to take her weight back off of her feet and sit down again, frightened due to Maagda's request made between howls, or possibly experiencing a bout of intestinal discomfort. Maybe all three.

"Ceremony is to end," announced the Kop. "Hwee'o oondeetah!"

Mercelle looked at Bewapen, and he whispered, "Is mean 'welcome little one'."

"I see," she replied. As the crowd of onlookers repeated the phrase over and over, she quickly caught on and joined in. "Hwee'o oondeetah. Hwee'o oondeetah."

The young girls put down their cups. Klo, Leidra, Gera and Hidre took up small blankets, fanning Mother Maagda with them as Kop Stamhoof helped her to the ground. Mother's head servant, Wardig, led two other men in, all of them with long white hair pinned in tails at the back of their heads, and wearing nothing but their loin cloths and steel strip belts. Right away, the men surrounded Mother. Two held her legs, bent at the knees, to the sides of her chest. Wardig held her long locks of white up off of the floor, keeping her hair clean and stroking through it as she tensed and relaxed. It was all just like it had always been done.

Stamhoof removed his trench coat and the belt holding his trinkets, propping himself in front of her womb. Klo removed flaming chunks of sappidge from the fire, handing them to Leidra, Hidre and Gera. They dropped the cinders into the pots of sappidge juice around the room until all of the pots had tall flames on top. Thin puffs of smoke rose and filled the cave.

Bewapen, who had taken a seat beside Mercelle, said, “We is all born to smoke of sappidge. Sappidge is in our blood, is part of us. Ceremony is never had females before Mother Aeterna. Females is bring relaxation, ease to birth.”

“Females tend to be a bit more comforting,” Mercelle agreed.

The girls lowered themselves to their knees in a semicircle behind the Kop. As witnesses to the birth, they were to take in every stretch, tear, revelation of skin and spill of blood. Their eyes and smiles were wide, beaming with happiness to watch the birth of the next Kop. Mother Maagda’s head was at Mercelle and Lito’s feet, with her hair pulled to the side and held up from the floor. All together, the men and girls surrounding Maagda began a breathing routine that included them taking in two short puffs of air through the nose, and slowly blowing the whole breath into her face with a long, collective hum.

With each blow of air, Mother’s eyes rolled into the back of her head as the collective breath relieved her of her pain and eased her into the ethereal realm little by little.

Stamhoof pulled her dress up over her stomach, bunching it onto her breasts and under her neck. Their glistening skins were exposed, the birthing assistors and daughters were rising and falling in unison with each breath, and the shivering body of Mother created a palpable energy, bringing Bewapen waves of euphoria. He wondered if Lito or Mercelle could feel it.

Beside him, Lito was watching with intensity. Thinking about it, he figured that this was the very first time the Order God would be able to see one of His creations initiate life. Before he knew it, Lito was swaying to the rhythm of the room. This was truly a magnificent day.

"I've always known women to receive a neural inhibitor when they go into labor," explained Mercelle. "That way they can give birth with minimal pain. Your Mother is brave."

"Mother is accustom to labor pain," he said. "Other hoomans is easy birth, slow. Mother's is tough birth, quick, grow fast in womb. Mother is doom for pregnancy pain, always."

"She never gets a break does she?"

"Never."

"Then I'd say she's more of a warrior than anyone else in your Clan. Wouldn't you?"

He'd once heard a supposition from a friendly warrior that women shared a collective mind. What Mercelle had just said told him otherwise: that they were each empathetic, sympathetic and wise in their own regards. "I is say yes. Is stronger than men, than warrior. Is Mother."

"How many times has she given birth?" she asked, beginning to sway with him.

"Is hundreds. She is birth five at same time, is only happen once. Is sometimes two or three."

"That must have been difficult. Five at once?"

Lito perked up, scanning the room with blistered eyes. "I feel a quake building beneath us. We should get out of this cave."

"Is life!" Bewapen shouted above the hums of the assistors and daughters. As expected, the cave shivered, flames reached the stone ceiling from the pots of burning sappidge, and small pebbles began levitating inches from the ground.

Mercelle's hand went to his, and he squeezed it as he watched Mother Maagda groan low, and push. The sound was primal, like that of a monster. From where they sat, he could see the muscles in her body tense, tremble and then relax.

"What's going on?" Mercelle asked, looking around at the tall flames and hovering pebbles.

"Baby is crown. Vision is start." There wasn't anything in the world quite like being in the presence of new life. The light skinned humans had their potent drink – the Clan had their birthing ceremonies. As one of the best warriors in the Clan, Bewapen was delighted to have a saved seat at every one, despite the cave only capable of holding a handful of spectators.

Mother Maagda's neck bent backward, and they

could see her entire face. The whites of her eyes fogged through the black irises and pupils until they took on the grey tinge of the sappidge smoke. Her head turned toward Mercelle.

"What is she seeing?" asked the curious Order God.

"I is not know. Vision is end after birth end. Mother is sleep then, is rest, is tell us of vision later."

The groaning, entranced Onyx Queen reached both hands back, reaching around Wardig to grab Mercelle's ankle and Lito's foot. For a long moment, Maagda pulled at them, tensing up and pushing to the rhythm of the room's breaths.

"Mother is invite you to join ceremony," he told them, motioning for them to lie down on the floor with her.

"I...uh." Mercelle hesitated.

Lito leaned forward, putting His hands on the floor and lowering Himself next to Mother. Bewapen took Mercelle's hand, gingerly pulling her forth along Mother's other side, making sure not to disrupt her bandaged feet.

"Oh, okay then," she said, wincing as Mother squeezed her palm. Mercelle awkwardly looked around at everyone, taking on their breathing and blowing pattern.

"Hwee'o oondeetah! Hwee'o oondeetah!" they chanted.

Mother cried out a long, low groan, curling her toes

and causing the cave to tremble. The smoke building up above them formed layers and waves as the vibrations hit.

With Mercelle and Lito at Mother's sides, Bewapen saw the Kop's eyes widen, and the muscles in his arms flexed with the weight of something dropping into them.

Stamhoof pulled the slimy mass into his chest, sobbing and rubbing his cheek on the babe's face. An assistor procured a blade, and cut the attaching cord, severing the tie between Mother and child, and ending Mother's vision.

Bewapen had been so excited the day Geboor was born that he'd nearly forgotten to wait until the cord was cut to take him away. The placenta dripped down his body, and he lay with Mother for days while she nursed Geboor, smelling of newborn and sappidge smoke until she decided it was time for the next mating ceremony. He'll never forget the vision Mother described: fields of colorful plants, spanning as far as the eye could see, and tiny, buzzing animals hovering and feeding from their ornate centers. She had said that she didn't know whether it was the future or the past. It could have been either, he thought.

"Litar," said Mother Maagda, panting. The chanting stopped and her eyes had gone back to their normal black. She was struggling to keep them open. She turned to Lito. "His name is Litar, after you." She gave

Him an exhausted smile before relaxing into the floor and passing out.

The Kop wrapped Litar in a blanket, and left into the adjacent room with him.

"Is she okay?" Mercelle looked concerned for the sleeping Mother.

The daughters poured cups of water over the pots of sappidge, staunching the flames. Then they went back to watering Mother, cooling her hot skin.

"Is rest. When Mother is awake, is nurse new baby, is tell us about vision. Then baby is raise by father until old enough to become warrior. Baby is next Kop when Stamhoof dies."

Lito and Mercelle stayed by Mother's side until she woke up, then they all limped over to the nursing room together where she spent some time with Kop Stamhoof and baby Litar.

LITO AND MERCELLE had gone to join the celebration which was now happening under the stars. By the time the birthing ceremony was over, Lito had healed enough to help Mercelle along in her bandages. Every time Bewapen looked over at Lito, His skin had healed a bit more. It was undeniable yet unbelievable, and Bewapen imagined the sappidge juice helped.

He walked with his Kop and First Prime Neemoor,

traversing the caverns to the valley outside. After hearing what the Queen saw in her vision, they had to discuss how it would be addressed before speaking with their guests.

Part of what Mother Maagda had told them was about a vision of three people walking through a leveled rebel city at night, and a glowing blue rain falling from the sky. It wasn't as important as the other half of what she saw: she described it as a voice from the ethereal realm that told her to be careful of false Gods, and that the one true God would be able to transcend a bridge between life and death.

Mother told them what part of her vision included. She had seen a pair of hands, glowing bright red, lowering onto the blurry face of an Onyx boy as he woke from a deep sleep, who then died while the red glow faded and the hands disappeared into darkness.

Bewapen asked if they were to tell Lito and Mercelle what Mother Maagda had seen, but the Kop ordered them to stay quiet. Stamhoof told the pair that he would divulge some of the vision, but not all of it.

Always tactful, Bewapen suggested that keeping secrets could be regarded as a bad relationship precident should they follow through with their alliance. Neemoor stepped in, suggesting Bewapen obey orders and adding that they must first find out what the light skinned were hiding from them, if anything, before revealing the entire vision.

Bewapen hung his head in silent obedience, ignoring the inner self-admonishment that came along with it.

THE KOP HAD a private fire built in the sandy valley below the entrance into the mountain. He had it surrounded by a circle of his most loyal warriors to create a space quiet enough for him to speak to his guests. All while Bewapen and the Primes remained quiet, as ordered. Typically, Bewapen would have started his daily morning routine of scouting out the many square miles surrounding the Clan's encampment to look for Chaos tracks, but the Kop had him stay instead.

Lito and Mercelle were retrieved from the celebration, and seemed anxious to hear about the Queen's vision. They sat beside the Primes while Kop Stamhoof told them of the portion of the vision which wasn't suspicious: she saw three unknown people walking through a destroyed rebel city, and blue lights came down from above, accompanied by a heavy sense of dread.

Stamhoof stopped there, purposely leaving out the rest of what they had been told by Mother Maagda. Bewapen wanted so badly to dash his orders to the side and tell the whole truth.

Lito and Mercelle looked at each other, wrinkling their brows at the same time.

"You saw it too," confirmed Mercelle as Lito opened His mouth to speak.

"I did."

"We is think means war is cause apocalypse," the Kop explained. "Hoomans is destroy Demigods, but is destroy Earth too. No life is left. No hope is left."

"Hold on," said Mercelle, shaking her head. "Mother Maagda saw three people walking through a destroyed city as blue lights fell from the sky?"

"Is right," assured Stamhoof.

"How is that possible?" she asked.

"Did you see it also?" questioned Lito. "You did, didn't you?"

Her eyes widened as she explained, "Y-yes. I saw it over and over after we took down the southern tower – while I was walking back to Sandra. Every time I closed my eyes I saw the same thing, dreaming it even. It stopped once I got something to eat. I just thought I was seeing things. I...how is that...what does this mean? I couldn't tell who the other two people were. One of them must be Lito. But, then, does that mean the third person is Maagda?"

Anticipation welled up in Bewapen as he waited for Lito to shed some sort of divine light onto the vision, explaining exactly what it was supposed to mean. But, beyond His meager suggestion, He looked as confused as Mercelle.

"I also had the same vision while walking through the desert, just before I found Bewapen," added Lito.

"That doesn't make any sense. It has to mean something," she insisted.

"Fee'u gee. Is your fate." The Kop shook his head. "Is no way to know fur sure. Ethereal realm is only show to Queen. If you is see it too, maybe you is also divine."

"Lito is, but I'm definitely not divine," Mercelle said, scoffing at herself.

"No," replied Bewapen. "You is destined to save hoomans. I is know it."

"Well," she replied with a sideways eye. "I don't know about that."

"When I saw it I only saw myself and two others," Lito added. "I couldn't tell who they were either."

"Same," Mercelle answered. "I remember that dreadful feeling of darkness approaching once the lights hit the ground. Did you feel that?"

Lito nodded.

"It must be the future, because the only leveled city I've been in is Lanna, and we were alone once it was destroyed. Nobody was with us. I just wish we knew who the third person is, and which city we're in." She took one long, pensive look at the ground, then picked her head up and shook it, changing the direction of the discussion. “How’s Litar doing?” she inquired. It was something Bewapen was allowed to comment on.

The Kop beat him to it. “Litar is good, is nurse with Mother. I is no wait for Litar is open eyes in few weeks. Baby’s eyes is most precious sight.”

“They are adorable, aren’t they?” Mercelle was utterly taken by the ceremony, just as Bewapen had hoped.

He pictured her holding a baby. A light skinned child who wailed and cried while its mother smiled and swooned. Warmth wrapped around his heart, and he found himself fantasizing about having another child, a daughter perhaps. He quickly shook the thought from his head.

“Mating ceremony is in few days,” said Bewapen. “Is once Queen is rested enough. Queen is becoming pregnant with new baby. You is stay?” It had already been a long day, but he still had so much more to show them of his Clan. He still wanted Lito and Mercelle to meet his son, Geboor.

“Perhaps we could return,” answered Lito.

Mercelle piped up. “Um. We really do have a lot of things to attend to in the coming days. I’m afraid we’ll have to leave by nightfall, but I really hope we can be there for the next birth. That was a really touching experience. I’ll never forget it.”

The sounds of drums and celebratory cries echoed

through the valley, and reached them as they stood in the brightening light of the rising sun.

"Hopefully the next child will be born into a world without Demigods," Lito threw in.

The Kop seemed happy to hear that. "I is hope so also. We is have faith in hooman rebellion, in Mercelle, in Lito, in Order. Clan is want war to end soon, is want to make alliance with hooman rebellion."

Lito stood and shook his hand.

"That's great!" Mercelle beamed. "You can come to the summit meeting in Naselba. Maybe you can help us teach their army a few things about real warriors."

"Kop is no leave Clan, cannot lose Litar. Litar is next Kop. I is send strongest warrior, is token of loyalty to Order, to rebellion." He looked back at Virou-Malik.

The leader of the Kop's army stood, dangling jewelry glinting in the firelight from his countless piercings. He slung a lock of hair over his shoulder, and answered the Kop's silent question. "I, Second Prime Virou-Malik, is declare warrior Bewapen to be strongest."

They locked eyes.

His chest stung. It couldn't be happening. He couldn't leave the Clan. Geboor... A cold sweat squeezed from his pores, covering his skin in a microsecond.

"Bewapen is leave Clan," Stamhoof declared. "Is to live among light skinned hoomans as ambassador and communicator. Is to tell us when we is needed for battle."

"Ni heedsvu Clan fa! I is no leave Clan!" Bewapen argued. The feeling of rising against his Kop for the first time made his soul and his body clash in a fiery collision of love and loyalty. "I is no sacrifice son!"

"Wait," Mercelle said, standing with her hands up in the center of the conversation. "What is this talk about sacrifice?"

Silence swept the group.

He thought of Geboor's face, sweet and young. The boy didn't deserve to be that part of the changes happening in the world. His fists clenched as he forced himself to be quiet.

"The last time I was here," said Lito. "They told me that if a member of the Clan leaves for the outside world then that member must sacrifice someone from their bloodline. Since Bewapen's father is no longer with us that would leave only his son, Geboor. They call it a sacrifice for severance."

"But it should be Bewapen's choice." She limped to stand in front of the Kop. "It isn't fair to punish him for being helpful, or for being a good warrior."

"It is not punishment," corrected the Kop. "Is honor. Sacrifice is symbol of severance from Clan, is opening of Clan to Order and rebellion."

"Okay, well, he isn't leaving for good," argued Mercelle. "He isn't abandoning his Clan. In fact, it isn't necessary for him to come with us at all. We can send a convoy to let you know when to prepare for battle. I could leave behind a radio, or a transmitter."

"I is insist. As Kop, I is gift best warrior to Order God."

"Then, as acting ambassador, Bewapen will be allowed to return to the Clan after the Demigods are beaten. I don't see the point of ending a life. Isn't what we're doing here supposed to be *preserving* life?"

The Kop sighed. "For hundreds of years, no one is leave Clan out of fear for Chaos. Now is time for Clan to know our light is shine in world. I is show by give warrior. Vision is show third person is with you. Bewapen is have to go. Is your third."

"How are they all supposed to see the light if they're all being sacrificed for no reason?!"

Stamhoof got to his feet, and raised his voice. "Clan is same for millions of years! Is no change now! No for light skinned!"

"Everything is changing," said Lito, calmly. "Fighting that change will only take away from the fight against our real enemies. Every human life is important, and we need all the numbers we can get if we want to win the war."

Failing to make the sacrifice would dishonor the Clan, turn Geboor into a pariah, and keep Bewapen from ever returning to the Clan again. On the other hand, his son was the most valuable thing to him –

the most precious asset taking up space in his heart.

"I is understand need for sacrifice," Bewapen spoke with eyes to the ground. "Millions of years is how long Clan is stay alive, stay pure, is wait for return of Order God. Countless souls is come, is gone. Geboor is have honor to be one of gone souls. Afterward – only afterward – is alliance possible." He let a tear crest over his white lashes. To wipe it away would have shown fear of vulnerability, and the only thing he feared was losing Geboor.

"That shouldn't be up to the Kop, or you!" Mercelle continued. "We can ask Geboor if this is something he wants. I of all people can understand the need for a warrior's death to be meaningful. Let's see what he has to say, and *I'll* make sure his decision is respected! Even if we have to take him along to Sandra with us too."

"Enough, Mercelle," said Lito. "We can't interfere any further. This is their way, and this is how they choose to honor the new alliance. Who are we to tell them otherwise?"

"This is a child! I thought you were the one who said that free will is the only power we humans have?"

"Free will is being exercised here. As a part of the Clan, Geboor has agreed to honor its traditions, its practices. Just as everyone else has. We need to respect that."

"And what? If Geboor declines are you going to sit back and watch them drag a child to execution?"

Lito didn't answer.

It was an honor to have their guests argue about whether or not his son would be sacrificed; however, the plain fact remained that it was not up to them.

"If sacrificial ceremony is no perform," the Kop threatened. "Alliance is not made. I is no let decision rest with child."

"Yeah? What would you have done if one of your relatives was forced to leave when you were young? Huh? Would you have marched happily to your death knowing your Clan would be without a Kaisering Kop?"

Bewapen stepped into the center of them, creating a calm divide and stopping the flow of angry words. "If that is happen, then Kop is dead, is sacrifice. Then Clan is travel along different path. But, is no happen. Everything is happen for reasons. We is part of bigger being, together. Future is together. I is understand sacrifice."

With a heavy sigh, Mercelle sat back down. "If you forge this alliance with the rebellion, you know you'll have to leave the Clan at some point, right? What will happen then? To Litar?"

"I is do as my people is need," the Kop replied, coldly staring directly into her eyes.

"Including killing them?" she asked just as coldly.

Bewapen couldn't let this go on. He opened his mouth to speak, but the Kop spoke over him.

"Quiet, Bewapen." An aggressive wince arose up one side of Stamhoof's face, and he gritted his teeth, keeping his stare steady on Mercelle. "You is leave by next nightfall. If Bewapen is stay, if Geboor is alive, alliance is no happen, rebellion is alone in war. This is everything." At that, he turned and walked away from the fire, into the bustle of the ongoing celebration outside the circle, which was still going strong into the cool, early morning. The three Primes kept up behind him as he disappeared into the crowd.

When Bewapen tried to follow, he was stopped by a firm hand on his shoulder.

"You don't have to do this," she told him. "We can take both of you with us."

"I is have to." He couldn't look at her, to let her eyes try and sway him. "Is the way of my people, of the Clan. Skin color is no matter, but Race is important."

NOBODY ALIVE HAD EVER WITNESSED or attended a sacrificial ceremony. For hundreds of years the Clan hadn't lost a single member to severance. It was the time before then – a time before the planet was a ball of dust – when men would sacrifice an elderly progenitor already on the brink of death in order to explore the outside world.

They would be gone for years, decades even, before

returning with accents and tales of other worldly machines and foods. The only stipulations being that they could not take on a lover, or speak about their people, to anyone on the outside. Bewapen suspected that some disobeyed those stipulations, mostly the ones who never returned from a freer life outside the rules of the Clan.

Stamhoof and Maagda were the only two who held the knowledge of exactly how the sacrificial ceremony was to be performed. Having passed it down through countless generations, the Clan hadn't used the information for nearly a millennium.

The two of them had the entire Clan gather in the valley after dusk. Lito and Mercelle decided to stay with the Onyx people until morning in order to ensure the alliance, and, Bewapen suspected, try and dissuade them from performing the sacrifice.

Standing at the head of a wide, flat clearing of desert ground surrounded by legions of warriors, Kop Stamhoof addressed the silent masses. His words were given even more power by Bewapen, Lito, Mercelle, the Primes and the Queen standing behind him.

Queen Maagda wouldn't allow her daughters to attend. They were left to care for baby Litar during the ceremony.

"We is show respect for new allies by perform ceremony in shared language," the Kop shouted to his people. "Since time is begin, Clan is true to law, to lore.

Is first time in many centuries that sacrifice is made as severance from Clan."

The crowd shoved spears and hammers into the air, sharing a communal, "Fee'u!" that came from deep within their cores. Bewapen's heart sped up further with each word spoken.

Stamhoof continued. "Strongest warrior Bewapen is to leave with light skinned warrior Lady Mercelle of Lanna, and Order God Lito. Is to form alliance with hooman rebellion against Chaos. Together, we is unstoppable force!" He put both hands up to the sky as his people gave another short, collective shout of support. "Together, we is end Chaos! But before, sacrifice is to be made. Son of Bewapen, by name of Geboor, is sacrifice for severance!"

"Fee'u! Fee'u!" Their chants were deep and loud, and they beat the butts of their weapons into the sand while Bewapen struggled to keep from losing his breath. At the far end of the opening at the center of the crowd, Geboor stepped out. Wearing the steel loin cloth of a new warrior, he walked to the center of the circle, and when the Kop started toward him, Bewapen, Maagda, Mercelle, the Primes and Lito followed. All nine of them congregated around the midpoint of the clearing.

The boy was grown, and just about to reach full maturity. It had been nearly four decades since Bewapen knelt between Mother's thighs and caught his son as he entered the world. This would be about the time he would be receiving his warrior status and completing training.

All of that, Bewapen thought, just to be snuffed out for the sake of an alliance which was meant to save lives. But, how could he argue with his leaders? He thought about how this would be the last time he would see those short, white spikes on top of Geboor's head, the matching grey marks across his chest, or the way he still wiggled his toes in the sands whenever he stood still. The eyes – the same two eyes that saw Bewapen before anyone else when they'd first opened – smiled at him again, and he melted.

Tears streamed down, and Bewapen couldn't stop them from forming rivers over his cheeks. It felt like an uncompromising mixture of pride and devastation.

He wished they could stand there forever, never moving forward from this moment. It was no burden for him to keep still and stare at his son's proud face for the rest of eternity. A small, hopeful part of his mind thought his wish might come true, until the Kop began speaking.

"Young Geboor, descendant of warrior Bewapen. You is to be sacrifice for alliance between Clan and light skinned."

"You could just call us rebels," suggested Mercelle.

Stamhoof went on, "When your soul is enter realm of dead, alliance is bring together army of Order. Army is impenetrable, undying, is great force against Chaos, is last hope to save Earth. Is you understand? Is you accept?"

The question was merely a formality, as there was only one answer. Anything else would lead to either a life of being shunned, or a death without meaning.

"You can say no," Mercelle threw out. "The choice is yours, and we'll respect what you want."

The Kop looked back at her in the flicker of his torch's light, but she ignored him, waiting for Geboor's answer. Bewapen appreciated her concern for the boy's free will to choose, but knew it was in vain.

"I is understand meaning of sacrifice," his son said, jutting his chin and chest out with juvenile confidence. "I is having honor to die for alliance. I, Geboor, descendant of Bewapen, is beginning of end of Chaos."

Studying the Queen's books for centuries wouldn't have provided Bewapen with the words he needed to describe what he felt. The closest could have been esteem, dignity, honor and respect. As father and son, they now had two roles imperative to the future of the Clan, and the planet as a whole. He would have switched places in a heartbeat if he could, and sent his son out into the world.

Geboor was his affirmation of faith, not just in Order, but in the Onyx people, his Kop, the rebellion and in himself. In his son's death, he would provide proof of life. He was evidence of the power of the human spirit, of free will.

He was a Testament.

Mercelle was hesitant in her acceptance, but once Geboor agreed there was nothing more she could say. And Bewapen was glad about it.

He put his hands on Geboor's face, holding it close to his as he said his final goodbyes.

"My son. Geboor. You is my light, is my warmth in darkness, is my blanket in cold." The same streams running down his face began on Geboor's smooth cheeks – the same cheeks he got from his father, although he had Mother's kind eyes and brave smile. "You is better warrior than me. You is more thoughtful than your Kop, is more caring than Mother. Clan is never forget you. I is love you forever, Son."

"I is love you, Father."

They wrapped arms around each other, sobbing and saying farewell in full view of the entire congregation. The Clan needed to see it. Tears dripped down each other's backs, and Bewapen couldn't imagine his days to come. Not wondering how Geboor's training was coming along, whether he had found a lover, and when he would get his first hairs below the top of his head. He ran fingers through his son's short spikes, knowing he would never get to see them grow long and proud.

After a few more arduous moments of raw emotion,

loosening and then tightening their grips on each other, the Kop ordered them to separate. Geboor gave his father one last gallant smile, and Bewapen gave him a lasting kiss on the ear, rubbing his cheek against his son's, and breaking away to wipe his face and stand beside his Kop.

The moon had separated from the horizon, glaring at him from behind Geboor, rays of white light bursting from his silhouette as he stood tall and spirited. Stamhoof handed him a wide-tipped spear, and after an instruction to do so, the boy began to dig a grave. Holding back sobs, Bewapen was more proud of his son than he had been of anything in his ninety years on Earth. Bits of sorrow and pity came, and he fought them away, choosing to hold his son's decision in a higher regard.

"He *is* brave," said Mercelle. That's when he saw wetness building on her lashes. "I will make sure he lives on in our alliance, and in our defeat of the Demigods. Our people will know of him, and will never forget. I promise." She wiped her eyes.

Bewapen's chin quivered, and he nodded a silent thank you to her, trying to rationalize how someone from outside the Clan – someone who'd had such polarizing words to say earlier – could possibly comprehend what was about to happen. He could tell that she felt for both of them, but he didn't just want her pity; he needed it. For some reason it lightened the weight of the moment with the sensation of someone helping to carry his burden.

Leading with a graceful toe, Onyx Queen Maagda – Mother Aeterna – gently put a hand on Bewapen's shoulder, and he stepped out of her way.

Slowly, the crowd of warriors closed in on the group, squeezing together to fit as many faces as possible. Those who couldn't see or hear were being dictated to by those who could, and the Kop ordered a handful of them to erect burning torches around the grave.

"My son," Maagda greeted Geboor warmly, touching her nose to Geboor's as he stood in the fresh grave. "I know it's been so long, but I still remember the day you were born. It was the first and only time I ever saw flowers. I'm not sure what kind, but I know they were flowers. In the ancient times, the light skinned people would bring flowers to celebrate a loved one's life after they died. At the funerals, members of their family – their Clan – would pile fresh flowers atop the casket of the deceased. I can't help but feel like the vision was trying to tell me of this day; the day I would have the honor of being your Mother, and of standing before the entire Clan beside you, my son." Geboor's head dropped, and he wept. She pulled him back up by the chin. "Head up, Geboor, son of Bewapen. Today the world owes you the largest debt, which will be repaid to you with the salvation of mankind. Your head shall never fall."

“Yes, Mother,” he sniffled.

It had been almost a decade since Bewapen had seen his son embrace Mother. With the embrace Bewapen’s heart received another twisting, searing needle.

She broke from their hold, turning to speak to the crowd. “This is the first sacrifice for severance in centuries. The body shall not be burned. His soul will not be allowed to pass through the portal to the unknown beyond. Instead, he will be buried amongst our dirt, to preserve his soul in the realm of the dead on Earth, with his people, with his Clan!”

The warriors erupted with shouting, howling, whistling and waving flaming torches about. A working frenzy was kept under control by her commanding presence, and the strength radiating from Geboor’s tenacious stance in the foot of his grave.

Mother faced him, tearing her gown from her body and bearing the whole of her skin to the Clan. She handed Geboor a blade, and lowered herself down into the grave at his feet.

Air was thinning around Bewapen. Breathing was a labored task, and he shook like a dried sappidge husk in the wind. He wanted one last embrace, one last feel of his son’s white spikes on his fingers.

Geboor adjusted his feet, then brought the blade up to his neck and ran it across his throat with little hesitation. Blood spewed from the opening line of flesh and covered Mother Maagda. His face never changed from that confident, faithful boy Bewapen always knew.

He felt a hand move inside of his, and he held it, knowing Mercelle was trying to comfort him. It was a bold try, but useless.

When Geboor's body weakened and fell atop Mother in the grave, Bewapen's knees gave out. He watched from the ground – Mercelle's arms around him – as his son drained out, and turned the color of ash.

He closed his weeping eyes, feeling Lito's rough hands on his back. The Kop knelt before him, one arm over Bewapen's shoulder. Soon, men from the crowd emerged and joined in the embrace. One at a time they latched on in a connected hold of sympathy and hope that filled the valley.

Geboor was gone, and an alliance was born in his place. All Bewapen could do now was make sure it would all amount to something worth his son's soul being trapped in the land of the dead.

HE LOOKED PLACID, lying in the hole he had dug to rest in for all eternity. Geboor's body was covered in a blanket up to his chin, and Mother had her daughters bring out the Clan's entire stock of dried sappidge husks. Friends – brothers – of the deceased son lined up to place the husks around Geboor's grave.

Mercelle, Lito and Stamhoof all joined in, and when there were only two husks left, Mother and Bewapen held hands, and put the husks over Geboor's closed eyes.

"They were the closest thing I could find," Mother said. "I think he would have liked the idea of flowers on his grave."

"I is know he is like it," Bewapen responded. His emotions had shifted from a depressed sinking to a surreal floating sensation. The option to stop the ceremony and remove Geboor from the situation had come and gone, and all he had left to do was accept the way things were now.

He hoped that Geboor was at peace. His son's face was relaxed, and the corners of his mouth had fallen into the shape of a smile. If it weren't for the boy's ashen complexion, Bewapen could almost imagine that he was simply sleeping.

The moon was floating freely in the early morning sky. It was a beautiful dawn, with thin clouds building up in opaque patches. It could even rain for a moment or two before sunrise. Was it Geboor in the sky? Was he watching over them?

"I is ready to put in dirt," said Bewapen. "Geboor is lay to rest."

Mother turned to Kop Stamhoof, giving him a secretive nod.

"First," announced the Kop, removing a short blade

from his belt and holding it out. "We is need a sacrifice of living blood, from new allies, is seal grave."

"I think that's enough sacrifices for one day," Mercelle sneered at him. "Don't you think?"

Bewapen had never heard of that tradition before, only of the ceremonies pertaining to specific large events like mating, birthing and sacrifices for severance, but never anything to do with sealing a grave. Then again, the Clan always burned their dead and joined the ash with the desert sand. It was best that he didn't speak up against the Kop now. He just wanted to bury his son, and leave with Lito and Mercelle.

"We is only need a small shed of blood from new allies," the Kop repeated. "Nothing more."

Mercelle sighed, reaching for the knife. But, the Kop pulled it back, much to her visible disapproval.

"I is wonder if Lito is willing," he said, pointing the blade's hilt at the Order God.

Lito took it, running the blade over His palm in the same place as when the Kop ordered Him to share His blood with Bewapen. Was that the Kop's goal, to have Lito open the same hand with the same blade every time He came to the village? Bewapen ran his finger along the scar on his own palm where Lito had healed him a few days prior.

Once the hand was dripping blood, Lito held it out over Geboor, running a stream of thick, red liquid over the dried husks. He moved His hand around in a strange pattern, creating a symbol of some kind. Bewapen assumed it was some sort of letter, or maybe even the glyph of Order. It didn't really matter what it was.

"I is put in dirt now," the grieving father requested.

Mercelle took a wide tipped spear from the ground. "Here. I'll help you."

"Alone, please."

"Of course," she responded. Before limping away with Lito and the others, Mercelle wrapped an arm around Bewapen's back, and rested her head on his shoulder.

He felt comfort, leaning in to rub his head on hers. Oh, how she smelled wonderfully.

Everyone left him. Even the crowd dispersed to give Bewapen some privacy to bury his son. This wasn't how it was supposed to be. Geboor was supposed to grow old, find the kind of love Bewapen had never experienced and outlive his father. None of those things would ever come about, and Bewapen let a warm flow of acceptance blanket him as he lay down beside Geboor.

The depressed sinking returned to him, and uncontrollable sobs exited his throat when he touched Geboor's cold cheek.

"I is love you so much," he whispered into a dead ear. "Your father is never forget you. Your father is make sure you is not die in vain."

He didn't want to get up. It meant he was done, and he would never be done saying goodbye. With the morning going by, Bewapen held his son. Once the sun was clear of the western cliffs, he decided it was time to leave Geboor to rest.

The dirt went in slowly. Push by push, Bewapen covered Geboor's feet, legs, torso and then his young, innocent face. When the last of the dirt went on, he tamped it down with the wide tip of the spear, tucking in his son for one final rest.

THEY ASKED him how he was doing, but he couldn't answer. He simply nodded, and helped Mercelle to re-bandage her feet, packing them tightly so she could operate her transport vehicle with him on the back.

Bewapen tried not to dwell on his past, and to focus on the future of Earth, as it was partly his responsibility now too as the Onyx Clan Ambassador of the alliance.

With a heavy head, a sunken heart and the hope of a newly formed alliance, Bewapen rode away with Order God Lito and warrior Lady Mercelle, his large Onyx hammer strapped to his back.

15

ZAKOPAT KRAJ V

Managing to stay hidden wasn't the easiest of tasks, although the lower levels were much less populated with replicas. After falling even further down into the tower's underground floors, he crept along empty corridors full of old refuse, hiding out in vacant rooms anytime he thought he heard steps closing in from around the many corners.

Eventually, he found a hatch that gave him access to the ducts. He climbed down into abandoned floors of the tower's deep sublevels, found a spot inside the walls, and slept for hours. Every little stir of a noise woke him; most of them were imaginary, but he came to attention anyway.

The rest was much needed, and it was the longest he had slept since arriving in Glaven Grad. He only hoped that it would help him to clear his head and find a way out of the Chaos city.

With a full six hours of sleep behind him, Kraj exited the ducts. He opted to traverse the empty floors on foot since there was no sign of life this far down, only mazes of unused storage rooms and vacant experimental chambers that looked as if they had been deserted after some series of explosions or radioactive events. Each room was damaged in its own unique way, and as he went from one to the other he examined them.

One chamber had melted walls, while another had chemical burns throughout the various machines, gurneys and glass partitions. Many had black scorches among the skeletal pillars, and Kraj imagined that it had either taken the Moras quite a long time to determine that humans were vulnerable to flames, or perhaps the chambers were used to incinerate failed experiments. Wires and loose hanging wall panels were left the way they were. Why not? There were thousands of levels built above him to support their experiments. They didn't need these anymore.

Ascending what felt like hundreds of floors of dark and humid corridors, he decided that it was about time to prepare himself to encounter some replicas. He wasn't quite sure what his plan of escape was, but that would have to be his next thought after arming himself. In a chamber that smelled like well-rotted flesh, he found two short, metal rods. They were sturdy and coated with a bit of rust and what looked like small chunks of human tissue. After tearing the sleeves off of his Crassa uniform, he made four strips that he used to tie the short rods to the outsides of his forearms. Not only would that make them easier to carry, but they would help him to deflect any sudden strikes from unseen Bleds or Valks.

In the complete silence of an empty floor, he sat to come up with a plan. In all of his time navigating the ducts he had never seen one with access to the outside of the tower. Windows and doors to the exterior only existed on the ground level and higher, which meant he would have to fight his way through, and then figure a way out of the city after being spotted. Vents were less than a foot high, making it impossible for him to fit.

Stealth was his greatest asset, and he would have to use it to the best of his ability if he wanted to survive.

KRAJ KEPT MOVING, observing his surroundings as he went to try and put pieces together and formulate a hidden path out of the tower. Getting outside was the first step, then getting out of Glaven Grad would also have to be improvised. The further he could get without being spotted, the better chance he had of surviving. As long as he could get out into the open desert he could find his way to the nearest tribe before dying of dehydration.

A large part of him wanted to know what had come of the information he'd sent out to Lady Feres. It made it difficult for him to decide whether or not to return to Sandra or to go home first. He would have to make up his mind before leaving the city, because his decision would dictate his direction of travel.

A few more floors up and he began to hear the humming of machines, which meant that replicas were probably nearby. He slowed his pace, and started peeking around corners. The humming grew closer, and went in and out, sounding like some kind of pumping system. That was music to his ears. Plumbing meant draining, and drains had to lead somewhere.

Around the next corner he spotted a tube about five feet wide, with a round crank atop it. No replicas were around, so he approached it, pressing an ear to the side. From within he could hear the sweeping sound of something flowing.

"Ees perrfict," he said to himself, finally free to use his real voice instead of the manufactured accent he'd used so far in Glaven Grad.

He spun the crank, and opened the hatch to look in. The hatch was round and small, but he could fit through if he squeezed. That smell was familiar to him, and when he stuck his hand into the rushing liquid he was disappointed to find that the large tube was full of

Newlyn goo. Kraj had stumbled upon the draining pipe for the massive amounts of jelly that slid off of Newlyns as they sat and worked at their terminals.

The goo only came about halfway up inside the pipe, which provided him more than enough room to keep his head free, but there was no telling what kind of twists and turns he would have to swim through. As an Oasian, he was one of the few humans on Earth who had ever been completely submerged in liquid, and one of the very few who even knew how to swim.

He slithered into the pipe, pulling the hatch down behind him, leaving him in darkness. The goo was thick and was surging with such ferocity that he was swept away instantly. It felt like he was suspended, not moving at all, but when he reached out to touch the walls of the pipe he could feel how fast he was actually going.

Just as he had suspected, there were turns and drops that rustled him about. Goo got into his mouth, and he held back gags as his head hit the inside of the pipe over and over. Fear that he was simply being drained back down into the sublevels of the tower struck him, until the flow finally stopped, and the pipe filled all the way to the top. He held his breath.

Feeling along the walls, he found that he had ended up at the bottom of a vertical pipe. He swam up the dense liquid, which was particularly easy to move through even though it stung his eyes and assaulted his nostrils. The taste was like an old protein wedge that had been left in the sun and sprinkled with chemical cleanser.

Up and up he went, with the slow flow assisting him in ascending. His head went into something solid, and he felt a metal grate covering the end of the pipe. There was no other direction in which he could swim, and there was no way he could make it back down to find air. His chest began to ache, but he didn't dare exhale what air he had held within him.

He slid a rod off of his forearm and jammed it through the grate. The metal was weak as the flow pressed him against it, and he twisted and pulled the rod to open the hole he had created. Shoving left, then pushing right, the grating gave little by little. His lungs reached their limits, and all the air he had held onto escaped his mouth. Goo went down his throat, and he swallowed it down to keep it out of his windpipe.

Still beneath the goo and unable to see, he heard the snap of the grate's bolts coming loose. It fell past him, and he pulled himself through.

Swimming up, and up and up, he thought he would never find air. But, the fresh sensation of freedom cooled his arms and his face as he surfaced and coughed up goo. The first inhale was painful, but after steadying his breath the pain in his lungs subsided.

Small specks of light bled through the ceiling and allowed him to see that he was inside of a giant vat. He floated atop the goo, looking around to see solid stone walls, and no hatches. The ceiling was damaged a bit, and the rusted steel above was pocked with holes. As long as the goo-level continued to rise, he could get up to the top and kick his way through.

The vat began to shake, and he felt something heavy slam beneath him. Goo was no longer flowing in, and the rising had stopped. A loud buzz came from outside the vat, and he found himself being pulled down as the goo drained.

Unable to grip the slick walls or floor, he was carried through another pipe, holding his breath and using his elbows and knees to keep his head from bouncing about. He was whipped around a corner, and was suddenly falling free. Slamming into the surface of a large pool of goo, he went under and swam back up.

After another coughing fit he wiped his eyes to look around. Above him was the drainpipe he had fallen from, and a glimpse of the sky, and all around him were walls of moist dirt. Goo was being drained into a pit in the ground. It had to be extremely deep, because even as more goo flowed from the pipe, the level wasn't rising. He was going to have to climb out.

Swimming over to the wall, Kraj felt the dirt. It was pretty solid, almost clay-like, but not too firm for him to press hands and feet into. It was an easy climb, and the light from the sun got him moving faster and faster as he made his way up the clay wall. He reached the top within minutes, rolling onto the ground and staring up at the sun. He was somewhere just outside the tower, and seeing the building's exterior wall extending all the way up into the clouds nearly gave him vertigo. To have the warmth of the sun on his skin again was an amazing feeling, but the Newlyn goo coming up from his stomach made him wretch until it all came out.

It was a noisy affair, and it only took a moment for a Valk to pop up from around the corner of the building.

Kraj hadn't even had the chance to see where he was before getting to his feet and sprinting away from the tower. It was daytime, mid afternoon to be exact.

He wasn't sure what the plan was as he ran toward a collection of transport bays. As long as they weren't too inundated with replicas he could find a place to hide. It was a matter of seconds before he had a swarm of Valks on his tail, their aggravated grunts communicating the presence of an enemy to pursue.

Entering the garage, he darted up a set of tall stairs to get to the roof and assess his position, and to find the closest exit out of the city.

Glaven Grad spanned for hundreds of square miles, with the massive tower sticking up out of the center of it. Flat buildings covered the ground, mainly housing vehicles and defense weapons that needed room for testing and storage. Vehicles from payload convoys pulled in and out of repair bays, Newlyns opening them up, reaching in and making adjustments.

There was no way he could get to the outskirts

without being surrounded. And even then, how would he get through the perimeter's security? Checkpoints opened up gaps in the walls around Glaven Grad, and only approved vehicles were let out.

Suddenly, a plan came to him. The only way out of the city was to be inside one of the convoy's transports. All he had to do was get inside one – or under one – and wait for the checkpoint to go by. Then he would be free to leap off as soon as the transport was far enough away from the city.

First things first: he had been seen entering this building, so he would have to sneak out somehow. He looked over the edge of the roof. Valks were entering quickly, stomping through the many entrances to fill the garage and find him.

Luckily, the buildings were very close together, making it easy for him to leap to the next one, run along the roof and leap again. Once he got a few buildings away, he spotted a line of transports pulling out below him. It was a long procession of storage tanks with large axels that would be perfect to hold onto.

Kraj entered the building through another staircase, only to find that it was empty, and only the tail end of the convoy could be seen pulling out of the tall door.

A deep breath of clean air, and he pushed himself off of the wall, taking long strides and dashing toward the exit. He crossed the room in seconds, barreling toward the opening.

Shifting arose in his peripherals. A Bled became visible, lunging out of a corner with blades out to catch him, but he was too fast and the replica landed on the ground at his sprinting heels. Through the doorway, sunlight beamed down on him, and he was blinded by the beautiful rays.

To his right the convoy moved away from him. To his left Valks were closing in.

He turned to run after the convoy, but more Valks blocked his path. With no other choice, he darted down the only alleyway between him and the Valks, surprised to find it clear and hoping to round the building and find a path back to the convoy.

He kept bounding forward, even as he felt the stomps of Valk hooves coming his way. The ground shook, but he couldn't stop. Stopping would mean the end of him. Narrowly dodging the corner of a repair building, Kraj spun around it, and kept on his path to span the block and intercept the vehicles as they made a turn which put them across the alleyway's path up ahead.

The alleyway was still empty, save for the replicas which he knew were hot on his tail. He couldn't tell if they were far behind or right on him. Far ahead, at the end of the alley, the convoy flew by. He veered left, taking a branching back street in order to try and head it off. As long as he could catch the tail end of the convoy he could sneak underneath the trailer and hold on until the checkpoint went by and they were far into the desert.

There were plenty of places for him to stop and hide, allowing the chasers to pass. But, he thought that if he stopped, the convoy would get away, and there was no way he could stay hidden until the next one departed, whenever that might be.

Another four way intersection, and he went forward, seeing the tip of one of the silver vehicles that made up the convoy passing the end of the alley far ahead of him yet again. This pace wasn't going to cut it. He shoved himself into overdrive, running, pushing, stretching his legs into a wide stride until he thought the smallest pebble could throw him off his rhythm and cause him to go tumbling.

There was one last intersection to cross, and as he came through it a Valk leapt out from around the corner of the building. Kraj used his momentum to kick off of the wall and do a rolling flip over the replica's head. He was clear of the Valk, until a claw came forward and pulled him onto the ground by what was left of his Crassa uniform.

He kicked up at the Valk, then brought his knees to his chest and flung them forward to hop back up onto his feet. The middle vehicles of the convoy were passing by, but he had to take care of his attacker before he could pursue them.

More replicas were grouping together, running

toward him from the tower. He was almost out of time. If they got to him that would be it. He couldn't possibly take them all on at the same time.

Valks were slow, and being very familiar with their movements it only took him a few seconds to disarm and kill the one before him.

He dipped into the Valk's range of motion, tempting it to swing the sword. It took the bait, and he shimmied to one side, stopping the blade with the rod still tied to his forearm. He swept the rod sideways, striking the Valk in its snout before spinning and taking out one of its knees. The replica went down on all fours. From there he stepped on the Valk's claw, wrapped a leg around its head, and twisted about its body until he heard a sharp crack of bones.

The large mass of dead meat went down, and he planted hands on the dirt to catch himself. After his feet were grounded, he turned and dashed toward the end of the alley. Just as he reached the road the rear vehicle of the convoy went by.

He rounded the corner, kicking up sand to try and catch up. No matter how hard his feet hit the dirt, no matter how hard he pushed off of each step, the rear trailer kept moving farther and farther away, the growing distance bringing his doom closer and closer.

It was over. There was no way out.

Stomping to a halt, Kraj gasped for air, putting his hands on his knees and watching as the vehicles turned another corner toward an exit checkpoint. The trailers and pulls all sped away. The convoy disappeared, out of sight, along with any chance he had of escaping.

"Sshhhheeet," he muttered, relenting to his end.

Something solid struck him in the back of the head, and he was shrouded in darkness.

Sustenance: a requirement of human beings. It gives them energy, helps them to think clearly, and keeps them healthy. His favorite way to re-energize was munching down some seared protein wedges, with lots and lots of salt. He loved salt, but sweet cane was his favorite. At this point he would have gone for a raw soy steak, or an old, dusty pack of vitamins, even if they had been soaked in clipper fuel and rolled in steel shavings.

Grumbling noises arose from his insides. Starvation was turning from an irritation to actual agony. His mind wandered, and he had to stop himself from thinking that his delirium was due to a lack of oxygen, and remind himself that it was the lack of nutrients in his body that was playing tricks on him.

There were a few things he knew for sure. First: he had woken up back inside the Glaven Grad tower, and was inside of an empty interrogation room. Second: since the room didn't have a table or even a chair, he knew that they weren't going to be asking any questions, or wanting to know if more of his memories had returned. Third: something had been implanted into the underside of his right arm. It was a small, tubular device held into place by cauterized flesh. If it had been stitched, Kraj would have been able to simply pull the stitches out and remove the device, but it had been meshed with the muscle tissue beneath his skin. Fourth: he knew this would be the last room he would see before being executed.

He didn't have a clue as to how long he had been in there – it had to have been days – or what it was that the Moras had implanted within his arm. There was a moment when he thought that banging on the walls or screaming for help would lead to the door opening, but decided to save his strength in case another opportunity came along for him to run. Given everything that had already happened, he doubted they would make that mistake again. He also doubted that he would have any trace of energy left to try anything. Simply lifting his swollen arm off of the floor where he lay was laborious.

What had they done to him? What were they going to do to him? How would they execute him? Decapitation? Would he be impaled and thrown into a hole? Anything but the experiments. Turning into a slave of Chaos was his worst and only fear. He had infiltrated Glaven Grad to help the rebellion, not to become a pawn used against it.

There was no way for him to contact anyone – he

was on his own. He had agreed to it though: the danger and possible fatal consequences of his mission. When he'd spoken to Feres about potentially taking on the position of a mole within Glaven Grad, part of him knew his end would come in the awful city of replicas. Seeing home again was something he'd tried to let go of before he even left.

He thought about all of the intelligence he had sent to Feres, and hoped some of it could do some good. At the very least, the rebellion would be more aware of what to expect when facing Chaos in battle. But beyond that, he just wanted to provide them with information that would bring about the end of the war in the form of a victory for the humans.

Knowing the outcome of his efforts was something else he would need to let go of.

Kraj was resigned to his death, and welcomed it as long as it would end his starvation. Cekanja and the kids would have to go on without him, but it was a fair trade for the advantages he'd provided to Feres. He hoped that whatever came after death would eventually reunite him with his family, and that he would see them again.

In the midst of his mind picturing the end, the door slid open. A Valk stepped through. Outside in the corridor, he could see another four Valks, waiting to see if he fought back. He didn't. Instead, he just gave the Valk an elbow and let it pull him off the floor and out of the bright room.

As they walked him down the corridor of tall windows, he stumbled and waited for them to toss him out of one. Each time they came to another window, he was sure it was the last. But they kept going, bringing him down multiple floors to a room with a glass chamber inside of it that he recognized as one of Mora's experimental laboratories.

No, he thought. This can't be!

Too tired to resist, he let the Valk push him into the chamber, and into a line of other tired humans waiting to die. The same human woman he had seen perform experiments on her own kind entered the chamber, placing a vial of pink liquid on a small table along the wall.

"How ees dee daily grind?" Kraj asked, chuckling sarcastically with what little energy he had to do so. "How long unteel you betray Chaos?"

She ignored him, pulling up a holographic tool and scrolling through it. The other humans were shivering, malnourished skeletons. It didn't even seem like they knew where they were, or like they even cared. Some had the same cauterized implant under their right arm, same as he did. They were doomed no matter what they did, and they knew it. Just like Kraj.

He wondered if the others were defectors, or if they

were simple captives. There really was no difference at this point.

The woman closed out the hologram, and plainly addressed the pitiful humans as a whole. “Today, you will all serve the purpose which you came here to serve. You will all become conduits to the destruction of humankind, and to the rise of Chaos. The Demigods thank you for your participation in this experiment, and we hope your help will allow us to leave this planet in ruins sooner rather than later.”

Kraj doubted that any of them had volunteered to participate.

“You know dat dey won’t bring you along weeth dem once Earth is deepleeted. Don’t you?” He couldn’t help but poke at her once more.

Stifling her annoyance, the woman put an elbow in Kraj’s gut. She wasn’t particularly strong, but it still sent him to his knees.

“Today we’ll be trying something new,” the traitor continued. “Some of you have been implanted with acetylators which will help facilitate the experiment, and some of you have not. However, you should all be proud to serve your Demigods with your lives.”

Moras filed into the chamber, lining up in front of the humans and each standing before a sickly individual. Two Valks came in also, each grasping Kraj by an arm and pulling him back up to his feet. Then they walked out and left the Moras and humans there, staring at each other.

When the traitor approached Kraj, she said, "Your D.N.A. seems to be the most compatible with the acetylator, Crassa. I look forward to seeing how you-"

A blind surge of furious energy blasted through from his chest to his right arm, and he found himself with his hand around her throat. Clenching her airway shut, he smiled through the pain of his cramping forearm muscles. Valks rushed back into the room, but the Mora standing beside the traitor put its hand up to stop them.

"Run a preliminary access attempt," it ordered, staring curiously at Kraj.

Another Mora pulled up a holographic operating system via a handheld device and began manipulating it. Kraj didn't pay any mind to them, focusing on holding his grip tight as the woman began uselessly pounding on his arm with her fists. It winded him to keep his arm muscles solid and his fingers locked, but her swelling eyes and bulging veins made it all worth it. Soon he would have one last kill under his belt before dying in this glass room.

Without warning, his fingers betrayed him, fighting his strength as if someone was pulling them away. He struggled against the invisible force until his knuckles cracked and his pinky snapped backward, breaking.

"It's working," announced the staring Mora. "We've

successfully accessed the acetylator. We can now control his functions."

The traitor jerked from his grasp as his other fingers bent all the way back, separating the bones from his hand beneath the skin. Kraj cried out in pain. What the Hector had just happened? His hand went limp just as the second Mora closed out its operating system. The closest he could imagine as to what had just happened was that his body was hacked. That's what it felt like when his fingers fought his commands and did just the opposite.

He grunted, wordlessly trying to take his mind away from the pain in his hand. The woman coughed and rubbed at her neck. Before he could even defend himself the woman's fist connected with his cheek. It wasn't enough to put him down, but when he turned back to her she put another one straight into his nose. The cartilage snapped, spewing blood over the floor and down his throat. His eyes immediately filled with what little water he had left in his body.

"I knew this was the one," announced the traitor, still catching her breath. "Mora won't be disappointed this time." She took the lid off of the pink vial on the table, and a strange smoke emitted from it. Then she stepped out of the door and said, "You may commence."

With his whole body cramping, stomach churning, hand shattered and nose shoved into his sinuses, he held his bloody face and choked down blood. Kraj looked up at the Mora standing over him through blurry tears. It leaned its head all the way back, opening the hole at the front of its throat. A burning, acid-like substance sprayed out over him, getting in his eyes and all over his skin.

Screams erupted around the chamber. His eyes felt like they would scorch right out of his skull, and his skin was on fire. The bit that got in his mouth caused his saliva to foam up, and it all slid down his throat, delivering a sharp, twisting stone to his gut. It made breathing nearly impossible.

He was so tired of being out of breath in this Kaisering tower.

Solid muscle cramps ran up his left side, and he toppled over, expelling involuntary bile all over the floor. Footsteps hurried out of the room. When he finally peeled his swollen eyes open he saw the treacherous woman observing from the other side of the glass with a smile.

He regretted not taking out as many of them as he could before it came to this. Even in his weakened, starving state, with what little adrenaline he had left, he couldn't even have dispatched that one, singular woman. Regardless, he wanted nothing more than one last chance to show the replicas the true meaning of chaos.

The blood in his veins got hot, and his bones ached as if they were breaking down into dust inside his body.

He gurgled a bubbling cry of pain, trying not to choke on his own stomach foam. With nothing but the blurry bodies of the other writhing humans around him, and the terrible taste of the foaming acid, Kraj readied himself for death, telling himself that it was almost over, and that the pain he was feeling would be the worst of it.

He was wrong.

Even through his closed eyelids, he could still see the green light as it pulsed throughout the chamber. The cells in his skin started to boil and change. They weren't dying; they were becoming something else. His muscles tore, and he could hear the ligaments crunch and separate as his body changed shape.

Ringing stabbed his ears, and before his vision went out he caught one last glimpse of the sizzling subjects around him. Fluids in his brain rushed around, slamming against his skull like a hammer. His hair fell out, and what remained of his epidermis was burned, bloody carnage.

What was all of this? He wouldn't even know what his cause of death was, only that he was bombarded by chemicals, poisons and some kind of radiating light that was quite harmful to the flesh of humans – according to what he was experiencing.

He always assumed people felt weak and exhausted when they approached death, slipping into a deep sleep from which they would never awaken. Eventually the body would just give up, knowing that by clinging to life it is only damning itself unto further affliction.

If that were true, then why was he starting to feel stronger than he had ever felt?

Twice as thick as they were seconds ago, his muscles throbbed with such intensity that he could feel his whole body jerk with the beat of it. Everything attached to his physical being was a different shape, and his teeth were replaced by sharp blades that sliced up the inside of his mouth.

As more and more of Zakopat Kraj diminished and reformed, he fell away from himself. Just like the glinting silver of the convoy's rear trailer pulling away from him, he sunk back into his subconscious, only able to watch his actions as they occurred.

Kraj was no longer able to will his unrecognizable limbs to move.

They moved on their own.

16

ZAKOPAT KRAJ V

High Cleric Astor Seemik III

WIND SWEPT in from the west, bringing clouds of dust about Sandramedius. Even the solar panels covering the city couldn't keep the blasts of granules from penetrating through to the ground. Small openings between the panels let much of the sand and wind in.

Seemik pulled a hood over his head, closing it to only expose his nose and mouth as he walked from the Library to the front gates. A frustrating occurrence kept repeating itself back in his labs: while running every kind of test on the Shard, his equipment would break down, mysteriously malfunctioning until it ceased working altogether. So far, the Shard had broken x-ray scanners, electrical current builders, short wave analyzers and his most precise radar emitter, among other things.

The pile of junked machines was building up behind the Library, and yet no results had been rendered. It seemed the one object capable of examining the Shard without breaking was the human eye. Only one thing was worth noting, and all it did was raise more questions. Seeing one of the lights move seamlessly through the glass, exit the Shard and zoom away, was the only observable piece of information he was able to gather from the elusive artifact. It was definitely something he would have to bring up to Lito.

Only Lady Feres, Captain Shou and Seemik were allowed to access the city's gates, and as soon as he heard that Lito and Mercelle had arrived he headed over to approve the opening of the entrance.

The crow's nest was being hit hard with waves of sideways flying sand, so he went to the office beneath it. The officer inside provided him with a feed from a vesp struggling to stay in a hovering position outside the gates. On the screen were two clippers, sitting and waiting to come in.

On one clipper was Lito, barely even squinting in the sandstorm. The other had two occupants, and at first he assumed it was Mercelle and Ashlan, but after closer inspection he saw a large, dark human holding onto Mercelle on the back of the clipper. He had no hair, but there were bright white eyebrows that stood out on his hardened face. Sand whipped against his cheeks, but he looked used to it, and seemed more amazed at the vesp moving about than the actual sandstorm.

Mercelle had a cloth wrapped around her head, with only her goggles showing. Her feet were huge. Swollen? No, bandaged. She had gotten herself injured, and he would have to get a medical Scholar to look at her feet right away. A blatant rising of joy filled him up to know that she had made it back okay.

Apparently, not everyone was so lucky.

"Open the gates, please, Officer," he ordered the man twice his age.

Seemik's joy was peppered with an irritated resentment for the strange man who had his arms around Mercelle's waist as the clippers came through. He wanted to ride on the back of her clipper, no matter how foolish he would look. At least she would see him being brave.

Why couldn't the man have ridden with Lito? Should it matter? Was he letting his age show? All the experience Seemik had – and at only nineteen years old – but he had none whatsoever in the category of females.

Everyone has to start somewhere, right? Only, his heart yearned to start and stop with Mercelle. Nobody had ever caught his eye and held his attention like she did. Mercelle and Order theorem, that was all the High Cleric needed in life.

They pulled in through the gates, and he greeted them promptly before closing the entrance to Sandramedius once again.

"Welcome back. I'd ask if there is any good news, but I see that you're down a man."

"Lost one," Mercelle said. "And gained another. This is Bewapen, from the Onyx Clan Lito told us about."

Bewapen clumsily got off of the clipper. "Hwee'o. I is Bewapen, is warrior of Onyx Clan. I is Ambassador of alliance, is sent by Kop Stamhoof."

He was wearing nothing but a piece of underwear bottoms that looked like they had been fashioned out of bent steel strips. Muscles were chiseling through his jet black skin, and a peculiar grey claw mark went across one of his round pecs.

Ashlan must have died during the attack on the magma tower they were going after. And to replace him they brought back Bewapen? Seemik wasn't happy about that, and hesitated when the new man held out a hand.

"Nice to meet you," Seemik told him, reluctantly shaking Bewapen's extremely strong hand. "I think. My name is High Cleric Astor Seemik, call me Seemik. I'm currently second in command over Sandra in Ashlan's absence. We'll have to let Lady Feres know that she'll need to promote a new First Officer." Seemik led the trio into the gate's control room to get them out of the whipping sand.

Shaking the dust from her head cloth, Mercelle ran fingers through her brunette waves, which were much shorter than the last time he'd seen her. The ends of her locks looked burned. "I'm surprised you didn't order full steel when you saw us pulling up with a stranger."

He had to admit to himself that he'd been tempted. "I wouldn't do that. I trust you enough not to bring anyone harmful or untrustworthy into Sandra." He tried to give her a playful look, but she was busy brushing herself off and stretching her muscles after a day and a half long clipper ride.

She sighed, popping her back as Lito greeted soldiers who stopped to say hello, and Bewapen gazed at the structure around him in astonishment.

"I thought Ashlan was already out of the tower when I blew the charges," she explained. "I don't know what happened to him. The Onyx Clan sent search parties after him, but there was no sign. No body or anything. I'm thinking a piece of the tower may have landed on him after he got out. Maybe his chute failed to deploy properly. He might have burned up. I'm not sure."

"That's a shame," Seemik responded gloomily. "I'll have to contact his family members and let them know."

"What family did he have?" she asked, matching his gloom.

"A father and a young daughter, I believe." Seemik looked at Bewapen. "He was one of our best warriors. He died with honor."

"I is agree. I is sorry for fallen warrior, for family." The dark man bowed his head, seemingly remembering something that shook him a little bit, and whispering something in a foreign language.

Seemik couldn't help but feel the pain in Bewapen's saddened eyes. Although loss was a part of everyone's lives, he always thought that no one ever deserved to feel the accompanying emotions that came along with it. They could be torturous at times.

Suddenly, the man became more of a comrade than an obstacle. "We've all lost someone," he said. "Whoever you lost, I'm sorry."

"We do have some good news," Lito joined in. "After we attacked the tower, Bewapen's Clan took us in and got us medical help. We met with their Kop – their leader – and they agreed to an alliance with the rebellion. They are awaiting a messenger to let them know when they are needed."

"Can't we contact them by radio?"

Mercelle laughed. "They don't use technology. All they need is metal working, combat, Order and loyalty. Feres is going to love them. They're going to be a great asset once we coordinate with Naselba and Kerk."

Was she laughing at him? Of course not. He didn't like the ego his lustful thoughts were bringing about. He reminded himself that he wasn't Naselban and he wasn't going to get what he wanted simply because he wanted it. Entitlement didn't suit him well, and it would only contribute to the detriment of his image as a young High Cleric.

No one deserved to experience loss, and no one deserved to have their role besmirched.

"Perhaps we can help them to advance their resources once the war is over," he said. "It's always been assumed that the Black Race had disappeared along with the Grey and Crimson. This is a great discovery."

"We didn't quite discover them," Lito corrected. "More like they chose to be found. They survived for millions of years by staying hidden in underground caverns, caves and magma flow systems deep below the surface."

"That's fascinating. One of the theories I've proposed about the Book of Order is that the texts are directly linked to our blood, and the Races that make up our genetic codes. See, I think it's possible that only those with that particular Race making up their D.N.A. can translate the writing. It's almost like a latent, inherited ability to see the glyphs' meanings. We'll have to put that to the test."

"Have you learned anything from the Shard yet?" Mercelle asked, always curious for progress.

"Not much. All we know for sure is that it causes any machine or device used on it to malfunction and break down. I'm not sure if that's informative. But, there was one reaction that occurred just after we arrived yesterday. So, the Shard is filled with those small, blue spark-looking lights, right? Well, just before we brought it into the Library to start the tests, one of the sparks came through the glass around the outside of the Shard, and took off. I tried to get eyes on it, but the last we saw it was travelling at great speeds away from the city, heading northeast."

"That's where we were," Mercelle pointed out. "Do you think it's related? I didn't see anything go by us. You?"

Lito and Bewapen both shook their heads.

"Lito, do you have any idea what that was?" Seemik asked. "Or what it might have meant?"

"I couldn't say. What would you theorize?"

"Oh." He sighed, moving the cogs in his brain to catch up with Lito's question. "So far I've thought about time passage: it's possible that it used to have many more sparks inside and that one leaves every so often. Of course, the implications of that would be that time is running out, or that it's counting down to something. Daunting, I know. Another potential theory is that it's a homing beacon sending a signal into space, maybe Leto, but let's hope not. Lastly, they could be bits of Lito's powers or memories slowly returning to Him. Which begs the question: could we smash it open to get the rest of them out?"

"I vote against the smashing," Mercelle said with a finger up.

"I vote we do nothing with it until we can be more sure we won't ruin it. I'll give it back to Lito and see if it reacts to His extended presence in any way."

"If that's all we can do," she replied with a shrug.

"It is. I can't risk damaging any more equipment on it. In the meantime, I'd like to take Bewapen here down to the Library and have him look over the Book. I want to see if he recognizes any of the glyphs. Maybe he can help us make some sense of the Black Text."

"I is go only where Lito is go," Bewapen said.

"I'll come along," Lito agreed.

Mercelle yawned, itching at the edges of her bandages along her ankle. "I'm pretty tired. But, I can't miss this. Let's go."

He knew that she was stalling. Ever since she'd shown up in Kerk she had avoided the topic of her medical results. The last he had heard was that they were in, but some of them were being double checked, which usually wasn't a good sign. The last thing he wanted was to upset her by apprising her of the status of the results.

"Afterward," he stated. "I'd like to sit down and talk

with Bewapen about his Clan. Their history and lineage are things we need to add to the digital history catalogs of humankind. I think we have a lot to learn from each other."

"I is happy to talk," Bewapen told him.

"Great. I'll let Lady Feres know that you've arrived safely. She's been waiting for you."

"I'm sure she wants to talk to me about my test results."

"We should also have your bandages looked at," Seemik suggested.

"It can wait. This is more important anyway."

This was what happened when a headstrong personality faced a situation beyond their control. Denial, avoidance and procrastination. None of which were going to help, he thought.

"THAT'S INTERESTING," Seemik said to Bewapen as they walked up the steps to the Library. "You say that the Onyx Queen who gave birth to the first Grey-Black hybrid child prophesied the coming of Mother Aeterna? If the Grey Race was integrated into the Black Race's bloodline, then some of the Grey genes may still carry on within you. If you're a descendant of that child, that is."

Bewapen pointed to the grey claw marks across his

chest. "Much of Clan is descendants of hybrid child. Few is not. Kop is not, is pure Onyx, no Grey. Litar – Kop's son – and all females but one is pureblood."

They reached the entrance, and Seemik pushed the ornate double doors open. Bewapen stopped to admire the soldered design in the metallic material. Inside the doors was a woman in a fitted uniform that clung to her long arms, sitting behind a reception desk.

This Library was much different from the Great Library that used to stand in Lanna in that it didn't have anything on display. It was more of a building for offices, classrooms, laboratories and meetings of the High Court. All of the digital records of human history, geography, technology and Order were stored there for the public to access anytime via a convenient terminal.

"If Seemik's theory is true," pondered Lito. "And you have the Grey genes in you, then that would suggest that you could translate both the Black and Grey texts."

"Theoretically," Seemik supposed.

Mercelle, who was limping along behind them with an arm around Lito's shoulders, replied, "If only everything could have been that simple. Look at how long it took us to translate the Yellow Text. Assuming that we were only able to do it because of a latent Yellow gene in our D.N.A., we should have been able to decipher it as easily as the other Texts. Right?"

"Not necessarily," Seemik answered, happy to clear up her confusion. "To add to my previous theory linking genes to abilities to translate the Sacred Texts, it's possible that the amount of genes present corresponds with the individual's ability to translate said Text. For example: the main human population is a mixture of Brown, Tan, White and Yellow genes. Yellow may be the least prevalent, therefore, the Yellow Text would be difficult to comprehend, but not impossible. If Bewapen's Grey D.N.A. is too latent, it might not work. Again, it's just a theory."

"It depends on the human," added Lito. "One's capacity to connect with their genetic background may determine their ability to translate. Consider that the Scholars who translated the Texts weren't able to fully access their Yellow genetic makeup hidden deep in their subconscious, because it was recessive to the other genes. They weren't able to decipher the Yellow Text on their own because of that, but they were able to create a program to help. As long as Bewapen is clear headed, it's very possible he could do it on his own, especially since his blood is more pure than most other humans."

"And considering the Onyx Clan's deep connection to their genetic heritage," Mercelle said. "He's probably a better candidate than most."

It all made perfect sense within the parameters of his theory. "I agree," Seemik threw in, taking them up a flight of stairs to the second level where the Order artifacts were stored.

"I is clear in head, is happy to try my hardest."

"That's the spirit," Mercelle said with a light punch to Bewapen's shoulder. "At the very least, you can help us construct another translation program. We could always use another one of those."

Seemik suddenly found himself dreading the tedious task of trying to explain to Bewapen what a program was, or even how a terminal worked. Perhaps that was why Lito was so taken with the man and his Clan: because human technology was as foreign to Bewapen as it was to Lito when He first woke up.

"It would be a long process to construct a new program with someone who doesn't even understand electrical signals." He sighed, entering a hall with high ceilings, and doorless rooms branching off. "We'll see what we can do in the lab first."

"I have faith in Bewapen," Lito assured.

"I is thankful," Bewapen replied.

ALONG ONE WALL of the room were seven tall screens going from the floor to the ceiling. Each screen was bordered in a different color that indicated which page it corresponded to.

The first screen was outlined in Crimson, the second in Black, and the third in Grey. Those three only showed scans from the pages in those colors, as nothing had been translated from them.

Continuing with the order of the Sacred Writings, the next four had full translations of the Brown, Tan, White and Yellow Texts, respectfully. The incomplete story of Order was the centerpiece of the laboratory, and Seemik watched as Bewapen looked over each screen with wet, curious eyes.

"As you can see, we've finished the last four pages of the Book," Seemik explained. "But, we've hit a wall with the first three. Many Scholars, myself included, believe that the most important information lies in the first pages. Suffice it to say, we're very glad that you're here."

Bewapen gave him a you're welcome smile.

Mercelle went into further detail for him. "The Brown Text explained that Lito was defeated by His brother Leto, who we believe to be Lito's twin, and the God of Chaos. Afterward, Lito was sent to Earth in an asteroid to die. The Tan Text talks about the creation of the Seven Races, and the Chaos creatures left behind which evolved to make up the fauna of Earth for millions of years. Next is the White Text, which says that Lito went into a deep sleep after creating the Races, and a temple was built to house His body." She stepped down the line of screens as she explained each one. "The Book of Order was created as a record of humanity's origin, the Races split up to populate the Earth, oh, and it talked about the Shard being hidden somewhere on the planet.

"The last page of the Book – the Yellow Writings –

indicated a location of where the Shard was hidden, and told us that the Shard would provide Lito with a direct connection to the 'Source' and to His power. We obtained the Shard, but we still don't know how to use it, or even what this 'Source' is exactly."

"You know your Texts," Seemik flirted with a cute grin. "Why am I not surprised?"

"Well, if your whole life revolved around a single, ancient document, wouldn't you remember every detail?"

"We have quite a lot in common, don't we?" He raised eyebrows at her, but she looked away, causing his chest to feel like it had just been impaled by a hot stake. Clearing his throat, and trying to refocus, he asked Bewapen, "So, do you know *how* to read?"

There must have been some unintentional aggression in his voice, because Mercelle looked at him like he had just slapped her mother.

"It's a fair question," he defended with a regretting shrug. "I need to know where he stands with interpretations. We don't want him dictating 'up' when it really says 'down'."

She nodded in hesitant understanding.

"Clan is only speak, is no write anymore. I is learn some ancient symbols with Kop and Queen, is not many though." Bewapen rubbed the white stubble sprouting atop his head. Was he getting nervous?

Seemik kind of enjoyed the feeling of making such a

large, strong man question himself. Muscles weren't everything. If only Mercelle could see that.

"Nobody understood any of the glyphs in the Book when we first discovered it," Mercelle told Bewapen. "There wasn't a person alive who was familiar with the languages written inside. But, something within the Scholars allowed them to figure out what we have today."

Lito added, "It's an innate sense of self and species that lives in the subconscious."

"That sounds like something *you* would create," she replied.

"Some believe scientific efforts will allow us to translate the remaining Texts," Seemik added. "Others believe that it is fate for humankind to finish translating the Book." He already knew what Lito was going to say.

"Free will is always going to serve you just as well as fate. True free will is being able to decide for yourself what you believe in. Trust in your heritage, and it will help you in return."

"I couldn't have said it better myself," replied Seemik. He punched in the access code to the glass case against the wall that housed the Book of the Seven Races. The clear front panel slid to the side, and he withdrew the Book, turning and handing it to Bewapen. Then he pulled a mechanical arm down from the ceiling and aimed it at him. "I'm going to record this, if you don't mind." Bewapen shook his head as if he had no idea what he was being asked. "Great. This will capture your visuals and audio, just stay seated and don't move out of the frame." He adjusted the arm into the perfect position, trying to contain his excitement.

The buzz of this important moment kept him from dwelling on Mercelle's rejection. This was, after all, one of the biggest moments of his life after being promoted to High Cleric. To witness the translating of an ancient Text was something very few people would experience, which was why he opted to record the attempt.

Bewapen opened the Book to the first page. It was Crimson on the front and back, and he paused to take a breath before flipping it and revealing the front half of the Black page. His rough finger pads touched the symbols there, and he traced them diagonally from corner to corner.

"I is..." Bewapen started. "...see words."

Seemik smiled ear-to-ear, and asked, "Can you tell us what it says? What words are you seeing?" He held his breath.

Bewapen squinted into the page. "I is see words in my head. More I is look, more I is see. I is no understand."

The High Cleric exhaled. "Not understanding what, Bewapen? Are the words not making sense?"

The Onyx man shook his head again.

"He isn't understanding how he's able to see it in his head," Lito answered for him. "He's never read anything before, but the instinct is taking over." He crouched down beside the struggling man, putting a hand on his bare knee. "Take another breath, Bewapen. Clear your head."

Bewapen did as instructed, letting his shoulders drop a bit as well.

"Remember your heritage," added Seemik. "Close your eyes and recall all of the lore and stories you've been told of your ancestors."

Mercelle even got in on the coaching. "Try picturing your Queen all those millions of years ago when she gave birth to the first Grey-Black hybrid child. You are that baby's ancestor. Your blood is the same."

Bewapen breathed deep, and opened his eyes.

Seemik froze as the man's eyes and fingers went to the page. There was a moment when none of them blinked or moved, waiting for something to come from Bewapen's mouth.

After what felt like an eternity, he finally spoke a single sentence, but in the Clan's language.

"What does that mean?" asked Seemik with a hint of skepticism.

Lito translated, "*As Lito is the origin of humans...the Source is the origin of power in the universe.*"

"He's got it!" shouted Seemik, taking up his tablet and scribbling notes into it. Lito remained pensively staring, and Mercelle's hands went over her mouth.

"Wow, Lito picks up on new languages very quickly. Go on, Bewapen. What else does it say?"

The calm man cleared his throat, and continued examining the page closely. After every sentence he would stop and wait for Lito to interpret. "*The Source is the origin of power in the universe...the Source was hidden from the twin boys by the God King, their Father...the King intended to appoint a successor, and bestow the Source to a single son...but the God King died before He could appoint or bestow...the twins searched for the Source...*"

Bewapen stopped to turn the page.

"I'm struggling to put it all together," inserted Mercelle, rubbing her temple. "At least we know what the Source is now, kind of."

"I think what he's saying," began Seemik. "Is that the Source is the origin of Lito's power, and of Leto's power. We already know that the Shard is Lito's conduit to the Source, which is why His power comes from it, somehow. It sounds like their father kept it from them, and died before naming His successor and bestowing the Source upon them, so the twins searched for it together." He looked to Lito to confirm, forgetting that if He was capable of confirming such things then they would be miles ahead of where they were now in regards to their translation progress.

Seemik's eyes locked onto the Onyx man with glorious anticipation, and the reading and translating continued.

"*The twins searched for eons...*" Lito went on while Bewapen read the other side of the Black page aloud. "*The twins found the Source together...agreed to share the power...the Source bestowed power unto the twins and made them into Gods...one became the God of Chaos...the other became the God of Order...the Source was broken into two...*"

Bewapen stopped to turn the page again.

Seemik's heart jumped a beat as he watched the man's eyes scroll across the back of the Grey page. "Wait. Are you reading the Grey Text?" He flipped the page back as the Book sat on Bewapen's lap. "This part here," he pointed to the front of the Grey page. "Is this what you were just reading?"

Bewapen nodded. "I is no realize. Grey is okay to read too. Words is appear in my head, symbols is change, I is understand it."

"So then it *is* true." Mercelle glowed with a smile. "As long as the bloodline exists in the person, they can read, or at least decipher, the Text."

"That's very good, Bewapen," Lito told him. "Your hybrid blood is allowing you to read multiple pages."

"Astonishing," added Seemik, giddy and trying to steady his shaking hands. Up until he saw Bewapen flip that Grey page, he was sure the Grey Text would remain untranslated like the Crimson. "Keep reading. Let's see what else it says."

Bewapen went to the back side of the Grey page.

"*The Source was broken into two...*" Lito translated.

"Chaos tried to kill Order...but Chaos failed...near death...Chaos replicated a giant monster...the monster decimated the armies of Order..."

Bewapen stopped, looking at the next page made of Brown stone.

Seemik was happy to put it into perspective, reading from his notes as Mercelle's face began scrunching into a pensive struggle, likely putting the same pieces together as he was. "So," he pointed to Lito. "After you and your brother found the Source, you agreed to split it in half, creating two pieces. Which means that there's another Shard out there, probably being used as Leto's conduit to the power of the Source. You both became Gods, and when Leto tried to overthrow you He failed and almost died. But, He ended up using His Godly powers to replicate a giant monster and kill Lito's armies. The Brown Text is next, and it goes on to explain how Lito was sent to Earth in an asteroid to die. It's all starting to come together."

Mercelle slapped Bewapen on the back of his shoulder. Even behind her force he barely moved. "We almost have a complete picture of the history of Order," she said.

"Technically," Seemik replied. "We have the entire history of Order. The Black Writing explained how Chaos and Order both came to be."

"Which only makes you more curious to find out what the Red Text says."

"Exactly. What came before Chaos and Order?"

Lito stood up, staring at the floor with hands on His hips. "The theory about bloodlines making one capable of translating the Texts is true. This means that there will never be a way of reading the Red Text. According to the Kop, the Red Race died out millions of years ago after refusing to taint their bloodline."

This was true. If Seemik didn't have access to a member of the Red Race, then he would be stuck trying to create translation programs for the rest of his life. None of them would work. Perhaps if he had access to some of their D.N.A., he could find a way of either breeding a hybrid or reverse engineering a lab clone. Either process would require intelligence beyond what he was capable of understanding, as well as a blood sample from a long extinct Race.

That would all have to come later. Now, he was in the midst of a moment worth celebrating. He couldn't wait to report to Feres and the rest of the rebellion what they had just learned. Bewapen was going to be a hero in Sandra.

"Thank you, Bewapen," said the High Cleric. "You don't know how you've helped the faith of Order. I and everyone in Sandramedius will always be grateful for what you've accomplished today."

"Hwee'o gee," replied the Onyx man. "You is welcome."

He was just a tad jealous of Bewapen. After all, the

dark man not only caught the eye of Mercelle, but he also had the honor of easily translating two of the Seven Texts of Order. There was something to be learned from the dark man, and Seemik felt his jealousy roll over into a type of respect and admiration. The High Cleric was smarter than jealousy; he knew that looking up to Bewapen and learning from him would better serve everyone and everything he worked to uphold.

Humility, he thought, was never easy for anyone, especially a nineteen-year-old High Cleric.

"We should report this to Lady Feres," advised Lito.

Seemik was simply buzzing with elation. "I'll forward her the recording immediately."

17

DREDGER IV

Kerk's economy, although stimulated by the recent giving up of prisoners to Chaos, was declining. The people couldn't tell, but those within the Board of Marshals over the city were preparing for the first recession they'd ever experienced. With the war heating up and two of the rebellion's cities leveled in the last few weeks, work wasn't being offered to Dredger or his team of diggers.

Soon their rations would run low, and their fuel would start to become scarce. Dredger had already spoken to the Transportation Marshal Blomstre about converting all of their vehicles to solar power, but the larger machines would be more difficult, as solar power tended to take away from torque and horse power unless larger modifications were made which he wasn't sure Kerk could afford at this time. It would also require a great number of their vehicles to have access to the sun instead of their typical underground storage. He would be needing mechanical supplies for the work as well, which were dwindling along with their stores of rations.

In his desperation for work to support his city, he had put a call in to Deputy Secretary Vtoro in Naselba. Sitting in the Outward Projects office, he listened while Vtoro explained that Naselba had no construction jobs at the current moment.

"Do ya think that might change by the time the summit comes around?" Dredger asked. "I could do some work for ya while I'm there."

"Hmm," considered the Naselban. "Our communications building could use some updates. While you're here you'll be a guest of our city. In return you could do some work on it. How about that?"

The man was having fun, making a joke at Dredger's expense. If he didn't need the work as bad as he did, he would have hung up the call right then and there.

"Look, I don't really want to come to your little meetin'," Dredger told him. "I was convinced to. I'm willin' to do the work on your buildin', but I would need to be paid for it. Kerk is headin' toward a financial hole we may not be able to dig ourselves out of. We could really use the help."

"We would have to see how the meeting goes, and whether or not the Empress allows it."

Dredger bit his tongue, but then let it loose. "If the summit don't go well, then ya may as well tear down your communications buildin', I'm sayin', because neither Kerk nor Sandra will have any reason to communicate with ya further."

"I don't see why the summit wouldn't go perfectly fine." Vtoro's nonchalant tone made Dredger's temples heat up. "As long as everyone gets what they want I don't foresee any issues."

"Ya mean as long as your 'Empress' gets what she wants? I'm not sure if ya know this, but the purpose of gettin' all us figureheads together is to plan an attack on Glaven Grad. If we don't do somethin' to preserve mankind now, we may not get another chance, I'm sayin'." He was starting to sound like Mercelle and Seemik.

"Empress Edeen isn't afraid of Chaos, and she has a plan for the future which she would like to discuss with you all."

"If that plan don't include a coordinated attack, it'll fall on deaf ears." He couldn't believe what he was hearing.

"Then we'll just have to see, won't we?"

Dredger rubbed his forehead and sighed. "I guess so. Look, Secretary, I-"

"Deputy Secretary."

"Sure. That's all I really needed to discuss with ya. I'll see ya in Naselba."

"We look forward to it," replied the stuck up Naselban.

He began to say something else, but Dredger cut the call off. He leaned back in his chair. Having been the one to build and install Naselba's communications hub, he was the best qualified to provide maintenance and updates to the structure. Now, he had no idea where Kerk's next round of provisions would come from. Sandra didn't need any work, and he didn't feel much like reaching out to Feres anyhow, not after she'd sent her whole posse to Kerk to convince Dredger to attend the summit.

No one else had ever been to Naselba – a city created by the offspring of the unholy Kaisers – only Dredger, and the city wasn't big on letting their people out. Mercelle had seen the outer walls with him once when travelling to a dig site, but only he had been inside, and it had been years. Citizens used to try and move there, the same way they would bring their families to another rebel city and adapt to their ways of living. For years, families flocked to the city of opportunity, only to be captured by Lady Edeen and her tyrannical laws. The worst of which being that once someone agreed to become a citizen of the city, they were not allowed to leave without express permission from the "Empress" herself. This permission was rarely granted, which made High Scholar Maalamon's presence in

Sandra quite suspicious. Dredger figured he was a spy for Edeen, and that Feres was well aware of it.

Many of the immigrants were forced into servitude, cleaning up after and tending to the needs of any Naselban descended from the Kaisers. Dredger could only hope that Edeen didn't try that with them when they arrived. Mercelle and Feres would take down the entire city before allowing themselves to be subdued.

With no work to be done for the other cities, Kerk would have to evolve into a more self-sufficient municipality. By expanding their turbine systems and irrigating some of the moisture beneath Kerk upward, they could try and start their own soy fields. During the years of digging deeper into the Earth and growing Kerk, Dredger had always hoped to come across some kind of precious mineral that would have provided a staple that could be sold when work was slow or nonexistent, like now.

Chaos must have done quite the number on the planet, because he hadn't found so much as a salt deposit. All he had was water, and not nearly enough to sell or profit off of. This was more stressful and scary than when he had risen up against Cakram and created an independent city, free from the rebellion. If something drastic didn't change soon, Dredger feared he may be facing his own uprising.

He needed something to bring his spirits up, something to remind him why he gave everything he had every day.

Attaching his tablet to the stand on his desk, he dialed Kizi. Her face came up on the screen when she answered. A thin scarf wrapped around her hair, she beamed and greeted him with her warm smile. His heart fluttered a bit, and any worry he had sunk away.

"Hello, my love. How are ya enjoyin' the new apartment?"

"It's just great," she said. "The stove works perfectly, and I just got the sun monitor set up. I can't wait to give you a tour when you get home."

"I'm glad ya like it. And I'm sorry – again – for the way I acted. Been under a lot of pressure lately, and I just wanted the best for ya. I promise I won't do that again."

"What? Destroy all of the electronics?" She gave him that look, which told him she knew more than she was leading on. "I know there's more to it than just you being under pressure. It's okay, I trust you. I know that everything you do is to protect me and the baby. Here, look." Kizi put her tablet on its mount, and stood back from it so her entire belly showed. "She says 'hi daddy'."

What she said was true. Everything he did was for her and the baby. The main reason he agreed to attend the summit was to make sure he was giving every effort to end the war before his daughter was born. He wanted nothing more than to raise her in a Chaos free world.

Qabda walked through the open door to Dredger's office, sitting quietly in the chair on the opposite side of his desk. She gave a subtle smile to let him know that she wasn't here because of something urgent.

"I want her to have a tribal name," Kizi continued. "One from my family's lineage. Something like 'Lutka' or 'Mir', maybe even 'Nebesa'. What do you think?"

"I like all of those names," he replied. He would have loved anything Kizi came up with. "But, I love 'Nebesa'. What does it mean?"

"Nebesa? It means 'heaven'."

The glint in her eyes as she said the name warmed his insides. She was going to be the best mother, and he was certainly going to be a better father than the one he had been stuck with. Their daughter would never feel as if she was stuck with either of them, he thought, because they'll always be there to bring her up and support her in any way possible. With Chaos gone she'd have a freedom he never experienced, and would be the first generation to live without war since the reign of man began over fifty thousand years ago.

"It's perfect. Why don't we go with that one?"

"Nebesa," Kizi whispered, rubbing her belly. "Are you my little Nebesa?" A small jump. "Oh! She kicked! She loves it too!"

Qabda looked up and made a face like she wanted to cry from witnessing something overwhelmingly cute, but Dredger didn't think she was capable of it. A hand went to her chest and her mouth opened with an inaudible “aw”.

He couldn’t hold back a laugh, and he took one last, long look at Kizi before sitting up straight in his chair to show that he needed to get back to business.

“My love,” he said into the tablet. “Qabda just walked in. We won’t be long, I promise, and then I’ll be comin’ right home. Okay?”

“Qabda’s there? How is she?”

“I’m well,” answered Qabda, leaning over the desk. “How have you been feeling? Not long now is it?”

“I’m always doing great. Once I’m done settling into the new apartment you can come over and spend an evening. I haven’t seen Patni in some time, bring her and the kids along. I’d love to see you all.”

“I’d really like that. Maybe you can tell your man to give me some time off so I can come visit.”

They chuckled together playfully, and said their goodbyes. Dredger told her one last time how much he loved her, and that he would see her soon.

Once the call ended, Qabda stood to close the door. “Obviously the courier made it to Sandra just fine. Feres was able to send Lito and Mercelle to tear down the tower where the frequency weapon was being held?”

“Yep,” he said through a smile. “Thank ya for contactin’ Kraj for me. He did his job, and did it well.”

“He saved a lot of lives. I wonder where he is now.”

“Probably at home with his family, enjoyin’ the

trucks of rations I sent over to his tribe. Ya heard about Sandra translatin' a couple more pages of their Book?"

"Yes I did."

"At least someone's makin' progress."

"Hmm." She squinted at him.

"Hmm...what?" he asked.

Qabda put both hands into the air in a small, yet dramatic, shrug. "So?"

Dredger had no idea what she was getting at. "So...what?"

"So, I haven't seen you since before Feres's posse left a few days ago. I heard they were quite aggressive in persuading you to go to Naselba, but I wanted to ask you personally how it went."

He sighed, and ran a hand through his beard. "It was rough. First Feres's new High Cleric came at me, spoutin' his rhetoric about 'you have an obligation to humanity'. Him and his little band of Scholars told me that if Kerk doesn't fight, then the city will die either way. I didn't want to admit that I knew they were right, not until Mercelle came in."

"I'm sure she had much to say about it. Feres knew that if anyone could persuade you to do something you didn't want to, it would be Mercelle. That's why she sent her."

"And she got here just in time, I'm sayin'. I was about to kick 'em all out. But, she reminded me of everythin' we'd been through – reminded me that her parents sacrificed themselves to help save Kerk, same as Feres's. How could I deny that?"

Qabda stirred in her seat. "I'm sorry you had to go through all of that. If I was there I would have backed you up, no matter what."

"Ya. I know. Maybe it's better ya weren't there. I broke down, and I said I'd go. So I'm headin' out tomorrow to meet the others at Sandra so we can travel together. Feres wants us to put up a united front when arrivin' in Naselba. We just have to keep this quiet so Chaos doesn't realize we're workin' with the rebellion again."

Her face scrunched up in disapproval. "You agreed?"

"I had to. Seemik's right. Even if the rebellion wins the war without us, who's gonna help us improve our economy? Who's gonna pay us for work, or provide us fuel or rations? The rest of the world'll turn its back on us." Now he was starting to sound exactly like Mercelle and Seemik, repeating their exact words, telling someone they have no choice in the matter, and urging them to use logic to justify their path. In turn, he feared he was making Qabda feel attacked, the same way he'd felt before and after agreeing to attend the summit. However, Qabda had a more impersonal approach with her logic than an emotional one. "Besides, if I can help bring an end to Chaos before my daughter's born, I will. I need to."

She looked away from him, licking her teeth behind closed lips. It wasn't like her to have to stop and think about her words. Answers were typically on the tip of her tongue. "Kerk is barely scraping by as it is," she said with a heavy tone. "Even the new projects you've proposed will take time and resources that we just don't have. Joining in the war effort will ensure allegiances once the Demigods are eradicated. Our economy only has a few months left at the most before it collapses." The hatred for her own words showed on her wrinkled brow. "I would just hate to lose everything that you, me and the other Marshals have fought so long to protect. We created Kerk so that the masses of unclaimed lives in this world would have a place to come and be accepted, protected. To lose all of that..."

"We'll lose a lot more than just that if we don't budge, and now. Feres is barely holdin' the leftover parts of the rebellion together on her own, and we don't even know how Lady Edeen will react to our pleas for help in an integrated attack. It's going to take everything humanity has to give just to put up a decent fight."

"So we sacrifice our neutrality?" She looked up at him, with those hard eyes she loved to challenge with. "We give up everything we've built?"

"Either that or it'll be taken from us. We don't have any choice, not anymore, I'm sayin'. Neutrality was a temporary fix, and we used it to help us avoid war while we built our city and cared for our people. That won't keep workin', not like it used to." Sweat dripped down his forehead, and he wiped it away, trying not to shake while holding down a mixture of resentment and fear. "Part of me hoped that we could stay neutral until Lanna or Sandra took out the Demigods, but once I met Kizi, and especially when she became pregnant, all of that started to slowly change. I couldn't live with myself knowin' I didn't do everythin' within my power to protect my girls. Wouldn't ya do the same to protect Patni and your siblin's?"

Qabda and Patni had taken care of Qabda's three young siblings ever since her parents failed to do so, abandoning them to live a free life with the Oases tribes. The children may as well have been theirs.

"If I were in your position," her voice was more tamed and focused now. "I would do the same. I just wanted to make sure you knew why you were doing it. It isn't to protect your people, or to pay Mercelle or Feres back for the grief they experienced from losing their parents, it's to keep the ones you love safe. That's all anyone wants in times like these. Naselbans only want to protect themselves. Remember that when you're there."

He didn't know how, but Qabda always had a clearer perspective to provide, and the way she went about bringing him to his own point was immaculate. "Thanks for your understandin'."

The A.L.A. Marshal waved a hand in the air.

"Always. And don't worry about Kerk when you're gone, I'll take good care of everything for you. I suggest you take a fleet of construction vehicles just in case you're able to barter some work while you're out there."

"Nah," Dredger responded. "We can't afford the fuel, I'm sayin'. I'm just takin' a small security team, nothin' too big."

"Smart. It'll help keep you under Chaos' radar. If they find out you're helping plan an attack on Glaven Grad, they're likely to plan their own attack on Kerk. I'm surprised they didn't attack us right away after the tower was taken down. They must have suspected that Feres and the others had discovered it on their own. But, just in case, I'll make sure our Patrol and Defense departments are ready."

An idea came to him, one he couldn't find a flaw in. "I'm leavin' Marshals Muso and Taksin in charge while we're gone."

Just as expected, she cocked her head to the side and glared at him. "I've always overseen operations in your absence."

"I know."

"Then why-"

"You're comin' with me to Naselba."

Qabda's eyes got wide, and she shook her head. "I haven't left Kerk in years."

"Then I'm thinkin' it's time. I need someone who can make better points and use their words better than

I can. Ya can navigate all of those politics, and ya can argue a point perfectly, even when you're wrong. I'm just not as good at arguin' anymore."

"All true," she agreed. "And as a woman I'll be much better received than you. The Naselbans don't always take well to male leaders, not since the fall of the unholy Kaisers, and won't be likely to listen to anything you have to say with all of those other women around you."

Dredger shrugged in agreement. "It doesn't help that I'm a filthy construction specialist who used to dig ditches for Cakram."

Standing up from her seat, Qabda gave a proud posture and straightened the wrinkles from her uniform top. "You're the leader and founder of this great city, and I'm honored to come along and make sure you are treated as such. I'll help you out."

"I know ya will. Be ready to leave by mid mornin', and take the rest of the day off to be with Patni and the kids. I don't know how long we'll be gone."

With a nod, she turned and left the office, leaving the door open behind her.

The reasoning he gave for wanting Qabda by his side was all true, but he was surprised that she hadn't picked up on the other reason he hadn't mentioned: he simply needed someone he trusted. Having another person on his side would assure that he wouldn't be ganged up on again, not by Feres, or Lito and His followers, and hopefully not Edeen and her elitist High Court. Qabda would defend him to the ends of the Earth.

Lito had Mercelle, Feres had her Scholars and Dredger needed back up also. One thing he wanted to avoid at all costs was Qabda and Feres getting into some kind of debate or disagreement. Two unstoppable forces tended to break apart when slammed together. It would have been quite the spectacle to watch, if the fate of humanity didn't depend on them coming together.

Dredger shut down his office, and went home to spend the evening with Kizi, and their unborn daughter Nebesa.

18

LADY INIS MERCELLE X

To her surprise, her feet were almost entirely healed up when she got back to her A.L.C.O. and unwrapped the bandages. Whatever was in that sappidge juice was a miracle. It was almost as if Lito's ability to heal had been synthesized into a plant. After a few stretches, her feet were ready to kick some more ass. Blisters and tender skin still existed on her soles, and she wished she had more sappidge to put on it, but plain old ointment worked just fine, and the pain was nearly nonexistent.

After two nights with very little sleep outside of Sandra, Mercelle thought it best to call it an early night, despite not having even a touch of tiredness. The bed in her A.L.C.O. was much more comfortable than the open desert or Bewapen's cave. Lying down on the thin pad, wrapping herself in her sheet and hanging an exposed foot off the edge, Mercelle closed her eyes, letting every muscle go limp.

It was all pointless if her mind refused to switch off, but she just couldn't shut herself down enough to fall asleep.

It had been exciting to witness two of the remaining pages in the Book of Order translated with little effort by Bewapen. The news quickly spread throughout the city, and even reached Kerk and Naselba almost in congruence with the information's release. She didn't think a single soul was unhappy to hear about the progress.

That wasn't what kept her from falling asleep though. Her test results were still pending re-examination, which told her that something was wrong – the medical Scholars just needed to be sure about what it was.

It was an easy decision for her to get out of bed, strap boots over her newly healed feet and venture into the training area below the cafeterias. A good workout was the best thing she could do to occupy herself until morning, and perhaps it would wear her out enough to help her sleep afterward.

It was evening, and the sun was going down, spraying color across the sky over Sandramedius. She was surprised to see so many people exercising and sparring throughout the large training floor. There was even a class of young teenagers following instructions from a trainer on combat stances and best blocking techniques. She thought about standing in the back and following along, but she didn't feel much like socializing.

The training level was a large floor with sections of exercise machines, empty mats, sparring areas, stretching bars and even a roped off ring in the center of everything where a couple of men grappled with each other as a few others watched on. Shower halls and toiletry accommodations were through the door in the corner, and she took note on how to navigate through the sections to get to it.

Unsure of exactly what kind of workout she wanted to get in, Mercelle found an empty stretching mat against the wall, and began a routine of randomly working her muscles looser and looser.

She put flat hands on the wall, applying pressure to her calves one at a time until they felt strained and warm, then she bent in half at the waist to hit her thighs and lower back. Powering through her arms, chest and core, Mercelle got on one knee with her hands out in a pose that she was told couldn't be held for more than a minute by many workout partners. She loved to prove them wrong.

Her arms were perfectly straight, back semi-arched, legs tensed in the appropriate spots, and her neck was at the proper angle. Holding this position would allow blood to easily flow to her muscles, awakening them from stiffness and giving her the energy to operate which-ever machine she ended up on.

Medical Scholar Rakta's face flashed into her head. The things she had said to Mercelle about the possibility of radiation poisoning were bogeys she couldn't quite pinpoint. Having an enemy she didn't know how to fight was her worst fear, and she didn't even know how to go about formulating a strategy.

Two things were certain. One: she couldn't find a path to victory over this enemy until she knew for sure what it was. And two: her truth was that she didn't really want to know. Fighting was in her blood, and she reminded herself that she could battle through anything that came her way, no matter the physical effects it had on her.

Another truth that existed deep inside Mercelle's flow of thoughts was the fact that this could be the strongest she would ever be if her health steadily declined from this point forward.

"You should try straightening your back a bit," came a woman's voice from behind Mercelle.

She opened her eyes to see a tall woman with dark brown skin and black hair in a bun atop her head. The woman had to be a good decade older than Mercelle. Tight silgen workout gear clung to her skin, and the bulge of her exposed muscles were something to be envied.

"That stance kinda works best when you don't arch, it lets the blood flow more freely through the diaphragm. Here, let me show you."

The woman put a hand on Mercelle's chest, just between the base of the ribs. Mercelle flattened her torso, feeling her breath move more easily.

"How's that?" the woman asked.

"Better," replied Mercelle. "Thank you."

Reaching the end of her stamina, she stepped out of the pose and went to loosening up her shoulders some more, hoping to be left alone.

"You're Inis Mercelle, aren't you?"

She didn't feel like talking, but as soon as the woman asked her that, she immediately took herself away from the thoughts which had led to her coming down here in the first place.

"I am," she answered. "And you are?"

"I knew it was you. I saw you in the recording of that man translating the Book of Order earlier today. A lotta buzz that generated around the city. What was his name?"

"Bewapen."

"Bewapen. Right. From the Onyx Clan Lito discovered." She paused for a moment, shaking Mercelle's hand with a smile. "Sorry, I'm Bari Vayreni. I should say 'First Officer Vayreni', but you can just call me Bari."

"Nice to meet you, Bari." It actually made her feel less heavy to engage with someone, and she decided not to be so closed off, as this woman seemed quite happy to meet her. "I didn't know Lady Feres had promoted a new First Officer already. That was fast."

"I know." Vayreni shook her head. "Gotta be prepared though. It was a shame Ashlan didn't make it outta the tower. He was a good man. We all looked up to him."

"I wish I could have done more to help find him. I'm not exactly sure what happened, or where he went. I shouldn't have blown the charges so early."

The First Officer put a hand up to stop her from going on. "I read your report. You all went into that tower on your own accord, and when you split up like that it's every soldier for themself. Ashlan knew this. He wouldn't want you taking responsibility for what happened to him. You took down that tower and showed those Kaisering replicas who's boss. That's what matters."

"Thank you," Mercelle forced a smile. "I appreciate that. I just wish I knew more. We searched the entire area around the tower and found nothing afterward."

"I wouldn't worry about it. I'm sure he took out a tonna replicas before going down himself. What do you say we take your mind off of it? You looking for a sparring partner?"

Pummeling someone sounded great, and Mercelle

looked Vayreni up and down, sizing her up and deciding that she'd be quite the opponent.

"I'll take that as a yes," said Vayreni.

They laughed, and Mercelle told her, "That sounds like fun, actually."

Vayreni clapped her hands together loudly. "Let's go then! I've never trained with a Lanna soldier before. And don't think I'm gonna take it easy on you just because you're a Lady."

"Please don't. I kind of need to blow off some steam."

"I know what you mean. Come on, follow me."

Mercelle went with Vayreni to a wide mat next to the ring at the center of the floor.

"This mat's free," said the First Officer. "You loosened up enough?"

"Oh, I'm ready, Bari." Mercelle hadn't gone hand-to-hand in a few days, and couldn't wait to get started. "I hope you are too."

"Bring it, Lady," Vayreni teased back.

They both breathed deep, facing each other and taking their stances. Bari had open hands, as many experienced fighters did. It indicated a tendency to block and counter quickly or even simultaneously, since open hands worked best for deflecting a blow or grabbing a wrist. Mercelle preferred a more brutal tactic, balling up two fists and raising her shoulders to put the strength of her upper body behind them.

The two women stared each other down, each waiting for the other to swing first.

Just before Mercelle moved her foot to distract from an upper strike, she heard laughter coming from the ring next to them.

"Shouldn't you be training in dresses?" shouted an enormous man. He was standing over his unconscious opponent, perspiring heavily from solid flesh. His neck was as wide as his head. Devoid of a shirt, his silgen pants were soaked with sweat, and his pompous grin showed a perfect row of teeth which Mercelle imagined re-aligning with the sole of her boot. "Don't pull each other's hair, now. I'd hate to have to separate you two."

The group of men surrounding the ring all shared a communal guffaw. There had to be nearly twenty of them, each waiting their turn to spar in the ring. All of their eyes were on the pair of women, waiting for them to respond, or cry, or maybe run away in shame. Mercelle looked at Vayreni, expecting her to get embarrassed, but she just shook her head.

"To Hector with sparring," the Lady told the First Officer. "Be my tag team partner."

Vayreni scoffed. "I don't need your help to kick his ass."

"I don't just mean him."

"I like how your mind works." She lowered her arms. "Which ones you thinking of taking on?"

"Everyone," Mercelle mumbled, stepping over to the

ring and pulling herself up by the rope. "How about a wager, Fatneck?"

"Ha!" he laughed. "How about I pin the both of you?" He looked around at the other men. "If you know what I mean."

She really was going to have fun with this one. "Okay. Fine. If you can pin either one of us, I'll spend the night with you and let you do whatever you want to me." It may have only been obvious to her, but she was never going to be bested by any man in any ring. She simply needed to draw them in, and what better to offer than her own body?

Fatneck was shocked at first, but then began shouting in celebration and slapping hands with the other imbeciles who had no idea what was coming their way. "I'm getting some tonight boys!"

Mercelle couldn't help but laugh along with him – moreso at him. "How about this?" She raised her voice so the whole floor could hear her. "If any of you Emmetting assholes can pin First Officer Vayreni or myself, I'll gladly take you to bed." It wasn't a bad way to get laid. After all, a man that could best her in a fight would certainly be good in the sack.

The group of men went quiet, looking at Vayreni with surprise in their eyes.

"Um, Mercelle," she said with a tap on her leg. "I was just promoted this afternoon. Nobody knows yet."

"Oh. Oops." Mercelle shrugged. "Sorry, Bari, but they do now. Feel like showing them how to fight?"

Vayreni shrugged back, pulling herself up next to Mercelle. "You can have us both if you can pin just one of us. How's that sound?"

Bellowing hollers of testosterone-fueled merriment circled the ring. Mercelle was in it for fun, therefore, she was already winning. Her new friend was quite the find, and she couldn't wait to see Vayreni's skills.

"Alright soldiers," shouted Vayreni. "Line up. You're first." She pointed at Fatneck, who made a crude gesture with his fingers before telling her to hop into the ring. "You wanna take this one?"

"Nah," Mercelle answered. "I think I want to watch you hurt him a bit before I get in. Just make sure to give him a few for me."

"You got it." Vayreni winked at her before hopping the rope.

A long line of gleeful men built up behind Fatneck, peering over each other to get good views of the ring. The unconscious man on the floor came to, and crawled away to rest. Mercelle hoped he wouldn't be the kind of idiot to get in line for another knock out.

"Ready?" asked Fatneck.

"Ready," Vayreni replied.

They squared up, locking eyes to see where the other one may try to strike. Feet moving, both fighters began circling the ring. Mercelle's heart pounded for some action.

Fatneck swung a meaty arm, which Bari deflected easily with one hand, while slapping him across his face with the other. This embarrassed him, which was sure to bring him to anger instead of tact. It worked, and he ran at her, grabbing wildly, and putting a shoulder into her waist. An arm wrapped around her legs, and he picked her up.

When he went to slam her body into the floor, she held onto his giant neck, rolled back, and in a stunning display of strength and weight displacement, tossed the man upside down into the ropes. The whole ring shook when he landed on his head and flopped over onto his stomach.

"Yes!" Mercelle cried out over the roaring crowd of men. "Get him Bari!"

Fatneck wasn't injured, just stunned as they both got to their feet. Without thinking, the brute faked another lunge, then recoiled to try and get Vayreni to move forward into his space. It didn't work, and his strike proved fruitless. As his thick arm came at her with great strength, she spun around and used her momentum to put both forearms in its path to stop it. Then she kicked her inside leg up into the back of his shoulder, dislocating it, and then brought her boot down into the back of his knee.

His cries of pain were music to Mercelle's ears.

Watching him tell Vayreni "Enough!" was even better. She imagined he would think twice before taunting another woman.

Vayreni, who wasn't out of breath in the least, came over to Mercelle as Fatneck climbed gingerly down from the ring. He was going to have to head up to the medical bay to have his shoulder reset. She pictured a small team of medical Scholars holding him down while he wailed and dripped tears.

"See? Easy as Hector. You gonna get the next one?"

Mercelle didn't even need to answer. Climbing into the ring, she slapped Vayreni's hand, tagging herself in. "Who's next?"

Another muscle-bound soldier happily hopped into the ring. Didn't they know muscle wasn't everything? He was tall too, hovering over her by a good foot. Working the legs would be her best bet.

"I like to be bitten during sex," he said as they took their stances.

"You got it," she responded right before sweeping the legs.

He jumped over her boot, throwing an elbow at her as she came around, just as she expected. She put her own elbow into it, then wrapped her arm around his and pulled him backward. With a knee planted behind his legs, he toppled over, allowing her to get on top of him. Her legs went around his waist, her forearm went into his neck, and if she could have kept it there long enough he would have passed out, but he crossed his legs up over her head and pulled her back.

She somersaulted over, landing on her feet. When he stood she gave him a flying kick to the chest. He caught her foot with both hands, and she used the leverage to lift herself off the ground and swipe a boot into his face. Spinning around, he went to his knees against the ropes with his back exposed. Mercelle hopped on and pressed her chest against his spine, leaning her head over his shoulder.

The men in line laughed as she grabbed him by the hair and bent him over, biting his shoulder and straining his neck into a position that made it hard to breathe as well as staunching the blood flow into the brain. Her teeth dug into his flesh, just short of breaking skin, while his hands held onto the rope to keep himself from sliding down flat onto his front side.

This was what he liked, right? Only, she was doing it her way. This was her sex, better even, and he had asked for biting. The boorish taunts of the other men fed her soul, and she reveled in her happiness. This was the most entertainment she'd enjoyed since beating the snot out of Klaed.

He tightened one arm, planting it on the floor to hold all of their weight, while reaching back and tapping her on the back of the head with the other. Disappointed, she unclenched her jaw and let him go, wiping drool off of her chin.

The poor soldier pulled himself up by the rope, catching his breath. His face was bright red and his eyes were full of moisture. After a small cough he said, "That was good for me. What about you?"

"Meh." She shrugged. "It was alright." She hauled forward and kicked him in the gut, sending him backward. The soldier flipped over the rope and fell to the mat outside of the ring. "*Now* I'm having fun though."

She really was. Causing pain was the best, but only when they deserved it. All she had to do was be careful not to kill or maim anyone too badly. Vayreni still needed soldiers to order around, not crippled men with broken bones and swollen eyes.

"Too Hectoring easy!" Vayreni shouted at her when she reached to tag her in. "Take another! You know you wanna!"

"Yes, First Officer," Mercelle said back with a bit of playfulness.

Without hesitation, she welcomed her next victim, taking him down with a knock out knee to the forehead.

Watching Vayreni's methods of speed and flexibility was a learning experience, and she compared that to her own style of force and agility. Together, they took down a handful of men, one at a time.

The entire training level was alight with cheers and onlookers. Even the class of youngsters had stopped, and their whole group was piled up at the edge of the ring, urging the women to "Hit him again!" and "Take on one more!"

Mercelle didn't think she was going to get laid tonight, her moves were too on point, and there was no chance of her getting pinned. She thought about the fact that she was more likely to orgasm in the ring than in bed. One after another, the soldiers filed in, only to be thrown or booted out. She wasn't even getting tired or sore.

Vayreni tagged her in, and she found herself staring down a lean but swift man with quick feet. He jabbed and she dodged. He kicked, she shimmied and ducked. She wore him out, holding back her strikes until she was sure his shoulders were tired enough to let one through.

When he finally dropped his shoulders for a split second she went in, catching him in the chin and sending him into the ropes, but it didn't take him down. She spread her feet, ready for his counter, and as he came at her, her vision blurred. Frozen in place, the room spun around her. It was difficult to even determine whether or not she was breathing, and she got cold as her heart pumped a million miles an hour.

The next thing she felt was a fist in her side. It wasn't particularly hard, but without proper sight or balance, it put her on the floor. She lay there, looking up at the movement of the ropes and ceiling tiles, as if she was experiencing a waking dream. Trying to move was useless, and frightening. Paralyzed, she saw Vayreni's face, and then a brief shaking brought her back.

"What happened?" she asked with numb lips.

"Does this mean I win?"

"Back off, idiot," said Vayreni. "She was out before you even connected. I don't think she's well."

"I'm fine," Mercelle told them, trying to get her bearings. It was hard to hold her head up, and her entire body shivered. Was this what it was like to feel weak? She had beaten every opponent willing to stand against her, but now she lay on the floor of the ring, unable to put weight on her legs.

"Give her some space," Vayreni ordered, fanning her face.

The air felt good, and helped to bring clarity back to her vision. Helplessness enveloped her. Wasn't there something she could do to defeat this plague ravaging her body?

Finally, the room stopped rotating around her, and she planted her feet. Vayreni lifted the rope to help her down. She hated needing help, especially when she wasn't injured. Injuries and scars were at least an indication of sacrificing one's body in combat, reminders of triumph. Without visible damage, it was nearly impossible for her to accept her feeble state.

"I'm sorry," said the lean man who had planted the fist in her side. "I didn't know she was sick."

As soon as her feet hit the floor outside the ring, she walked as fast as she could toward the shower halls.

"Wait up!" called Vayreni. But Mercelle was out of there.

Walking with such speed made it hard to breathe again, or perhaps it was the thoughts rushing through her head. She imagined dying alone, or in her sleep, with no explanation, no legacy, and no way of helping to destroy the Demigods.

Lanna was gone. Dirig, Agnitius, her parents: were all gone, and the pain of their losses clouded her brain as her powerful frailty allowed it to come through. She was the last of her name, and the last living Lanna soldier. Falling to an unseen enemy couldn't be her fate. What if she was only sick enough to prevent her from fighting? She would fight anyway, she thought, but the idea of it made her feel even heavier. It felt like someone had fastened a rope or strap around her chest, and they just kept pulling it tighter and tighter.

Shoving the door to the toilets open, she found a stall and went inside, locking it behind her. The toilet rotated sideways, and rolled around in front of her. The dizziness had returned.

A gulp seized her throat, and pressure from her stomach built until she couldn't hold it back anymore. Yellow, foamy bile spat out into the toilet. Her lips hardened and went numb again. She turned around and sat down, trying to get her hands to stop shaking so violently. They refused, and it made her angry.

She hated this, and convinced herself that she didn't want to know what it was. Something from the tower at the South Pole had infected her. She could feel it in her blood. Maybe, she thought, she was too far into the atmosphere and got some kind of space poisoning. If her body had taken in something synthesized by Chaos, then there would be no possibility of treating it, or slowing its progression.

Those thoughts weren't helping her to catch her breath. She was going to have to manage her vitals on her own, by controlling her thoughts and inducing a relaxing reaction.

In her mind, she pictured Bewapen translating the Texts, and remembered the hope it instilled in her for the future. Her body warmed, and she was no longer freezing. She recalled the sound of Klaed's glass helmet cracking as she struck it with a pipe. Her hands stopped shivering and relaxed. She relived the sensation of her boot connecting with the first man she took down in the ring earlier. Her skin stopped pumping out sweat. The feeling of a tower crumbling to the ground behind her as she and Lito ran from it. Her breathing slowed to a comfortable rhythm.

Lastly, she summoned to mind the end of the Demigods. With the image of her boot on Valk's skull, she softened her tense muscles, leaning forward to hang her head between her knees.

It passed, and she came back to herself.

Two soft knocks rapped on the stall door.

"Mercelle?" came Vayreni's voice. "You okay in there? You took off kinda fast for someone who just passed out."

"I'm fine, Bari," she answered, wiping her mouth before opening the stall door. The automatic toilet rinsed itself out as she slunk past Vayreni and went to the nearest sink, still a bit heavy in the legs.

"The Hector was that?" Vayreni asked. "Kinda came outta nowhere. You got thin blood or something? Nutrient deficiency?"

"Nothing like that." She rinsed her hands, splashing water over her face. "I got infected with something when I took out that tower at the South Pole." Saying it out loud made it real, and set her mind into motion to try and compartmentalize the stress the way she would any other grief or anxiety.

"The one that was disrupting our comms?"

Mercelle nodded. "They ran some tests, but I don't have the results yet. I'm still waiting, but the symptoms come and go."

"That's gotta be hard. Why don't you let me help you back to your A.L.C.O.? I know a way to the rear stairwell so we won't have to go back out onto the training floor."

"That's probably a good idea."

Bari pulled Mercelle's arm around her shoulders, and helped her through the bathroom door.

"Bari?"

"Yes, Lady."

"Thank you."

"No. Thank you. I had a Kaisering great time this evening. We should do it again sometime."

"What? Beat up a bunch of men?"

"Hector yes!"

19

LADY TI-ERIN FERES IV

Her favorite part of the day was just after the sun went down. Pinks and purples highlighted the distant dunes and the wall around Sandra, bringing rare bits of color to an otherwise bland landscape. It was much more exhilarating to see it reflected off of the multichromal surfaces of Sandra's solar panels. Sharing the moment with Lito on the steel walkway that wrapped around her A.L.C.O. building was especially nice. They were on the eighth floor overlooking the city. Hers was one of the few buildings that extended above the panels, and her A.L.C.O. was the only one up that high. She loved it up here, where the bustle of the streets couldn't reach. Sometimes it was the only place where she could clear her mind to make room for her heart.

This evening, her mind was anything but clear.

She still couldn't figure out what had enticed her to invite Lito up to share the view. It was more like she didn't want to admit why she did it. She just wanted to be alone with Him, and to temporarily disregard the endless responsibilities she held within Sandra, if only for an evening.

Was a single sunset too much to ask for? Did the people of Sandra need more from her?

Lady Feres always questioned herself – which was part of what made her so good at self-assessing – to make sure she was being the best she could be for the people she chose to protect.

"I'm surprised you got Bewapen to leave your side," she said to break the silence. "He must have been tired after the rough couple of days he's had." She was torn about how she felt regarding being left alone with Lito for the first time.

The Onyx man had tried as hard as he could to stay by Lito's side, but the Order God never slept, so it would have been impossible to keep up. Once Bewapen's eyes had started to flutter shut, Lito sent him down to His A.L.C.O. with His armor and the Shard.

He watched as the horizon slowly took the sun away. "Bewapen's a good man, and he's shaping up to be a strong representative for the alliance. By translating two texts today he is already a hero to the rebellion."

"Word of the translations has already reached Naselba. Even if they consider themselves the head of the rebellion, there's no arguing about who's contributed more. If they think they're going to push us around at that summit, they really don't know who they'll be pushing."

"We have Dredger from Kerk, you for Sandramedius, Bewapen representing the Onyx Clan, and with Mercelle and me at your backs they won't have much to stand on in regards to demanding authority. We all love our people, and want to protect who we can." He looked away from the colorful spray of sunset in the distance, locking onto Feres's eyes. "I still have a lot to learn about this ideal of love."

She sighed. It would be a Kaisering task to explain to a God exactly what love was. To Feres, it was assumed that love meant different things to different people, depending on what kind of love it was. There was love for one's purpose, family, culture or people, but love for another individual that exceeds the heart's capacity and eclipses all other emotions was something she hadn't felt. Or, at least, she hoped it was something she would never feel.

"I guess, love isn't something you really understand until you experience it. Even then it could make very little sense." She looked away from Lito. "That's why I think we should try and keep our distance. We don't want to...never mind."

Feres couldn't stand the way He looked into her eyes, unmovingly seeing her to her core.

"We don't want to what?" asked Lito.

She knew that being vague wouldn't help Him understand anything. Forwardness was more His style. Pure, unfiltered information was what Lito needed to get certain things through His head.

"Look, Lito. Ever since you saved my life from Baqil's exploding transport I've had...feelings...toward you. I've never felt this way about anyone, and I tried not to let it take me over, but something about the way you do what needs to be done, and the way you sacrifice everything you have to do what's right...I don't know. It's rare. And it makes me want to do things that I simply can't do."

"Why can't you do them?"

He wasn't asking what she wanted to do, therefore, He had to have some kind of idea as to what she was getting at.

"I can't afford to be distracted from the war," she answered. "Neither of us can. Humanity needs our focus, not our lust. Everything I do...everything I've ever done has been to prepare the rebellion to face the Demigods. Some things are just more important."

She wished it wasn't the case, and wanted to disappear into a world where she wasn't accountable for the fate of humanity, but those with the power to help, she felt, had the responsibility to do so. Mercelle understood that better than anyone she knew.

"You're a warrior for humanity," Lito told her. "You fight for yourself also, never forget that. By denying your own humanity you only betray yourself. Based on what little I know of love, one should never shy away from it. If I created humans, and humans created love, then it was for a reason. Don't take that away from yourself."

She wanted Him to be right, wanted to leap into His arms and take Him right there on the steel-grated balcony. Everything she had sacrificed to be able to control the kind of power she had in her hands couldn't be risked. Her entire head had convinced her that her heart was getting in her way, especially in this moment.

"You don't understand."

"I believe I understand more than you may assume. When you described the way you felt toward me over the radio, I couldn't help but match my own feelings to yours. I feel a strange, but good, way about you also. I just want to understand it more."

Her solid exterior was beginning to thicken, and she refused to look at Him.

"We can't," she insisted, unable to find other words to help her justify resistance.

"I want to taste your skin," He said, honest and forward as always.

The thumping of her heart was so loud that she feared Lito could hear it. Heat in her ears made her hate herself for not relenting.

"Well, I don't want to taste yours," she lied, trying to hide the fact that she was salivating.

"It's your choice to sacrifice pieces of your life for the war, to maintain your head in lieu of your heart. I will always respect any decision you make."

On one hand, she thought He was being a condescending, pushy, self-righteous child. And on the other, how did He know what was going on inside of her? He wasn't just in her blood, but in her head. Could He also sense her veins throbbing throughout her loins? They pulsed up and down her spine, landing on an appendage which she kept tucked between her legs.

Feres was vulnerable. Nothing she did now could keep her behind her thickened exterior because Lito clearly saw right through it like polished glass. He only asked questions to get her to know herself better, to get her to bring her decisions to the fore of her mind instead of the back, and to consider them with both her head and her heart.

All she could think to say in return was, "Thank you for your honesty, and for respecting my wishes." A lump swelled in her throat.

"Of course," He replied. "Free will is what humanity-"

She grabbed His wrist from the railing, moving it from her path as she stepped into His space and pressed her chest into His. Her hand went to the back of His head, pulling her closer so she could feel the softness of His lips on hers.

They were strong but supple, dry but velvety, human but Godly. She wasn't sure if she was feeling some sort of power of Order emanating from Him, or simply taking in the rush of the moment.

At first, His lips didn't move. Shock must have overwhelmed His senses when she lunged at Him. He must not have seen this rising up within her as He could her thoughts, and after holding her lips against His, He tightened the luscious pads and kissed her back.

She exhaled, realizing she had stopped breathing, and relaxed in Lito's embrace.

Her brown hands were in His black hair. His fingers were on her cheek and pressing into her back. Cracks sounded out from her spine, and Lito pressed just enough to make her shiver and hurt a little. It was quickening, vitalizing, *exhilarating!*

A hand came up to the back of her neck, and the other beneath her knee. Her leg lifted, wrapping around His waist as He leaned her back over the railing. Firm fingers held her tight, and Lito's lips slid down to her neck. Her head hung back, and through a shaking, upside down vision the sunset looked more like a sunrise.

Light penetrated her eyelids when she closed them: purple, pink and yellow.

Lito pulled her face back to His, and she pressed her

lips into His firm cheeks, spinning around until her back was against the door to her A.L.C.O. She rubbed the inside of her thigh on His leg while reaching up to hit the engage switch. When the door went open, Lito lifted her up. Feres's feet came off the floor, and as her ankles linked behind Him they went through the door's threshold, landing among the sheets on Feres's bed.

THE SUN WAS UP. Much to her delight, she had gone all night without some kind of emergency page or alert reaching her tablet.

Lito's head lay on her chest, and she stroked His neck while thinking of the night before.

They had kissed and caressed for hours, staring into each other's eyes. He hadn't tried to remove her clothes until she began tugging on His, loosening His buttons and zippers until He was bare before her.

She was happy when He took off her blouse, and had avoided any self-conscious inklings as He slid her pants off one leg at a time. His lips massaged her chest, tickling her dark nipples and making her moan in peaceful absorption of His energies. Then, His eyes locked back onto hers, and she reached up to unclip her wig from her head, exposing the ever curly locks that she had hidden beneath. At first, she was afraid that His reaction to her true self would make Him doubt the feelings they shared, but instead He smiled, and pressed His body into her even harder.

Lito didn't make love with one part of Himself, but with His entire body. Every muscle and every inch of skin was in play. It was electrifying, and she swore she could feel ticks of sparks in her head during the whole interaction of sensual pleasure. It wasn't carnal, it wasn't rushed, it was what she believed making love felt like.

Remembering her thought process leading up to kissing Lito, she was both worried about having left her position unattended for the night, and satisfied that she had actually realized how happy she could be. She allowed herself to enjoy something – or someone – without it having to contribute to the war.

Lito wasn't asleep. He was running a firm hand over Feres's stomach, tracing the outline of her scar. "Your heart is still racing," He said softly.

"I've never been with a man before," she admitted, a smile adorning her satiated face. "Let alone a God."

He turned His head to face her, rolling onto His other side. "You've never allowed yourself to be with a man? Why is that?"

"I've been with women, but that was a long time ago, before I knew who I was."

"You mean before you recognized that you were a woman, and what you wanted."

Even after seeing every part of her, He still called her a woman. Her flat chest, and well-endowed anatomy of a man between her legs, didn't define who she was in His eyes. His blatant acceptance of her was both comforting and confusing.

"How is it that you created the Seven Races with only two genders, and yet, when something that refuses to fit into either one presents itself to you, you somehow accept it just the same?"

"You will never be an 'it' to me," He said, squinting with concern and brushing a dark curl away from her forehead. "Never forget how weak I was when I created humans. If I could do it over again I would make them all in your image."

"That would just be selfish," she laughed.

"Free will, remember?" He smiled at her.

Was He beginning to understand how to joke? She could never believe He would use His Godly powers like that, but enjoyed the flattery just the same.

The inevitable buzz came from the tablet on her bedside table. She sighed, flattening a palm on Lito's cheek one last time.

"I've been dreading that sound all night," she said. "Time to get back to reality."

Lito lifted Himself up, and she shifted to a sitting position, hanging her feet off the side of the bed and pulling the tablet from its charging dock. A message was waiting for her. It was from the medical Scholars – from Rakta herself.

She tapped the message to open it, and sped

through the report. It was regarding the findings of Mercelle's scans. It detailed the process of cellular breakdown and the presence of radiation throughout the body. The initial tests were shown beside the second round, displaying exactness and making it impossible to deny the results.

Feres's heart stopped racing, and slowed to a heavy thud that she felt all the way to her feet. Without finishing the report, she messaged Mercelle right away, telling her to come up as soon as possible.

"Emmett's ashes," she whispered with a hand on her forehead. "I should have never let her go into that tower."

"Something wrong?"

She didn't answer. She didn't need to. She held Him again, trying not to cry. A strange balancing of logic struck her: the weaker Mercelle became, the stronger Feres would have to be. Without her sister, Feres was alone. She was Feres's constant, her link to a history and a past that would surely lose meaning without her.

Together they were impenetrable, unstoppable. Apart, Feres didn't know who she would be.

"What did the message say?" He was trying to share her burden, to make it lighter by taking some of it Himself. But, this was hers to hold, and no amount of sharing would make it any easier.

All she could do was shake her head. Despite making love for the first time, and to a God, there was still no one closer to her than Mercelle, and she needed to tell her sister about the test results before anyone else.

"I'm sorry," He said to her. "Whatever it is, I'm sorry you have to bear it alone."

"Thank you," she said back, staring at the lines of bolts holding up steel panels on her ceiling.

A knock came from the door, and then it slid open.

"Oh," came Mercelle's voice, a surprised grin on her face. "I didn't know...I'll just give you a minute."

"No," Feres stopped her. "Just sit." She sat up, looking at Lito and remembering that He was still naked. "Sorry, I-"

"I know," He replied. "I can go."

"Thank you. I'll come find you in a bit."

Mercelle sat on the foot of the bed, biting her lips together to hold back a teasing smile, while Lito stood, gathered His clothes and left to dress Himself outside.

"Wow," Mercelle said as soon as the door closed. "I wasn't expecting to walk in to *that*. I have so many questions." She kicked off her boots and climbed into the bed. "Judging by the look on your face I'm thinking it wasn't all that great."

Feres pulled the sheets up to cover her chest. "It's not that. It *was* great. I don't even know how to describe it, honestly."

"Then what's with the face, sis? Do you think He, maybe, didn't enjoy Himself?"

"No. It's not that."

"Then *what* is it?" asked Mercelle. It was obvious that she was excited to know more about Feres's night and what may come of it.

"How are you feeling?" Feres didn't think to ease into it.

Mercelle's smile sagged into a disappointed stare. "You got the report from the medical Scholars, didn't you?"

Feres simply nodded, pointing to the tablet on the table. They didn't always need words to communicate.

"Well," Mercelle said, standing from the bed and tying her boots back on. "I don't need to read it. I feel great. I felt great last night when your new First Officer and I took on half your infantry in the training hall. I didn't feel too well this morning, but once I got moving and came up here everything went away. As long as it doesn't say something about pregnancy, I think I'll be fine."

"You're not pregnant."

"See? I'm fine." She put a hand on the door's switch.

"Inis, please just sit down."

Mercelle hung her head to the side, glaring at Feres as she slowly crouched back down onto the foot of the bed. "I know...I should read it. I just...I don't know."

Her sister had the same tendencies to avoid things as she did. Only there was more pain behind Mercelle's eyes because of it. Once Mercelle knew what she was up against, she could always fight it.

"Here, sis," said Feres, picking up the tablet with a shaking hand. "I can read it for you."

When Mercelle nodded, a single tear fell onto the bed.

20

KOP STAMHOOF I

The moist caves were cool, but stagnant. Burning the sappidge plants at the center of the fields helped to keep the caverns slightly dry. It also provided some much needed light to help the other sappidge plants grow. Since the underground system of lava flows didn't exist anymore, the now-named Onyx Clan had to improvise to keep propagation and cultivation at a high enough rate. Third Prime F'Briek did a great job of overseeing such projects and keeping the fields plentiful.

Mercelle and Lito had just left the day before with Bewapen, having lost their friend Ashlan during their takedown of the magma tower. He felt sadness toward their loss, and chose to see it more as a sacrifice to ensure their allegiance, much like Geboor.

Bewapen was the first to leave the Clan in centuries,

and the only one to leave under Kop Stamhoof's leadership. No one had ventured outside of the Clan since emerging from the underground centuries ago after the magma flows dried up. They used to bury their dead in the slowest parts of the subterranean lava rivers, and when they stopped flowing, they began burning their deceased instead. Geboor was the only Clan member he had ever seen buried in the dirt, as burials were meant to trap the soul on Earth's death realm instead of allowing it to rest in the warm embrace of the afterlife beyond.

Geboor's soul was the collateral that allowed their alliance with the rebels to start strong. Only honesty and loyalty could keep it that way, and the Kop held subtle doubts that those ideals had been held up by the other side.

He walked through the sappidge fields by the entrance of the caverns. The black casket was held to the wall high above him with ropes, and he stopped to appreciate the ornate carvings of fading glyphs he couldn't read on the outside of it. The casket had been passed down through countless generations, and it was his secret weapon. It only required perfect timing – and the perfect enemy – to be released. Part of him believed that that time and enemy had finally been substantiated.

Lying to Mercelle and Lito wasn't easy for him, but it paid off in the end, exposing the truth he had tried to obtain by easier means. He hadn't told them about Queen Maagda's entire vision. The part he had left out included her hearing a warning from the ethereal realm, which instructed her to be wary of false Gods, and that the true God of Order would have the ability to transcend a bridge between life and death.

Stamhoof already knew that Lito's blood could heal, but if it couldn't resurrect, then that had to mean that Lito wasn't the true God of Order. Whether Lito was aware of that fact or not, the reality of it all was that the Kop and his people had been lied to; they had been provided with a false hope that would only bring danger and death to the Clan. Sacrificing Geboor was necessary to test the so-called God's merit, and Stamhoof had hoped with everything within himself that Geboor would hop up out of that grave as proof of the coming of Order. His guilt was heavy, but he knew it had to be done.

It was the right thing to do to protect the Clan.

Crouching down to collect the dried sappidge leaves at his feet, he thought to pay respects to Geboor one last time before lying down to sleep for the night. Bewapen would have wanted him to place leaves there to remind his son's soul that his father would never forget his sacrifice.

Kop Stamhoof left the caverns, entering the cool night and nodding a "Hwee'o" to the groups of men who preferred to sleep outside by fire light. On the outskirts of the valley, some men sparred under the stars, teaching their eyes to see clearly in the darkness. Through the forest of dunes and into the vast empty patch of sand where Geboor was buried, he stopped to also let his own eyes adjust to darkness without the light of flames.

This was his Clan's burial ground, fitted with a single, lonely grave of a sacrificed son. Stamhoof opened his eyes, now able to make out the subtle drifts of sand humps that wavered throughout the empty desert. Geboor's soul was here, wandering the Earth, carrying the burden of the Clan's new allegiance with the rebellion.

Was the alliance real? Could he require his people to hold it up and respect it even though Lito had lied about being the true God of Order?

Lito had failed the test – His blood hadn't brought Geboor back to life. Perhaps, Kop Stamhoof thought, Lito was a Demigod. His abilities surely were comparable to that of a Chaos Demigod in that both could replicate beings in their own image. Chaos Demigods created replicas just like themselves, and Lito had done exactly that when He'd created the human Races. From what he knew about Chaos, their God had the power to create Demigods. Why didn't Lito have the same power? He didn't even have the ability to create replicas any longer.

Regardless of that, a sacrifice had been made, and

an alliance forged from it. His thoughts went to Bewapen, and he assumed that Bewapen would be dead by now if the alliance was as false as Lito's claims of Godliness. Was He lying in order to secure allegiance?

Walking through the empty valley, the Kop tried to make sense of it all. The state of the world had never been the Clan's problem, but now that the war between the rebellion and Chaos was coming to a head, spilling over into their Clan, it was time to fight or die. There was no in between.

With or without allegiances, it was time for the Clan to take action, and engage against those who wished them harm.

He approached Geboor's grave, where the lump of sand had been piled up not two days ago. Freezing in place, he dropped the dried sappidge leaves, not because placing them on Geboor's grave would honor both the sacrifice and Bewapen's wishes, but because the grave was open and vacant.

The sand had been pushed away from where Geboor had been put to rest. Instead of a lump, a hole lay empty and exposed to the night. Footsteps and handprints led away from the open grave; something had crawled away in a horrifyingly crooked fashion.

Before he could consider what he was seeing, a terrible scream came from the valley by the caverns.

Kop Stamhoof turned tail and bolted back toward the valley. Taking the shortest route through the sand dunes, he followed the sound of the screams until he came to a group of men huddling around something, threatening it with spears and large hammers. "Eestoo!" he shouted. Taking out his knife, he pushed through the huddle to see what they were hollering at.

At the center of the crowd was a burning sappidge. Its light blinded the Kop at first, but it only took a second for his sight to adjust. Next to the fire was a small dark mass. It was a young man, crouched down with his hands in the flames. The boy was covered in dirt, filthy from head to toe. The dancing flames showed the glint of dried crimson on his chest, and when the boy turned his head to look at the Kop, the open wound on the boy's throat became visible. It wasn't bleeding, as it was crusted and coated in sand.

He looked into Geboor's eyes: red and black, and wider than any eyes he'd ever seen. Geboor's skin was also an ashy-grey color, like that of a dead man. His previously white spikes had taken on the color of the sand. Teeth were bared and covered in dripping saliva. A low growl exited Geboor's throat. The boy no longer resembled a Clan member.

"Eestoonil alldeetah!" the Kop ordered, instructing everyone to back up. Stepping closer to the animalistic boy, he kept the knife ready.

Geboor didn't blink once, he only stared up at the Kop as if he was considering striking out. Stamhoof was ready, although he didn't want to hurt the boy who he had already condemned to death once before.

If he was alive, then it had worked. Lito's blood had successfully resurrected a descendant of His own creations. But, in what state had Geboor returned? The boy before him looked devoid of a soul, and the Kop feared that something else had returned from the afterlife in Geboor's place. Something dark.

The Kop let Geboor know that he didn't want to hurt him, and asked if he was okay.

A rumbling moan came from deep inside Geboor's chest, and Stamhoof held his blade tight.

With a slow movement, Geboor shook his head side to side.

Makeshift sleds were built to transport large amounts of sappidge, some still rooted and growing in pots. The Kop left Queen Maagda in charge, having convinced over two-thirds of his Clan to accompany him, including the three Primes, and the men hastened themselves to prepare for a long journey on foot.

Stamhoof fashioned a rope around Geboor's waist to ensure that he wouldn't wander off or disappear. The boy seemed fine with it, but determining how Geboor felt was difficult because the only way he could communicate was with a series of grunts and snarls. The boy had become a monster, rubbing sand over himself constantly and rolling his head into the ground like he was trying to scratch a terrible itch within his brain.

Something awful was inside Geboor, trying to claw its way out.

The last item to be tied to a sled was the black casket from the cavern entrance. Taller than three men, it took dozens to pull the casket. Kop Stamhoof's secret weapon was coming along, and he intended on using it. Lito needed to be aware of what kind of monsters He was creating, and the casket would surely help send that message.

All of the rules pertaining to the sacrifice for severance were discontinued, and by daybreak, his mobile Clan was following the tracks left behind by Lito and Mercelle's transports, heading toward Sandramedius.

21

LADY INIS MERCELLE XI

Feres's A.L.C.O. was where Mercelle sat, the bed sheet dotted with tears. Her sister had already left for the medical bay to find Scholar Rakta and have a room set up for an in-depth assessment of Mercelle's infection, but she couldn't bring herself to go, not yet at least. Having left a few moments ago, Feres had given her a little bit of time to process, alone, as she had requested.

On the bedside table lay Feres's tablet with the medical report still pulled up. Mercelle's eyes went to it, then away. An urge to pick it up and reread it tempted her, but she knew there wouldn't be anything different than what Feres had read to her. She didn't need any further details. All she needed to know was that she was sick, and there was nothing more she could do to combat it. There was no doubt in her mind that Feres,

Lito and Rakta would try and convince her to stay strong, but much of her physical, emotional and spiritual strength had dwindled since leaving the South Pole. The report simply told her why.

The few minutes she'd been alone felt like hours. Each second created an overwhelming sensation of heaviness. She wanted to lie down on the bed, curl into a ball and wait for the poisoning to break her down. Also, she wanted to battle it – to will the infection away – but, the skills she had spent a lifetime acquiring weren't going to help. By keeping her mind solid and ready for what comes next, she could persevere. Her mind was the last bit of herself she felt she could keep under control; however, that too was beginning to slip from her grasp.

Loosening the involuntary fists she was clenching, Mercelle felt pressure building. Her head and her chest rushed with an unwelcomed excitement as the weight of the world slammed against her shoulders and flooded her thoughts. For the first time in her entire life, she didn't believe she knew how to carry it any longer.

Onyx Queen Maagda had helped her and Lito confirm that a vision had been shared between the two of them, one the Queen had seen as well. Maagda had experienced countless visions in her time, and Lito was a God. Why had Mercelle, of all people, been included in the premonition? She had no powers, no ethereal abilities and no long lineages of pure blood to induce visions. It could only mean that she was more important than she had originally believed, or that something *else* was happening to her that she didn't understand. Control was beyond her grasp, as was her ability to maintain the ever growing pressure of heading the war against Leto's Demigods.

She just wanted it all to go away.

All she craved was to stand in the midst of battle, and shed replica blood upon the sand, as she had done her whole life. It was what she was born to do. Perhaps, she thought, her purpose had been served. Maybe she was meant to have perished in Lanna, and Lito was supposed to be the lone survivor. Her innate ability to survive was becoming her downfall, putting her in a position of dying slowly, instead of honorably as she had intended.

What would her parents say? Would they push her to go on? Or would they convince her to retire from a life of battle? They had died in battle, as warriors were supposed to. If she couldn't do the same, then what was the point of going on?

Her lack of control extended to the darkening thoughts encroaching on her psyche.

Guilt flowed through her heart at the thought of convincing Dredger to attend the summit in Naselba. If she was the cause of his neutrality being compromised, and Kerk being at risk, she would never be able to forgive herself. Was she causing more problems than she was capable of solving at this point? Dredger wouldn't even hug her after their heated discussion.

She missed Agnitius, First Officer Dirig, and the smell of Lanna's open-air markets. None of those things would ever grace her presence again.

Lito and Feres were clearly close now, and it was a relationship which she didn't feel a part of, but apart from. They were capable of heading the rebellion's campaign without her, and she thought that the rebels would be more successful following their lead than hers.

Teeth clenched, her tears flowed freely onto her lap.

Why couldn't she have died in Lanna? Why couldn't Lito have taken down the other towers alone and been the warrior the rebellion needed? Why hadn't she found peace in her end after awakening the God of Order? Was that not the extent of her purpose, to awaken Lito? Now that she had accomplished that, she felt she only had the potential to be a burden going forward.

The darkness she was cultivating in her own heart only allowed her to see the worst, almost as if she was subconsciously trying to convince herself not to go on. She didn't want to go down to the medical bay for yet another exam that would only serve to prolong her suffering. She was tired, and wanted her suffering to end.

Tears ceased falling from her swelling eyes. The

cold, blank realization of her decision washed an apathetic indifference over her. She released all of the burdens of her lifetime, thankful for the little bit of strength she had left to end it all.

Mercelle stood from the foot of Feres's bed, walking to the door and opening it up to the steel-railed balcony that overlooked the city of Sandramedius. Her hands on the rail, she knew this was the only way.

The morning sun beat down on her as she climbed atop the rail, balancing herself.

Lito and Feres were the leaders of the rebellion now, and anyone who still believed in Mercelle would only be setting themselves up for disappointment, and she wasn't accustomed to disappointing those she was meant to protect.

This was the only way.

Soon, her pain would be over. Soon, the rebels would move forward to victory over the Demigods. Soon, she would be at peace, with her parents.

Oh, how she missed her mother and father. As a child, when she would find countless ruins throughout the world with Dredger, and constantly be in the midst of failing to find the Temple of Order, her parents would tell her that her failures were simple stepping stones to her success, and that they would amount to something. They had, and she was the one who awakened Lito. They always found a way to bring her up when she was down, and convince her to go on another excavation with Dredger, to try and try again.

A shiver tickled her spine as she reached into her pocket and pulled out the picture of her mother and father. Smiling, she touched their faces, ready to feel their presence once again. A light floating sensation enveloped her, and she found elation to be a comforting feeling as she looked down at the ground far beneath her, and took her last breath.

This was the only way...

She closed her eyes, and imagined what her mother would say to her when they found each other on the other side of life. Would she say how proud she was of her daughter? Would she praise her for finding the strength to bow out with grace? Suicide wasn't exactly graceful, but Mercelle didn't know any other road out of this dark place.

Her arms went out to her sides, and she stood atop the railing, a cross against the sky.

Her mother's warm breath caressed her ear, and she whispered through the warm breeze, *My daughter. My warrior. My heart and soul. We're here. We've always been with you, and we will always be with you.*

Shaky hands pulled her picture out of her back pocket. Her mother and father played joyfully with her younger version in the sand. It was impossible for her to recall the innocence she once had.

"I miss you, mom," Mercelle whispered back, breathing once again. "I can't wait to see you."

You must wait. We aren't ready to see you yet. This isn't your time.

No, sweet Inis, came another voice. *You still have fight left in you, and it cannot be wasted.*

"Dad?" Her weightlessness disappeared, and the burdens of the world and of the war returned to her. A sickening feeling arose in her stomach and pushed on her throat. The darkness was still there, waiting for her to accept it back unto herself, and she began to cry again. "But...I can't do this anymore. I'm tired. Haven't I done enough?"

You've done more than enough, he answered. *But you can do more. You can always do more.*

Never doubt yourself, her mother told her. *Your strength has never lied in your muscles, or in your brain, but in your heart. It is what will carry you on to your own salvation.*

"Mom, my heart hurts," she sobbed heavily, her tears dripping into the wind as she swayed back and forth. Her voice cracked as she screamed into the sky. "It's empty! Drained and lost! What if I *can't* find my place here?! What if I no longer have a place or a stake in this world?!"

Her father answered, *You will always have a place, as long as you have the will to find and fight for it.*

Everything begins with free will, her mother

reminded her. *Remember the choices which are within your ability to make, and you will never be lost.*

"This *is* my choice!" she cried out.

It was her decision to make, her free will to exercise, and she was going to do what she felt she needed to do for the rebellion.

She leaned, letting the wind push her. The rail rubbed against the soles of her boots as she went over, and vertigo overtook her senses. Air rushed passed her face, brushing her cheeks and tossing her hair up. The sensation of being suspended in air comforted her for a split second.

The fall was quick, and when her butt struck the balcony's landing she stared up at the sky, sobbing hysterically behind the thought of carrying this darkness around with her. She was alone again, waiting for more whispers which wouldn't come.

Her limbs were lead, her clothes were constricting, and her brain was ricocheting between walls of panic and emptiness.

For a while she stayed there, trying with what remained of her will power to find the strength to stand and descend the stairs to the medical bay.

22

LITO IX

He had to admit it to Himself: last night was an experience He never thought He'd have. Creating the humans with the best of intentions, and trying as He could in His weakened state all those millennia ago, Lito had made Races of similar beings, yet He saw only original traits in Feres. She was her own creation, a product of vision, perspective, heart and heat. If anything was going to distract Him from reality, it was the way she made Him feel.

It was a consistent, pounding want for another level of closeness, and once He achieved it, He wanted nothing else. Her wet skin pressing against His was sensational, and the things she did to Him were unimaginable. He tried as He may to do the same things back, in the way He tended to mimic gestures until guided to correctness. She was a great teacher, correcting His every move until nothing but moans and squeals came out of her. It was an evening He'd never forget, and one He'd prefer to repeat as often as possible.

Something about the encounter made Him feel different. As a God, there were no means for Him to grow, however, Lito felt more human than ever before. His humanity, He felt, was bigger than anything else He could accomplish as the God of Order, aside from destroying Chaos. Reality was a distant focus, His surreal elation taking precedent over it.

A lovely distraction, perhaps too distracting.

Lito pulled His attention back to the medical bay, where much more important things were happening.

The room was small, meant for observation and protection from certain particles emitted by certain machines. Feres said they'd be safe behind the glass window, and on the other side Mercelle sat on an examination table, staring blankly ahead, with medical Scholar Rakta sewing up a piece of her shoulder and tending to intravenous tubes connected to each arm.

Bewapen stood silently behind them as they watched poor Mercelle being subjected to multiple scans after a partial blood transfusion. If Lito didn't know better, He would have assumed Mercelle to be brain dead due to her complete apathy and lack of reaction. His heart manifested pain as a reaction to her suffering.

"I think she's still in shock," said Feres. She nervously bit at the end of her thumbnail, tapping her foot on the floor repeatedly. "What was it exactly that you saw that told you she was sick? It was something you sensed, wasn't it?"

The more information He could provide, the better off the Scholars would be in treating her. He had already given His report to Rakta, and it was time to extend it to Feres. "A short time after parting with Mercelle inside the tower, I started to feel that she was in danger. This danger was different than the typical situations we've been in. I sensed that she was being attacked from the inside, and the more I concentrated on her, the more I could feel her molecules breaking down and dying. Her own body was attacking itself."

"That sounds like radiation poisoning to me." Feres shook her head. "I should have put more pressure on them to rush the results. Letting it go on this long without invasive treatments could have killed her. I never should have let her go to Kerk."

Lito rubbed a finger on the back of Feres's nervous hand, feeling and trying to absorb her anxious energy, and she clutched it.

"I've never seen Mercelle so scared in all the time I've known her," she said. "I don't think I've seen her afraid of anything before, only angry. If we lose her..." Her eyes shut, and she squeezed them tight.

"We would all be lost without her," Lito replied,

looking to Bewapen, who nodded in agreement. "But, I believe Mercelle won't die without giving everything she has to end the war. She still has a lot left to give, this I know for certain."

Medical Scholar Rakta untied the thick apron that covered her body, and waved for them to come in.

"They're finished," Feres told Him. "We can go in now."

Without waiting for the two men, Feres walked through the open door into the corridor, and went into the examination room next door. Lito and Bewapen waited in the doorway to avoid crowding the women. Feres stood by Mercelle's side, waiting for an update from the Scholar.

"Well," Feres opened. "What treatments are we pursuing?"

Scholar Rakta slid a finger over her tablet's screen. "I've just finished installing a subdermal scanner in her right shoulder. This is going to help us keep track of how invasive the poisoning is within the blood, and allow us to better administer treatments as needed. Right now the breakdown of her cells is slow enough to be considered stable, but it can increase or decrease depending on environment, stress levels, exposure to illnesses or infections, things like that. We have a cocktail we would need to administer intravenously each day or more if levels spike. There's always the option of transfusions when the poisoning gets bad enough. It all depends on how you're feeling, Mercelle. If you begin to get sick, come to the medical bay immediately so we can assess you."

Feres rubbed Mercelle's arm, and although Lito couldn't see a reaction, He knew she was taking everything in.

"What's in the cocktail?" asked Feres, since Mercelle wasn't speaking just yet.

"It's a mixture," answered Rakta. "Mostly radiogardase and potassium iodide compounds tailored to her blood type and level of infection, as well as a substantial amount of D.T.P.A. to help move some of the poisoning out of the body through the digestive system. We've only treated minor cases of this kind of infection, nothing this severe. I have a panel of Scholars discussing better treatment options, as well as working to perfect a more effective cocktail."

Lito's eyes went to Mercelle, who finally spoke up. "Thank you," she said plainly, without looking away from the floor. "I understand."

A sigh came from Feres. "What is the likelihood of an improvement, or even the eradication of the infection? Is there any chance at remission?"

"Not that I can tell," replied the Scholar. "In our more minor cases, survival is guaranteed with treatment, but even in those instances it's nearly impossible to obtain full recovery from radiation with what resources we have. It's very possible that this infection can take years to incapacitate her. The more research we do the more we can improve the way we treat it, though. We have quite a lot of her blood, and examining it closely should help."

"I can still fight, right?" Mercelle asked, bringing her eyes up to meet the Scholar's.

Lito wasn't surprised that she had asked that. Everything in Mercelle's life revolved around her being able to participate in battle.

"It all depends on the advancement of the poisoning. It could be seconds or even days before your numbers spike again. There's even the possibility of none of our treatments working at all. It all depends on the body, and the individual. I recommend that you not leave Sandra. You'll need to stay close in case we need to transfuse you or administer a cocktail. I'll try to monitor your stats from my tablet, but in the meantime, try to avoid exchanging any bodily fluids with anyone else, as the poisoning has the potential to spread. Here." She handed her tablet to Feres. "The internal scanner I implanted is functioning. It'll show me the level of cellular breakdown, and if there's a sudden spike I can contact you, or have a medical Scholar sent to your location immediately to bring you in."

Feres looked over the screen, and Mercelle even glanced an eye up at it.

"Come look at this, Lito." She motioned for Him to come into the room. "Is this what you were sensing?"

He stepped inside, walking over to the examination table. When He looked at the tablet, it showed a heavy flow of red blood cells. Some of them turned black and shriveled. Dying before their eyes. “Yes. This is what I felt was happening after we separated. Her body is attacking itself.”

“That’s one way to put it,” said Scholar Rakta.

As Lito watched the screen, the blackening of cells stopped. Instead of seeing a few die each second, He was only seeing a healthy flow of red.

“Hold on,” Feres whispered. “Something’s wrong. The flow changed, or something.”

“Let me see.” Rakta took the tablet back. “That’s strange. I might need to recalibrate it. One moment.”

“Lito,” uttered Bewapen from the doorway.

Lito went to him as the Scholar examined the scanner’s feed.

“What is it, Bewapen?”

“Lee’al Mercelle ahm veem?”

“We don’t know how bad it is yet. She hasn’t given up, though. She’s trying. All we can do is stay close, and be there for her when she needs someone. I feel that may be all the time. If she’s your friend, then you need to make sure she knows it. Okay?”

Bewapen nodded.

“There it goes,” assured Rakta. “You can see the breakdown again. It’s working fine.”

Lito went back into the room. Rakta gave Him the tablet, which showed the same thing as before.

The red cells were breaking down and dying – many of them at once. Then, it slowed again. Lito gave the tablet back to Rakta.

"It's doing it again," sighed the Scholar. "I think it might be malfunctioning."

"Wait," ordered Feres, taking the tablet from her. "The breakdown has nearly stopped." She looked up at Lito, then at Mercelle. All three of them shared a look of potential realization, and Lito believed He knew what they were thinking. "Lito, could you step out into the hallway for me?"

He was right, and she was testing the effect of His proximity to Mercelle. Walking past Bewapen, Lito turned to look back into the room.

"Ooh'ohum keesun?"

"Not sure, Bewapen. I think something might be wrong with their machines."

"Look at that," beamed Feres. "You see that?" She showed the screen to Rakta.

"I see it," replied the Scholar with a confused scrunch on her face. "What am I missing?"

"Just keep watching," Feres advised. "Lito, come back in."

Just as He was told, He came to their side again.

"See?" Feres pointed to the screen. "A decrease in

the breakdown. The scanner isn't malfunctioning. It's Lito."

"Huh?" Scholar Rakta was trying to apply logic, and Lito could see the wheels turning in her eyes. "How is that possible? The decay is nearly halted when He's near."

Mercelle perked up, staring at the screen and beginning to smile. "Are you sure?"

"Yes!" cheered Rakta. "We just saw it work three times. The infection went from moderately invasive to borderline nondetectable within a matter of seconds. I can't scientifically explain it, but based on this little experiment I can highly recommend staying within fifteen feet of Lito at all times. How amazing?!"

"Are you sure?" Mercelle repeated. "Is it Lito or the Shard? If it's the Shard then I could just wear it, couldn't I?"

"I don't have the Shard here," Lito responded. "I left it in my A.L.C.O. and I haven't been back since leaving Feres's this morning."

Scholar Rakta turned her head to look at Feres, making a face that Lito could only determine to be suspicious, yet mischievously accusatory.

Feres gave Rakta one of her famous, squinting glares, and the Scholar averted her eyes. Lito had to assume that He had just indirectly given away a piece of information which Feres wished to keep private. He would have to be more careful in social situations, as

Feres likely wanted to avoid word of their relations getting out to the public. Honestly was good, but discretion was better.

Lito tried to change the energy in the room. "As long as we fight side by side your illness won't advance." Reaching out His internal senses, He felt another change within Mercelle. It was as if she was allowed to shift back into herself. Perhaps it was the hope of her next fight returning to her.

She began to sniffle behind restrained tears. "I couldn't imagine fighting alongside anyone else for the rest of my life. However long that may be."

"It won't be just me," Lito declared, trying to show pride in His words. "Since Bewapen won't leave my side it will have to be the three of us from now on."

Mercelle laughed. She actually laughed as tears ran over her cheeks. "I'm fine with that."

Feres's chin shivered for a moment before she straightened her back and pulled her emotions back inside herself. "You're the three best warriors in the rebellion right now, as far as I'm concerned. I believe that the most deadly enemies of Chaos are all within this room right now, and together you'll be unstoppable."

It was obvious, even if only to Lito, that Feres was helping to convince Mercelle that the end was far from this day. Her words solidified the three of them as an inseparable team.

Feres put her arms around Mercelle, who reached up and pulled Lito into their embrace. He mimicked them, and joined in the hug with His arms over the two sisters. When He picked up His head, He looked back to see Bewapen stepping into the room hesitantly.

"Get over here," Feres ordered, and with that, Bewapen brought his large, dark arms around the three of them.

"Aw," came a coo from Scholar Rakta. She put down her tablet, and came closer to them.

Feres put a hand up at her. "Not you," she said.

"Of course," Rakta responded with a timid chuckle. She laced her fingers behind her back, and respected the moment the four of them were sharing.

Feres's head pulled up from the tangle of arms. "Prepare a full treatment plan, with contingencies, and have it sent to me and Mercelle within the hour."

"Yes, my Lady." Medical Scholar Rakta left the room.

Lito didn't want to let go. With Bewapen at His side, and Feres and Mercelle within His embrace, a warm sensation collected within His bosom. Resting His head on Feres's shoulder, the thought of staying here forever, in this room, entangled with His favorite people, crossed His mind.

Within the last twenty-four hours, Lito had experienced two different sensations of love. It was something He could bring Himself to understand now, His experience of it at least. What's more, He better understood all of humanity because of it.

One thing was clear: when He created the humans, He didn't create love. It had only come to be through the work of His creations, and in turn, His creations were teaching it back to Him.

23

NEWLYN II

Summoned, once again, to the control room of the Mastership, Newlyn waddled down the corridor. He knew what this was going to be about, but was quite confident in his ability to argue the fault away from himself.

The Newlyn that was killed for helping a Crassa access unauthorized information was a replica he hadn't seen since its creation. If the Demigod was going to be blamed for something like this, then it was a good time to bring up the fact that he had very little control over his own replicas, especially since Mora was in charge of overseeing operations in both the maturation bay and in the handling of Crassa within Glaven Grad. The only replicas Newlyn actually kept charge of were the ones trained to conduct transportation missions and mining assignments. Valk would have to see things his way.

As expected, Mora was there when he turned the corner into the dim control room. Valk was staring out the large glass wall, looking down on Earth. Knowing Mora was there validated his suspicions that she had sold him to Valk in return for her exoneration from any guilt. She was clever like that, and he wasn't surprised that she would turn on him to protect herself. It was the Chaos way.

Standing behind Mora was a humanoid monster – one of her creations she had likely brought up here to gloat about. It looked like a human man, but its exterior was scaley and rough in most places. Muscles swelled out of each limb, splitting through the skin with thick scar tissue attempting to cover the open wounds. Some replica skin may have been used to graft over the openings. The legs were massive, wrapped in a black, reflective material that was probably keeping the distended flesh from falling free. The elbows and knees protruded sharp bits of bone. Its lips were gone, its nostrils ripped wider than normal, and only the monster's straight, white teeth showed through the mouth. Its eyes darted around the room as if it was looking for something, or waiting for something, orders perhaps.

What ever it was that Mora had done to this man, it truly was a monstrous creation.

"Hello," Newlyn opened. "Where is Bled?"

“Bled is engaged at the moment,” Mora answered. “He’s working on a special project that I’ve been helping him with.”

A sudden swell of betrayal swept through Newlyn, even stronger than the one he’d felt after realizing Mora had turned on him yet again. How could Bled be working on something with her without even telling Newlyn about it? Why was he being kept out of the loop?

He wasn’t being included in everything like he used to be, and that made him nervous. It was supposed to be him and Bled working against Mora. A small part of him believed that Mora could have been lying to him, if only to put him on edge.

If that was the case, then it was working.

“I see,” was all he could think to say back. He kept near the door, just in case Valk planned on killing him. At least he’d have a chance at running away, although he didn’t have any idea how far he could possibly get.

A low, daunting tone came from Valk. “The weak one still roams the Earth,” he said calmly, but with a pinch of annoyance. “You aren’t doing enough to stop him, Newlyn. And you, Mora, your experiments still fail to render successful results.”

Good, Newlyn thought, the focus was on Mora too, and not just on him.

“Actually,” Mora replied through a devilish grin. “I think I’ve reached a breakthrough. The liquid to vapor gamma-tachyon mixture has finally been perfected, as has the acetylator implantation procedure. I was able to use them to create this human-Chaos hybrid you see here. He's capable of understanding and carrying out orders, just as you asked. He's stronger than any Valk, faster than any Bled, and he's even been infused with poison from a Mora's throat gland without succumbing to complete organ failure. I believe the success of this trial depended on the subject's blood type and body fat ratios, but we're looking further into it to formulate a way of making more just like him. Many more." Her eyes went to Newlyn. "This man was the Crassa by the name of Olim Jasusa, although we suspect that to be a false name given to hide his true identity as a spy."

Newlyn became even more nervous at hearing that. Now he knew exactly why she had brought her monster up here: she wanted to rub in his face the fact that his mistake was her opportunity for success. Olim Jasusa was the reason he was up here to begin with. It didn't matter, though, because he knew that once he explained everything to Valk, he would know that Newlyn wasn't at fault for the breach.

Mora motioned for the monster to step forward. It did, and held its hands behind its back like an obedient soldier.

"As soon as we identify the D.N.A. markers that facilitated the stable change from human to hybrid we'll have the capability of replicating the experiment with the same results. You'll soon have an army of monsters, my King."

Valk turned away from the glass, looking the Jasusa monster up and down. "You said it obeys orders?"

"It's the only tamable being to come out of my experiments thus far," Mora told him. She stepped into the threshold of the door, speaking to someone out in the corridor. "Bring him in."

Two Valks entered, each holding the arm of a human man and pulling him roughly into the room. He had on a torn human military uniform, and looked like he had put up quite the fight before being apprehended. Half of his face was swollen and purple, while open cuts on his shoulders and torso bled slowly onto the floor.

"We found him wandering around one of our magma towers just before it was destroyed," she explained. "He has said nothing during questioning beyond who he is."

"And who might that be?" asked Valk, stepping closer to the man and staring down at him.

The man puffed up his chest, staring right back at Valk with little fear in his eyes. "My name," he said. "Is First Officer Castnik Ashlan, Head of the Armies of Sandramedius, and Second in Command beneath Lady Ti-Erin Feres."

"Not anymore, I suppose," taunted Valk.

"A capture like this can prove to be very advantageous," said Newlyn. "He definitely has vast knowledge of the inner workings of Sandramedius, and he could be an asset of information if questioned *properly*." He glared at Mora.

"As if I hadn't thought of that?" Mora pressed. "All high ranking officers of the rebellion are trained to withstand heavy interrogations and even torture. Besides, loyalty is the currency of Sandramedius." She looked at the First Officer with disgust. "This man would happily die without divulging a single thing."

"Believe it," the man said, tugging at his arms as they were held in place by the Valks. "May as well kill me, because you won't get a thing out of me."

Valk seemed to enjoy hearing that. "Very well. Leave him and go." The two Valks let the man go and left the room, pressing the button to seal the door. "I think this is the perfect test for our new experiment. You, Crassa." The Jasusa monster stepped forward, facing Valk to receive its orders. "Kill this man."

The Jasusa monster whipped its head around to face the First Officer. Mora and Valk backed away to give them space, and Newlyn pressed against the wall as flat as his rotund figure would allow.

The monster walked blankly at the man named Ashlan, reaching out to snap his neck, but the man was too quick, ducking out of the way and coming up behind the hybrid. A swift twist, and the hybrid swiped at the man with the sharp bone sticking out of its elbow.

Ashlan ducked beneath it, striking in quick succession and putting a rain of fists into the monster's gut before pivoting away once again. The monster was unfazed, turning to face the man no matter where he went. A step closer, and the man was dodging another strike, leaping up to put a boot into the scaley face of his enemy. One stitch popped free from the monster's face, and a drip of blood ran off its chin, but it still didn't blink as it continued to step toward the wily man.

The monster kicked and missed as Ashlan leapt backward, bumping into Newlyn. He elbowed the monster in the back, recoiling from the pain it caused before kicking the back of the monster's legs, jumping into the air and dropping another elbow onto its head.

Nothing seemed to hurt or effect the thing, as it stood still and took countless blows with no reaction and very little movement.

Finally, it turned its head toward the panting man. Two swift steps toward him, and it brought a knee into his midsection.

Ashlan threw both arms down to stop the blow, pressing against the meaty part of the monster's thigh, but it was too strong and Ashlan was sent flying backward into the wall. A wound formed on his chest from the protruding bone on the monster's knee.

Even Newlyn had to admit that this experiment had

proven to increase the strength of the subject by at least six fold. He couldn't believe it. If more of these could be made, their decimation of the human Race could be expedited. Although, he didn't like the idea of Mora's head getting even bigger.

To his surprise, the man recovered quickly, blocking the monster's massive hands from gripping his neck, and attempting to kick its legs out again. The only thing that resulted from that was the sound of a snap coming from the man's shin. An open hand from the hybrid struck the side of the man's cheek, toppling him over and bouncing his head off of the floor. When it picked him up with a single arm and held him to the wall, his eyes were rolling about incoherently.

A scaley hand went to Ashlan's neck, and his eyes snapped back awake, but there was nothing more he could do. He would soon succumb to the strength of the monster. His face turned red and purple, and bulged with pressure as air and saliva spat out from his mouth.

Blood trickled from beneath the hand that held the man's neck, indicating a tearing of the skin. With a sudden crunch, the light went out from his eyes, and his body fell to the floor. When Newlyn looked back up at the monster, it was still holding the man's head.

Slowly, it turned and handed the head to Valk, who was grinning frighteningly. He took the head, and said, "Very good, Jasusa. I see your humanity is no longer a liability. Mora, your experiments will continue, and with full resources. I'll be keeping this one for myself."

"Thank you, my King!" she shouted before giving Newlyn a look that could only mean that she wished him dead. "We have all the samples we need to locate the required markers. There should be more just like him in no time."

"Excellent," Valk declared. "Let it be known to all of the other Crassa in Glaven Grad that this is what will become of any traitors – they will be made to kill their own. Chaos, however," he looked at Newlyn, who went cold and tried not to choke. "Will not be given second chances. Just like the Newlyn who assisted the Crassa, all Chaos traitors will be killed on sight."

This was it. Valk was waiting for Newlyn to explain himself. Simple.

"I can explain that," he began.

Valk came toward him with slow steps. "It was your replica who aided the Crassa in the breach."

"It wasn't under my charge. Nor was it-"

"A communication device was found among the traitor's possessions," Valk inserted, drawing ever nearer.

"I know. If I could just-"

"There is no possible way for us to determine how much information was leaked to the rebels."

Newlyn pressed against the wall, praying he would simply go through it to the other side and get away. "It wasn't my fault! Please. I haven't even seen that replica since-"

"Your replica! Your fault!" Valk's nose was right on Newlyn's.

"Was it Mora who convinced you of that, my King?" he asked, grasping at anything to save his own life. "Sh-she's the treacherous one. Always after your affection and your power! She-"

Valk put a claw around Newlyn's throat, tightening and tightening until the internal flow of goo was plugged, and his head began to swell, just like the headless human's had. Newlyn looked to the decapitated man on the floor, waiting for his own head to pop off just the same. It couldn't be the end. He couldn't have lost to Mora's double-dealing gambits. This was what she had wanted all along, and Valk only needed a reason.

"Your replicas are becoming hindrances," Valk growled into his face. "I can't tell you just how *angry* it makes me when my own Demigod has gone against me."

Newlyn mouthed the words "please" and "no", but it did little to quell Valk's short-sighted wrath.

"You won't let something like that happen again. Will you?" asked Valk.

He shook his head as much as he could in the reptilian Demigod's tight grip.

"Good," Valk said, beginning to calm the rumble in his throat.

That was it. Valk was going to let him live. If only he could be spared, he could work to show Mora's true colors, and in doing so ascend his position with Valk. Perhaps he could witness her death instead. That would make all of this worth it, he thought.

But, Valk's grip on his neck didn't loosen.

"Jasusa," ordered Valk. His tone was lulled and strangely composed. "Come." The monster obeyed, coming to his side immediately. Mora held back laughter in the corner of the room. "I want you to do something for me." The monster grunted its reply. "I want you to remove Newlyn's eye for me. Could you do that?"

Newlyn wriggled, trying to get free, but even with the goo excreting in large amounts through his skin, Valk had him in his claws like a vice. There was no way he could speak or cry out in pain, and when he saw the monster's hand coming at his face, he tensed up, which only made everything worse.

Without responding at all, the monster shoved its fingers into the socket around Newlyn's right eye. The eye was about half the size of the monster's fist, but it worked the fingers deep into Newlyn's head, unsympathetically tearing at the nerves and tendrils that kept it attached.

Like a screw being driven through his head, and

exploding into acid-edged shrapnel, a thrust of sharp pain shot through him. Strangely enough, once the nerves were severed the pain dulled. But it wasn't over.

The worst part came when he watched with his left eye as the Jasusa monster crushed his right eye in his scaley hand. It turned to black water, and splashed upon the ground.

It was humiliating, and while Mora laughed out loud, Valk dropped Newlyn to the floor, turning to look out the glass once more. Finally able to speak, Newlyn whimpered, covering his leaking eye socket, only to feel his eyelids torn and hanging loose from his face. He pushed himself back against the wall, sliding around like a newly born replica.

The hate he held for Mora intensified, and he even found himself hating Valk for believing her. Newlyn was smarter than the both of them combined, and from now on he was going to start using his intelligence to put himself above them. Somehow, he was going to be the one to end humanity, and then he was going to take down Valk and Mora when they least expected it.

Bled was another story, and Newlyn just assumed he had been manipulated by Mora the same as Valk. Whatever the case, the burning strain in his head fueled him further.

As angry as he was at this moment, he imagined Valk was even moreso, because the Demigod King shook the room, shouting as loud as he could when he spoke his next words:

"You have all proven to be useless in the task of killing the weak one!" He didn't look away from the glass as he bellowed the words out. Mora stopped laughing to herself. "Because of that, I will go down to Earth myself! If I am unsuccessful in ridding this planet of His pesky existence, then you ALL shall be prepared to face Leto's wrath!" He turned to face them. "Because Leto is on His way here as we speak!"

"Oh no," Mora trembled.

This wasn't good at all. Leto couldn't arrive before they ended all life on this planet, including Lito's, and depleted its resources. That would mean the death of all of the Demigods at His hand. None of them would be allowed on another campaign, or even allowed to survive, after such a failure.

"How did He find out about Lito?" asked Mora.

"He is a God!" Valk shouted. "He is THE God! He knows all He needs to know to survive and rule the universe! We do not question that!"

Newlyn stood up, turning toward the wall and hiding his face in eviscerating shame.

"Leto has left the Great Wall, and will be here in due time! By then, this planet shall be decimated! Or it'll be your heads delivered to Leto! Now, be gone! I'm finished with you!"

Newlyn scurried to the door, hitting the button to

open it, and shuffling down the corridor as fast as he could.

HIS REFLECTION WAS DIFFERENT.

After locking himself inside of an empty room, Newlyn stared at himself in the glass of a powered down monitor. The screen went from floor to ceiling, and in the dark chamber he could clearly see the hollow pit left behind on his face by the Jasusa monster.

Ashamed by the entire interaction, he couldn't believe Mora had bested him. She had managed to blame the entire breach on him, and because she brought Valk a new pet to kick around, he ate it up. For all Newlyn knew, Mora could have planned this, orchestrating the breach from the time she received the replica in the maturation bay. Who knew if the Jasusa Crassa was even a traitor?

She was good at manipulation and deception, and he would have to be better. He was lucky to be alive, but still fumed with rage.

The goo inside of his body reached a warm temperature, and he felt the oncoming of a replication. His wet hands went flat onto the glass of the terminal, and he tensed up, feeling his liquid insides begin to solidify into chunks and make their ways through his softening, gelatinous skin. One by one they plopped themselves on the floor, each no larger than his foot, and he kicked them into the wall in front of him, bouncing them away until there was a pile of over fifteen of them at his rear. It wasn't a particularly painful process, he just wasn't in the mood, causing him to replicate such a small number.

He watched in the reflection of the terminal. The pile got bigger as the wet chunks each grew in size. They slid off of each other, forming four limbed replicas. Fingers sprouted out of the hands. Small ear holes and nostrils developed within seconds. The mouths opened and tiny cries of birth came out of them. Lastly, each of the newly born replicas sprouted a pair of bulbous black eyes.

Even as newborns, his replicas still held a physical advantage over him, as he would never be able to regrow his missing eye. They would always be created in a better image than their creator. This is the curse Valk and his new pet had bestowed upon him.

Looking at his only eye in the reflection of the screen, he felt weak. Newlyn had to be the weakest Demigod of the four, and possibly of all that Leto had created. Why had he been designed like this? Why had Bled betrayed him by working with Mora on some secret project? He had never felt so pitiful in his entire millennium of existence.

Leto was the one who had made him this way. Creating beings through Chaos was never consistent, or controllable, even by the God of Chaos Himself. Still, Newlyn couldn't help but resent his creator for his own shortcomings. His hatred increased with each throb of his vacant eye socket.

The replicas got to their feet, struggling at first to stay upright, but quickly learning the function of balance. They looked to him for guidance. This was typically when he would send them off to the maturation bay, but the thought of putting them under the control of one of Mora's learning and propaganda programs made him shake with rage.

"I won't have them turned against me," he declared to himself. "Not this time!"

Newlyn balled up a wet fist and slammed it into the terminal's screen, shattering it into a pile of shards on the floor before him. Whipping around, he fired pellets from his wrists at the small crowd of replicas, piercing their midsections and causing goo to leak out of them heavily. It was so quick that not a single one even had the chance to react.

He fired at them until their skins gave in and collapsed, pushing what goo remained inside of them out. In a way, Newlyn had reclaimed a small bit of his self-respect by destroying his own replicas.

If only he could get a pellet or two into Mora.

24

KOP STAMHOOF II

The group of traveling Onyx men had stopped for a few hours before the sun went down to eat and rest briefly. Kop Stamhoof tried to get Geboor to take some sappidge, but the boy wasn't having any of it. He wouldn't drink the juice either, which led the Kop to fear that he may become sick soon. The rope tied around Geboor's waist had to be held at the other end at all times to keep him from wandering off, and with night falling, Stamhoof didn't want to lose track of the boy.

Once the cool night breeze began sweeping across the desert floor, the convoy began moving once again. The tracks left behind by Lito and Mercelle's two-wheeled transports were easy to see and follow. Travelling at night was less taxing on the men, and he figured they would rest the next day in the shadows of the dunes.

At the head of the procession were his trackers, under the command of Second Prime Virou-Malik. Dozens of men with lit torches led the way, keeping their eyes on the ground. Before leaving the caves, the Kop had instructed them to snuff out their flames at any sign of danger.

Behind the trackers was a group of the most experienced warriors, with another group bringing up the rear with First Prime Neemoor in case of an ambush. In the center of their convoy, the Kop led the younger warriors, who dragged supplies and the large, black coffin along on steel sleds. Third Prime F'Briek stayed by the Kop's side as a last layer of protection.

Geboor had crawled on all fours the entire way, his head moving about to look this way and that, as if he was completely unaware of where they were, or what might come at them out of the darkness. The Kop needed Geboor to stay safe, and in one piece, at least until they reached Sandra. He wanted to make sure Lito could see what He had created, and exactly what Geboor had become.

With the bulk of the Onyx Clan with him, he thought about the men and children who stayed behind, his son Litar, and his beloved Queen Maagda – his Mother Aeterna. The mating ceremony would be commencing within the next couple of days, and he regretted that this would be the first one at which he wouldn't be present to bestow a blessing. He'd been to every one in the last century and a half since becoming Kop of the Clan, and he pondered whether or not it would be any different without his presence.

Everything would be different, he thought, from now on.

He looked up to the sky. Stars glinted down on them, blessing their journey with a victory he couldn't help but look forward to. The procession dipped into a valley. Mountains encircled them on all sides. Such a calm night it was, as they hadn't seen a single dust storm since the night before. The breeze, however, was steady, and brought him a slight chill. This is why they travelled best at night, because sleeping in such cold conditions was nearly impossible for the Onyx people. At the caves they could at least curl up next to a hot sappidge flame.

The Kop had heard stories of their ancestors sleeping alongside magma flows, or even atop them. That was back when the hot rivers still ran deep below the surface of Earth. This generation was a bit more accustomed to the cool night air, but still not entirely comfortable in it.

Coming out of the valley, the Kop could see the light from the trackers' torches far ahead of them, and they ventured through a maze of skinny dunes that had been weathered down to pillars over the centuries. Mercelle and Lito must have traversed these parts very carefully, as some places were quite narrow, and heavily populated with the stone pillars.

The worn down dunes thinned out, and they made their way through the desert with ease, until the torches up ahead went out.

That was the signal he dreaded to see. A voice called out, but it was too far away for him to make out the words.

"Aahast!!" he shouted, and the procession came to a halt. He continued forward, cutting through the crowd of warriors at the front of the group, F'Briek on his heels. Geboor hummed low and deep, and the Kop soon realized the boy was growling. Drooling, biting at the air, and snarling at something up ahead, Geboor stayed close to the Kop without having to be pulled by the makeshift leash, and once they got closer to the head of the convoy, they stopped and listened.

Stamhoof could hear the granules of sand bouncing off of his cheek, but he couldn't smell anything in the wind. Geboor's nose went into the air, and his nostrils flared before his growling intensified. Something was ahead of them, and only the boy could sense it.

"Shh," Stamhoof told Geboor.

In the silence of the night, he heard nothing, and waited for another holler from the trackers up front. It never came. Instead, he heard heavy footsteps coming at him in the pitch dark. Taking a battle stance, the warriors around him took the cue and did the same.

Directly in front of them, a handful of trackers approached, running at full speed and joining in the wall of warriors. F'Briek handed the Kop his hammer, which was seven feet long, with a small anvil at one end that could outweigh a young man. He took it in one hand, and held tight to Geboor's rope with the other. All of the trackers faced the darkness ahead and held up their hammers and staffs.

"Chaos," Virou-Malik whispered to him. "Valks!"

Once they were all in position, the heavy footfalls didn't stop. Kop Stamhoof could still feel the beat of hooves in the sand. He called out, "Chaos!" just as the tall reptilian replicas came into sight.

They held their positions, waiting for the enemies to get near enough to be overwhelmed and easily dispatched. The creatures were the same ones who had built the magma tower, and the Kop had never seen one this close up. These were the formidable replicas Lito and Mercelle referred to as Valks.

Geboor dug his knuckles and feet into the sand, waiting to lunge while dripping saliva through bare teeth, and making throat noises the Kop hadn't heard come from any human before.

Holding tight and solid at the center of the front line, Stamhoof's eye caught the dark maroon of Valk scales as the horde slammed into them.

He spun around, swinging the hammer horizontally and knocking two Valks in the head with a single swipe. Geboor's rope wrapped around the Kop's waist, so he spun the other way, landing the anvil of his hammer in the gut of another replica. F'Briek, Neemoor and the trackers encircled him for protection, and the experienced warriors shot forward to push the line back.

Surrounded by Valks, he felt the tug of Geboor on the rope, and looked to see the boy wrapping his legs around the neck of a reptilian creature, rotating around to its back and twisting the neck until the head snapped off and blood ran over his face.

Pulling the rope to keep the boy close by, he found it rather difficult to overpower Geboor with one hand. The ravenous boy growled, trying to pull away from the Kop and enter the fray of battle.

"Geboor!" cried the Kop. He commanded the boy to stop pulling, but it was no use.

Geboor's teeth went to the rope, gnawing and tearing at it wildly as his eyes bulged and his throat moaned with the hunger for violence.

A Valk broke through the front line, trying to get the Kop with its heavy blade. His hammer was heavier, though, and with one hand the Kop blocked the strike with the long handle. Another strike and another block, and he felt the other end of Geboor's rope drop to the ground. He let it go, gripping the hammer with both hands, bringing it up and smashing the Valk into the sand with little effort.

Looking around, he was clear of enemies. Some of the younger warriors had rushed to the head of the convoy to partake in the melee, and out of the corner of his eye the Kop saw Geboor scamper through the swinging swords, hammers and staffs, disappearing into the dark night with a small length of rope dragging behind him.

"Geboor!" he called out. Without the boy, their trip was futile. The whole reason for uprooting nearly his entire Clan was to show Lito what He had created, and what He had done to this innocent boy. All he heard in return was the boy's thunderous roar fading into the distance, and the clashing of steel weapons against Chaos hardware.

He stepped into the ocean of movement in front of him, knocking a sword away with one end of his hammer, and stabbing the other end into a scaled torso. When a replica grabbed Stamhoof by his white dreadlocks, Neemoor twisted its arm off like it was nothing, and tossed the freed appendage into the sand before crouching to dodge the next sword.

A hoof caught the Kop in the side, and nearly knocked him over, but he kept footing, kicking backward to disable the Valk's other leg. When it stumbled, he shoved his hammer forward into its head, putting it on its backside. A young warrior stepped on the creature's neck, and pulled its head off, throwing it into the face of the next replica that came at him.

With this being the Kop's first direct interaction with Chaos, he decided that these Valks weren't much to take on at all. The way Mercelle spoke of them, it was as if they needed two or three light skinned people to take even one Valk down. Their centuries of living in fear of Chaos were for naught. If the light skinned had stood up to them sooner, they could have been regarded as the saviors of humanity. Now, Chaos ran rampant all throughout the deserts of Earth. It was no wonder as to why they had intercepted a Chaos convoy.

Neemoor led the rear of the procession of Onyx as they flooded forward, making light work of the reptilian replicas and overpowering them with numbers and strength. He was proud to witness their heritage of battle training in its full display, and the fight lasted but a few more moments before the ringing of hammers on swords and the splattering of replica blood ceased.

Once the battleground was silent, the Kop began searching for Geboor.

WHILE THE THREE Primes gathered the convoy back to order and assessed injuries,

Stamhoof searched the nearby mesa, finding a fleet of Chaos vehicles hidden behind it. A few of the trackers assisting him in the search fanned out, inspecting the transports. Oddly enough, the area around the fleet was sprinkled with Chaos bodies. Kop Stamhoof hadn't seen anyone come this far in this direction, and to kill so many creatures would require at least a handful of his warriors.

All around the vehicles were fat creatures which were leaking some kind of thick liquid, skinny, greenish creatures which were torn limb from limb and a collection of Valks that had been absolutely destroyed. Some of the monsters even had their midsections ripped open, and their entrails dragged out over the sand.

Kop Stamhoof tried to imagine what could have done this, and thought that there may have been an even bigger Chaos creature around here somewhere that got out of control.

Low snarling came from the other side of a long, green-glowing transport. The Kop and his trackers all held the killing ends of their weapons out in its direction. They crept, slowly, around the rear of the transport, and what he saw on the other side told him that there was no bigger monster. There wasn't some gargantuan creature that had lost control and killed its own keepers.

Crouched on the ground next to a Valk's body that had been half shredded, was Geboor. He had a reptilian arm in his mouth, gnawing at it with a mad hunger. The sounds of the boy's snarling faded and returned with the rhythm of his rabid, bare-toothed chewing.

What the Kop was seeing wasn't Bewapen's son, it was a beast, and to watch the boy feasting on Chaos flesh was another level of insanity he thought he'd never be able to get out of his mind.

The trackers held their weapons at the boy.

"Eestoonil," the Kop instructed, telling the others to keep their distance. He approached the end of Geboor's rope, quietly reaching down and picking it up from the sand. It was coated in Valk blood, sticky and frayed.

The boy's face when he whipped around to look at the Kop was distant, ravenous and unaccepting of being pulled away from his meal. His eyes went back and forth, looking at the Valk's corpse and back at his Kop again. For a moment, Kop Stamhoof thought he was going to have to pull the boy away. But, in a surprising display of obedience, Geboor took what remained of the corpse by its leg, turned toward Stamhoof and crawled, dragging the replica behind him.

25

LADY INIS MERCELLE XII

Small bits of darkness remained in her heart, unavoidably tainting the vision she had always held for her future. They shrank and throbbed, testing her strength every moment. As the day went on, her mind straightened out, putting the weight of her previously depressed state into perspective as she repeated her parents' words in her head, over and over. Everything had a purpose, and each step she took was a step toward salvation for not only herself, but for Earth. One moment she believed, and the next she was convincing herself of it yet again.

The single thing she was sure about was the fact that every time she pictured herself standing on that steel railing, looking down at the opening between the solar panels beneath her, she was nothing more than disappointed in the temporary weakness she had allowed to take her over. She had the power to battle almost anything, and the darkness was her next enemy. Even if it took every second of every day, Lady Inis Mercelle of the legendary city of Lanna wasn't going to let the darkness step back into her path.

The highest point in Sandramedius was the signal tower above Feres's A.L.C.O. building. With such a steady, moderate breeze coming from the west, they couldn't stand to waste the night. All together, Bewapen, Lito, Feres and Mercelle climbed the caged ladder that reached over seven hundred feet to the railed off access point. From here, a communications Scholar would typically cross the zipline wearing protective gear to get to the antenna in the case of any malfunctions.

Tonight, the access point was theirs, and they looked out over the entire city. Small pillars of street-lamps bled up through the cracks between the solar panels, and aside from that, the only other light flickered down from the stars. Smoke rose from stacks in the manufacturing district, and disappeared into the cool breeze of the otherwise warm evening. Low murmurs of transport engines, and the cranking of metal machinery in the recycling plant were the only sounds.

The access point was also the only place where Mercelle thought the air smelled the most crisp and fresh, with no interruption of sand making its way up her nostrils. Breathing the air deep felt revitalizing, and since Lito hadn't left her side all day she had been her normal self, with no dizzy spells or nausea, not even aches of muscle pain from her workout the night before. It was as if she was alive again, and ready to kill something. As long as Lito was nearby, she would be fine. Using the restroom had been slightly awkward, especially since she had eaten quite a lot throughout the day due to the energy provided by Lito's proximity, and was extra hydrated from the transfusion and subsequent electrolyte treatments. She preferred not to think about that, and enjoyed the wind on her face instead.

Since Lanna had been destroyed, it seemed as if Mercelle hadn't had a single calm day, her grief buried by distractions, and today was no different. Learning about her diagnosis and Lito's curative effects on the poisoning within a few hours of each other was enough, but Feres had shared a piece of information: her placement of a spy within Glaven Grad. Part of Feres's reason to scale the access tower had been to find a safe place to share the information without fear of being overheard or recorded. Where Lito went, there was usually a number of recording devices, accompanied with giddy citizens who loved asking Him questions about His favorite weapons, or where His large, dark friend came from.

"Kraj sent us back a lot of information," Feres explained. "I couldn't get any audio from the transmitter he took with him, but he relayed hours of video files. It looked to me like he was working with Newlyns on some kind of translation think tank. They're intercepting our communication documents, both public and private, somehow, and trying to make sense of them. Kraj was manipulating most of the data he came across to throw them off."

This was smart, and Mercelle found herself questioning how she didn't see something like this coming. Feres was good at hiding things, even from her, and Mercelle understood.

"What kind of intel did he manage to send back?" she asked. "Anything useful?"

"They've acquired a large number of humans," Feres answered. "I'm not sure how, but with the number of experiments Mora's been performing on them, I'd be surprised if they haven't perfected some kind of monster manufacturing process. They even use their own replicas in the tests, killing most of them. And they seem to be happy to participate."

Lito, as always, shed some logic upon the implied question. "With large numbers of replicas being created out of nothing, the Choas won't put much value on a single life. I'm sure the participants are conditioned from creation to believe that dying in an experiment is their purpose."

That made sense to Mercelle. The ability to manipulate any type of thought process had to be an advantage. Humans weren't as capable of the hive mind mentality. At least, she'd thought so until she met the Onyx Clan.

"Creator is tell creation to die?" asked Bewapen, disapprovingly.

"That's Chaos for you," Mercelle replied. "All they care about is killing us and ruining our planet so nothing can ever survive here again."

"And they plan on leaving soon," said Feres. "The biggest piece of intel Kraj sent back was a file showing their plans to convert the Glaven Grad tower into a space vessel. I think they want to leave with their armies intact as a way to be prepared for the next planet they plan on taking over and destroying. It also means they don't plan on staying much longer. They may be getting ready for another attack, one they feel will be the final battle of the war."

"We're ready," declared Mercelle.

"No," Lito countered. "We're not. If the Demigods threw everything they had at Sandra right now, we would surely lose. All they would have to do from there is go after Kerk, and then save enough numbers up again to take down Naselba."

Mercelle shook her head. "And with Naselba's complete lack of battle knowledge, they wouldn't stand a chance."

Feres scoffed. "I'm starting to wonder why they haven't been taken out yet. They're the biggest human city left on Earth, yet they're the smallest threat. Valk probably sees no point in wasting time on them since they pose very little danger to him. We'll have to try and talk some sense into this 'Empress' at the summit. Tomorrow I'll start preparing the convoy. We leave within a couple of days."

"I is help." offered Bewapen with a wink. "You is let me know."

"I will, Bewapen. Thank you."

Mercelle couldn't help but ask, "Are we even sure we can get any help from them? I mean, what exactly are we planning to say at this summit? The Naselbans are pretty comfortable in their luxurious lifestyles. Sometimes I think they know the end is coming, and they're just trying to enjoy their time before Earth is uninhabitable."

"Well," Feres started. "I'm really hoping we can work something out with them. They can't be *entirely* useless. Naselba has to have something to offer, even if it's simple medical or nutritional support for the soldiers."

"Ha!" she laughed. "Good luck with that. You already spoke to their secretary. Edeen is calling herself 'Empress' now? Her ego runs that city. We'd be lucky if she didn't take us into custody as soon as the gates closed behind us. She'll turn us into her personal servants."

"I is no let that happen. If Naselba is no help, then

we is abandon them. We is fight without them if they is cowards."

"It isn't that easy, Bewapen," Feres responded. "We need them. They have numbers and technology which could give us a huge advantage over the armies of replicas we'll have to face. Our best bet at winning this war is in a singular, coordinated attack on Glaven Grad, and giving it everything we have."

The prospect of battle enticed Mercelle, and she felt the exciting anticipation of taking an enemy life. But, she would have to be patient for blood. Any hasty decisions would surely ruin the advantages they'd fought to obtain thus far. Maybe if Lady Edeen opted out of assisting in the attack, Feres could make an enemy of her, and launch a full scale attack on Naselba instead, just for the practice. Mercelle would be at the front line.

These were the happy thoughts which helped her keep the darkness out.

"I agree," Mercelle said, banging a fist on the steel railing. "We fight and we win, or we die trying, with or without Naselba. Besides, convincing a Naselban to put their life on the line for anyone but themself will be even more difficult than convincing Dredger to attend."

She shook her head, feeling as if there were better ways of spending their time than attending the summit. The more she thought about it, the less useful the summit had the potential to become. But, she wasn't about to allow herself to succumb to such gloomy ideals.

Mercelle could feel Feres's worrisome eyes on her.

"How are you feeling?" she asked.

"I wish people would stop asking me that," Mercelle replied back. "I feel fine. If I don't, I'll let you know. How about that?"

"I'm just checking in." A page came through on Feres's tablet. She pulled it off of her belt and checked it, sighed and clipped it back. "I have to go, of course. Look, sis, I'm proud of you. You've gone through more than anyone, and you've put more of yourself into this war than your parents did." She squeezed Mercelle's hand. "I just don't want you to worry about yourself. The summit in Naselba is our best bet at accumulating more allies, and if it doesn't work I'll still fight by your side. Got it?"

Not wanting to accept her sister's pity, Mercelle stared out at the solar panels beneath them. All Feres was trying to do was find the old Mercelle that still lived deep inside of her – the Mercelle who laughed, and celebrated each victory no matter how small – the version of her that existed before the fall of Lanna. That woman was gone, and Mercelle missed her too.

Everything was different, and most people were unrecognizable from their former selves. One thing that still rang true was Feres's devotion to her sister and to the inevitable victory over the Demigods. Mercelle had to remind herself that they all wanted the same thing, and that her sister was simply trying to keep her spirits in the right place.

Mercelle looked up at Feres, forcing a smile and a nod. "I know. Thank you, sis."

"I love you, but I have to go deal with this right now." Feres pointed to the tablet. "Apparently some of the power storage facilities are draining electricity. If I don't get it resolved by morning we may be out of power by tomorrow night."

Feres squeezed Mercelle's hand again, and Mercelle squeezed back, showing a real smile this time. Next, Feres stepped in close to Lito, leaning her forehead onto His cheek for a moment before saying good night to Bewapen and beginning her descent down the caged ladder.

"May humanity and Order reign!" Feres called up to them.

The two men came to the railing, standing on either side of Mercelle.

Lito spoke first.

"I think the Naselbans will see reality for what it is once they hear what Lady Feres has to say, and once they learn everything we know about the Book of Order. Logic will set in, and they'll see they have no choice but to join us in battle."

"Even so," Mercelle replied, shaking her head. "Their warriors are Kaisering useless. We wouldn't have time to train them properly. Besides, you're missing one key detail: Naselbans aren't known for listening, they're known for talking and ordering. They may act like they're listening, only to manipulate what they hear into something that benefits them and their lifestyles. It's a city of narcissists run by descendants of the unholy Kaisers." There had to be other options, and Mercelle couldn't help but suggest one. "We should come up with a back-up plan in case we aren't heard at the summit, something drastically different than what we've tried before."

She looked left, to Bewapen, who was making a face of disinterest, likely trying to cope with the political nonsense in which he was now involved. The Onyx Clan hadn't experienced war in hundreds of thousands of years, according to Kop Stamhoof. This was all very new to them, despite them probably being the best warriors of the Seven Races.

"Expanding our abilities is always something worth trying," posited Lito.

"Or is something unavoidable."

Mercelle nearly laughed at the rush of thoughts flwoing through her head. "In the case of our shared vision. I still think we're missing something – something that we're meant to see. How did you feel at the end of your vision?"

"Sad," He answered. "Like all hope had been lost."

"What if it isn't? What if there's more to it than that?

We saw blue lights falling from the sky. The same blue lights that are inside of your Shard. What if we're meant to get them out somehow?"

"Don't forget that we were walking through a leveled city. If we pursue this vision, then we risk existing in a timeline wherein another city is destroyed."

That was a good point, she thought. The vision meant something, at least to her, and the longer she went without addressing it seemed to make her itch and irritate more. "We have the Shard, and we have the three of us. Mother Maagda said that Bewapen was the third one in our vision. All we need is ruins, and a way to get the lights to come out of the Shard. Didn't Seemik say that one of them came out during examination? How do you suppose that happened?"

"Lito's blood is heal," Bewapen said, avoiding eye contact while staring contemplatively at the horizon. "Maybe blood is more powerful with Shard. They is work together."

"Hmm..." Mercelle added. Agnitius had taught her to always review the facts to get to the next hypothesis. "The Shard is your conduit to the Source; therefore, it channels your power to you. Right? Maybe, if you concentrated your power into the right things, you can do more than just heal. What do you think?"

"It's worth a try." The God was giving them nothing,

continuing with His quest to instill free will in everyone around Him. "What do you suggest?"

"You is try to bring dead back to life," Bewapen randomly threw out. He was facing away from them, almost speaking into the wind. "Is only thing left to try."

Mercelle sensed she was missing something. She locked eyes with Lito and squinted at Him. "What aren't you telling us, Bewapen?"

Capitulation in his sigh, Bewapen turned to face them. "There is something I is not say before. Kop is order me not to say, but I is feel I must say."

Her eyes were now digging into Bewapen with impatience. "What did the Kop order you to keep from us?"

"It's about the vision, isn't it?" asked Lito.

Bewapen nodded slowly. "Kop and Queen is say that vision is more than what they is tell you. They is say-"

"Wait," Mercelle put a hand up. "The last thing we need is the Alliance Ambassador going against his own Kop. If the Kop suspects you've been turned or that you've betrayed his trust it could jeopardize the whole alliance between the rebellion and the Onyx."

"I is have to say," Bewapen insisted. "Is important so Lito is get more powerful."

Something about the Queen Mother's vision related to Lito getting more power? It didn't make any sense to Mercelle, but she decided that if Bewapen was willing to give the information then she wasn't going to refuse to accept it. "What does that mean, exactly?"

He took a deep breath before answering. "As I is understand, other part of vision is tell Mother how to test if Order God is true." He made a face that showed he was skeptical to provide more.

"A test?" Lito perked up with curiosity. "They were still doubting me."

"Mother is say that vision is tell her to test if Order God is able to bridge life and death. Kop is say that true Order God is bring dead alive again."

Dots were connecting in Mercelle's mind. "That's why he ordered you to come along as Ambassador; he wanted to perform the sacrifice for severance on Geboor and convince Lito to spill His blood over the corpse. But it didn't work. He failed the test."

"I didn't have this." Lito held up the Shard.

Lito's blood was already powerful, and could also be considered somewhat of a conduit of His power, seeing as it had effects on open wounds and other injuries, and lingered on within those who had taken His blood into themselves.

The question as to why the Kop and Queen would keep this information from them was no longer relevant to Mercelle. She started racing through ideas. "I think maybe you should try channeling the lights outward from the Shard, and into something else? Trying it on a cadaver would tell us to what extent you have the ability to heal. If you can keep me from death then maybe, just maybe, there's a chance you can bring others back from it with the Shard's help."

"This line of thinking makes sense to me," said the Order God. "And the risk is low."

"I agree. You can't exactly do more damage to a dead body. The only problem is finding one."

"Is no dead bodies in Sandra?" Bewapen asked.

"No. Feres isn't much into taking up useless space. All bodies are operated on, examined and then incinerated. The only close place I know to have cadavers for sure would be-"

"Kota Kara," inserted Lito.

"Kota Kara," she confirmed. "I just don't know what condition the bodies will be in. But, it's our best shot."

"How is we get there?"

"Clippers. We can get there in under four hours and be back by morning, as long as we maintain top speeds."

Her adrenaline pumped with the excitement of her next mission. Medical Scholar Rakta had told her that the cocktail she was given would likely keep her up all night. It was meant to increase blood pressure and entice the movement of cells within her veins to keep them active and avoid further breakdown. She had Lito, and that was all she needed to keep her energy up.

"It sounds like a good plan," agreed Lito. "Let's try it."

"I'm in," said Mercelle, looking to Bewapen. "I know you're coming, right? Unless you want to stay behind and help Feres with preparing the convoy."

"No. I is come, as long as I is ride with you."

His white eyebrow went up. The face he made was strange, but he seemed happy to be a part of the team, and she hadn't minded his arms being around her when they had ridden the clipper through the desert to Sandra.

"I wouldn't want it any other way." She grinned at him. "You're a great riding partner."

"I'm quite good at riding clippers by now, even on my own," added Lito.

"Great!" She banged a fist on the railing again. "Bewapen and I will eat something first, then we need to stop by the weapons depot and check some things out of inventory before heading to the garages. If we start now we can leave within the hour."

"I'll take Bewapen to the cafeterias," Lito advised, walking over to the ladder. "We'll get some electrolyte and vitamin tablets and meet you at the garage."

"Deal. I'll hit the weapons depot and then find us some clippers."

IN NO TIME AT ALL, Mercelle was loading up the small holds in the sides of two clippers with guns, bombs and ammunition. They were well prepared in case they intercepted a Chaos convoy or encampment. Bewapen carried his hammer with him, always strapped to his back, and would probably be better off with that than any weapon they could offer him.

Once Bewapen and Lito arrived with a small amount of provisions, they were ready.

Under the cover of night, they approached the gates. Mercelle had a brief conversation with Captain Shou, convincing him that Feres was aware of their secret little mission. Either way, none of the three of them were under Feres's control. They were all considered guests of Sandramedius and couldn't be held, which was one of the many reasons why she'd kindly declined Feres's offer of a position on Sandra's Court. Shou checked his area scans and agreed to open the gate a few feet to allow the pair of clippers to go through.

With Bewapen on the back of her clipper, and Lito on His own clipper beside her, they rode off into the night. Mercelle used the screen between her knees to navigate the terrain in order to avoid turning on their lights.

Aside from a few stubborn building supports, the city of Kota Kara was flattened. Chunks of concrete covered the ground for miles, twisted steel jutted up here and there, and even the main gates had been toppled and broken into pieces. The tips of each peak were scorched with the blackened remains of fire. Once they had given up their nuclear reactor core, there was no way of powering up their sophisticated automated weapons systems.

Mercelle recalled destroying the tower where Kota Kara's core had been taken. Another memory came to her, and she wasn't able to push away the image of Lanna's burning buildings. She had become so accustomed to bullying down her grief that she compartmentalized the image to the back of her mind, not forgetting, but not allowing it to weaken her either. Anything she had gone through was only meant to make her stronger, and she was going to facilitate that in any way she could.

"I don't see any bodies," she pointed out. "The fires must have burned most of them away."

Lito closed His eyes for a few seconds, then opened them and said, "There are some bodies still intact beneath the rubble. We need to go further in."

The three of them climbed over fields of destruction. It was rough terrain to say the least, but if they wanted to test their little theory, they needed to do as Lito said, and get closer to the intact cadavers. There wouldn't be much point in trying to resurrect a mangled body. Even if it did work, the mangled bodies wouldn't operate properly. It was all a foreign concept to

Mercelle, as she had never thought to suggest attempting a mass resurrection.

Then again, a month ago she didn't think she'd be travelling around Earth with a God, killing replicas, saving humans, and even finding a lost Race.

Times were always going to change rapidly. She just needed to stay prepared.

Her boot slipped on an angled piece of concrete, and when she looked down, she saw the slightly tarnished plaque that read "Main Command". The rest of the building was among the ruins on the ground, all around them.

"This was their command center," Mercelle said.

"Is where they is make last stand," Bewapen suggested.

Lito grabbed Mercelle's hand and pulled her up a steep embankment of rubble. Then she reached back and pulled Bewapen up.

"This is where we'll try it," Lito advised, standing still and looking around.

The top layer of debris included many scorched bodies. But, He must have sensed many more bodies beneath them, still in good shape despite whatever injuries they had succumbed to. Lito had told them that as long as the body wasn't rotted or decayed, then He should be able to heal any injuries upon their resurrection, but none of them were entirely sure about this.

"Are you sure this is the best spot?" she asked, staunching a shiver trying to crawl down her spine.

"Yes," He answered. "It looks like a large number of their soldiers died when the building collapsed."

She remembered the Great Library, and how the last of Lanna's soldiers gathered inside until it fell. The Kota Kara soldiers must have had the same mentality with their military command building.

The vision struck her with a rush of familiarity – she had been here before. Two other individuals were with her, and when she angled her neck to gaze into the sky, the stars and the horizon were exactly the same as she remembered them.

"This is it," she whispered in amazement.

"Is what?" asked Bewapen. "Is what you see before?"

"This is what I saw – what *we* saw – in our dream. Mother Maagda saw it too. That's incredible." It was reliving a dream. She didn't know what to make of it. Soon, they would have an answer. Either blue stars were going to rain down from above or they weren't. Her breath shook, needing an outcome to grace her here and now.

Lito took the Shard from the chain around His neck, and held it up in front of Him.

"How many lights do you think are in there?" she questioned.

"It's hard to tell," He answered, staring through the glass and watching the flowing, flickering light bounce around within. "It looks like hundreds, although, when I think I've counted them all, more seem to come out from behind others. It's strange."

"No wonder it kept breaking Seemik's machines. The thing wants to stay a mystery."

"How is they come out?" Bewapen wondered aloud. "Is you break glass?"

"Honestly," Lito said, turning the Shard over in His hands. "I have no idea. I'd rather not break it open if I don't have to."

"What if there's a way to get them all to come out on their own without compromising the Shard itself?"

Lito nodded. "I'll try reaching out to the lights, using just my plain will. If they're under my control then they'll react." He clutched the Shard in both hands, closing His eyes.

It was a stretch, she thought, and for a moment, nothing came of it. Mercelle looked around to see no movement, and she felt no change in the air around them. Then the ground shook with a small tremor. She held onto Bewapen's strong arm, and they held each other up until the shaking stopped.

A few rocks fell over, and some piles of concrete pieces shifted, but there was no significant result.

"It isn't working," Lito told them. "I can sense the lights, and follow their movement, but I can't get inside of them. They aren't allowing me to will them out."

“Blood,” said Bewapen. “Your blood is heal, is powerful.”

“Yes!” Mercelle agreed. “Bewapen’s a genius. Use your blood. Maybe that’ll act as a catalyst of some sort.”

Lito drew His knife from His belt’s sheath. His hands had gone through plenty of injuries which had since healed back to normal. Even the deep scarring from catching a Newlyn’s pellet had faded back to perfectly smooth skin, despite His entire body being submerged in molten lava.

He handed the blade to Mercelle, and held out a palm. She pressed the blade into His skin, splitting it open. Knowing she didn’t have to be careful made it easier. Lito would simply heal this wound as well.

Blood trickled onto the ground, and Lito flattened His palm over the face of the Shard, smearing the red liquid over its entirety. It formed a layer of crimson over the glass, and the blue, flickering lights within took on a much more green hue to them as they swirled about.

Lito turned back around, facing the empty field of rubble. He held the Shard up with both hands again, hanging His head in concentration. “I can feel them.” His voice quivered through trembling lips.

“That’s good, Lito. Now, can you will them to come out this time?”

“I’m trying.” His head shook, and His eyes clutched tightly shut. “I’m speaking to them, but they aren’t listening." The veins in His arms protruded as His grip intensified on the Shard.

"Tell them that they are one with you. Remind them who they work for, why they're here. They belong to you, Lito."

Low mumbling came from His lips, as if He were praying or incanting a spell. "They're resisting." His voice broke beneath the intensity of His grip and concentration. "Out! I command it! OUT!"

With a sudden jerk of Lito's arms, the Shard pulled upward toward the sky. His elbows went taut, holding onto the Shard with all of His strength. She thought to help Him, but didn't want to taint any kind of cosmic magics the God was manipulating at the moment. For all she knew her involvement could cause a fatal disruption.

From the top end of the Shard, a streak of blue shot out, and as if the Shard had become weightless, Lito's arms dropped. The blue lights were flying up and away from them in a thick line of cerulean that went higher and higher, until it disappeared into the stars above.

"What is happen?" asked Bewapen, looking around warily. "Is work?"

"I don't know," replied Lito. He showed them the empty Shard. With nothing inside, the talisman was dark and hollow. "They're gone."

She looked up, taking note of each and every star in the sky. None of them were moving. Flickers caught her eye here and there, but there was no sign of the blues above them.

"Is that it?" She put her hands on her forehead. "Did we just break the Shard? Lito, your hand."

Lito brought His hand up to His face. It was still bleeding profusely. None of the wound had healed in any way, unlike the previous wounds He'd incurred. Usually, they would stop bleeding within seconds, and begin healing shortly after. This one was untouched by any kind of Godly healing energy.

"It's not closing," He said.

"Calvin's carcass," she grumbled. "What does that mean?"

Had Lito lost His powers along with the blue lights? How weak had He become? What would they do without their Order God?

Pressure built around them, and they all felt it. Bewapen lifted his arms and looked at the sweat accumulating heavily upon his skin. Mercelle's stomach tightened, and heat rose up in her head and chest. Lito looked her in her eyes, communicating with a glance that He was feeling it too.

A rush of weighted particles fell on Mercelle's face from above, tickling her cheeks and forehead. The vibrating sensation flowed down her shoulders, and trickled down to her toes. She looked up to see glints of light blue falling down from the sky. Directly above them, encircling their position, were hundreds of stars, falling in straight lines to the ground. The three of them stepped in closer together, watching as the lights decorated the landscape with cobalt shimmers and tiny shadows. Night had become filtered dusk, and the streaks stretched from the cosmos to the leveled city of Kota Kara.

Mercelle's suspended breathing kept her from speaking as she watched the hundreds of glittering meteorites strike the ground around them with little impact. When they landed, they each scrambled to find passage through the solids and into the dirt. Every twinkling speck reached the ground, burrowing down among the remnants of Kota Kara until the streaks faded. Once the last of the lights had fallen and dug in, the landscape went mute, with only the heavy beat of her heart throbbing in her ears.

Along with the shroud of night returned another form of darkness.

"Lito?" She was beginning to panic, remembering the part of her dream where hopelessness had become a palpable sensation. The only thing that could ever make Lady Inis Mercelle of Lanna panic was the fear of the unknown, and these lights were capable of anything, especially if they were miffed about Lito trying to impose a certain will upon them. "What are they doing?" She couldn't feel any movement beneath her feet.

"They're finding bodies," He answered. "They're doing what we asked."

How He was able to sense this she didn't know.

The sky glistened with the clarity of the universe. Only shimmering stars and the sound of boots digging into debris could be heard as they pivoted with keen eyes. In a vacuum of anticipation with just her, a God and a foreign warrior, they couldn't speak, they could only watch out for movement of any kind.

Out of nowhere, the soles of Mercelle's boot tickled her feet. Bewapen looked at the ground, as if something had disturbed his focus as well.

"Something's wrong," Lito said. "The ground is unsettling! Quick! We need to get to higher ground!"

He grabbed her by the elbow, and turned to run up the steep incline behind Him. They scaled it to the top, Bewapen on their heels. Once they were looking down on mounds of the broken city, they began to see arms and legs emerge in large numbers from beneath stone and dirt.

The limbs rolled rocks, and pushed debris out of their way as they pulled up the torsos attached to them. The mound the trio stood upon began to sink, and the stones rushed out from beneath them.

With quick legs, and while gripping each other tightly, they managed to stay atop the sinking heap. It dropped out from under them, and they all fell along with it, rolling along with the concrete chunks and coughing up dust, struggling to get back to their feet.

When everything stopped, and she looked around, dust was settling, and strange creatures were walking crookedly through it in their direction. A man with a damaged leg limped heavily over a chunk of rubble, his bones cracking with each step. Another one pulled himself along with an arm while the rest of his body lay limp, dragging behind him. She whipped around to face a woman with pieces of her face missing, showing teeth through vacant cheeks and dripping bloody drool about the ground and over her torn Sergeant's uniform.

On reflex, she put a boot in the woman's chest, sending her back and away from the trio.

They reformed their triangle, putting their backs to each other and facing their enemies.

She handed Lito His knife back, and pulled her handguns from their holsters. This wasn't the kind of battle she was excited to engage in. These were humans, kind of.

Bewapen reached up to grip the heavy end of his hammer, yanking it free from the strap holding it to his back.

As the undead covered the surrounding land and crept closer to them, they held their positions, ready to take them on.

26

LADY TI-ERIN FERES V

A faulty coupler was found inside one of the junctions beneath the power storage facility. It took Feres all night to locate the right one and dismantle the casings in order to remove, repair and replace the coupler. Once she was done with that she left it in the hands of her engineering Scholars to close the casings and secure the flow of power.

Now, the energy being absorbed and processed by the morning sun on the panels wouldn't go to waste, it would be stored.

"You three got this?" she asked the Scholars before leaving. They all gave her a confident "yes" so she made her way out of the facility and to her rover. All she could think about was climbing into her bed and trying to sleep away some of the morning before helping to ready the convoy to Naselba. She was hoping Lito would be there waiting for her. What else did He have to do today? They'd cuddle for a few hours before she came back down to start preparations.

Her thoughts went to Mercelle as she shifted into gear and drove down the road toward her A.L.C.O. The idea of begging the Naselbans for their assistance in a coordinated attack on Glaven Grad didn't seem to sit well with Mercelle. Feres saw it on her face that she wanted to put her efforts toward something else, something more useful. How could Feres blame her? Part of her felt it was a lost cause also, but they needed to explore every advantage they possibly could. They would only have one chance at destroying the Demigods, and it was going to take everything they had to be successful.

Like Mercelle had said, they were going to fight whether or not Naselba was on board, and they were either going to win or die trying. It was better for humanity to go out with a fight, as opposed to slowly deteriorating and going extinct over time.

She rolled her eyes when her tablet buzzed and chimed loudly, indicating a possible emergency. "What now?"

Pulling over and unclipping the tablet from her belt, she immediately saw the yellow indicator flashing, and answered the call.

"You got Feres."

"Lady Feres. This is Captain Shou at the main gate.

Scans are showing a group of a few thousand approaching the city. They're a couple of miles out, and they're on foot. No trace of Chaos signals."

Feres sighed, pressed the gas and turned the rover down an alleyway to head in the direction of the gates. "Do you have a visual feed?"

"I do. They look human, might be Bewapen's people. Their skin is pitch black, and their leader looks to have long, white hair. I can see weapons, hammers and fighting staffs, but no vehicles."

"Copy. That'll be the Onyx Clan. Put a call in to Mercelle and have her meet us at the gates with Lito."

"My Lady," came a hesitant voice which told Feres she wasn't quite aware of something. "Lady Mercelle and Lito were seen leaving the city last night on clippers. They took the Onyx ambassador with them."

"Did they say where they were going?"

"All we have is the feed showing them leaving, my Lady. They didn't tell anyone. Would you still like me to put the call in to her tablet?"

"Damn it! They're the only three who have met and dealt with the Onyx Clan. I don't know how to get the Clan to trust us without them. Don't bother contacting her if she isn't here. Give me a few minutes and I'll be there. Out."

She cut off the call, and placed another one, steering swiftly around the corner of the Library.

"This is Rakta," answered the medical Scholar.

"Rakta. It's Feres. I need you to activate the tracker you put in Mercelle's arm. Can you tell me where she is?"

"Yes. Let me pull it up quickly. One moment. Ah, here it is. She's outside of the city."

"I know that. Can you tell me where she went outside of the city?"

"Expanding the scan now. She's east of here. It looks like the path to Kota Kara."

"The ruins? Why would they go to the Kaisering ruins?"

"I couldn't say," replied Rakta. "If Mercelle's levels increase we won't be able to-"

Feres cut the call off, gripping the steering handles with both hands to steady the rover while maintaining a high speed. All three of them had left without saying a word to her. How could they? Were they on another rogue mission to continue taking down towers? Did Mercelle get bored and go looking for a fight, dragging Lito and Bewapen along with her?

There were so many questions, but none of them would yield any answers until they returned. Now, she had other issues to address, and coming at the leader of their newest allies with a face of confusion wasn't going to help their situation.

She pulled up to the intake checkpoint at the gates, hopping down from her rover and scaling the stairs to the crow's nest on the second level. Shou was already there, waiting with his tablet showing the feed from a vesp he had deployed to scout out the large group. First Officer Vayreni came up behind her.

"Orders, my Lady," said Vayreni.

"Arm the top level, but nothing too intimidating. We don't want to scare them off. Remember: these guys are our allies. We only fire if threatened first. Understand?"

"Heard," replied Vayreni, before turning to head up the steps to the third level parapets.

On the feed from the vesp, Feres could see the Onyx people. Their Clan was a few thousand strong, and as she flew the vesp over the length of their group, she could see men young, old and in between, all with the same dark complexion and bright white hair.

Dirt was built up on their skin, and she could see rust on their huge steel hammers, which they carried with little effort. The sun's heavy morning rays made them all scowl. They looked mean, angry, but Lito and Mercelle spoke highly of them, and she had the utmost respect for anyone willing to join their fight. Even Bewapen had proven to be much more than just a warrior, with a heart and a conscience which craved justice, regardless of the necessary sacrifices.

At the center of the procession of Onyx was a large sarcophagus-looking item. It was being dragged by long ropes, and held glyphs and symbols she couldn't quite make out. The leader with the long, white cords bunched atop his head led the group to the wall, and they all stopped at the gate, where they stood and waited.

That's when she noticed that the man at the head of the group was holding a rope, and on the other end of the rope was a boy, crouched down low to the ground and darting frantic eyes in all directions. He looked sick, with grayish skin, but she wasn't here to judge, she was here to secure the alliance which Bewapen, Mercelle and Lito all swore to.

If only they were here to help.

She handed the tablet back to Captain Shou. "Keep everyone alert and on stand by."

"Why do you think they're here?" he queried.

"I don't know. They were supposed to wait for our contact after the summit. Maybe something's happened. Their Clan may have been attacked."

"Do you think they're pulling out? Coming to get Bewapen back?"

"I hope not."

Feres stepped to the railing that looked over the main gate's entrance. Thousands of the Onyx were lining the front wall of Sandramedius, admiring the steel construction as if they had never seen anything like it.

"Welcome," she shouted down to them. "My name is Lady Feres. I am the ruler of Sandramedius. We are grateful that you have chosen an alliance with us. Our cooperating peoples will be a formidable force against Chaos."

The leader at the front of the pack stepped forward. "I is Kop Stamhoof, is leader of Onyx Clan. We is also grateful for alliance. We is talk to Lito and Mercelle."

"Yes, they told me about you and your great warrior Clan. I'm afraid the two of them aren't here at the moment, they've left on a mission for which they failed to provide details. Your friend Bewapen went with them."

"Then I is talk to you, alone."

"Of course." Feres turned to Shou, ordered him to open the gates and said to close them behind the Kop. "I don't think he's happy about them not being here. I'll do my best to keep things cooled, but stay close by. If I feel threatened I'll call out for you."

"Yes, my Lady," he replied, tapping on his screen to crack open the gates beneath them.

The Kop handed his rope to another man behind him, and walked across the empty entrance to the gates. Once he stepped through and the gates were closed again, Feres gave the rest of the Clan a bright smile, then turned around and gave Shou a look of intensity, showing she wasn't entirely sure what was going to happen.

Down the metal steps and into the intake just inside the gates, Feres approached Stamhoof. He held out a hand, and she reached out to shake it, but his hand went to her forearm, so she mimicked the greeting.

"I'm very pleased to have you and your people here in Sandramedius. I hope everything is okay."

"When is they return?"

"I'm sorry, but I'm not sure. They left last night without saying anything. Mercelle is somewhat of a free spirit, and doesn't like to sit around much. Since none of them are under my command they're fine to do as they please, and I trust them in anything they do." She just wished they had left her a message or a note of some kind. Their timing was atrocious.

"We is come to talk to Lito and Mercelle, is fight beside Order God. I is come to summit with you."

That was certainly different than what she had been told. "I was under the impression that Bewapen would be representing your Clan at the summit meeting."

"New information is come to light," he said. "Is testament of Lito's power. Is Fee'u."

"Fee'u?"

"Fate."

"I see. So, you were doubting Lito?"

"You is come. I is show you."

He walked around Feres, and she rotated to keep her front to him. The cryptic man, who was armed with a large hammer, was trying to say something profound, but instead of coming out and saying it he was putting up a front. Stamhoof went up the stairs, and she followed, knowing that Shou was already up there watching them.

"This is why I is want to speak to Lito," he said at the top of the stairs. "I is fear you is not believe me, but Lito is know."

They went to the railing, and she glanced at Shou in the back corner of the crow's nest, just to make sure he was still there. He mouthed the words "you okay?", to which she responded with a mild shrug.

"What is it that Lito knows?" she asked, looking out at his people.

Kop Stamhoof pointed at the boy with the rope tied around his waist. "You is see this boy?"

The young man was on all fours, digging in the dirt. Once his hole was big enough, he turned over, lying in the hole on his back and pulling sand over his body. His mannerisms were that of a much younger individual.

"I do," she answered. "Why is he tied like that?"

"Is son of Bewapen. Is not well."

"I see. He mentioned that he had a son."

"Name is Geboor. Boy is sacrifice to secure alliance."

"There's no need for that," she immediately replied. "Unnecessary bloodshed is-"

"No," he stopped her. "Boy is *already* sacrifice."

It may have been the language barrier, but what she was hearing wasn't making any sense. "I don't understand." She left it open to his explanation. All Bewapen had said was that he had a son, she hadn't been given any further details, but sensed the kind of melancholy in Bewapen that had indicated a recent loss of a loved one. It was starting to make sense...kind of.

"When member of Clan is leave, a sacrifice of bloodline is made."

"Okay," she responded. "Your traditions are important to you. But, did you say that the boy was 'already' sacrificed?"

"Yes. Geboor is sacrifice before Bewapen is leave with others. Is Lito's blood that is bring him back. Boy is not same as before. He is have life, though."

"Lito's blood has the power to bring people back from the dead?" The more time went on, the more abilities Lito seemed to have. It'd been weeks since He had been woken up, and His Godly powers were only getting stronger. Perhaps the Shard was more of a help than they originally thought.

"Lito is not tell truth about powers." The Kop looked directly at her, as if trying to hammer a point. "Lito is hide things, is lie."

"He doesn't know," she told the man. "Since He woke up He's been struggling to remember anything before Earth. We've all been hoping beyond hope that He'll be powerful enough to help us defeat the Demigods, but His abilities have to be relearned. According to the Book of Order He used to have the ability to replicate humans in His image, but He doesn't seem to be capable of that anymore. With time, perhaps."

The wheels were turning behind Stamhoof's eyes, and he nodded in acceptance of her explanation. "Now we is know. Now we is stronger, together. Onyx is loyal to Lito, He is Order God, and is confirmed. Lito is say He is loyal to Sandramedius. Now, we is loyal to Sandramedius."

Relief washed over her. "I'm glad to hear it, and once Lito returns we'll-"

"My Lady!" shouted Captain Shou. "There's a massive group a few miles out, heading toward us, quickly."

She slowly turned her head to glare at him. "Excuse me, Captain. But, there's a delay on your feed. Check your timestamps. As you can see I'm already speaking with their leader. Now, let's open the gates and let them all in."

"No!" He rushed at her with his tablet, turning it to show her. "It's a Chaos signal."

She looked over the desert landscape, and saw minute puffs of dust kicking into the air a great distance away. All of the Onyx people on the ground whipped around, collecting into battle formations and arming themselves with their steel weapons.

"Enemy is approach," the Kop said. "They is feel hooves on ground." With little effort, he hopped over the railing, dropped the thirty or so feet to the sand, and rushed forward to join the formation.

Chaos must have spotted the accumulation of Onyx outside the city and decided it was a good time to attack. Without Lito, they were absolutely right.

She looked at the tablet's feed as the vesp flew closer to the encroaching enemy horde. Legions of Valks covered the valleys to the north, and kicked up enough dust to nearly shroud their armies beneath the brown clouds. Chaos replicas were within a couple miles of Sandramedius, and she wasn't prepared.

"Full steel!" she cried out. "Arm the gates! Sound the alarms!" Climbing the steps to the parapets on the top level, her heart threatened to leap out of her chest. She wouldn't be able to stand watching their new allies fall to protect the city, but there wasn't time to get them all inside the gates. Besides, their weapon choices called for a more direct combat, and her automatic turrets would be able to provide suppression fire. "Send signals to Naselba and Kerk! Someone scan for other hordes in case this one is a decoy! Get those turrets manned now! Shou, rifle!"

Soldiers were rushing up the stairs, filing into the parapets and aiming their weapons out into the desert. The turrets were filled immediately, and large explosives launchers were heaved into position. Buckets of ammunition were carried up and placed every few feet along the parapets, and once the entire upper level was filled, they waited for the horde to approach.

Shou handed her a rifle, and she crouched down, putting the scope to her eye and looking toward the Chaos army. She zoomed in, watching as the horde stopped just over a mile away. She scanned their crowd, looking for a reason as to why they had stopped.

Much like the Onyx Clan below them, Valks had a more melee approach to their fighting strategies. If they came to a halt with this much distance between them, then they may have found other means to attack. The darkest part of her mind thought it best that Lito, Mercelle and Bewapen weren't here, as their absence may be what saved their lives if the attack proved successful.

There, at the center of the horde was a monster with the mangled yet recognizable face of Zakopat Kraj. It was tall and ferocious, but it was standing beside something much taller and much more ferocious – the most frightening thing she had ever seen. He was the reason the horde had stopped, and it was their reason for doing anything that they do.

It was a Valk, but this one was twice the normal size, and it wore crimson guards on its arms and legs – the only Valk with any kind of armor on.

"Oh no," she whispered to herself.

It wasn't just another Valk.

Seeing an actual Demigod for the first time in her

life, Feres struggled to steady her breathing. What made it worse was the devilish smile, adorned with sharpened teeth, that stretched across his face in a most terrifying display of his thirst for carnage.

Feres couldn't help but gulp her anxiety down into the pit of her stomach, readying herself for the battle to come as Valk's blood thirsty eyes stared down her front gates.

27

LETO II

The vastness of space was a wonderful yet excruciating thing, especially the empty voids between galaxies. From the eons of harvested materials, He and His oldest Demigods had built the Great Wall, and it was growing so large that its gravity was swallowing more planets and systems on its own. Nothing had ever pulled Him away from the Great Wall since it had been built, but the knowledge of His brother's awakening drew Him, and Leto couldn't keep Himself from facing Lito.

Not long after banishing His brother to Earth, Leto took down His first civilization. It was an enormous planet, layered with reflective stone and oceans of liquid glass. Originally a spherical planet, it looked as if a long asteroid had lodged itself into the mass at some point early on in its development, sticking out of the planet at two ends, elongating the once perfectly round sphere. The atmosphere was relatively young and weak, and its clouds shimmered with hues of orange and yellow.

At its core was the most solid, durable stone He had ever found, and there was enough of it to make not only His own massive ship, but fleets of space travelling vessels. The only issues were the pesky lifeforms that inhabited the planet.

His campaign against the nine-limbed, semi-intelligent species was short and simple, with legions of His own creations descending upon them with brute force and heavy machinery until the thin atmosphere dissipated. Much of the surface was removed and shipped away to get to the precious, dense stone at the center. It was one of His easiest conquests, and one He would have since forgotten if not for the relic He'd kept from it.

The strongest of the stone was at the center of the giant asteroid, and it took effort and ingenuity to carve through it, but once His ship was done being constructed out of it, it was undoubtedly the most massive vessel in the universe. His next campaigns began with intimidation as He flaunted the ship about, convincing many civilizations to simply surrender before decimating them anyway.

At the head of the ship, Leto stood patiently, staring at the spread of approaching galaxies ahead. He had been here before, but it had been over sixty-five million years ago. Somewhere within these galaxies was Earth, and Lito. When He'd first learned of Lito being woken up, He thought to leave Him be. He would have, if not for the humans His brother had created.

These humans had put up more of a fight than any other species He'd come across, resisting four of His Demigods. Valk had done a great job at clearing out the planet at first. Instead of waging war, the Demigod had offered the humans a chance to flee. They took the offer, and the bait.

Once the allowed century had passed, and the fleet of ships emerged from Earth's atmosphere, each ship was quickly shot down. The small number of humans who remained were left unchecked, and during that time they'd managed to build a substantial resistance against Valk and the other Demigods.

They were Lito's creations, and He had no doubt in His mind that His brother was weakened after so much time spent asleep. This would leave Lito open to easy manipulation, or maybe even enslavement. Either way, Leto wanted these resilient humans on the side of Chaos. Killing Lito wasn't an option, and had never been, which was why He was left on what Leto thought was a dying planet. As it turns out, the planet survived the impact, and was now teeming with more pesky inhabitants who He thought would be very useful.

Anything with worth was always something that

drew Leto's greedy inclinations into action. The goal was to obtain ultimate power over the universe, and since the universe was always expanding His work would never be done, and He liked it that way.

He willed His ship forward, into the collection of relatively young galaxies, keeping an eye out for the one that held His brother.

Want to know more about the author and the next book? Check out the next page...

ABOUT THE AUTHOR

It could be paranormal, it could be romance. You could find yourself amidst a war, whether it be societal, subconscious or science fiction. Whichever path you choose, Ronin Romero's unique take on humankind will keep you from your complacency, and keep you up long into the night with thoughts and nightmares to last and last. Find all of his work at RoninRomero.com, and on Amazon.

Also by Ronin Romero

Revelations Book 1: Glyph Series

Find book one of this series here.

One Night At The Banshee

The PennyRoyal Banshee is a supernatural brothel, run by a human named the Hag. When a Maggopod called Muck seeks to mate with another of its species, the only option is to enter the Banshee in hopes of finding a fellow Maggopod under the Hag's employ. With the disreputable O'Grady's Enchantments swiping all of the Maggopods off the streets, Muck has to tread carefully, and be wary about who can and cannot be trusted.

My Book

Getting Out

When her aunt's lawyer proves her charges false, Reanne is released from prison into a world in which she is no longer invested, and doesn't recognize. Her short stint was enough to gain her sobriety, but can she hold on to it while she copes with the loss of her mother and father, who both passed away while she was incarcerated?

My Book

Daniel

Society has taken on new leadership, and new laws that undo the equality built over so many years. As the world falls apart around him, our main character must fight for the survival of himself, his people, and of tolerance. Military police are no match for a strong spirit and the will to uphold justice. He'll find the end of his own tolerance while being hunted by the very government who turned on him.

My Book

Debt to the Dead

An ancient King has conquered his enemies. But, not all victories are clean cut. How will he cope with the demands of the dead after a necromancer brings his demons to the surface? Centurions can protect their King from death, just not from his own guilt.

My Book

The Problem

Gerald isn't happy in his marriage. It seems his wife, Susan, isn't happy either. When Gerald decides to consult with a member of the supernatural community to figure out The Problem, he gets more than he bargained for. A story of spite, deep thought, and a struggle for happiness, Gerald will take you through a journey of realization that will bring you back around to the source of The Problem.

The only question is: can he resolve it?

My Book

Last Shot

His desert village is being sacked by a hostile enemy. As the sole villager who stayed behind to defend his home, a young man fights through starvation, exhaustion, delirium and the memories of his family, in order to hold on to one last shred of hope.

What will he do with the final round in his chamber?

What will he do with his Last Shot?

My Book

Baby's Cry

After encountering a baby with fangs and an affinity for shrieking, Sacha rethinks his dream of raising children in his secluded mountain home. Will he survive the night, or will he succumb to his fears?

My Book

The Dwellers

New to the small, backwoods town, Spencer is invited by a group of young teens to play a harmless game of hide and seek in the woods. It's the kind of night he was never able to see in the city where he's from, and with a new crush by his side he's confident enough to take his friends up on their offer, even after Chad tells him the tale of the Dwellers.

When many of his new pals go missing, Spencer is forced to see for himself whether the dark hills hold monsters or tricks. After venturing through a barrier of thorns, Spencer comes across an abandoned cottage with a candle burning in the attic window.

Is it a prank? Is he hallucinating?

The more important question is: will he find his friends and make it out of this secluded forest alive?

My Book

Disclosure

In the future, Sergeant Amanda Hilt is the sole survivor of a militarized attack on an encroaching settlement of E.T.s. After waking from her coma, she learns that she will soon die if she doesn't agree to undergo a series of experimental operations to install fabricated parts, essentially turning her into a human-machine hybrid, and the first of her kind. Amanda signs the Disclosure, and goes through with the procedures, only to find that she isn't being told everything.

Disclosure is a one-of-a-kind, psychological thriller that will keep you rooting for the good guys, as long as you can figure out who they are.

My Book

Tangible Despair

From the first page of TANGIBLE DESPAIR to the last you'll experience nine short stories and four poems, each revolving around journeys of self discovery via the human spirit. Every form of salvation differs from the next, as every path to liberation from one's demons is personal, trying, and unforgiving. Whether it's the oppressed finding their place within battle, a King discovering the weight of victory, a Wife learning the limits of her rage, or lovers fighting for freedom, it'll be impossible to keep yourself from laughing and crying throughout. From Science Fiction and Horror, to Romance and War, TANGIBLE DESPAIR will show you a reflection of humanity that you've never quite seen at this angle. Don't worry, questioning the nature of your species is just par for the course.

TANGIBLE DESPAIR contains all of Ronin Romero's short stories published before the end of 2020.

My Book

Made in the USA
Columbia, SC
23 February 2023

12874595R00272